Symbiosis

Symbiosis

Justice Keepers Saga Book I

R.S. Penney

@Rich_Penney
keeperssaga@gmail.com
https://www.facebook.com/keeperssaga
Edited by:
Jourdan Vian
Gina Fusco (Re:Word Communications)
info@reword.ca
http://www.reword.ca/

Contents

Prologue

(Western Kenya, April 6, 1954)

The sun was a crimson sphere on the Western horizon, painting the sky a mosaic of colours, amber fading to red, then purple and blue. Stalks of tall grass swayed in the wind that swept across the field.

A small ridge overlooked a dig site where men in straw hats laboured with shovels in the oppressive heat. They would not be pleased to be pushed so hard, but there was no getting around it. Either they returned home with something of value or Cambridge would not fund another excavation.

Kenneth Barnes stood on the ridge.

A tall man in beige pants and a white shirt that was plastered to his back with sweat, he scrubbed a hand through his slick dark hair. "Keep at it, Crawford!" he shouted. "I've got no time for dawdling."

Kenneth felt his face heat up. He closed his eyes tight. "Idiots, the lot of them," he muttered, shaking his head. "Utterly useless unless you have a mind to part with money."

"You're too hard on them."

He turned.

A young woman stood three feet away with her hands clasped together behind her back. Tall and slender, she wore a black skirt and a white shirt that was somehow free of sweat stains. Her face was a perfect oval, framed by long red hair that spilled over her shoulders to the small of her back. "Do be patient, Dr. Barnes," she admonished. "I am *quite certain this trip* will prove fruitful."

Kenneth felt his lips curl, then bowed his head to her. "You genuinely believe that, do you?" he asked, brow furrowing. "Then perhaps you can articulate the reason for your constant badgering."

From the moment they had set foot on this dig site, Chelsea Lawrence had been a source of constant frustration. Appointed by the Parliamentary Expenditures Committee, her job was to ensure that the Crown's investment in this project did not go unrewarded. How a woman managed to achieve such a position was unclear to him, but there were days when he could feel her gaze on his back.

Wiping his forehead with the back of his hand, Kenneth winced and turned his face away from her. "Not to worry, Miss Lawrence," he went on. "I'm sure the knowledge we gain from this will be-"

"Knowledge is the province of scholars, Dr. Barnes." She lifted her chin to stare at him with gray eyes that seemed to drain the heat from the air. "My interest lies in making sure the funds you've been granted are spent wisely."

"You're questioning my methods?"

Folding her arms across her chest, Chelsea Lawrence pursed her lips as she studied him. "You're surprised?" she asked, eyebrows rising. "You may not have realized this, sir, but the Mau Mau are a serious threat."

"I am well aware of-"

She stepped forward until her face filled his vision, held him pinned in place by the force of her gaze alone. "The soldiers we employ to protect this...dig site," the derision she invested in those last words was obvious, "could be put to better use hunting down the Crown's enemies."

Dealing with this woman was like trying to walk around with a splinter in your big toe. When he met the man who assigned Chelsea Lawrence to this project, he was going to punch the fool in his fat face.

"Dr. Barnes!"

He spun around to find a man staring up at him from the dig site, a tall man with a straw hat over his head. "You need to come down here, sir!" the fellow went on. "There's something you should see!"

The trek down to the dig site only worsened his annoyance. These idiots tended to call him when they found a stone that looked like an arrowhead; it was highly unlikely that they had produced anything useful.

He found Crawford standing with two other men next to a hole in the ground with piles of upturned earth nearby. The wiry fellow was nodding quickly as he spoke to one of the other workers.

Scrubbing a hand over his face, Kenneth frowned and blinked a few times. "I take it you found something?" He felt his mouth tighten, shut his eyes and shook his head. "Another 'arrowhead,' Mr. Crawford?"

The man went red in the face, then lowered his eyes to the ground. "Well, sir...no." He scraped a knuckle across his forehead. "You're going to have to see for yourself. This is...there are no words."

Kenneth stepped forward.

In the hole, he found a triangular piece of metal that would stand as tall as a grown man when set upright with sinuous grooves running over its surface. The sight of it held him transfixed.

Clamping a hand over his gaping mouth, Kenneth squeezed his eyes shut. "This is not right," he said, shaking his head. "Call Captain Langford down here. I want a report on anyone who set foot on this dig site."

"Sir?"

The red light of the setting sun glimmered on the triangle's reflective surface. "This thing was man-made," Kenneth went on, "which tells us someone put it here. So, unless you think the hunter-gatherer tribes of Eastern Africa had secret knowledge of metallurgy, someone has been tampering with our work."

A thousand tiny stars twinkled in the night sky, and the quarter moon provided more than enough light for Kenneth to make out the pits and piles of dirt scattered throughout the dig site. Up on the ridge, tall grass swayed in the breeze. The men had gone to their tents hours ago.

Kenneth was still awake.

The triangle had been stood upon its base in the middle of the dig site, moonlight reflecting on its surface. He found himself fascinated by the sight of it. The discovery they had made yesterday had set everyone in the camp abuzz with theories on its origin. Miss Lawrence was beside herself.

Lifting a mug of coffee in one hand, Kenneth closed his eyes as steam wafted over his face. "At least the woman kept quiet." He brought the mug to his lips and took a sip. "A day of silence is its own reward."

Kenneth stepped forward.

Nibbling on his bottom lip, he lowered his eyes to the ground. "Now, how long do I have with you?" he asked, creases forming in his brow, "before someone carries you away to some dusty storeroom?"

The triangle stood silent and ominous, silver moonlight reflecting on its top corner. An archaeologist's dream! That was, of course, if the bloody thing wasn't just some hoax perpetrated by disgruntled Kenyan natives. Or possibly the Mau Mau. They would do just about anything to make the Crown look incompetent.

He clasped his chin in one hand, then shut his eyes tight. "With my luck, you'll be appropriated by some hot-shot from MI-6." The thought left him feeling disgruntled. "So they can hide you away before rumours spread."

Some of the more colourful tales circulating through the camp involved little green men from Mars depositing this thing in the middle of the African grasslands. Nothing but the products of unrestrained imaginations, but Kenneth did nothing to discourage his men from sharing those theories. It wasn't his job to-

The triangle began to hum.

Half a moment later, the grooves along its surface began to glow with fierce white light. Little green men indeed! A gnawing sense of terror in his belly commanded him to run away, but he couldn't.

He approached.

Shielding his face with one hand, Kenneth peeked at the thing through the cracks between his fingers. "Hello?" he called out. "Can anyone hear me? Hello? My name is Dr. Kenneth Barnes of the-"

When he got within three feet of the triangle, a bubble formed around his body, a perfect sphere of rippling air that made it seem as though he were viewing the dig site through a curtain of falling water. The ridge was a shadowy blur off to his right, rippling and wavering. "Heaven help me," Kenneth whispered.

He was pulled into oblivion.

(Present Day)

Another night down in the storage room. There were days when being a security guard just plain sucked. Whether it was hours of boredom or the exhaustion of working the night shift, sooner or later the job would kill you. Still, it was hard enough to get any job in this economy, and this one offered thirteen bucks an hour.

Doug took a bite of his hamburger. He closed his eyes, chewing mechanically as he savoured the taste. "Mmm...mmm...mmm..." he said, shaking his head. "Ain't nothing in the world like Greasy Joe's."

The storage room where he had been assigned to complete his shift was located in the sub-basement: a huge room about the size of a high school gymnasium with concrete walls. Over a dozen wooden crates were spaced out on the floor. What exactly they held was not important to him.

The one thing that did bother him was the strange triangular object in the middle of the room. Nearly as tall as a man with grooves along its metal surface that reminded him of veins, the thing practically glimmered under the fluorescent lights.

Wiping his mouth with a napkin, Doug winced and shook his head. "Rich folks and their toys," he muttered, leaning against the wall. "Who in God's name would ever buy a hunk of crap like that?"

His bosses, of course.

Penworth Enterprises was one of the largest shipping companies in the country and had dominated the market since the late nineties.

5

They carried stuff over the Atlantic and back again. Doug's job was to keep it safe

Clenching his teeth, Doug turned his face up to the ceiling. He squinted at the harsh fluorescent lights. "Vinnie, I'm getting tired of this," he muttered as if his boss could hear every word. "Just once I'd like to be somewhere other than the-"

A strange humming caught his attention.

The grooves along the triangle's surface were suddenly glowing with blazing white light. With every second, they got a little brighter until he thought it might explode. How in God's name...

The hamburger hit the floor.

Before he could speak, a bubble appeared from out of nowhere, a rippling pulsating bubble that had jerked to a halt just in front of the triangle. When he focused, he thought he could see someone standing inside.

The bubble popped.

A man stood just in front of the triangle. Tall and slim, he wore a long dark jacket. His fair-skinned face bore the faint creases of a man just into his middle years, and gray hair crowned the top of his head.

Lifting his chin, the man frowned as he studied Doug. "*Kom Jen endi?*" he said, creases forming in his brow. "*Kom enday Wesley Penn-field ay kay tan enda? Nom ademi dasa.*"

Doug drew his pistol.

Thrusting his arm out, he squinted as he took aim. "Now, that's enough of that," he said, shaking his head. "Who are you?"

The man offered a sly smile, then shut his eyes and bowed his head to Doug. "*Nom velens, men beli,*" he said, stepping forward. "*Nom dobera tosk vek deesa elinsinai en del vorad.*"

The man raised a hand.

Something was fused to the skin of his palm: a strange circular device with blinking lights on its surface. A screen of energy appeared just in front of the man. To Doug's eyes it looked like the static you saw on dead TV stations.

The man thrust his hand out.

Just like that, the wall of static came racing forward. Doug had half a second to fire off a shot before it hit with all the force of a freight train. The next thing he knew, he was flying backward.

He collided with the concrete wall, then dropped hard to the floor. He fell over onto his side, curled up and aching from head to toe. "God help me…" Doug murmured. "My God, please help me."

The bubble came to a halt, and she found herself in a brightly lit area, encapsulated by a sphere of rippling energy. Through the shimmering curtain, she could make out what appeared to be boxes.

Then the bubble popped.

Dressed in gray pants and a black shirt under a long brown trench coat, Anna Lenai looked around. Her fingers closed around the grip of a pistol in a holster on her right hip. With any luck, she wouldn't need it.

Her round face was framed by thin strands of strawberry-blonde hair with bangs falling over her forehead. "All molecules intact," she said, eyebrows rising. "The Companion be praised for small wonders."

Anna pursed her lips and glanced over her shoulder. She narrowed her eyes to thin slits. "The damn thing still works after ten thousand years," she muttered. "You've got to hand it to those Overseers."

The SlipGate stood silent and ominous behind her, light fading out of the grooves along its triangular surface. After being buried for so long, you would have thought the thing would have stopped functioning, but when her shuttle had detected its presence on the surface, she had known where Denario had fled.

She appeared to be in a large warehouse with wooden crates spaced out across the white floor tiles. Fluorescent lights in the ceiling flickered. *So, these people had reached a state of post-industrial development. Good to know.*

Closing her eyes, Anna let her head hang and forced out a breath. "Can you hear me, Dex?" she inquired. When no answer came, Anna tapped her earpiece to re-establish the connection. "Dex?"

Static.

"Great."

The Nassai within her stirred, no doubt apprehensive at being stranded on a strange planet with no notion of what to expect from the locals. Scans from orbit had confirmed that they were human. *A colony world this far out? Why had there been no record?* But that told her nothing about their temperament.

With her Nassai's assistance, Anna was able to project a mental map of the room, a 360-degree image of her surroundings. Spatial acuity was one of the many benefits of symbiosis. She could see every crate, every piece of junk and every last light in the ceiling without turning her head.

No movement.

After making her way around a few boxes, she found a hallway that led out of the room with the body of a man strewn across the mouth of the corridor. He was rolled up on his side, groaning in pain.

Anna rushed over to him.

The man wore a pair of black pants and a white shirt with an odd flapping garment around his neck. A guard? Most definitely Denario's latest victim. The poor fellow let out another groan.

Shutting her eyes tight, Anna drew in a rasping breath. "You're gonna pay for this, Denario," she said, kneeling next to the fallen man. "Hello? Can you hear me?"

The man stared up at her with his mouth agape, his dark eyes wide with fright. He blinked a few times. *How bad are his injuries?* The fellow tried to speak, but all she heard was some guttural gibberish.

A shout made her jump.

When she looked up, a trio of guards was marching through the corridor. Dressed identically to the man on the floor, they wore sour expressions on their faces. The one in the middle let out a growl.

He stopped in front of Anna.

Drawing a pistol from the holster on his belt, he thrust an arm out to point the gun at her. Words came out of his mouth, followed by a jerk of his head, and she had the very distinct impression that this wasn't going to go well.

Craning her neck, Anna stared up at him. She blinked a few times, considering her words. "I'm not your enemy," she began in a soft rasp. "I'm here to help. This man needs medical attention."

The guard snarled.

Anna got to her feet.

In that moment, the other two marched past her to inspect the storeroom. With her heightened sense of spatial awareness, she was able to keep track of them both. No good being taken from behind.

Baring his teeth, the first guard scrunched up his face. He let out a low hiss before proceeding to bark at her. Whatever it was this man said, she was pretty damn sure that he was running out of patience.

"Can't you see that I'm cooperating?" Anna said. "I don't want to hurt you, but you're making me antsy."

The man shoved his gun in her face.

I don't have time for this.

Anna fell backward.

Slapping her hands down on the floor tiles, she brought her legs up to catch the gun between her feet. She tore it out of the man's hand and sent the weapon tumbling through the air.

Anna snapped herself upright.

She jumped and kicked out, driving a foot into the man's chest. The impact sent him stumbling backward, landing hard on his ass and sliding across the floor tiles. He let out a painful groan.

With heightened spatial awareness, her frenzied mind projected the image of one of the guards coming up behind her. A big man with a barrel chest, he spread his arms wide as if to catch her in a bear hug.

He charged at her.

Anna reached back over her shoulder, catching his wrist in one hand. She bent over and flipped him over her shoulder, dislocating his arm in the process. The man landed on his backside with a shriek.

She spun around just in time to see the third guard trying to draw his pistol from its holster. Sweat glistened on his face as he stared at her with his mouth agape, fear visible in his eyes.

He managed to pull the weapon free.

Anna kicked the gun out of his hand. She spun like a whirlwind, driving her elbow into his nose.

The man's head jerked backward, blood dripping from his nose. He stumbled about, then fell over sideways. Now there were *four* security officers on the ground. A fat lot of good she'd done here.

Anna felt her mouth tighten as she stared down at him, her blue eyes flicking back and forth. She winced and shook her head. "I didn't want to do this," she began, "I'm on your side here."

She spun on her heel.

Charging up the corridor, she kept watch of the fallen men with the assistance of her Nassai. The one she had taken down first was getting to his feet, hunching over as he searched for his gun.

No threat there.

She rounded a corner.

Good fortune had been with her today; she had been able to elude the three guards without having to resort to some of her flashier abilities. Justice Keepers such as herself had a vast arsenal of talents beyond simple hand-to-hand combat, but each use taxed the Nassai and the host. Overuse could be fatal. Much better to disarm an enemy with your hands than to risk passing out.

With a little luck, she would be able to find Denario before he got too far. This city would be a maze to both of them, and it was a good bet that the people here would not be prepared for the technology he had at his disposal. Her greatest concern, however, was for the prisoner he carried with him.

She had to recover it.

After a long trek up to the first floor – one in which she had been careful to avoid the attention of any security guards – Anna found herself in a lobby with a set of double doors that looked out on a city street. Through the glass, she could see what appeared to be automobiles on the road.

Tall buildings in the distance rose up toward the night sky, some with tiny lights in their windows. What level of threat should she expect from these people? The thought of going up against the locals left her queasy.

Anna jerked to a halt.

Pursing her lips, she stared through the window, then narrowed her eyes. "A whole lot of civilians," she said, shaking her head. "And a bloody good chance that someone is going to get hurt."

She pushed through the door.

Once outside, Anna found herself on a columned walkway with marble pillars that supported an overhanging roof and steps that led down to the sidewalk. Automobiles that were parked along the sidewalk blocked her view of the road.

She drew her pistol.

Anna stepped forward with the gun raised in both hands, pausing at the top of the steps. *Now, where is he?* she thought, looking around. *He only had a few minutes' lead on me. He can't be-*

She spotted a man a short ways up the sidewalk, crouched behind one of the parked automobiles and scanning the road as though looking for a chance to run across. The gray hair on the back of his head was unkempt.

"Denario!"

He turned.

Clenching her teeth, Anna felt her face redden. She squeezed her eyes shut. "Stay where you are, Denario!" she screamed. "You move so much as one inch and I swear by all that's holy, I'll end you!"

He rose and spun around to face her. The force-field generator fused into the palm of his hand was still blinking away. "This won't work, Agent Lenai," he shouted. "I have no intention of coming with you."

A grin bloomed on his weathered face as he craned his neck to study her. Denario Tarse narrowed his eyes. "Harm me," he went on, "and the creature I carry dies as well. Your gunfire could break open the stasis pod."

"I might just risk it."

Anna fired.

A screen of white static appeared in front of the man, intercepting her bullet at the very last second. The slug bounced off and fell to the sidewalk. "Foolish girl!" Denario growled, thrusting a hand out.

The force-field sped forward, up the steps. Anna spun around and put her back to a pillar just in time to feel the energy wave strike the other side. Chunks of granite fell to the ground.

Anna felt her face crumple into an anguished wince. She tossed her head about in frustration. "Bleakness take you, Denario!" she said. "Your tricks aren't going to serve you this time!"

She lifted her gun. "E-M-P!"

The pistol's sleek black surface reflected the street lights. LEDs on the side of the barrel suddenly lit up, turning white. If her luck held, the charged rounds would short out his generator.

Anna spun around the pillar, raising the gun.

This time, when she fired, white tracers zipped through the air, causing Denario's force-field to wink out as they passed through it. The man stumbled backward, pressing his body to the side of a parked automobile.

Denario clenched his teeth, his face turning red. He shut his eyes tight and shook his head. "Idiot girl!" he screamed at her. "Do you really think I wasn't prepared for your interference?"

He pulled his jacket aside, revealing a thick armoured vest with three smoking slugs mashed against its fabric. "I have many tricks," he said, revealing a small gray sphere in his left hand.

Anna felt her eyes widen.

The sphere suddenly floated up into the air, orienting itself to point a lens at her, a lens that began to glow with fierce orange light. Anna threw herself behind the pillar and dropped to a crouch.

A beam of orange light burned through the granite just above her head, striking the building's front wall and shattering a window that looked in on the lobby. Shards of glass fell to the ground. When the light winked out, the acrid stench of scorched air hit her like a blow to the face.

A Death-Sphere! The man had brought a bloody Death-Sphere! Anna had to think fast. If she ducked out from behind the pillar, the damnable sphere would target her and fire before she could blink. She needed time.

Anna closed her eyes.

Calling upon her Nassai for assistance, Anna threw up a warp bubble, a sphere of rippling air that formed around her body. Time moved faster for her than for anyone else; minutes here passed as mere seconds out there.

Unfortunately, her mobility was limited. Once it was in place, the bubble could not be moved, and though its surface was permeable to anything but Anna herself, she would be unable to escape.

Anna spun around the pillar.

Through the warp bubble's rippling surface, she could make out Denario's sphere as an amorphous gray blob. It was trying to reorient itself, trying to focus that lens upon her once again.

Her temples began to throb.

Crouching down, Anna raised her gun in both hands. She squinted as she took aim, then fired. Glowing white bullets appeared beyond the bubble's surface, spiralling as they floated gracefully through the air. Each one was on course for the Death-Sphere. The pain in her head made it clear that Anna could hold this Bending no longer.

She let the bubble pop.

The floating sphere was suddenly knocked off course, blue sparks flashing over its body as the EMP rounds shorted its circuitry. The thing dropped to the ground, landing on the steps, then exploded.

Raising a hand to shield her eyes, Anna grunted. She turned her face away from the blast, ignoring the heat. "Damn you, Denario!" she whispered. "When they finally decide to space you, I'll push the button myself."

She got to her feet.

A huge black scorch mark now decorated the concrete steps. She spotted parked cars along the sidewalk but no sign of the fugitive. No doubt he had made his escape while she had been busy with his little toy. And he carried a captive Nassai with him. Her symbiont grew restless at the thought of harm coming to one of its brethren.

Something caught her eye.

A streak of light blazed across the night sky, bright like a falling meteor – a streak of light that exploded somewhere high above the city. The flash was intense but faded away in an instant. Her shuttle? Perhaps Dex had been shot down. Anna felt a sharp ache in the pit of her stomach.

Now, she was alone.

Part 1

Chapter 1

The sun was a blazing disk nearly halfway to its zenith, sending out waves of light that glinted off of every window. Huge buildings rose up to tickle the clear blue sky, tall spires of tinted glass and concrete.

Ottawa was a bustling city at any time of day, but 10 a.m. – that joyful hour when people had finally settled into their workday routine – was a little calmer than rush hour but still annoyingly busy. With all the traffic on the packed city streets, no one noticed as an old Honda Fit pulled into a parking lot and rumbled to a stop.

Pressing his back into the driver's seat, Jack Hunter closed his eyes and took a deep breath. "Oh, happy day…" He reached up with both hands to massage his temples. "I just love operating on five hours' sleep."

A quick once-over in the rear-view mirror confirmed his unkempt appearance. His thin angular face was marked by high cheekbones and bright blue eyes, his dark hair cut short with messy bangs crossing over his forehead. "Well, if they wanted me to look nice, they probably shouldn't have called me right after a late shift."

He got out of his car.

Jack wore a pair of blue jeans and a gray t-shirt with a V-neck, its fabric clinging to his back from sweat. *Oh, I love the late shift…* He wiped sweat from his brow with the back of his hand. *There's nothing like going against your very genetic makeup to make you feel more like a man.*

The parking lot was a flat sheet of black asphalt baking under the fierce sunlight of a warm spring day. His view of the river – and the Parliament Buildings along its bank – was obscured by tall concrete spires in every direction, and the noise was enough to make him groan. For the fifteenth time since crawling out of bed, Jack noted that human beings had a way of building stress factories for themselves.

He spotted a beat-up old hot-dog cart on the street corner. The thing was dented in several places, the yellow tarp that formed a makeshift rooftop ripped and torn, but Jack knew the proprietor.

Approaching with hands clasped behind his back, Jack closed his eyes and bowed his head to the man. "Hey, Tony," he said with a shrug, "you think you can scrounge up one of those Italian sausages?"

The man behind the cart flashed a grin.

A wiry-looking guy with copper skin and a crop of silver hair on his head, Tony let out a chuckle. "At ten in the morning?" he said, eyebrows rising. "Kid, you're gonna give yourself a heart attack if you keep this up."

Pressing a fist to his mouth, Jack winced and let out a sputtering cough. "You're the one who sells them," he informed the other man. "I'm just the loyal customer who puts your kids through college."

"Isn't that the truth?" Tony looked down to watch the grill. Smoke wafted up to caress his face, but somehow the man ignored it. "Did you hear the latest story on the news?"

"You mean the one about the cops trying to Sherlock what happened down at the Penworth building?" A wolfish grin bloomed on Jack's face. Squeezing his eyes shut, he barked a laugh. "Yeah, I saw it. Including the part where they interview some guy who claims he saw a big orange laser."

"People will believe anything."

Tony grabbed a well-cooked sausage with the tongs, then dropped it into a bun. He thrust a hand out, offering it to Jack. "Happy breakfast, my friend," he went on. "I think you're gonna need it."

Chewing on his lip, Jack shut his eyes and tried to ignore the surge of heat in his face. "Don't remind me," he said, shaking his head. "I'd prefer to avoid the thought of rejection for as long as possible."

For the last three months, he had been meeting with an Admissions Official for the University of Ottawa, and each visit to Miss Grimes's office began with a stop at Tony's hot-dog cart. For the last three months, he had been searching for some loophole that would allow him to enter the university's Computer Science program despite his abysmal performance in high school. As time went on, it became less and less likely that his efforts were going to pan out.

Academics had always been a source of boredom and frustration for Jack; none of his classes throughout high school had been very challenging. So, at the age of fourteen, he had simply stopped paying attention. A bone-headed maneuver – he realized that now – but try talking sense to a fourteen-year-old. Lord knows, his father had tried.

A year working at menial jobs that came without a bachelor's degree had done wonders for his outlook on life. "Thanks for breakfast, Tony," Jack mumbled. "They say a little protein goes a long way."

He reached into his blue jeans' pocket, pulling out a ten-dollar bill with two fingers and stuffing the money into Tony's tip jar when the man wasn't looking. Jack had a pretty good memory and he recalled the other man mentioning a teenage daughter. She deserved to go to college as much as he did.

Maybe more so.

"Maybe you should dress up a little," Tony said with a wry grin, a touch of colour flaring in his cheeks. "Make a good impression."

"Zoot-suit," Jack teased. "White jacket with sideburns five inches long."

The cramped little office that Miss Grimes used to meet with prospective students was sparsely decorated. A wooden desk with chips in its finish sat in the exact centre of the white-tiled floor, bathed in the segmented light that came in through the blinds on the window along the back wall.

Miss Grimes looked up when Jack came in. Her face was a perfect oval of creamy skin, framed by auburn curls that spilled over her shoulders. "Ah, good, you've made it," she muttered. "Have a seat."

Jack strode into the room.

He sat down across from her in an old metal chair, with his hands folded in his lap, trying hard to keep his face smooth. "Tell me you have good news," he said at last. "I've been living in Suspenseville all morning."

Hunching over, Miss Grimes planted her elbows on the desk, then rested her chin on laced fingers. "I'm sorry, Jack," she replied, "I've gone over the admissions guidelines and there's nothing that applies to your case."

Her reply hit him like a punch to the abdomen, driving the wind from his lungs. So. There went his chances of getting away from this menial existence. "You know, for future reference," he said, "this is really the kind of conversation that we can have by telephone. Hell, text messages would be okay."

The woman wore a serious expression as she studied him, her eyes trying to bore a hole in his skull. "This is no time for jokes," she said. "I admit that your test scores are nothing short of excellent, but that doesn't change the fact that your grades are poor."

He blushed.

"I would love to help you, Jack," she went on in tones that were more than a little patronizing. Though, Jack had to admit that he was hardly an unbiased judge of character at the moment. "But when an admissions officer looks at transcripts like yours, the very first thing he sees is laziness."

The standard replies about not judging a kid by mistakes that he made when he was fourteen came to mind, but when Jack considered them, they rang hollow in his ears. "But there has to be a method for appeals," he offered. "Some way to reverse a mistake that I made when I was too young to know better."

"Why should a school take you? Honestly now."

Tilting his head to one side, Jack flashed a wry grin. "Well, you could start with my Zoosk profile," he said, eyebrows rising. "My page gets over twenty visitors per day, and I have some great head shots."

"Another joke."

"Well, to be perfectly honest with you, most of them are just the same shot of me against different Photoshopped backgrounds." He barked a laugh that sounded bitter in his ears. "But 'Jack goes to Mount Rushmore' got fourteen likes on Facebook."

"Enough!"

Miss Grimes leaned back in her chair, folding arms over her chest. She held his gaze. "I've had enough," she said. "If you refuse to take this seriously, I cannot help you."

He stared into his lap for a long moment, wetting his lips and trying to hold back the tears in his eyes. "I'm sorry." He rubbed his nose with the back of his hand. "I'll be on my way."

"Jack."

When he looked up, Miss Grimes wore a sympathetic expression. "You could try taking some community college courses. It will be difficult since high school students are given priority over those with community college backgrounds, but you could try."

"It's good advice, ma'am," Jack replied. "I'll take it under consideration." And with that, there was nothing left to say, so he left the office with a heavy heart and a sense of guilt that gnawed at his insides. He shouldn't have been so flippant with the woman; she was only trying to help.

No, Jack Hunter had gotten himself into this mess – him and nobody else – and it was his burden to bear now. His and no one else's. How exactly was he supposed to tell his sister about this latest setback?

The hallway on the seventh floor stretched on to a stairwell in the corner, its white-tiled floor dingy and scuffed in many places. Fluorescent lights flickered in the ceiling, giving off a soft hum.

Leaning against the wall, Jack folded his arms. He tilted his head back, squinting at the ceiling. "You've done it now, boyo," he muttered to himself. "Despite all odds, you've found yet *another* way to piss off your betters."

Heaven help him.

Chapter 2

McDougall's Pub was a quaint little restaurant down in Centre Town, a hot spot for people who wanted to enjoy a quiet meal and a beer after work. Faux lanterns were hung up on the wood-panelled walls, casting soft orange light upon the wooden tables that were spread out across the blue carpet.

There were booths along each wall, most of them filled with young couples sharing a romantic evening, and the noise of soft conversation permeated the room, settling into a hum in the back of Jack's mind.

The young hostess stood at her place just inside the front door. Skinny as a post, she wore a pair of black pants and a matching shirt that clung to her body.

Her sun-darkened face was framed by long dark hair that dropped to the small of her back, little flecks of body glitter sparkling on her cheeks. "Hello, Jack," Genevieve Stevenson said coyly. "Working late again?"

Folding his arms across his chest, Jack lifted his chin. He squinted at her, steadying his nerves. "Genevieve," he said, nodding once. "And how is my favourite grade-twelve student this evening?"

"Eighteen in two weeks," she said. "In other words... soon to be legal."

Jack snapped his fingers. "I'll have to write Parliament about that."

He left before she could come up with a reply, clocking in on the small touch-screen terminal on the back wall. After that, it was a quick jaunt to the middle of the room where he found several tables in a state of disarray. Nothing like a little manual labour to take your mind off things you'd rather not think about. School and grades and seventeen-year-olds who didn't know when to quit.

"Do you work here?"

He spun around.

Mopping a hand over his face, Jack scrubbed fingers through his hair. "Yes, ma'am, I do," he said, blinking a few times. "Is there anything I can help you with? Do you have a table?"

The old woman who stood before him wore a winter coat despite the warm spring weather. Her leathery face was marked by a mole on her cheek, and the curly hair on her head had turned white. "My hamburger is all wrong," she explained. "I specifically told the waitress no pickles. Are you all deaf?"

Red-cheeked with chagrin, Jack smiled and bowed his head to her. "We'll get you another one right away," he said. "My apologies, ma'am. Allow me to offer you a free dessert."

"I don't want dessert."

The old woman folded her arms over her chest. She lifted her chin and stared up at him for a long moment. "I want you to get my order right the first time. My husband and I have been waiting twenty minutes!"

"Right away, ma'am."

He made his way back to the kitchen, trying to stuff the bile back down into the pit of his stomach. These were the joys of the service industry! Without some kind of higher education, he could look forward to a long life of taking abuse from senior citizens who had forgotten that to err is human.

The kitchen was a white-tiled room where fluorescent lights in the ceiling gave off enough illumination for the half dozen or so cooks to scurry about like a swarm of bees gathering pollen. A deep-fryer on the back wall was operated by a man in a white uniform with a hairnet on his head.

The head chef stood at her worktable, chopping carrots. A gorgeous woman in her late twenties, she wore the same uniform as every other cook, but somehow made it seem a little more... spiffy.

Her round face was marked by rosy cheeks, and sweat glistened on her forehead. A hairnet held blonde hair in place. "Hey, Tracy," Jack called out. "We need another burger for that couple at table six."

"Seriously?"

"Sadly, yes."

A smile bloomed on Tracy's face, the rosy hue in her cheeks somehow deepening by several shades. "All right, Jack," she said softly, "but only because you ignore my cousin's attempts to throw herself at you."

"She can throw all she wants," Jack muttered. "I've never been good at catching. I'm more the guy who shouts, 'I've got it! I've got it!' then runs into the wall."

"The wall?"

"Mine is not a happy story."

His night went on like that for several hours: menial tasks coupled with a whole lot of self-recrimination. For whatever reason, he just couldn't get the events of that morning out of his head. Jack Hunter, the loser. Jack Hunter, the man who had managed to screw up his life before his age even started with a two.

When he wasn't waiting tables, he was putting supplies away, making sure that the condiments were stocked and cleaning up after people who really should have been old enough to know better. It was a lovely existence. At one point, he crossed paths with old Lou, the restaurant's owner. A grunt and a stiff nod were all he received after wishing the man a good night.

The supply room wasn't much bigger than a closet, its walls lined with old brown bricks, and steel shelves made it hard to move around. He spotted a box of napkins up on the highest shelf. *Good thing I'm tall.*

Craning his neck, Jack squinted at the top shelf. "All the way up there, eh?" he said, nodding to himself. "Well, good thing natural selection decided to bless me with a tall and lanky physique."

"Hey, Hunter."

He whirled around to find another man standing in the doorway that led back to the kitchen. Marc Norris was a large fellow with a scruffy beard on his sun-darkened face. "Your sister's here."

Jack buried his face in the palm of his hand. He let out a groan that reminded him of a dying weasel. "Just what I need," he muttered. "A little mothering by proxy. Let me guess, she has food."

"Go easy on her, man," Marc shot back. "Wish my sister cared like that."

"Yeah…I know." Jack pushed past the man, making his way into the kitchen. The steel door in the back wall led out to the small parking lot that the staff used. When they *could* use it. Half the time, customers sneaked in there, and it wasn't like you could tell them not to.

Once he was outside, Jack took a moment to savour the sweet caress of cool wind on his face. The night was crisp and clear with a thousand tiny stars decorating the sky, barely visible thanks to the glow of city lights.

The small parking lot was packed, each space taken up by some-one's car – many of them too big to maneuver in such close quarters – and Jack wondered why anybody even bothered to drive to work. He spotted his sister maybe twenty feet away from the back porch, waiting for him.

Lauren Hunter was a slender woman wearing black pants and a short-sleeved shirt. Her long dark hair was tied back to reveal a pale face with sharp blue eyes. "I come bearing gifts," she said, lifting a plastic bag. "Chicken soup. And I expect you to eat it."

"Or what?"

"I'll kick you."

Jack rolled his eyes.

"I have something to tell you," he began with a touch of hesitation in his voice. He had been meaning to put this off as long as possible – anxiety was like a drill punching a hole in his chest – but now that the opportunity had presented itself, he had to get it over with. "The university turned me down."

"Oh…That's not so bad."

Jack turned away from her.

Marching up the steps with his arms folded, he stopped on the wooden deck. "Not so bad?" he said, glancing back over his shoulder "I seem to remember a whole army of guidance counsellors saying the opposite."

Lauren stood in the parking lot with hands clasped behind her back, her eyes fixed on the pavement. "You yourself said guidance counsellors don't know anything," she told him. "I know Dad will have a fit, but you'll work things out."

"If you say so."

"Stop being so hard on yourself, Jack," she snapped. "There are many schools and there are many ways to survive in this world without going to any of them. Our parents might have had all these lofty ambitions, but things aren't the same for us and that's okay. You know we'll always take care of each other."

He did know that much. Many times over the last year, he had considered moving in with Lauren and her boyfriend Steve. The idea of living with a couple made him a tad uneasy, but his sister seemed in favour of it. It was Steve he wasn't so sure about. Still, it was good to know he had someone. "Thanks, sis," he said softly. "For the soup and the words of encouragement."

"Make sure you eat."

The evening wore down along with Jack's energy levels, customers gradually clearing out and leaving the pub in a state of dim silence with the scent of various dishes still lingering in the air. Somehow, he found time to wolf down the sandwich and guzzle the cup of soup before midnight.

His last few tables wanted nothing more than a pitcher of domestic beer and the odd appetizer, so he left them with their bills and set about cleaning up. With that done, he sat down to rest for a while. That was how he found himself talking to Genevieve.

Jack sat in a booth with his elbow plunked down on the table, his chin resting on the palm of his hand. "Not a bad day," he said, eyebrows rising. "Tips alone will cover groceries for a week."

Across from him, Genevieve leaned back against the leather seat cushion, a smile on her pretty face. "Or you could do something romantic," she teased. "You ever hear of the Star Registry? Last week, Lou bought a star for his wife."

"You know, one of these days someone's gonna purchase a star that happens to be home to some other species." His mouth stretched in a yawn that he stifled with his fist. Letting his arm drop, Jack smacked his lips a few times. "I wonder what's gonna happen when they find out about it."

"Are you always so glum?"

A wave of heat surged through Jack's face. He squeezed his eyes shut, bowing his head to her. "I like to think I'm realistic," he murmured. "But I guess I could buy a star. Galactic Domination has always been a goal of mine."

In a way, he felt sorry for Genevieve. He wasn't *that* much older than her – less than two years, to be honest; hardly a massive age difference – but deep down, he just couldn't bring himself to open up to her. Oh, she was gorgeous, but Jack knew that if they were to ever try a serious relationship, it would fall apart. "Look, kid," he said at last, "I promise it's not you."

Genevieve lifted her chin, her eyes as sharp as daggers as she watched him. "Then who is it?" she asked, raising an eyebrow. "Don't tell me you're going to fall back on the 'it's not you, it's me,' routine."

"Can't beat a classic."

"Har har."

"I'm not headed for a bright future, kid," Jack said. "Trust me, you do not want to board this train."

Genevieve lowered her eyes to stare down into her lap, her cheeks flushed to a soft pink. "You know," she began, shaking her head, "maybe you're right. Excuse me, Jack. I just remembered I have something to do."

She left without another word.

A heavy sigh escaped him as he buried his face in his hands and rubbed his brow with his fingertips. "Good one, Jack," he muttered to himself. "You're becoming such an expert in the fine art of diplomacy."

Chapter 3

Anna threw her head back with eyes squeezed shut. She let them flutter open. "Oh my…," she said through a gasp. "Well, that should just about take care of it. Thank you for the conversation."

The woman who sat across from her was positively lovely with a pretty face framed by long dark hair. "Are you alright?" she asked, raising an eyebrow. "You look like you might be sick."

Covering her mouth with the tips of her fingers, Anna felt her face grow warm. She shut her eyes. "Yes, I'm fine," she said, nodding to the other woman. "Just a little fatigue. Nothing serious."

The woman stood.

Slipping the strap of her purse over her shoulder, she watched Anna with a concerned expression. "Well, if you're sure," she said, turning away. "But if you need medical attention, I can call an ambulance."

"Thank you, but no."

The small coffee shop she had chosen for this exchange was sparsely populated. A dozen round tables were spaced out across a black-tiled floor, most unoccupied. Behind the counter, a young man in a black uniform stood with his face concealed by something called a…*Damn it! What's that word?* A magazine!

The face of a woman with a sultry expression dominated the cover, her long dark hair falling over her shoulders in waves. Objectification of women. If her knowledge of history was accurate – Anna cursed her decision to frequently doze off in Mr. Dae's class – her own people had faced similar problems once.

Through the window on her right, she could see people making their way up and down the sidewalk and beyond them a line of... *Cars!* A line of cars making its way along the road. *You can do this, Lenai.*

Her faint reflection in a mug of coffee wavered as she blew on it, ripples spreading across the surface. At least these people had discovered coffee. Their planet seemed very similar to her own.

The Nassai within her stirred.

Anna bit her lip as she stared into the mug, a lock of reddish blonde hair falling over one eye. *I know you're tired,* she thought at the symbiont. *I'm tired too, but we've got to keep at this a while longer.*

No reply.

Clamping a hand over her mouth, Anna shut her eyes tight. She took a deep breath through her nose. *Can't you at least acknowledge me?* she screamed in her own mind. *I'm all you've got down here.*

No reply.

The Nassai preferred to avoid direct interaction. Through their blending of minds, she was able to learn a complex language in days, but that was not something that Nassai did often. They preferred to allow their hosts to learn on their own. Only sheer necessity had changed that.

Pulling her brown coat over her shoulders, Anna got to her feet. She paced across the room to the door, pushed it open and stepped through. *I guess I'll just have to keep myself company.*

Once outside, she found herself on a street with tall buildings on either side, glass spires that stabbed the overcast sky. A yellow car sped toward her, carrying a young man who stuck his head out the back window.

His thin face was marked by a neatly trimmed beard, and spiky black hair crowned the top of his head. "Hey, gorgeous!" he shouted as he passed. "Five Twenty-One Lisgar Street! I'll be expecting you at seven!"

Anna flinched.

Such behaviour was considered taboo among her people. That wasn't to say there weren't any brash young men with difficulties respecting boundaries, but most would be compelled to keep their mouths shut by the stares and frowns they received from their peers. The driver of that car ought to have scolded him.

She looked down at herself.

Anna still wore the gray pants and black blouse that she had been wearing during her pursuit of Denario. "Except now they're starting to smell," she muttered in her own language. "I need to blend."

Not far ahead, the door to a shop swung outward, allowing a woman in a black skirt and white blouse to step out onto the street. Her face seemed frozen in a tense expression, golden hair falling to her shoulders.

A child came out behind her.

No older than four or five, the boy wore a pair of overalls and a red shirt, a tiny cap on his head. "I want McDonald's!" he shouted, stumbling up to his mother. "Mom, I want McDonald's for lunch!"

He looked over his shoulder.

In a heartbeat, he was waddling up to Anna, craning his neck to stare up at her with enormous blue eyes. "Who are you?" the boy inquired. "You got crazy hair! Why do you got crazy hair?"

She dropped to one knee.

Chuckling softly, Anna smiled and nodded to the boy."You shouldn't run away from your mother," she told him. "If you get lost, you won't be able to have any McDonald's."

"Why are you talking to my son?"

The woman strode forward with arms folded, her chin thrust out as she stared down her nose. "What's wrong with you?" she said, seizing the child by his shoulders.

Anna said nothing.

Such hostility. Did the woman actually believe that she would harm a *child*? What kind of people were these? Doing her best to remain inconspicuous, she started down the sidewalk again.

A queasy feeling settled into her stomach when she added the factors together. In two days on this planet, she had encountered all sorts of people, and every single one of them had displayed mistrust. Those first few interactions – when she had not yet grasped the rudiments of their language – had been particularly difficult. Thank the Companion for her Nassai.

A few minutes later, she came upon one of the currency-dispensing machines these people used, built into the concrete wall of a skyscraper. The bright blue screen displayed words in a language she could not yet understand. She could speak but she couldn't make sense of any of the letters. She looked around to make sure she had enough privacy; after a few months of this, she'd be as distrustful as anyone else in this city.

I cannot believe I've been reduced to this, she thought to herself. *A Justice Keeper made into a petty thief.*

She retrieved her multi-tool – a small metal disk that fit in the palm of her hand. After pushing a few buttons with her fingers, she watched lights blink on its surface. The tiny screen lit up with the words "scan mode."

A blue ray of laser scanned over the intake slot that she had seen people use to slip plastic cards into the machine. A moment later, her multi-tool went silent as it processed the slot's dimensions.

Tiny nanobots emerged from a groove along the tool's outer edge, trillions of them building on top of one another, forming a gray rectangle in the shape of one of the cards she had seen people use.

Anna fed it into the slot.

The screen on the disk blinked a few times. Her multi-tool was sending electrical signals, learning the currency dispenser's circuit architecture. In just a few moments, it brought up a series of menus.

Turning her face up to the sky, Anna blinked when the sunlight hit her eyes. *You're really going to make me do this?* she thought at the Companion. *No last-minute twist of fate to spare me the blow to my integrity?*

No reply there either.

Running the macro she had programmed, her multi-tool sent electrical signals into the currency dispenser. A moment later, a slot at the bottom of the machine popped open, offering three glossy green bills.

Anna took them.

That's three, she noted. *Three times I've stolen from these people.* The brief lull in pedestrian traffic allowed her to slip away unnoticed. If anyone had spotted her from a distance, they would see nothing more than an ordinary woman retrieving currency from her bank account.

The sun was halfway to its zenith, hidden behind a glass spire that seemed to be a shadow to her eyes. Not a cloud in the clear blue sky. On the road, a young man upon a bicycle – amazing that these people had invented a device almost identical to those of her own world – eyed her as he passed.

Anna continued on.

It wasn't long before she found a man sitting with his back pressed to a concrete wall. Lanky and slim, he wore a pair of old brown pants with a matching jacket. His face was covered by a scraggly gray beard and unkempt silver hair sprouted from the top of his head like a lion's mane.

He craned his neck to stare up at her with haunted eyes. "Excuse me, miss," he said before pressing a fist to his mouth to stifle a wheezing cough. "Do you think that you can spare me a few dollars?"

Poverty.

Throughout her life, Anna had known that word only as an abstract concept, a note in the back of a history textbook. No wonder these people had such difficulty with trust and openness. She knelt before the man.

Anna shut her eyes tight, tears running over her burning cheeks. "I'm so sorry for your pain," she said, pressing a twenty-dollar bill into his hand. "Please take this and buy yourself something to eat."

He watched her with his mouth agape, then shut his eyes and turned his face away from her. "You're awfully kind, ma'am." The man shivered as though her touch brought pain. "I thank you for it."

"It's my duty."

The look of confusion on his face made her want to explain further, but that would expose her as an outsider. Justice Keepers opposed suffering wherever they found it. No one should endure what this man had endured.

Bright sunlight came in through a window in the front door, leaving a rectangle of light on the steps that led down into the thrift shop. The floor-space was dominated by round racks of clothing up near the counter and tall metal shelves near the back of the room. A few bins in the corner held children's toys.

The morning shift was, in Jack Hunter's estimation, quite possibly the worst kind of cruel and unusual punishment ever devised by the human race. Especially on days when he had been working at the restaurant the night before.

Sadly, one job just wasn't enough to pay the bills in today's economy, so he spent most of his time transitioning from evenings at *McDougall's* to mornings here with four or five hours' sleep in between. Joyous. How this was possible was beyond him; on some level, he knew that something didn't add up.

How was it that people were buying enormous houses in gated communities with salaries that would barely let them keep ahead of the mortgage payments? Hadn't the big financial meltdown of ten years ago done anything to convince them of the need for more frugal practices?

Planting his elbow on the counter, Jack rested his chin in the palm of his hand. He closed his eyes, took a deep breath. *Welcome to my life,* he thought to himself. *There's no turning back.*

The only other person present was a little old lady who stood flipping through the clothes on one rack. Dressed in white pants and a colourful Hawaiian shirt, she wore her gray hair in a bun.

Jack could say this much: at least this job gave him time to think. Although, given the sort of thoughts that had been racing through his head, he wasn't sure if that was such a good thing. *Just keep on attacking your own sense of self-worth,* he told himself. *It can only help your situation.*

The door chime jingled.

He looked up to find a young woman coming through the front door. A short woman with a slender build, she wore a pair of gray pants and a shirt under her long brown trench coat.

Her pretty face was framed by red-gold hair that she wore tied up in a ponytail, thin bangs falling over her forehead. *Now there's something you don't see every day.* The girl looked about the room like a fox expecting hounds to come around the corner.

Is she casing the joint?

A moment later, she descended the steps.

She approached one of the racks near the counter and began flipping through old t-shirts with her back to him. There were scuff marks on the back of that brown trench coat and her hair looked dishevelled.

For the next five minutes, he watched the strange young woman out of the corner of his eye, watched her move from rack to rack without choosing anything. Every now and then, she looked up at the door as though she expected trouble to come rushing in on her heels. She never so much as glanced in his direction.

That made him very uncomfortable. Jack had no desire to recall the tedious training videos they had subjected him to on his first day, but one tiny tidbit popped into his mind: shoplifters had a tendency to hide their faces.

He waited.

The young woman stood with her back to him, hands on her hips as she stared up at something on the far wall. *Looking for cameras?* She took a tentative step forward. *Okay, that's it.*

Jack went over to her.

The young woman spun around. A tiny jolt of anxiety went through him when she met his eyes. Her expression was serene, without a hint of emotion, and for a moment he felt silly for going over there.

Crossing his arms over his chest, Jack grimaced as he studied her. "So either you're planning to steal something," he said, deep creases forming in his brow, "or you're the editor for *Torn Fabrics Monthly*."

"Why would you suspect me of theft?"

Chewing on his lip, Jack felt his face heat up. He squeezed his eyes shut, taking a deep breath. "Well, there's the way you keep eyeing the merchandise," he explained. "And the fact that most young women don't like second-hand clothes."

"Most young women have poor taste."

"I can't argue with that."

The girl scrunched up her face in frustration, then tossed her head about like a dog who had been sprayed with water. "I wish it were that easy," she said, turning to the rack. "Clothes shopping is something of a chore, you know. First I've got to find something in my size, then in my price range. And if by some miracle I achieve those first two things, maybe I'll consider whether or not I hate the sight of it."

"Maybe I can help."

Jack began flipping through the clothes rack. The hangers slid across the metal bar with a harsh scraping sound, offering him a glimpse of brightly coloured t-shirts in pinks and yellows. It would be the perfect selection if you just happened to be a female Power Ranger. Not much for the average woman, though. "Hey, I have an idea," he began. "If I can find something you don't hate, you tell me your name."

The girl craned her neck.

A smile blossomed on her pretty face as she stared up at him with big blue eyes that sparkled. "At least your attempts at flirting are clever," she said, nodding. "Most men just stare at my chest and think it's a compliment."

"Unsophisticated pigs!"

He flipped through the rack until he found a plain white t-shirt with a woman's face smeared across the front. A quick examination made it clear that he was looking at the Britney Spears of ten years ago. "How 'bout this one?" he asked, lifting the shirt for her inspection. "With this woman's face on your chest, I can guarantee you that no one will ever check out your boobs."

The young woman grinned, shaking her head. "An interesting choice," she said. "But while I do enjoy striking terror into the hearts of fools, perhaps we could search for something more subdued."

Jack put the hanger back on the rack.

After flipping through a dozen more garments, he came upon a pink tank-top with spaghetti strings that offered just enough fabric to make a hand towel. "Ah, here we are," he murmured. "This particular number is favoured by middle-aged women who want to attract sexually inexperienced partners. We call it the Man-Maker."

"Are we looking to become a man?" she asked, raising an eyebrow. "I'm afraid that I can't help you with that one."

"Sorry," Jack replied. "I didn't mean to give you the wrong impression. You see I'm saving myself for Jennifer Lawrence."

He returned the shirt to the rack and began sliding hangers along the metal bar. One more attempt and then it was time for his concession speech. Just as he was about to give up, he noticed a blue t-shirt with a green cartoon dinosaur on the front. Yoshi stared up at him with a glint in his eyes. "What about this?"

The young woman pursed her lips as she appraised the shirt, then nodded once in confirmation. "I love it," she said. "How much does it cost? Sadly, I have to be careful with money."

Jack shrugged. "Five bucks."

"You have a deal," she replied. "My name is Anna."

He spent the next half hour helping Anna find enough cheap clothing to last a week. After that first success, it wasn't hard to figure out her sense of style; if it was the kind of thing you'd find on a ten-year-old boy, she'd love it.

To his great relief, she was willing to pay for everything. He still wasn't quite sure why she had been glancing around the room, but with no harm done, he figured there was no use in asking.

"Anna."

"Yes, Jack?"

Jack smiled down at the floor, trying his best not to sound like a goof. "Well, I was wondering..." He looked up to meet her gaze. "You think you might like to grab a cup of coffee sometime?"

She stood before him with arms folded, blushing like the sun. "You know, I really would," she said, lowering her eyes, "but I'm afraid I won't be in town for very long, and I won't have time."

"Well... can't blame a guy for trying."

In the end, it was probably for the best. Just last night, he had told Genevieve that he wasn't boyfriend material and that wouldn't be any less true if he changed the woman involved. "Well," Jack replied. "Let's get you on your way."

A few minutes later, he found himself staring down at the receipt that he'd wrung up for Anna. The list of things she'd purchased was quite extensive. Five t-shirts, two pairs of jeans, a hat and several pairs of socks. It was almost as though she didn't own anything more than the clothes on her back.

The store was empty; he was alone with the humming fluorescent lights and musty old clothes. Through the window, he could see that traffic had come to a halt on the road. O'Connor Street usually got busy when mid-morning rolled around, and though he wished some of those people would come in and buy something – the more they sold, the more money would go to Good Will – it wasn't likely.

Just then, he noticed the folded up red t-shirt sitting on the counter and fought off a jolt of anxiety when he realized why it was there. Anna had purchased that one – had paid him for it – and he had been so distracted by his attempt to make conversation that he had forgotten to put it in her bag.

Great.

She had been gone for less than two minutes; if he hurried, he might just be able to catch her and fix his mistake. *Get a move on, Hunter,* he thought, snatching up the t-shirt. *Karma isn't a forgiving mistress.*

He bolted across the store.

Charging up the steps, he stopped just in front of the front door and tried to catch a glimpse of the young woman. *Oh, wonderful,* he growled in his own mind. *After tormenting her with lame dialogue, you short-change her.*

He stepped outside.

Jack turned his face up to the sun. He squinted, working it out in his mind. "Almost noon," he said to himself. "Bus won't stop here for at least fifteen minutes. She couldn't have gone far."

A moment later, he was running down the small walkway in front of the strip mall. Scanning the area, he spotted her. A young woman half a block down the sidewalk stood with her back to him as cars whooshed past nearby. Jackpot! The back of her blonde head made it clear that he'd found Anna.

So consumed was he by the search, he barely noticed that he had left the strip mall behind. It was only then that he realized he was standing in the wide alley that led to the parking lot behind the store. And something caught his ear.

Jack turned.

Two young men came out from the alley behind the store dragging a third guy by his arms and dropping him in front of an old green dumpster. The leader stood with his hands on his hips.

A wiry man in blue jeans and a dirty hoodie scowled down at the man lying on his stomach. "You think you can screw me," he said, shaking his head. "Do you think I won't come looking for payment?"

His face was deathly pale with a forest of dark spikes on his head and a birthmark just above his left eyebrow. "Get the fuck up!" he growled. "You owe me a hundred fifty fucking dollars, bitch!"

The accomplice was a bit more solid. Dark skin and hair, he pressed his mouth into a thin line as he stared down at the fallen man. "Better get up, Josh," he added. "No one likes a man who can't pay his debts."

Out in public?

If Jack's instincts were correct, he was now a witness to a drug deal gone wrong. The dealers in this city had gotten a whole lot braver over the last ten years – Genevieve had told him she'd spotted a shady-looking guy selling Synth out by her high school – but common sense would suggest that this was the kind of thing that usually happened in the dark of night. Then again, drug dealers weren't known for their common sense.

The man on the ground looked up.

His face was marked by a nasty gash just above his eyebrow. He winced, letting out a groan. "I'll get it, Tyler," he said, pushing himself up. "Twenty-four hours. Just give me twenty-four hours."

Tyler's lips peeled back, revealing crooked teeth. He narrowed his eyes as he stared down at his victim. " 'Twenty-four hours!' " he mocked. "How many times are you gonna make me listen to that line?"

Jack dropped the t-shirt – Anna would just have to deal with being short-changed – and retrieved his cell phone. Someone would have to put a stop to this before they were looking at a homicide.

Tapping at the screen with his thumb, he brought up the dialling menu and hit 9-1-1. The bloody thing took a moment to dial before he heard an operator's voice. "Emergency Services."

"I've got an assault at two thirty-one O'Connor," Jack barked. "Looks to be of the aggravated variety and I'm pretty sure one of them has drugs."

"Thank you, sir," the operator replied. "Units on the way."

Would they get here soon enough? Tyler was already kicking poor Josh in the ribs. The man seemed completely unconcerned by the fact that any passing pedestrian would witness his felony. And why should he be? There was no one on the sidewalk but Jack, and the motorists were focused on the road.

The smart thing to do would be to leave and pretend he hadn't seen a damn thing. A good thing Jack Hunter wasn't famous for doing the smart thing. "Hey!" he shouted. "Get away from him!"

Tyler glanced in his direction. "Fuck off."

Clenching his teeth, Jack squinted at the man. He shook his head in disgust. "Now would be a good time to move on," he said, striding forward. "Before I have a chance to memorize your descriptions."

Tyler spun around to face him.

The man lifted his chin, his nostrils flaring as he sized Jack up. "You've got to be kidding me," he shouted, moving toward him. "You're really gonna stick your nose in my business for a piece of shit like Josh?"

Jack flashed a grin, sweat matting dark hair to his forehead. "Well, it's more about sticking it to you," he said, eyebrows rising. "But I'd be happy to see Josh there get out of this in one piece."

Gritting his teeth, the other man snarled at Jack, his face growing redder and redder by the second. "That was a mistake," he said, shaking his head. "Who the bloody hell do you think you are, kid?"

He threw a punch.

Jack brought an arm up to hit the man's wrist and knock the blow aside. He ducked and drove a fist into Tyler's chest.

The man seized him by the shoulders.

Wincing hard, Tyler let out a hiss and slammed a vicious headbutt into Jack's face. Stars floated in his vision and the ground seemed to fall away. He fell, a flash of hot pain racing through him.

He landed on all fours.

Clenching his teeth, Jack felt his face heat up. He blinked back tears. "All right then," he said, pushing himself up. "First round to you. Better back off, boyo, now I'm mad."

Tyler stood over him, a towering giant that blocked out the sun. He pressed his lips together, shaking his head. "Stay down, you little shit." He delivered a hard kick to Jack's ribcage.

Pain flared.

Jack fell flat on his face, stretched out on the pavement. A fat lot of good he'd done here. Poor Josh was probably in for twice the beating now that Tyler was pissed. A part of him wanted to shout that cops were on the way – that would surely send the drug dealer running – but the larger part of him wanted Tyler to stick around. A piece of filth like him deserved the jail sentence that would come sooner or later.

"Kicking a man while he's down," Jack managed. "Who says chivalry is dead?"

Tyler jerked backward, his eyes widening in shock. He stood there, slack-jawed and confused. "What the hell is *wrong* with you?" he growled. "You want me to kill you right here in the parking lot?"

Somewhere in the haze of confusion and pain, all the pieces fell into place for Jack. Defiance: that was what it all came down to. When you got to the heart of the matter, Tyler wasn't so different from a caveman defending his supper with a club.

Regardless of the danger, if he turned and ran, he would be lessened in the eyes of his peers. This wasn't over until Jack decided to yield to a superior foe... which meant it wasn't going to be over anytime soon.

"Why won't you just stay down?"

"Because..." Jack replied in a breathy rasp, "you hit like a girl." Defiance: that was what it all came down to. In the end, it didn't matter if the bad guy was stronger. It didn't matter if resisting cost you your life; it was better to spit in death's eye than to live in a world where such injustice went unchallenged.

He braced himself for another flash of pain.

The map of bus routes that these people used to navigate this city was a convoluted mess. True, she could not yet read their language, but it wasn't difficult to determine the meaning behind the maze of colourful lines that spread out over the page. How they got anywhere in reasonable time was a mystery to her.

Anna sucked on her lower lip, her eyes flicking back and forth. "This is getting us nowhere." She tilted her head back, staring up at the sky. "These people have *the* worst transit system I've-"

The Nassai within her stirred.

Anna frowned, glancing over her shoulder. She squinted into the distance. *What do you sense?* she thought at the symbiont. *Danger? It would really help if you would deign to be more specifi-*

Only then did she notice it.

Around the side of the thrift shop, a woozy Jack stood with his back to her, facing a rather nasty-looking man. A few paces beyond him, a darker man stood next to one of those waste-disposal units with his foot pressed to the back of some other fool who was stretched on the pavement.

They were too far away for Anna to hear what was going on, but she had the distinct impression that young Jack had decided to put himself at risk to protect the battered man. *Young?* she asked herself. *He can't be more than a year younger than me. Carrying the weight of the world doesn't make you a crone.*

She ran.

When she got within fifty feet, she was able to make out their conversation. "Why won't you stay down?" the nasty man barked.

"Because..." Jack replied, "you hit like a girl."

Well, *that* was offensive; but she would let him get away with it on account that he was standing up to an obvious thug. "Tyler, don't," the dark man put in while keeping his victim pinned.

"Shut up, Dave!"

Tyler lunged at Jack, driving a fist into his belly. The impact made him double over and Tyler shoved him. Jack landed hard on his knees, staring up at his attacker. "That all you've got?

"Enough!"

Anna strode toward them, dropping the bag of clothes she had purchased. She drew herself up to full height – which, admittedly, was not very impressive – and closed in on the three men. "Leave! Now!"

Maybe it was the threat in her voice. Tyler backed away until he was standing just in front of Dave and the fallen man. A moment later, he regained his nerve. "Well...look what just came our way."

Dave frowned at her, then wrinkled his nose as if he detected something foul. "I don't like this," he said, stepping away from the fallen man. "Tyler, let's get out of here before someone sees us."

"You hear that, Josh?" Tyler mocked. "You have *two* guardian angels."

Pressing her lips together, Anna lifted her chin. She narrowed her eyes to thin slits. "You think you're strong?" she began. "You don't even understand the concept. Let these men go, and I will let *you* go."

"You can go, Josh."

Pain or no pain, the fallen man got to his feet and bolted off across the parking lot at a quick lope. Such cowardice. Not even enough integrity to stand beside the one who had come to his aid.

Tyler's grin deepened as he studied her, and for a moment, she wondered whether an ordinary woman would feel fear. It had been a very long time since she had cringed at the sight of a common street thug. "This one," he went on, "this one needs someone to teach her a thing or two about manners."

"You're welcome to try," Anna replied. She was cognizant of Dave moving around her left side. No doubt he intended to hold her while Tyler did the pummelling. A good thing she had eyes on the back of her head. "Come on, Tyler," she mocked, "show me what a big, strong man you are."

"You stupid little bitch!" he growled, face reddening until it looked as though he would burst a blood vessel. His fingers curled into a fist and he stepped forward. *Well... here it comes.* He threw a punch.

Anna ducked.

She punched him in the stomach with one fist then the other, then rose and drew back her arm. She slammed her open palm into his nose. The man's head snapped back, blood dripping.

Footsteps behind her.

Bending her knees, Anna jumped and rose into the air. She backflipped over the man's head, then uncurled to land poised on the pavement. She brought her fists up in a guarded stance.

Dave spun around to face her.

Anna kicked him in the belly.

Driven backward by the impact, he stumbled and collided with Tyler, the two of them falling down. In a heartbeat, the idiot pushed himself up and stood on wobbly legs. He doubled over and charged at her like a bull.

Anna seized his shoulders, stilling him.

She jumped and flipped upside-down over his head, using her own weight to force him to the ground. Flat on his face. Anna flipped upright, then brought up her fists. *How I hate slow learners.*

Tyler lunged at her.

Anna kicked him in the chest. She spun and hook-kicked, her foot whirling around to strike him across the cheek. The impact was brutal. Tyler fell over sideways, stretched out on the pavement.

Glancing over her shoulder, Anna smiled down at him. "I trust you understand your predicament," she said, eyebrows rising. "I hit like a girl."

Behind her, Dave was moving, trying to stand. Some people just refused to learn a very simple lesson. "Stay perfectly still," she spat. "I'd rather not have to knock you both into senseless oblivion."

She turned away.

Jack was sitting with his back pressed to the wall, head lolling. The poor kid must have been exhausted. *You've got to stop doing that,* Anna scolded herself. *Thinking of him as a child.*

Using her Nassai to keep an eye on the other two, she went to him. She checked his wounds and tried to ignore the worry gnawing at her insides. Concern for a man she barely knew?

His face was fine with the exception of a bit of blood that dripped from his nose. If Tyler had harmed it, the bruises were likely concealed by his clothes. "You're going to be all right," Anna whispered. "I'll get you to a hospital."

The harsh wail of a siren filled the air. Even as an outsider among these people, she knew that was a sign the authorities would show up soon. If she stayed, there was a good chance someone would connect the story of a tiny blonde woman who had beat up a pair of thugs with the story of a tiny blonde woman who had beat up a trio of guards. *I can't just leave him!*

She lifted Jack's shirt to reveal an ugly purple bruise over his rib-cage, but no major cuts or injuries. No sign of blood on his pants. There was no real chance he'd bleed to death. *Time to go, Lenai. Fortune favours the prudent.*

Jack's breathing was slow and steady.

She stood.

Anna frowned and tilted her head to one side, a lock of blonde hair clinging to her cheek. "I'm sorry to leave you," she said softly, "but some things are bigger than any one man…no matter how brave he may be."

She turned and ran.

The narrow alley behind the building was just large enough for three men to walk abreast, surrounded by the store's back wall on one side and a wooden fence on the other. Tyler and Dave were already hobbling away, the fair-skinned man limping with his arm around his companion's shoulders. Neither one saw her. Anna decided to let them go; if fortune was kind, the local authorities would find them.

She called on her Nassai and used its power to lessen the pull of gravity. That came without too much difficulty for the symbiont. With over twice the strength of an average human being – symbiosis had its advantages – she wouldn't need much assistance.

Let's go.

Bending her knees, Anna jumped. She somersaulted over the fence, then uncurled to drop to the ground on the other side. She fell into a crouch, releasing her Nassai's hold on local space-time.

Anna stood and listened to the sound of automobiles pulling into the parking lot. A moment later, voices started barking orders and footsteps hit the pavement. Half a dozen of them if her instincts were right.

Pressing her back to the fence, Anna shut her eyes. She took a deep breath to calm her nerves. *He'll be alright,* she thought, nodding to herself. *The police will take Jack to a hospital, and they will see to his wounds.*

But would they?

Anxiety clawed at her chest when she considered the question. On her world, Jack would be guaranteed medical treatment, but she had to remember she could not take anything for granted. If these people were willing to allow their own citizens to starve on the streets, there was no reason why they would feel compelled to treat any young man who came through the door – and unless she was very much mistaken,

Jack did not have much in the way of currency. There was only one conclusion.

She had to follow.

Chapter 4

"What do you have for me, Jeannie?"

The forensics lab was a narrow room with a long steel table in the middle, green tiles on all four walls and fluorescent lights in the ceiling. Jean Simmons sat at a counter along the wall, staring into her computer monitor.

Tall and skinny as a post, she wore a white lab coat over her pantsuit, her brown hair pulled into a ponytail. "Oh, I've got plenty," she said, nodding to him. "But I can't say you're gonna believe any of it, Detective."

Harry Carlson strode into the room.

A tall man in a black suit and white shirt, he slipped hands into the pockets of his jacket. His square-jawed, dark-skinned face was marked by a small scar on the cheek, and his black hair was cut short. "Go on."

Jean sniffed.

She wrinkled her nose as she stared into the computer screen, white light reflected on her face. "We've been going over the haul from the Penworth building," she explained. "Some of it... well, I'd have to show you."

Half the department had been going over that building with a fine-toothed comb for the last three days. The explosion that had gone off on the front steps had left a very large scorch mark, and one of the pillars along the front walkway had a three-inch hole through the centre.

At this point, it would be a miracle to avoid finding anything without tripping over half a dozen Mounties and CSIS agents. The media was positively abuzz with all sorts of theories. Harry had been forced to turn over most of the evidence, but he wanted *some* answers. When bombs went off in his city, he took it rather personally.

Harry smiled, tilting his head to one side. He studied her for a long moment. "You sound frightened, Jeannie," he said, brow furrowing. "Whatever it is, I'm sure we'll get to the bottom of it."

She swivelled around in her chair.

Standing up, Jean went to the steel table and stood there, gripping its edge with two hands. Only then did Harry notice the charred fragments of what had once been a sphere that could fit into your pocket. At least that was what the lab techs claimed. The casing was distinctly round.

"This thing is composed of a material that I've never seen before." Jean said. "It's some type of complex polymer, but there are no records of this compound."

"No records?"

Crossing his arms in a huff, Harry frowned down at the floor. "You're saying that you don't know what it is?" he asked, raising an eyebrow. "Can't you send it off to a lab for further analy-"

"No, you don't understand."

The look of worry on Jean's face gave him pause. She stared blankly at the wall as if a ghost had materialized right in front of her. "I *have* sent it off to a lab," she added. "The entire chemistry department down at Carlton is buzzing. They don't know what it is either, and according to Dr. Farah, the compound is light, durable and unlike anything we've seen before."

Harry frowned and looked up to fix his gaze on her. He felt sweat bead over his forehead. "You're saying..." The words came out in a rasp, "you're saying this thing is composed of material we've never seen?"

"Yes, Detective," she replied. "That is *precisely* what I'm saying."

Worry found its way into the pit of Harry's stomach. This case had been setting his teeth on edge for the last seventy-two hours, and every time he thought he had something pinned down, another layer to the onion made him want to cry.

The explosion had been simple enough – any homemade bomb could explain away the damage to the concrete steps outside the Penworth building – but how exactly did one account for the hole through the pillar? Harry knew of no weapon that could do that kind of damage.

Then, when you factored in the stories about "giant orange lasers," it began to seem more and more like he was living in an episode of the *X-Files*. He stifled a chuckle. *All I need is a pack of Morley's.*

With a heavy sigh, he tried to put that out of his mind and focus on the task before him. "All right," Harry said under his breath, "so, where does all of this leave us in terms of leads?"

Jean wore a frightened expression as she studied him, blinking like a deer caught in the headlights. "You haven't seen everything," she said, shaking her head. "Trust me, it gets even stranger."

She used a pair of tongs to lift a small nub of metal from a tray. For a moment, she just held it there so that Harry could get a good look at the thing. It seemed to have been flattened, almost as if… "Good Lord, is that a bullet?"

Jean smiled, bowing her head to stare down at the floor. She offered a half-hearted shrug of her shoulders. "That was quicker than I expected," she said. "Yes, that is a bullet but not one for any gun I've ever seen."

Harry bit his lower lip. He closed his eyes and gave his head a shake. "A slug from an unknown firearm." This kept getting worse and worse. "Well, Jeannie, there's just no getting around it now."

"Sir?"

"We're dealing with advanced technology." Sweat broke out on his forehead as he said that, juxtaposed by a sudden chill that raced down his spine. "So, that means either the government is holding out on us…"

"No, I can't accept that," Jean said, shaking her head with enough force to send strands of dark hair flying. "The government cannot be withholding this kind of information."

"Why not?"

"Because…Because…"

Pinching his chin with thumb and forefinger, Harry narrowed his eyes. "You claim the bomb is composed of an unknown material," he said, nodding as he thought it over. "The slug comes from an unknown weapon."

He could see the wheels turning in Jean's head. Her eyes flicked from side to side as she considered the question. Eventually, she would come to the very same conclusion he had; there were only two explanations.

"Keep working on it, Jean," he told her, clapping a hand on her shoulder. The poor thing shuddered as he did so. "This case is no different from any other. I want you to give me as much information as you can."

"Yes, sir…"

Harry left her to her work. Knowing Jean as he did, he was well aware that the best way to get through her anxiety was to just keep busy. *I'll have to check in on her at least once a day,* he noted. *The poor thing might just have a breakdown.*

Outside the lab, he found a long gray corridor with doors spaced at even intervals and bright lights that shone down on the floor tiles. One uniformed officer came shuffling toward him with his head down. "Detective."

"Yes?"

As the man passed Harry, he spun around to walk backwards. His thick face was lined by wrinkles over the cheeks and forehead. "Your wife's up in your office, sir," he said quickly. "Asked to see you with some rather…colourful language."

A flush burned through Harry's cheeks. Closing his eyes, he shook his head with exasperation. "Thank you, Simmons," he replied. "I'll try not to keep her waiting any longer than I have to."

"Your funeral, sir."

A well-lit stairwell led up to the third floor, and when he arrived, Harry felt a wave of mixed emotions settle into his chest. Nearly six weeks of cold silence had passed and now Della wanted to talk. The terms of their separation did not preclude contact, but there was something of an unspoken truce between them.

He had planned on speaking to the lieutenant before forcing himself to endure his wife's latest tantrum – if they acted quickly, they'd be able to keep stories of aliens from getting out of hand – but as Simmons had said, it was his funeral. If Della chose to kick up a fuss, she might just earn him a reprimand.

A long hallway stretched on from the stairwell to his office in the corner with a line of doors on the wall to his left. Some were open, allowing Harry to overhear the sound of his colleagues speaking on the phone.

He started up the corridor.

Harry frowned, looking down at the floor. *Well, this cannot be good,* he told himself. *If she came all the way down here, it means she's ready to spit bullets.*

His office was a simple room with white walls and a rectangular desk that faced the door. Sunlight came in through the window, filtered into thin bands by blinds that he kept half-closed.

He found his wife sitting in the chair across from his own. Dressed in a black skirt over dark stockings and a green blouse, she looked up to glare at him as he entered the room. Her face was a perfect oval, framed by golden hair that fell over her shoulders. "So good to see you, Harry," she said with a curt nod. "You're such a kind man to make time for the mother of your children. Such a kind man to try to prevent me from seeing my own daughters."

Tossing his head back, Harry shut his eyes and took a deep breath. "I don't want to force you out of their lives," he said. "But I think we both agree there have been problems."

"Problems?"

Crossing her arms with a sigh, Della craned her neck to stare at him. "And what problems would those be?" she inquired. "I do hope you'll enlighten me."

"Well, there's the drinking." He felt his face contort, then rubbed his nose with the back of his hand. "I'm sorry, Della, but a DUI is kind of pushing the limits of my ability to turn a blind eye."

His wife rose in one fluid motion and made her way around his desk. She stopped at the window with her back turned, looking out on the street. "Why am I not surprised? Once again I have to listen to your sanctimonious crap."

"Della…"

"You owe me a chance to see my daughters."

"How's that?"

"Maybe you haven't been keeping track," she muttered to herself. "I completed my last counselling session last week. We agreed to revisit the issue of custody when I did; so, I want the girls to live with me."

"Absolutely not!"

Harry felt his face redden as he stared down at the floor. Scrunching his eyes tight, he tried not to tremble. "You are not *fit* to be a parent, Della! A few months of counselling won't change that."

Spinning around to face him, Della lifted her chin to fix him with a frosty glare. "I thought you might say that." The menace in her voice made his stomach writhe. "Such a shame. But you can't say I didn't warn you."

"Warn me?"

Covering her mouth with her fingers, Della closed her eyes and giggled. Giggled! What the hell did he ever see in this woman? "You better lawyer up, Harry," she mocked. "Not that it'll do you much good."

She gestured to the desk, pointing at a thick manila envelope that had been left on its wooden surface. An icy jolt of fear passed through him when he realized what was likely inside. Divorce papers?

For months, he had been anticipating this moment – looking forward to it, actually – but now that it was finally here, all he could feel was…numbness. He wasn't sure what to make of it all. How did you redefine reality so that the person you had once thought of as "the one" was now a villain who wanted to take away your children?

Della glided around the desk.

She smiled and looked up to meet his gaze. "I believe the expression is 'you've just been served,'" she said frigidly. "Just remember which one of us has the funds necessary to sustain a protracted legal battle."

With that, she stormed out of the room.

"And one more thing, Harry," she called out from the hallway. "If Missy and Claire stay with me, they'll be living with a person of means. In a few short months, you will not be able to say the same thing."

Harry clenched his teeth, then buried his face in his hand. He let out a low painful groan. *A person of means,* he thought to himself. *But without a soul. And what will you raise them to be?*

He dropped into the chair that Della had vacated, his body suddenly unbelievably heavy. As though someone had cranked up the Earth's gravity knob. What was he going to do now? Della was right; he *didn't* have the funds to sustain a legal battle. Just about every cent he made went toward the girls.

How could she be so cruel to do this to them? Couldn't she see that ripping away his finances only harmed her own children? *No, she can't,* he told himself. *She never had to live without anything; everything she ever wanted was there before she even realized she wanted it.*

"Detective Carlson?"

When he looked up, a young woman stood just outside the doorway to his office. Dressed in a black skirt and white short-sleeved blouse, she tilted her head to the side as she studied him. Her copper-skinned face was framed by long auburn hair that fell to her shoulders. "I'm sorry to interrupt you, sir," she began, "but I have Mr. Pennfield at my desk asking to see you."

Massaging his eyelids with the tips of his fingers, Harry let out a grunt. "Send him in, Teresa," he replied in a rasp. "And there's no need to apologize. I was just distracted for a moment there."

The man appeared a moment later. Tall and slim, Wesley Pennfield wore a well-pressed gray suit with a pristine white shirt. His face was incredibly pale but also incredibly plain – unremarkable in every way except for a thin pair of glasses. "Detective Carlson," he said, "I'm pleased to finally meet you."

"I should hope so," Harry replied. "You've been ducking me for over a week now."

The man folded his arms, lifting his chin to stare down his nose at Harry. "My most sincere apologies, Detective," he said in clipped tones. "Certain internal matters required my undivided attention. You understand."

Harry felt a smile bloom. Closing his eyes, he nodded slowly. "Yeah, I suppose that I do," he murmured to himself. "So, what brings you down to my office today? Have you got something new to show me?"

"You might say that."

Wesley Pennfield walked past him to the desk. He set his briefcase down on its surface, then undid the snaps. "We've managed to recover some footage from the security cameras," he said softly. "You'll want to see this."

The man retrieved a photograph.

When Harry took it, he found himself looking at the glossy black-and-white image of a young blonde woman in the middle of a hallway. She was a pretty girl – barely more than twenty unless he missed his guess – and a little overdressed. That long coat of hers wasn't appropriate for late spring.

Tapping his lips with a single finger, Harry squinted at the photo. "This *cannot* be the suspect," he said, shaking his head. "Your guards described a woman who 'handled them like a kid playing with toys."

"You believe her incapable of it?"

"This... *child* is barely more than five feet tall." Harry said. "You expect me to believe that she took out three armed guards who were all twice her size?"

"I expect you to do your job, Detective," the man replied. "No more than that. And if you are unable to do so-"

Craning his neck, Harry fixed a smouldering glare on the other man. He narrowed his eyes. "Let me make one thing incredibly clear," he said, standing. "I am not one of your employees."

Standing toe to toe, Harry was almost as tall as the other man and yet somehow he felt very much as though he should shrink away. Something in the way Wesley looked at him through those lenses...Harry could almost see the calculations.

To Wesley Pennfield, this was all just one more variable in an equation that would stretch on for pages. It was hard to say just what the man considered important, but Harry was fairly certain the opinions of a second-class detective in Ottawa's Police Department weren't high on that list.

"Apologies, Detective," Pennfield replied in a voice drier than Arctic air. "I will leave you to your work."

Through the polished window, Denario could see a field of skyscrapers, and in the gaps between them, a river that sparkled in the afternoon sunlight. More city stretched on across the other side, but from what he had been told, the people there spoke a different language and followed different customs.

His own faint reflection stared back at him: the face of a man just into his middle years with creases in his brow. He didn't even realize he was smiling until he saw it in the window pane.

Clasping his chin in one hand, Denario closed his eyes. He took a deep breath. "So you spoke to the local constabulary," he inquired, "and set them on the trail of our dear little Anna."

He turned around.

The office was sleek, sterile and devoid of anything that would distract from work. A leather chair was tucked underneath a thin white desk in the shape of a kidney. He saw no pictures there, no ornaments. Gray carpets stretched across the room to a pair of couches that faced each other on either side of a glass coffee table. No works of art on the walls, no plant life of any kind. This was a place of business.

Wesley Pennfield stood just inside the door.

Crossing his arms in frustration, the man frowned down at the carpet. "I tried to set them on her trail," he said in perfect Leyrian. "Detective Carlson did not put much stock in the video records."

With a grin, Denario looked up at the ceiling. He squinted, shaking his head. "You cannot expect your people to defeat a Justice Keeper," he mused. "Chemically propelled bullets and bi-weave armour?"

"What of it?"

Denario waved a hand. "You may as well attack her with sticks!" he said, turning back to the window. Somewhere in this city – this barbaric, haphazard, poorly planned city – a Justice Keeper was trying to locate him. If she found him, she would put a slug through his skull.

With any luck, Anna Lenai had been far too busy trying to locate food and adequate shelter to bother tracking his movements. Common sense told him he should breathe a sigh of relief, but experience warned that doing so would be premature. She had chased him all the way through Dead Space, long after anyone else would have given up.

He paced around the desk.

Wesley stood in his place by the door, stiff as a statue, and watched him through the lenses of his glasses. "The danger is minimal," he said softly. "Lenai has managed to keep a low profile, but she will slip eventually."

"Lenai is only one of my concerns," Denario said. "I've brought you the Nassai. Now you had better pay me."

Wesley lifted his chin, sunlight glinting off those lenses. He shook his head ever so slowly. "I do not take kindly to threats," he replied. "You would do well to remember that you are a guest in my home."

Grinning like a madman, Denario squinted at the other man. "This is the part where you try to intimidate me?" He cocked his head to the side. "How well is that working for you so far?"

He turned his hand up to check the force-field generator embedded in his palm. The little device blinked at him, indicating a full charge. "It doesn't matter anyway," Denario went on. "I'm going to kill our dear Anna."

"What did you say?"

Denario felt his mouth tighten, then looked up to study the other man. He narrowed his eyes. "I'm going to kill Agent Lenai," he said, nodding. "I'm going to put an end to her meddling once and for all."

"That would be most unwise." Wesley marched past him, past the desk, and went to the window. He stood with his back turned, staring out at the city. "Agent Lenai will be dealt with by the local authorities. Pursuing her yourself will only put you at risk and possibly implicate me."

"I don't care about you."

"You should."

The man looked over his shoulder, his mouth a thin line as he watched Denario. "I am the one providing you with the new life you want." He nodded toward the surface of his desk. "Look."

Only then did Denario notice the simple brown folder tucked under the corner of the other man's keyboard. Had Wesley Pennfield finally managed to fulfill the terms of their agreement?

Opening the folder revealed a series of forged identification documents with text that Denario could not read. He would have to remedy that if he planned to live among these savages. The situation left him at a most uncomfortable disadvantage. There was no way to verify *what* those documents said or whether Wesley Pennfield had actually provided the monetary compensation that he had promised. Denario was not the sort of man to put much faith in the generosity of other human beings.

"As you can see," the man began as if it were all as plain as day. "I've provided you with a substantial amount of money in exchange for the Nassai. In addition to the initial five million, I am quite happy to manage your portfolio so that you may retain the benefits of a comfortable lifestyle. You will be able to live out your days in peace, and I assure you that the Justice Keepers will never find you." There was a slight pause while the man chose his next words. "All you need to do is exercise prudence."

Clenching his teeth, Denario looked up to snarl at the other man. "You don't tell me what to do," he said, backing away from the desk. "You don't dictate my actions."

Framed by bright sunlight that came in through the window, Wesley Pennfield was a shadow with his back turned. "So long as your actions affect my interests," he began. "I most certainly do."

Once again, Denario found himself staring into his own palm. The blinking LEDs on his force-field generator gave him pause. One thought and he could hurl the arrogant fool out the window.

"Do it."

Denario froze.

Wesley Pennfield stood there with hands clasped behind his back, not bothering to turn so much as an inch. "Activate that tawdry piece of technology," he went on in a dry voice. "See what it gets you."

A chill went through Denario: a sudden shiver that he decided not to examine too closely. The implications of Wesley Pennfield's...insight into the inner workings of his mind were not something that he wanted to consider. But Bleakness take him if he was going to let this man tell him what to do.

Leana Delnara Lenai was a threat, and since they were both stuck here on this backward little planet, the sooner he eliminated her, the better. Fortunately, that wouldn't be too difficult. The poor dear was probably unaware that her multi-tool was sending a distress signal through SlipSpace.

It had started shortly after their arrival on this Companion-forsaken rock, no doubt the result of her pilot activating a distress beacon before their shuttle exploded. After all, if Anna had known about the signal, she would have silenced it. Catching him would be impossible so long as her multi-tool was alerting him that she was closing in.

Of course, Wesley would say this was all the more reason to simply let matters attend to themselves. So long as the multi-tool was broadcasting, Denario was safe from Anna's wrath. *Honestly now,* he told himself, *you were expecting logic from a primitive like Mr. Pennfield?*

The tool's power-cells would run dry eventually, but Leana Lenai would pursue him until her dying day. Better to be rid of her now, while he could find her. The little bitch had earned a bullet through the skull. No one got in Denario's way.

No one.

"Do what you want, Pennfield," he barked. "But I guarantee you, Anna Lenai will be dead by morning."

Chapter 5

Darkness slowly faded into a haze of colours that bled together, blues and grays and whites swirling together in a whirlpool. Half a moment later, objects solidified in his field of vision and he realized he was looking at the ceiling of a hospital room with daylight coming in through the window.

Jack felt his jaw drop. He turned his head, mashing his face into the pillow. "Oh, God, what the hell happened to me?" he whispered. "Or maybe I need to ask the devil."

The girl from the thrift shop was sitting in a chair at his bedside. "I had the oddest dream," he went on, "and *you* were there! The Scarecrow and Tin-Man too! Although the presence of Ronald Reagan remains a mystery."

Anna. That was her name.

She flashed a smile, a flush creeping into her cheeks. Closing her eyes, she bowed her head to him. "Well, it's kind of a long story," she began. "You see, I needed a date to my cousin's wedding."

"Right..."

"And lacking social skills of any kind, I decided to corner you, knock you out and then drag you to the banquet hall." Anna hunched up her shoulders like a turtle shrinking into its shell, hiding the grin on her face behind the tips of her fingers. "Then it occurred to me that you wouldn't be a good dancer in that condition, so I brought you here. I'm not a *total* monster."

Sitting up on the mattress, Jack pressed a palm to his forehead. He winced and let out a groan. "A date to your cousin's wedding," he murmured. "That's quite a lot of work for arm candy."

"I didn't say I was smart."

Jack chuckled. "Good thing I'm a masochist."

"It's *very* convenient for me."

When he glanced over his shoulder, the girl was staring at him with her lips pursed, her big blue eyes practically glistening. "You stood up to a drug dealer," she told him. "A rather nasty man. And you did it to protect some poor junkie."

Jack clenched his teeth, his face suddenly on fire. He shook his head in frustration. "Yeah, that's me," he muttered under his breath. "Always doing the stupid thing and then suffering for it."

"Stupid?" she replied. "Try brave."

Anna wore the most serene expression as she studied him, blinking as though his words left her confused. "It was truly remarkable," she said, nodding to him. "You were willing to put yourself in harm's way for a total stranger."

Hearing that only made his embarrassment deepen. Jack Hunter was a bit of a goof and a whole lot of screw-up, but the word *hero* had no place on his résumé. Besides, the only thing he did was take a beating.

A true hero – not that he had the audacity to assume Anna would call him as much – would have stopped the crime rather than just defy it. Which, got him thinking…how exactly did he get to the hospital?

Glancing over his shoulder, Jack frowned as he studied her. He squinted, thinking the matter over. "What happened to the drug dealer?" he asked at last. "Did you frighten him off with your puppy-dog eyes?"

"No, I just flashed him."

Clamping a hand over his mouth, Jack squeezed his eyes shut. He trembled as a fit of laughter went through him. "I see…" he said into his palm. "How very…innovative of you. I would have never thought of that."

Anna grinned into her lap, her cheeks painted red. She closed her eyes and shook her head. "I keep telling you," she said in tones of mock annoyance. "Men are all helpless under my thrall."

"You wanna make with the truth?" Jack inquired. "Because I'm pretty darn sure you Vampire Slayered that guy into the next century."

"Vampire...what?"

Well, there was a shocker. How did a girl with such rapier wit not appreciate the all-consuming awesomeness of Buffy Summers? There was something about her, something he couldn't quite put his finger on.

Jack was about to bring up the point when the sound of a man clearing his throat brought an end to their conversation. A pity. He was really starting to think he could like this young woman. True, she was leaving town, but there was this magical thing called Skype that could solve that problem.

A doctor stood in the doorway to his room. Tall and slim, he wore a white lab coat with pens in his pocket, his sun-darkened face matched by brown hair that he wore cut short. "I hope I'm not interrupting," he said, striding into the room. "I wanted to look in on you, Mr. Hunter."

"Right as a rainbow, Doc." Jack replied. He was quick to dismiss any thoughts of getting to know Anna. After all, there was a zero-point-one percent chance that she would care about what he had to say now that there was a handsome doctor in the room. With a zero-point-one percent margin of error, of course.

"That's good."

The doctor scrawled a few notes on his pad with his pen. His brow furrowed with concentration. "We found no evidence of any major head trauma," he went on. "But just the same, it's good that you came in."

Grinning and shutting his eyes tight, the doctor shook his head. "I want you to take a few days off," he said, approaching the bed. "I'll write you a note. Just make sure you get some rest."

Anna seemed fascinated by this discussion. In truth, Jack could almost see the gears turning in her head. He filed that little tidbit away under the heading *things that make her a bit weird.*

The doctor noticed her for the first time. "Is this your friend?" he asked, giving her the once-over. "We called the store to check your emergency contacts. They gave us your sister's number, but she didn't answer."

"She may not be there," Jack replied. "She's frequently out of town, so you may not have been able to reach her."

"Well, we're willing to release you but…"

Tilting her head to the side, Anna grinned at him, her big blue eyes glittering with amusement. "I will make sure he gets home, Doctor," she said softly. "It's the least I can do considering the circumstances."

"Well, that's settled then."

Yes… Jack thought. *Yes, it is.*

Through the window on the seventh floor, Anna looked out on the street below. A dozen or so cars were lined up between this intersection and the next one over, moving at a crawl. She spotted pedestrians on the sidewalk – some old, some young – all whizzing about like bees collecting honey.

The sun was a blazing sphere in the western sky, hovering just over the tops of the tallest buildings. Evening would come soon and she could already feel a rumbling in her stomach. To their credit, the doctors had insisted on running every test on Jack just to be sure he was all right. Of course, that required a large amount of patience on her part, but she didn't mind.

Anna pressed her lips together, then lowered her eyes to the floor. She took a deep breath and let it out again. *You should mind,* she told herself. *Each and every second you waste with this young man is one more Denario can use to get away.*

Chastising herself would accomplish nothing. She had made a promise to see Jack home safely, and prodding the snarl of emotions that had settled into her chest would only bring unnecessary aggravation.

She had seen many things in her three days on this planet, most of them leaving her with a bitter taste in her mouth. There was vanity here, selfishness and a casual disregard for the well-being of other people... but also nobility, strength and kindness. Jack Hunter had proved that to her.

It was easy to thumb her nose at a society that embraced values her own people had long since cast aside, but that would be a mistake. Hard as it was for her to admit, she had allowed herself to grow complacent. The first step down a road that led to bigotry was a little too much confidence in one's own convictions.

So where did that leave her?

Her people believed in a simple maxim: serve the servants. By putting himself at risk for a complete stranger, Jack had demonstrated a willingness to take care of others, and now she was honour-bound to take care of him. But she was also honour-bound to pursue Denario with every breath. The man had captured a sentient being and there was no telling what he had planned for the poor Nassai he had taken. *A Justice Keeper must make the hard decisions,* Anna told herself. *She must control her emotions and act based on who has the greatest need.*

The Nassai had a greater need.

Of course, that did nothing to make her decision easier. She knew next to nothing about this city. Denario could have gone anywhere, and somewhere deep down Anna felt as though she had already failed. By now, the symbiont could be dead... or worse. If she was to have any hope of saving the poor creature, she needed help.

Is that why you arranged for me to find Jack? she thought at the Companion. When you had analyzed the situation over and over, added up all the factors and found yourself unable to make a decision based on logic alone, sometimes faith was the only thing you had left. Not faith in the Companion – to Anna, that was no more than an abstraction, an attempt by humankind to articulate truths beyond their understanding – but faith in the idea that there was a purpose to the universe.

Fate gave you a chance to make the correct decision; after that, it was up to you.

"Are you ready to go?"

She turned.

Jack stood in the small waiting area, dressed in his blue jeans and a brown coat over a black t-shirt. "That is if you insist on escorting me." He went red, then bowed his head to her. "You don't have to."

"No, it's my pleasure," she replied. "I think we could both use something to eat."

Chapter 6

Anna had never taken the opportunity to appreciate this city's beauty. After chasing Denario through Dead Space for nearly three days and then discovering to her shock that there was actually an inhabited planet out here among the wilderness – not to mention the skirmish after she pursued him through the SlipGate – she was in no frame of mind to be captivated by architecture.

No, she had been in fight-or-flight mode for almost four days, sleeping in alleys and deathly afraid that someone might knife her every time she shut her eyes. When you lived like that, it was easy to see everyone here as your enemy. A dangerous attitude, that. No one ever prospered by thinking in terms of "Us against Them."

In the distance, Ottawa's skyline was alight as tall buildings reached up toward the heavens. The sky was a deep blue that was quickly fading to black, and stars were starting to twinkle. Could she see her home from here?

Tall trees lined the sidewalks on both sides of Lyon Street with branches that nearly stretched across the road, creating a canopy of leaves above their heads. The houses here were almost…cute. Small, red-bricked buildings with gabled roofs and balconies on the second floor. Not the sort of place where you would expect to find barbarians.

Jack was humming behind her.

The young man walked along with his head down, a smile on his face, "So, are you gonna tell me your secret?" he asked with a shrug. "Or do I have to keep guessing until I pass out from exhaustion?"

Anna felt a blush come on. Closing her eyes tight, she shook her head. "I have no secret to tell," she said. "Besides, if I did share it, that sort of defeats the purpose, now doesn't it?"

"Well, that depends."

With a grin, Anna turned her face up to the heavens. "Maybe for you, it depends," she said, eyebrows rising. "But not for me."

Jack overtook her.

Clasping hands together behind his back, he travelled up the sidewalk at a measured pace, forcing her to stare at the back of his head. "Secrets are useless if you keep them to yourself," he explained. "At that point, they're nothing but emotional baggage. When you get down to it, the purpose of a secret is to tell just one person."

He spun around.

Anna frowned, then looked up to fix her gaze upon him. She blinked a few times. "So you think I should tell you," she said. "Tell me then, how exactly have you earned so much trust?"

He went red and then bowed his head to her. It was nice to be able to put the man off balance; after so many quips, she was beginning to feel like every conversation was a sparring match. "So, you *do* have something to tell," he said at last. "I'll have to put more faith in my powers of observation."

Bleakness take him!

When was she going to learn to guard her responses? Covert affairs were not the standard mode of operation for a Justice Keeper. She was used to flashing a badge and getting to business. "Jack, you're reading something into nothing," she mumbled. "Why would you even think I have a secret?"

Oh... bad move.

"Well, let's see," he began. "You needed an entire wardrobe. You were completely unaware that Canada offers universal health care. Then there's your accent. I have never heard one quite like it."

Anna bared her teeth, then lowered her eyes to the ground. She let out a soft, slow hiss. "All right," she said, nodding once. "So, you've noticed a few oddities about me. It doesn't mean I'm part of some conspiracy."

Jack's mouth curled into a small smile, his cheeks flushed to a rosy hue. "I take it back then," he said. "Forget I asked, and we can go on pretending you're just an ordinary young woman."

After a moment's consideration, Anna decided that it'd be best to walk in silence for a little while. Many people had looked askance at her over the last few days – noting her accent or her stumbling attempts to master their language – but her interactions with each of them had been fleeting. With each conversation, she had grown more familiar with this strange way of speaking, learning at an exponential rate.

Jack, however, had spent quite a bit of time with her. It would be all but impossible to prevent him from speculating. That left her with a predicament. Did she simply come clean, tell him everything and ask for his help in navigating this city? Or was it better to preserve his innocence?

The people of this planet were clearly unaware that human life had been scattered across the galaxy. Perhaps they had forgotten the Overseers or rationalized them away as myths of the distant past. It was even possible that these people actually *believed* they had evolved on this world.

Could she disabuse them of it?

They turned down a narrow street where small houses looked out upon a road that was just wide enough for two cars. Trees along the sidewalk swayed in the wind, sighing as the breeze passed through their branches.

Anna shuffled ahead with hands shoved into her pockets. She paused for a moment, keeping her back turned. "I don't mean to be cryptic," she said at last. "It's just that some of it is hard to explain."

"Try me."

Anna shot a glance over her shoulder, a small smile spreading on her face. "You've got a keen mind, Jack Hunter," she said softly. "But I'm not sure that you would believe me if I did so."

Grinning like a fool, Jack looked down at his feet. He scrubbed a hand through his thick brown hair. "Well, I can't promise I will," he replied, "but you'll never really know until you give it a-"

Something caught her ear.

In the distance behind him, a yellow automobile came to a stop in the intersection with the street they had just come from. The back door swung open and a man got out in a hurry. *This feels wrong.*

He stood up straight.

Just into his middle years, the man wore a loose-fitting jacket over black pants and a matching shirt. His brow was lined with creases and his short hair was slowly graying at the temples.

Denario.

Anna shoved Jack to the ground. He fell hard upon his side on some stranger's front lawn, then turned his head to glare at her. "*Et tu, Brute!*" he snapped. "What in the bloody hell was that for?"

"Stay down!"

She ran off the sidewalk, into the middle of the street, then spun around to face her opponent. If the fool thought he would get past a Justice Keeper, she would gladly school him in the basic laws of physics.

Denario marched along with grim determination on his face. He lifted his chin and sniffed at her. "I knew I'd find you sooner or later," he said. "Were you aware that you've been broadcasting a convenient signal?"

A signal?

Why in the Verse would she be broadcasting a...Dex must have activated a distress beacon before the shuttle went up! Elation bubbled up in her belly. This meant there was a chance she could be rescued; all she had to do was survive Denario and recover the stolen Nassai.

Her opponent sneered, shaking his head in disgust. "You're not going to walk out of this one," he growled, thrusting a hand out. The force-field generator in his palm let out a high-pitched whine.

A screen of white static appeared before him, so thick it seemed as though she were watching him through a blizzard of tiny snowflakes. It sped forward, threatening to crush her with the speed of an oncoming truck.

Bending her knees, Anna leaped.

She somersaulted over the wall of static, then uncurled to drop to the ground in the middle of the road. She brought up her fists in a fighting stance. "You wretched piece of festering *lasonch.*"

Clenching her teeth, Anna narrowed her eyes. "I'm going to make sure they throw you out an airlock," she said, tossing her head about with such force that tendrils of hair flew across her face. "In the middle of a plasma storm."

Jack was crouched on the nearby lawn. His face was bone-white as he blinked at her in confusion. "What the hell was that?" he exclaimed. "I... I... When in God's name did we make energy weapons?"

Soft laughter filled the air.

Denario backed away, keeping his outstretched palm focused on her. "Do you like my little toys, Agent?" He tilted his head to the side, a wicked grin splitting his face in two. "I have more."

The man lifted his other hand, revealing another blinking device fused into the skin of his left palm. Most of this was for Jack's benefit. She knew perfectly well that Denario had several force-field generators implanted in his body. The fool did love to show off for spectators. "In a few moments, the first one will be charged. But..."

A wall of white static sank into the ground, kicking up chunks of asphalt as it sped toward her. In a heartbeat, she was standing in a storm of debris, bits of black pavement flying toward her.

Crossing her arms in front of her face, Anna backed away. She sank to one knee in the middle of the road, ignoring the pain as a piece of shrapnel slashed a shallow gash in her scalp.

Her sense of spatial awareness provided a silhouette of Denario in her mind's eye. He drew his jacket aside, retrieving a pistol from the holster upon his thigh. He raised his arm, taking aim.

Anna called on her Nassai.

The air before her fingertips rippled, light twisting as though someone had grabbed a portrait of the street and crumpled it. She saw the blurry image of Denario's fire, his arm jerking from the recoil.

Bullets struck the wall of rippling air, slowed to the point where she could see them with her naked eye. One by one, in a line, they veered off to her left and hit the road with enough force to send pavement flying.

She let the Bending vanish.

Anna looked up to meet his gaze. She felt her face crumple in disgust. "You must be joking!" she rasped. "You're really going to bring a half-empty clip to a fight with a Justice Keeper!"

Denario pulled the trigger but the blinking LED on his pistol gave him pause. An empty mag, two drained force-field generators and one very pissed-off Keeper: the man must have been sweating.

Denario snarled at her, his teeth bared with spittle flying from his mouth. He shook his head. "This isn't over!" he said, backing away. "You hear me? The next time we meet, I'm going to end-"

Anna leaped at him. She flew like an arrow right into his chest. The impact drove him backward, and he toppled to the ground, landing hard on his ass in the middle of the road.

Gritting his teeth, Denario squeezed his eyes shut. His face went redder and redder by the second. "You little bitch!" he growled, trying to sit up. "I swear to the Companion that I will-"

His eyes popped open.

Denario opened his mouth to let out a sharp squeal that reminded her of a pig being slaughtered. He tossed his head from side to side. "Aaaaaaahhhhh…" His body spasmed several times before going still.

Slapping a hand over her mouth, Anna flinched. She felt a bead of sweat roll down her forehead. *He's dead,* she thought. *Those bloody force-field generators fried his entire nervous system.*

Funny how she had been willing to kill him in the heat of battle, but now that she was perched over his dead body, the sight of it made her sick...He wasn't even dead by her hand, and yet she felt responsible.

Anna stood.

Running across the road, she hopped onto the sidewalk and approached the lawn. She dropped to one knee in front of Jack. "Tell me you're all right," she whispered. "No shrapnel to the face? No oncoming heart attack?"

He seemed fine.

Jack winced, head hanging. He slapped a palm against his forehead and let out a painful groan. "I can't even begin to describe what I'm feeling," he said. "Anna, how in God's name did I get pulled into a Syfy channel original movie?"

"You care too much about strangers."

"Noted." He coughed. "You weren't speaking English..."

She wasn't? The conflict with Denario had been so intense that she hadn't noticed herself slipping back into her native tongue. What must poor Jack have thought? Sitting there, watching two people shout gibberish and hurl death at one another.

She gently laid a hand on his cheek. Jack closed his eyes, leaning into her touch. "I guess that solves one moral dilemma," Anna mumbled. "Do you know a safe place where we can rest? I think it's about time I gave you some answers."

Chapter 7

To say that Jack's apartment was small was a bit of an understatement. It was pretty much a closet, and whether you were standing in the kitchen or the bedroom depended a great deal on which wall you were looking at. Still, it was home. He had never needed all that much in the way of space.

Four red-bricked walls surrounded a couch that sat in the middle of a carpeted floor, facing a small television. His bed was in the corner, walled off by a set of white curtains on steel rails.

On the other side of the room, a line of cupboards was home to his small oven, and the fridge was humming contentedly next to the front door. Just enough space for a man to find a little peace. His apartment was the safest place he could think of, and now it was occupied by a woman who could make bullets curve.

He paced across the floor.

Pinching his chin with his thumb and forefinger, Jack closed his eyes. He exhaled through his nose. "All right," he said with a curt nod, "let's get on with the Q&A portion of our date."

He went to the couch.

Anna chose a chair across from him with its back to the TV, where she sat primly with her hands folded in her lap. For a moment, she was silent. Perhaps she thought it appropriate for him to begin.

Licking his lips, Jack stared down into his lap. The words were there in his mind, but he had to work up the nerve to say them. "How did you do it?" he began. "How did you make the bullets veer off course?"

Anna watched him with a face that might have been carved from ivory, perfectly serene in every way. "I'm not from this world," she said at last. "My people are well versed in the mechanics of bending space-time."

"You're an alien?"

"Not in the sense of the word that you mean." She stood, turning her back on him and facing the wall. Her posture was stiff, tense. "Genetically speaking, I'm as human as you are. I was just born on another planet."

"How is that possible?"

She froze in place, taken aback. Clearly she had expected him to know the answer to this question. That fact alone had several interesting implications, the most pertinent being that human civilization must have flourished on multiple worlds across the cosmos. Jack felt a rising sense of elation. Space travel was possible! There were other worlds to see and expl-

"My people were brought to Leyria by the Overseers," Anna replied. "Just as your people were brought here."

"Overseers," he said. "I've never heard of the Overseers."

Anna turned partway around, looking over her shoulder. "You think your people *evolved* here?" she mumbled. "You honestly believe that?"

"Anna, we *did* evolve here."

"That's not possible," she said. "Terra Prime was lost."

Jack leaned back against the couch cushions.

Throwing his head back, he grinned up at the ceiling. "Well, congratulations, sweet pea," he said, eyebrows rising. "Because you've just found it. This is the planet where our species evolved."

"You have proof of this?"

"There are extensive fossil records," Jack explained, "tracing our lineage back to our primate ancestors. I can't produce them for you right now, but no matter what those Southern preachers tell you, the theory of evolution is quite sound."

He found himself transfixed by the expression on her face as she worked her way through this new information. How would Anna's people have learned about evolution? If what she said were true, there would *be* no fossil records for them to examine, not for their own species anyway.

Then again, it could all be lies. True, he had witnessed something fantastic this evening, but fantastic events can have many explanations. Perhaps Anna was part of some government program investigating new weapons tech. That wouldn't quite fit in with her strange accent, but it was plausible. You couldn't just look at something fantastic and then accept the first explanation that came along. And if he thought the word *fantastic* just one more time, he would have to find himself a TARDIS.

Jack got to his feet.

He marched across the room – right past Anna – and let out a frustrated sigh. There had to be some way to make sense of this, to verify the woman's claims. Something that would appease his inner skeptic.

He stood before the wall with arms folded, chewing on his lower lip. "Something occurs to me," he said to himself, "you never answered my question. The one about how you bend the bullets."

He turned.

Anna stood in front of the couch with hands clasped behind her back, head cocked to the side as she studied him. "I carry a symbiont," she explained. "A life form called a Nassai that can bend space-time."

"A symbiont." Jack had to admit the thought left him with a queasy feeling in his belly. The human body wasn't really meant to be *paired* with another species. "So, what? It's like a worm in your belly?"

She actually giggled, shaking her head with amusement at the notion. "It doesn't work like that," she said, dropping onto the couch. "The Nassai are very different from what you would have imagined.

"The moon that orbits my planet has an atmosphere. On its surface, we found a thin mist with trillions upon trillions of tiny organic cells communicating with each other through a series of electric pulses. Naturally, human hubris kicked in, and we took a small sample back to be studied.

"This… sample… became a distinct consciousness, an individual being separated from the whole. It broke out of its containment unit and bonded with one of the scientists. That was its only option; the Nassai cannot survive in our atmosphere. Only then did we learn that the creatures were sentient."

Hugging herself, Anna rubbed her upper arms. Her eyes were downcast as a shiver passed through her. "The Nassai is not localized within my body," she went on. "Its cells are bonded with my own, throughout my nervous system, my blood, my bones."

"And it warps space-time?"

Anna nodded.

"The Nassai sometimes share with us fragments of their collective memory," she explained. "From what we've seen, they were engineered by the Overseers for that very purpose. Millennia ago, the Overseers experimented with organic technology, living ships that could bond with their pilots and be controlled with nothing more than a thought. The Nassai were part of their attempts to allow a living vessel to travel at speeds faster than light. Exactly how they do it has always been a mystery to us. Some of our physicists speculate that the Nassai can tap into vacuum energy.

"Even so, the process is very taxing for both symbiont and host. Overuse could kill my Nassai, and if it dies, I won't be far behind. That is why we only use a Bending when all conventional methods of defense prove ineffective."

This was just…

Jack was speechless. Absolutely speechless. Never in his wildest imaginings would he have dreamed up a story like this, and he had come up with some doozies. In his youth, he had turned in a Western story involving gunslingers calling upon the electromagnetic force and infusing their bullets with lightning. His sixth-grade teacher had not been very impressed. "The assignment was 'write about your weekend,'" her shrill voice echoed in his head. As if anyone wanted to read about Super Mario speed-runs and reprogramming the TV's parental controls to lock out the Justin Bieber concert. Lauren had thrown a fit. *I make no apologies,* Jack thought to himself. *What I did, I did for the good of humanity.*

But... aliens. Did he believe Anna's story? She sat there on his couch with the most earnest expression, like a girl trying to convince her teacher that the dog really *had* eaten her homework. "Why did you come here?"

Anna's face crumpled, tears streaming over her cheeks. "The man that I fought in the street," she said, shaking her head, "he captured a Nassai and took off in a shuttle. I pursued him to this system."

"Worst of all, he's dead," Anna went on. "Those implants he carried sometimes break down, and if that happens, they can short out your nervous system. Just one of the many reasons such devices are outlawed. Still... he's gone and I have no way to find out where he took the..."

She sniffled, rubbing her nose with the back of her hand. "I'm sorry," Anna hissed, turning her face away so that he wouldn't see her tears. "Normally, I don't have quite so much difficulty keeping my composure."

Jack approached the couch.

He dropped to his knees in front of her, then craned his neck to meet her gaze. "You think it's your fault," he said, blinking. "You blame yourself for whatever happens to that poor creature."

She stiffened.

So now they came it. Did he trust Anna? Was he willing to get mixed up in what was either a life-threatening situation or the biggest con of all time? Something about this woman seemed genuine. *Oh, to hell with it. What good is life if you never take any risks?* He just prayed it wasn't hormones fuelling his decision. "I will sleep on the couch," he said. "You can take the bed and I'll make sure you have clean clothes."

Anna stared at him with her mouth hanging open, blinking in confusion. "I don't... I don't understand." Another shiver escaped her. "You want to help me? Even knowing the risks? For all we know, Denario may have friends who want me dead just as much as he did. I've disabled the transmitter on my multi-tool, but they may still find me."

"A criminal kidnapped a sentient being," Jack replied. "Call me cynical, but I *don't* think he had anything pleasant in mind. If I can do something to prevent the Nassai from being harmed, I will."

He stood up and turned away from her, wheels spinning in his head. Anna had not been carrying the bag of clothes she had purchased; she must have dropped it after saving him from Tyler and his buddy. *Another reason to help, Hunter,* he noted. *You owe her.*

She tugged on the back of his shirt.

Jack spun around to insist that he was willing to help, but before he could speak, she stepped forward and slipped her arms around him. The hug took him by surprise. "I think I should point out that on my world, 'thank you' is usually sufficient."

She leaned her cheek against his chest and smiled. "Thank you," Anna whispered. "It's been a harrowing few days on this planet. I'm glad I found a friend."

No, this won't be awkward at all!

The instant she pulled up the covers, Anna felt the tension drain out of her body like water through a hole in a bucket. Aches and pains she had been ignoring for days slowly faded away. She suspected that a large part of it was the glorious feeling of being clean! After getting settled in, she had taken a shower, a real Companion's truth shower with hot water! Her heart went out to the beggar she had seen in the street. How long since he had been given a chance to bathe?

She snuggled into Jack's bed with the covers pulled tight. Her new friend had been kind enough to lend her a pair of his shorts and a t-shirt that dropped almost to her knees. A bit too big but it would do for sleeping.

The apartment was pitch black with blinds over the windows to shut out the street lights. She could hear Jack breathing in a slow and steady rhythm. He must have fallen asleep on the couch.

It surprised her to realize she felt at ease. She had expected an internal struggle in which she had to suppress the urge to stay awake and keep an eye on her host – sleeping in alleys tended to have that effect – but something about this little apartment made her feel safe.

Twenty-four hours ago, she had been willing to see the worst in the people of this world, but now she was ready to trust a man she hardly knew. What did it say about the human condition when a full belly and a warm bed made up the difference between optimism and cynicism?

She didn't know. And she was too tired to consider the question. Three nights on the street and another three in the cramped bunk of a shuttle.

Dex...

She had barely known the young pilot from Petross Station; they had not said very much to each other on the long trip through Dead Space. It had been nothing more than pure dumb luck that Dex had been assigned to her team when she had come charging through the docking bay.

He was a quiet man. In truth, she knew very little of what had happened after she passed through the SlipGate. Their shuttle had been shaking, the lights flickering. In the frenzy, she remembered hearing Dex say that Denario was firing on them. Then the trip through SlipSpace and her arrival in the storage room.

Three days on this planet had not given her much time to mourn. Dex popped into her thoughts from time to time...She wished she could feel a stronger sense of grief. He deserved better.

Anna said a quick prayer for the young pilot, then relaxed her mind. She needed to let herself rest. *It wasn't your fault...* The words rang hollow, but she said them anyway. They had been trying to save the life of an innocent. Dex had agreed to follow a pursuit course. It wasn't her fault.

Somehow, she just didn't believe it.

Crickets chirped in the distance, the sound carrying through the window on a breeze that made the blinds sway. It was still dark, but the odd birdcall made Jack aware that sunrise was only an hour away. He had slept soundly, but his body seemed to be used to short naps.

Temporarily energized by a few hours of rest, he found his mind wandering. A total stranger slept not twenty feet away, a woman with the ability to bend space and time, with a talent for kicking five kinds of ass. How did he feel about that? Was it strange that he was mostly okay with it?

Despite his usual tendency toward skepticism, he found himself starting to believe Anna's story. Aliens on Earth... and Jack Hunter, the smart-ass kid from Manitoba, was the one to stumble face-first into one of them. Amazing just how much could change in the brief span of twenty-four hours.

Just one day ago, his biggest concern had been scraping together enough cash for rent, and now he was fretting about the well-being of some gaseous life form. He had never considered that life could exist in a gaseous state, much less that it could be a thinking being.

He wondered what it meant in terms of the bigger picture. How would the people of Earth react when they learned that other human beings were zipping about the galaxy and bonding with aliens? Would it cause a crisis of faith for some?

Jack had never been a religious man – unless you counted a vague sense that there existed a level of reality beyond human perceptions – but he had seen Lauren recite the Lord's Prayer. Would this knowledge affect her? His sister was a bright woman with a keen grasp of science, but what about those people who believed the Earth was a mere six thousand years old?

The image of riots in the streets passed through his mind, protesters with big neon signs that read, "God hates E.T!" Hell, he himself had to chew on the issue to really wrap his brain around it, and he wasn't all that wedded to any particular philosophy.

Even now, a part of him still resisted it, still looked for other possible explanations for how Anna had deflected bullets with a thought. Not to mention the strange man with the force-fields. It was as though some part of him wanted to deny what was right there in front of his face.

Was this what it had been like for the people of seventeenth-century Italy when Galileo told them the Earth went around the sun? It was so easy to just dismiss them as a bunch of backward savages, but had human beings changed all that much in the last four hundred years? A troubling thought.

He mused on it for half an hour before drifting off again.

Chapter 8

Soapy water filled the basin of the sink nearly halfway to the top with the odd plate popping out from under the surface. Through the window above the tap, Harry could see a starry sky and the shadow of the house next door. A beautiful night. Even the chirping crickets seemed to agree.

Harry frowned as he stared through the pane. He blinked, trying to put his thoughts in order. *Unless your ex despises you,* he thought. *If that's the case, it's not at all perfect.*

He scrubbed a dish with a sponge, wiping the last suds away from the floral pattern. Della had insisted on taking the dishwasher when she moved out – it had been a gift from *her* father, after all – but Harry didn't mind. Doing the dishes always left him with time to think and wind down.

His small galley-style kitchen was little more than a narrow corridor between two lines of cupboards with the sink on one side and the fridge on the other. Not much room to maneuver, even for someone who had never really learned the art of cooking. It was a common feature in houses built in the eighties, and another sore spot for Della. Even now, he could hear her complaining that her father would gladly buy them a larger house. That might be so, but Harry had wanted to make it on his own.

"Dad!"

Claire came running through the space between the cupboards. Barely more than three feet tall, she was an angel in her blue dress. Paternal bias perhaps, but Harry wasn't about to amend that statement.

A grin bloomed on his daughter's round face as she stared up at him with big brown eyes. "Miss Collins said my painting was good." She lifted up a picture of a stick-figure cat on a field of green grass.

Harry cocked his head to the side, examining the painting. He felt his eyebrows try to climb up. "Miss Collins is a smart woman," he said, dropping to one knee. "You might be a famous artist one day."

Claire's smile was infectious as she came closer. She threw her arms around his neck, burying her nose in his chest. "Will you drive me to school tomorrow?" she asked. "I don't like taking the bus."

"I can't, sweetie," he replied. "Missy will look after you."

Harry sucked on his lip, nodding slowly to his daughter. "Now, you need to get to bed," he said, mussing her hair with the palm of his hand. As always, Claire let out a little squeal when he did that.

She stepped back.

Planting fists on her hips, Claire lifted her chin. She squinted at him. "You're in a lot of trouble now," she teased. "The other day, you said that messing up someone's hair was against the rules!"

Yes...he had told her that. Of course, 'the other day' had been last month, and at the time he had been trying to get Claire to stop tormenting her sister, but the rules were the rules. Amazing how much children retained. "Yes, I did say that," Harry conceded. "You have a very good memory."

"You told me if I kept doing it, I was grounded," Claire added. "Doesn't that mean you're grounded, Daddy?"

He pinched her nose, and Claire squeezed her eyes shut. She squealed like a pig in a frenzy. "I *am* grounded," Harry agreed, "which means I have to go to bed early, and you get to pick what we watch on movie night."

Fortunately, that probably meant nothing worse than a Dora the Explorer marathon. Missy would be annoyed, but she was usually good-natured about that sort of thing. She'd probably spend most of the night on her iPad. Of course, that meant frequent glances over her shoulder to keep an eye on what she was reading. He would never have imagined that parenthood would turn him into the Gestapo.

"Upstairs now," Harry said. "It's bedtime."

"But, Dad-"

"Claire…"

Without another word, Claire turned on her heel and marched through the narrow aisle. She paused just in front of the kitchen table. "Love you, Dad," she said just before charging up the stairs.

The smartphone on the counter lit up and began to buzz, rotating around with each vibration. Harry snatched it up and took the call. *God Almighty, this had better be pretty damn important.*

"Detective Carlson?"

"How can I help you, Bates?"

"We found new evidence in the Penworth case," Bates replied. "You're gonna want to get down here, Detective. Trust me when I tell you that you're going to have to see it to believe it."

"Fine," Harry muttered. "In the morning."

"But-"

Harry felt his face crumple, sweat beading on his forehead. He shook his head in frustration. "No buts, man. I've got the girls; I can't find a sitter, and they don't like it when I randomly take off."

"Detective," the voice on his phone protested. "You're really gonna want to see this. Someone managed to tear up whole chunks of a city street, and the neighbours claim they saw a man hurling lightning."

Could this week get any more bizarre? Holes punched in concrete pillars, tiny girls beating up grown men twice their size and now lightning bolts? This really was starting to sound like a cheesy *X-Files* plot. "I'll be there in the morning," Harry insisted. "No one is in any immediate danger, right?"

"Uh…no."

"Then I'll see you at seven."

The morning sun was shining down on small houses with black shingles on their gabled roofs. Under any other circumstances, this would be a peaceful neighbourhood on a warm summer's day complete with maple trees that sighed in the wind. Not today. Today, the place was roped off by police tape.

A thick layer of asphalt had been scraped off the road's surface, leaving a pit about the size of a child's bed. Several paces beyond that, chunks of pavement were scattered across the street.

Harry let out a grunt.

He marched around the pit with hands shoved into his pants pocket, pausing near a group of uniformed officers. "Well, this is a new one," he said, shaking his head. "Do we have any theories?"

Officer Brandon Mitchell was a heavyset man with stubble along his jawline. He reached up to grab the bill of his cap and pulled it down, shading his eyes from the sun. "I can't say we have, sir."

Tilting his head back, Harry closed his eyes. He took a deep breath then let it out again. "Not even a guess?" he inquired. "So we're just going to sit here and conclude that the hand of God came down and scooped up some pavement?"

Mitchell crossed his arms with a sigh. "Couldn't say *what* happened, Detective," he grumbled. "All I know is that somebody's trying to get in on the construction market."

Har har…

As he took in the sight of the massive pothole, Harry felt a sinking feeling in the pit of his stomach. He had ordered Jean to keep quiet about the strange devices that she had been examining – the last thing he needed was to start a panic – but with each new incident, a pattern began to take shape.

Clearly, they were dealing with technology that was decades ahead of anything they had ever seen before. So, either the military had lost track of some incredibly impressive hardware or… or Ottawa had just become centre stage in an interstellar turf war. That had its own set of implications.

If aliens really were walking the streets of Canada's capital, they had done so for nearly a week without being noticed. That meant they had the ability to look like human beings. Harry had always considered himself a die-hard Scully – show him a palm reader and he'd show you a con-artist – but with every passing day, Mulder's position felt more and more plausible.

Harry narrowed his eyes. "Get CSIS down here," he ordered, squatting down near the edge of the pothole. "They're going to want to take a look at this. And someone get me some coffee!"

"Detective."

A glance over his shoulder revealed a woman in a blue pantsuit striding across the road. Her round olive-skinned face was tight with anxiety. That was the sort of thing you noticed after a few years of interrogations. "I appreciate your professional courtesy," she began, "but CSIS has been here for the last four hours."

"Harry Carlson," he said, standing and offering his hand.

The woman took it and gave a single pump. She smiled up at him, holding his gaze for a long moment. "Aamani Patel," she said with a quick bob of her head. "I thought you might like to meet someone."

Harry arched an eyebrow.

Patel stepped aside to reveal a tiny old woman in a pair of pink sweatpants and a white t-shirt standing on the curb. "Detective Carlson," she said, stepping into the street. "I saw it all.

"It was a little blonde thing, sir," she went on. "She fought with an older man who...well I can only say he loosed thunderbolts at her. I went to my window when I heard the commotion.

"A blonde woman?" Harry asked. "In a brown coat."

The woman went pale before lowering her eyes to stare at the ground. Her gray hair was in a state of disarray. "Yes, sir," she whispered. "I take it you've seen her as well. She was...well, the thing about it is, she wasn't the aggressor, I don't think. That older fellow had her on the defensive."

"The defensive?"

"Yes, sir," she replied. "It was...well, I can't really put it into words except to say he made a wall of lightning and it...scraped up the pavement. I'm also pretty sure he pulled a gun on her."

Baring his teeth, Harry turned his face away from her. "Thank you for your statement, ma'am," he managed at last. "I'm sure it will be of assistance."

He spun around.

"Vitello!" Harry barked. "Mitchell!" Two of his uniformed officers who stood with their backs turned suddenly stiffened. There were times when people claimed that Harry's voice cracked like a whip. He tried to control it, but today was not a day to be walking on eggshells. "Call the station," he went on. "I want every report involving a blonde woman over the last ninety-six hours. Arrest reports, 911 calls, *anything*. If Marilyn Monroe was caught sneaking out of the prime minister's house, I want to know it. We clear?"

"Detective!"

When he turned, he saw Aamani Patel standing in the middle of the street with her hands clasped behind her back. "Look at this..." she said, tapping the road with her foot. "Very odd."

He marched over to find a few slugs embedded in the asphalt, having kicked up the pavement on impact. Who would fire at the goddamn road? "Very odd," Patel repeated. "I had one of our ballistics experts analyze the trajectory. From the angle of impact, the shooter would have had to have been on the roof of the house to your left."

"It just keeps getting weirder," Harry lamented.

"Oh, I think we can go one step further," Patel replied. "Come with me, Detective. There's something I'd like to show you."

Fluorescent lights in the ceiling shone down on a sterile room with white-tiled walls and a stainless steel operating table that supported what was clearly a man's corpse. The body was covered with a plain white sheet, the fabric tented where a large nose stuck up from his face.

Patel stepped into the room and stood in front of the table with fists planted on her hips, scrutinizing the body. "Several of your officers recovered this fellow last night," she said. "We had him transferred here."

Harry felt the blood drain out of his face. Closing his eyes, he nodded slowly, then let out a sigh. "From the crime scene, you mean." It wasn't a question. "Why wasn't I told about this?"

"Apologies, Detective, but you had…other priorities." The woman scowled but covered it in an instant. If he didn't know better, he might have thought he had imagined that brief flash of emotion. Harry stifled his anger. His family life was none of her concern. "I ordered a full autopsy, but so far, we've only done the most preliminary examinations. We can confirm that he is human with blood type B positive."

"His species was in question?"

"Take a look for yourself."

Harry donned a pair of rubber gloves, then pulled back the sheet to reveal a dead man's face. This fellow might have been handsome once, but his skin was pallid, his hair unkempt. Nothing about the corpse stood out to him. "Check his hands," Patel said from behind. "I'm an expert at reading the back of a man's head. Yours says you're wondering why I brought you here. Check his hands."

"Checking his hands," he muttered to himself. "Please tell me I'm not about to find ten-inch nails."

He seized the man's wrist and turned it palm up to reveal…something. A metal disk embedded in the man's skin. An implant of some kind? Who would graft a chunk of metal onto his own hand?

Suddenly, a thought jumped into his head. One of the guards from the Penworth building had mentioned something about a man with a metal disk in his palm. The poor guy had been so beat up that Harry hadn't put much stock in his statement, but now… "I don't suppose you know what this is?"

He turned.

Patel stood there with her arms crossed, a frown on her face. She shook her head ever so slowly. "We have no idea," she replied. "That little hunk of metal is *why* we have not begun an autopsy. I had a bomb squad check him out from top to bottom before I let anyone else in this room."

"Wise..."

Human. So, the man was human. That meant Blondie was probably human as well. The prospect of extraterrestrials seemed less and less likely, but it was abundantly clear that they were dealing with technology they had never seen before, and Aamani Patel seemed to be at as much of a loss as he was.

It was all well and good to imagine clandestine meetings between high-ranking government officials, and secret black projects where advanced weaponry was developed without the public's consent, but Patel was sharing information freely. She was trying to get to the truth, not cover it up. That being the case, he could only draw one conclusion: if there was a conspiracy here, CSIS wasn't in on it.

He needed to find that blonde woman.

Seems I've underestimated you, Goldilocks, Harry thought to himself. *But you can rest assured that's a mistake I won't make twice.*

Chapter 9

Morning sunlight came in through the large window along with the sounds of birds chirping and the sweet scents of summer, waking Anna from the best night's sleep she'd had in recent memory. Even with the troubling thoughts of Dex, she had drifted off into a peaceful slumber.

Anna smiled, then pressed her cheek into the pillow. She squeezed her eyes shut. *A few more minutes,* she thought to herself. *Just a few more minutes. I don't want to get out of bed yet.*

There was no denying it, however; she was awake. Awake and well-rested for that matter. Was it strange that she felt so safe in a stranger's home? She had never been one to trust too easily.

She sat up.

Raising her arms into the air, Anna felt her mouth stretch in a yawn. She tossed her head about, sending blonde hair flying. *On your feet, Lenai,* she told herself. *You've still got work to do.*

She hopped out of bed and took in her surroundings. The apartment was a bit more orderly than she would have expected from a young man like Jack: just a couch facing a television and beyond that a kitchen where wooden cupboards lined both walls near the corner, broken only by what appeared to be the oven and the refrigerator. At least, she thought that big white thing was the refrigerator. Appliances on this world looked so very different from those she knew. Still, she was happy. Unjustifiably happy given everything that had happened, but she decided to go with it.

Biting her lower lip, Anna nodded to herself. *There's an elegant simplicity to this place,* she thought, tucking her shirt into the waistband of her shorts. *Almost as though Jack doesn't want to be burdened by too many possessions.*

Anna fell forward, slapping hands down on the carpet and thrusting her feet into the air. She walked across the room on her hands, then flipped upright to land upon the chilly kitchen floor tiles.

A cheerful disposition put her in the mood for a hearty breakfast. Pulling open the refrigerator revealed a pitcher full of orange juice, packs of meat and cheese and a carton of eggs. Eggs! She couldn't remember the last time she had had eggs, and she had a mind to repay her host's generosity.

It didn't take long to locate a frying pan or to figure out how to operate the stove; within a few minutes, she was ready to go. Even tracking down the cooking oil had been simple enough. Just a dab on the finger and a quick taste to make sure it wasn't some sort of dish soap or something like that. She had never realized just how difficult life could be when you couldn't read.

Cracking an egg on the counter, Anna split the shell and let the yoke drop into the frying pan. Oil sizzled with a satisfying hiss and she got to work. Nothing demonstrated affection more than a home-cooked meal, in her opinion.

The door opened.

Jack stepped in with a plastic bag in his hand, dressed in a pair of dark blue jeans and a gray t-shirt. "Good morning, Anna," he said, shutting the door behind him and making his way into the kitchen. "You didn't have to cook. I would have taken care of that."

He smiled, bowing his head to her. Those bangs over his forehead were particularly messy today. "I got you something. Just consider it a welcome-to-the-neighbourhood gift."

Anna looked up to meet his gaze, slowly arching a thin eyebrow. "What might that be?" she inquired. "I wasn't aware that I merited a gift on top of everything else."

"I figured you needed something to wear." He snatched a t-shirt out of the bag and held it against his chest. It was the same t-shirt that had won her over – the dark blue one with the adorable green dinosaur. "What do you think?"

"So, you have a pretty girl in your apartment with almost nothing to wear and your response to this is to bring her *more* clothing?" The irony was delicious. "I don't know if I should be impressed with your chivalry or worried that I'm not as cute as I think I am."

Jack flashed a grin, his face growing redder and redder. He lowered his eyes to the floor. "Well, um…" he mumbled. "That is um…I just thought it would be appropriate to help you with-"

"I'm joking, dummy!"

Anna lifted the frying pan, then scraped up a large hunk of scrambled eggs with her spatula. She dumped them onto a plate. "Honestly," she teased. "It's like all they see is a cute behind. They completely forget my propensity for quick quips."

She handed him the plate.

"I'll go change into something 'appropriate,' and you can appease my fragile ego by telling me how gorgeous I am."

A few minutes later, she emerged from the bathroom in a pair of blue jeans and the t-shirt with the adorable green dinosaur. A little jolt of excitement went through her when she saw that her host enjoyed her cooking. He stood in the kitchen with the plate in one hand, scooping up the last of his meal.

Jack popped a fork into his mouth. He closed his eyes, chewing thoroughly with a satisfied grunt. "An," he said. "Can I call you 'An?' These are some incredibly delicious eggs. I didn't know you could cook."

Slipping hands into her pockets, she moseyed into the living room with her head down. "So what do you think?" she asked with a shrug. "Does it suit me? Will I blend in with a crowd?"

"Congratulations, An," he said. "You are now a ten-year-old boy."

Anna felt her face redden and turned her head to break eye-contact. "Well, I do have that boyish figure," she teased. "Smear some dirt on my face, skin my knees raw and I'll fit right in."

When she looked up, Jack was trying his best not to look at her, blushing as though the topic embarrassed him. Had she said something offensive? "Oh, you've looked," she said with a dismissive wave of her hand. "Don't be ashamed of it! You weren't vulgar like the people I met on the street and it's..."

She trailed off there, refusing to say anything more. The simple fact was she knew very little of the customs of this world, and nothing made people touchier than the subject of sex. Relying on her innate sense of what was appropriate would be a mistake.

When you got right down to it, it was nice to be looked at, so long as the one doing the looking saw you as a person and not a thing. The whole point of her comment was to entice him to... *well, flirting must work differently here.*

Biting his lip, Jack closed his eyes tight. He turned his face up to the ceiling and let out a sigh. "Anna..." he began. "You are... well, you're very beautiful. It's just that while you're a guest in my home..."

How odd.

He seemed to be feeling guilty. Was he completely oblivious that she had been *encouraging* his attention? After flirting with her so effortlessly not one day earlier? *What are you doing, Lenai?* A symbiont's life was on the line, and she didn't have time to puzzle out the thoughts of a young man. It was just... well, there was a good chance that she would be dead in a few days, and charming, honourable men were in short supply.

"There's nothing wrong with your body..." Jack went on.

Anna smiled up at him, holding his gaze. She batted her eyes to put him off guard. "I like the way I look, dear," she replied. "All joking aside, my ego is not so fragile that you need to stammer out compliments."

"I'm sorry," he muttered. "I should have realized you were just messing with me. Anyway, if you feel up to leaving the apartment, there's something I'd like to show you."

"What's that?"

Jack grinned. "Come with me."

A white-tiled floor stretched from the library's front entrance to a curved reception desk where an old woman sat with her head buried in a novel. Metal bookshelves lined the walls to her left and right, blocking out sunlight that came in through the windows, each practically overflowing with books.

And that was just the first floors. At the back of the room, a set of stairs rose up to the second story. Anna had never seen so much knowledge gathered in one place. On her world, e-readers were used to conserve paper. You could access just about anything from the palm of your hand. True, paper books still existed, but most were kept safe and never touched. A collector's item.

Anna grinned, tilting her head back. She felt her eyebrows climb up. "Well, this is certainly unexpected!" she exclaimed. "I wish I could spend days here just gobbling up every last scrap of knowledge."

She glanced over her shoulder.

Grinning down at the floor, Jack squeezed his eyes shut. He shook his head in wry amusement. "You've never seen a library before?" he asked, keeping his voice low. "Not once in your life?"

"Let's just say I have most of my books in soft copy."

"There's something sad about that."

Red-cheeked, Anna smiled down at herself. She brushed a lock of hair away from her face. "Guess I'm the most boring girl you've ever met," she said, "talking about how much I want to gobble up knowledge."

"*Boring* is not a word I'd use to describe you."

He led her to a wooden table in the corner that was bathed in warm sunlight from a window on each wall. A few old books – some with tattered covers – were stacked upon the table's surface. The leftovers of students who had been doing research? Libraries still existed on her world, but they were used mainly as a place of study. Physical copies of books were still printed, but they were kept safe in vaults so that the knowledge could be preserved in the event of disaster.

Anna dropped into a wooden chair. It felt a little strange to be learning how to read again, but if she survived the next few weeks, there was a good chance she would be living her life here. She would have to adapt. "Where do we begin?" she asked. "When I was a child, my favourite book was called *The Moons of Myria.*"

Jack sat next to her.

"I figured we'd start with something simple," he explained. "You already know how to speak the language, so now all we have to do is teach you to associate text with sounds. So, Anna, let me introduce you to the English alphabet."

"In a...hole...in the...groan...ground! In a hole in the ground, there lived a...hoe-bit?" Remarkable. Simply remarkable. After only three hours, Anna had advanced from learning basic vowel sounds to reading books that most people didn't tackle until their early teens. Jack had never seen anything like it.

She attacked each book with such gusto it made him want to cheer every time she mastered a new sentence. Apparently, this rapid progress would not have been possible without the assistance of her Nassai. *Remarkable creatures,* Jack thought to himself. *It must be an incredible experience.*

"A hoe-bit?" Anna muttered. "What's a hoe-bit?"

"Hobbit."

Planting her elbows on the table's surface, Anna buried her face in her hands. She let out a groan of frustration. "Why can't your language follow consistent rules? Small wonder you're all crazy."

Jack smiled into his lap. He shook his head, trying not to chuckle. "Well, believe it or not," he began, "you're actually doing quite well. You've gotten further in three hours than most people do in three weeks."

When he looked over his shoulder, Anna was grinning at him, her cheeks flushed to a soft pink. "Well, it's embarrassing," she whispered. "Always having to hide that I can't read this language."

"I can imagine."

Slouching down in her chair, Anna threw her head back. "Part of it is just survival; a woman who can't read would draw notice." She folded her arms with a soft sigh. "But the fact that I even have to pretend is irksome."

That made all kinds of sense to him. Jack imagined he'd feel much the same way when he got around to visiting Leyria – a task that had climbed to the very top of his bucket list. If there were other worlds in the cosmos, then he wanted to see them, to learn about a way of life beyond the one he had known.

For months now, a pervading sense of gloom had settled into his world and defined his every day. It had taken some soul searching, but Jack had concluded the source of that feeling was a belief that so much of what he did was pointless.

He had chosen a job in a thrift shop to help the poor, but honestly now, what did that do to address the root cause of poverty? Instead of treating the symptoms, society should cure the disease. Every time he said as much, people told him he needed to accept the things he couldn't change. A rather ugly paradox. It turned out the only way to make an idealist *accept the things he could not change* was to break his spirit.

Jack bit his lip and nodded once. "Let's try this one," he said, sliding a book across the table. If he knew anything about Anna, then J.K. Rowling would be perfect. "I think you'll really like it."

She scooched closer, close enough that Jack had to ignore the warm fuzzy feelings in his heart. Taking the book, Anna began to read. "Murr and Mriss Dursley of Number Four Privet Drive...

Jack grinned, slapping a hand over his face. He trembled as a wave of laughter went through him. "Those are abbreviations," he explained. "Short for *mister* and *missus*. I know, I know... you want consistent rules."

She punched his arm.

"So, you think violence is a form of affection!" Jack teased. "I didn't know Leyrians subscribed to the Ike Turner school of thought on marital bliss."

"I subscribe to the school of thought that says smart-ass young men get punched if they're rude," she muttered. "Honestly...laughing at a woman's attempts to learn a very difficult language."

It was difficult not to feel a little tense. A part of him just wanted to wrap his arms around her and soothe away her pains with warmth and affection – the poor girl had been through so much: violence, danger and now she was cut off from her own people – but Anna was a guest in his home. That made her dependent on him. She didn't know the first thing about getting around this city.

So long as she remained dependent on him, indulging those feelings of affection would be five kinds of sinful. Consent that came at a time of vulnerability was not really consent. He had to get some distance.

Jack stood.

He spun around and looked through the window. Through the glass, he saw a parking lot where cars filled almost every space, and beyond that a line of elm trees that marked the edge of the property. A beautiful summer's day. It occurred to him that he was using his time off – time that should have been spent resting – to strain himself further. To hell with it – he was never one to be idle.

Crossing his arms with a heavy sigh, Jack frowned down at the windowsill. "If we could just narrow down the search," he said with a shrug. "Come up with a theory as to where Denario took the Nassai."

"Believe me, I've tried."

Pinching his chin with thumb and forefinger, Jack squinted through the window. "I have an idea," he said, nodding. "You said that you arrived here by passing through some kind of short-range transit device?"

"A SlipGate, yes."

"Well, this may not have occurred to you – since those things are common on your world – but I've never heard the term *SlipGate* before

I met you, and neither has anyone else in this city. That technology is unknown to my people.

"So, it stands to reason that if Penworth Industries has a SlipGate in its basement, it might just be in the business of collecting other alien technologies. Say… a living creature that can warp time and space?"

He spun around.

Anna sat with her back to him, hunched over the table. "You're right; I didn't think of that." She slid her chair backward, then got up. "But I should have. Tell me more about this *Penworth Industries.*"

"On a hunch, I Googled," Jack explained. "They refine jet fuel."

"Propulsion technology," Anna whispered. "An organization like that will be very interested in the prospect of bending space…I think you had better share everything you know about this Penworth Industries."

Anna stood on the sidewalk with hands clasped behind herself, her posture stiff. He could only see the back of her head, but even so, Jack knew she was troubled. "So, this is the place where I came through the SlipGate…"

Across a busy street where cars zipped back and forth, a towering skyscraper rose up to touch the clear blue sky. Thirty stories of white concrete with windows that glinted in the sunlight. Though he couldn't see it from here, he knew one of the pillars along the columned front entrance had been damaged.

Jack craned his neck to stare up at the building. He narrowed his eyes. "Yeah, that would be it," he said, nodding to himself. "Penworth Industries Incorporated. One of the leading manufacturers of jet propulsion technology."

He stepped up beside her.

Jack frowned then lowered his eyes to the pavement. He ignored the sudden chill that raced down his spine. "I used to work in a call centre," he went on. "They had some pretty tight security. Given Penworth's reputation, the place is probably in lockdown. We may have to do some recon."

Anna stood beside him as still as a statue, the wind blowing tendrils of hair across her face. "Then I'll take a look around," she said. "If I find the Nassai, I'll make a quick exit."

Jack clamped a hand on her shoulder.

She spun around, glaring up at him with fire in her eyes. A spike of alarm pierced his chest when he saw her expression. It wouldn't do to forget that this woman could snap him in half in a heartbeat. "You're not going in there," he said before she could get a word in. "It's too dangerous."

Anna clenched her teeth and hissed like a mother cat defending her young. "You must not have been paying attention," she snapped. "It's my *duty* to go in there. Give me one good reason why I shouldn't."

Jack arched an eyebrow.

"The fact that your face will be recognized by just about anyone on their security staff?" he suggested. "This is a recon mission, not a direct assault. If they're holding the Nassai here, chances are they'll keep it in a science lab. Now, you've got thirty stories of floor space and no time for a room-by-room search.

"Most office buildings are organized so that individual departments occupy one or two floors. If I can locate Applied Sciences, that will narrow down the search. No one in that building knows me; no one has seen my face. I'm the best choice to get the lay of the land. After that, you can decide how you want to proceed."

Anna pursed her lips, then bowed her head to him. She heaved out a frustrated sigh. "You'd make a good Keeper, Jack," she murmured with only a touch of resentment in her voice. "Alright, we'll try it your way. But I want you out at the first sign of trouble."

"Won't be any trouble, An."

He stepped back, allowing her to take a good look at his clothing. Anticipating this possibility, he had changed into a pair of dark slacks and a matching jacket, a gray shirt with the collar left open. "I look like one of them," Jack explained. "Hundreds of people walk through that door, and I will be just one more. Just an ordinary man going about his business. So long as I don't try to poke my head into a restricted area, I'll be fine."

Anna nodded.

She slammed into him with a fierce hug that nearly took the wind right out of him, her hands gently caressing his back. "Good luck," she whispered with her cheek pressed to his chest. "I'll meet you at the coffee shop on the corner."

"Right."

At the crosswalk's prompting, he started across the street. Now that he was actually committed to the task, Jack felt his bravado begin to wane. He had assured Anna that this was just another office building – and in all likelihood, that was the case – but if he was correct and the Nassai really *was* in there, it meant these people were in cahoots with dangerous criminals who possessed advanced technology.

Once again, he found himself marvelling at the situation. The knowledge that human beings were already roaming the stars and kidnapping members of other species left him with a kind of disembodied feeling, as if this were a movie he was watching and not a genuine conflict.

He paused on the sidewalk.

A set of concrete steps led up to the front entrance of the building. Stone pillars supported an overhang that provided employees on their smoke break with a little relief from the sun's scorching rays, the first one on his right sporting a hole that let him see all the way through.

Jack started up the steps with his head down. *You can do this, Hunter,* he told himself. *Just an ordinary man going about his business.*

He found a set of double doors that looked in on a lobby, but the adjacent window had been shattered, and now a sheet of plywood filled the opening. Anxiety began to well up in his belly. He stifled it.

Jack stepped inside.

The lobby was a huge room where gray floor tiles stretched from wall to wall. To his left and his right, hallways branched off, and a staircase along the back wall rose up to a balcony that overlooked the front entrance.

There was no reception desk, just a computer kiosk in the corner. That should not have surprised Jack. Why pay someone to greet your visitors when you could use an interactive program to do it for free?

A pair of men in suits emerged from a hallway on one side of the room and walked across the lobby at a brisk pace. Jack spared them a glance, noticing each man had a key card clipped to his belt. So, that was how they got through the security scanners. It would be difficult to pilfer one, but not impossible.

Ideas flashed through his mind, but he stifled them. That kind of brainstorming was best when you weren't in the middle of another important task. Recon now, strategy later. When he got out of here, he and Anna could hash out the details.

Jack went to the kiosk.

When you got up close, it was little more than a computer monitor in a rectangular box with a keyboard attached. Next to that, he found a bowl-shaped pit in the floor, a pit made of some glossy substance that-

Light shot upward, resolving into the transparent image of a woman in a black skirt and a blue short-sleeved blouse. Her face was a bit too angular to be called beautiful, but she was pretty nonetheless, long dark hair falling over her shoulders.

The hologram smiled, then bowed her head to him. "Good afternoon," she began. "My name is Aveena, and I will be happy to assist you today. Are you currently waiting for an appointment with one of our staff? If so, I will contact him or her."

Pressing his lips together, Jack looked up to stare at the hologram. He blinked. "No, that's alright, Aveena," he replied. "I'd like some information on the company directory if it's not too much trouble."

"Certainly," she replied. "You may make your inquiry verbally or type your search query into the adjacent terminal."

"Where can I find Applied Sciences?"

The hologram flickered, rippling like one of those old TV channels that had been scrambled. A moment later, she solidified again. "The Applied Sciences Department is located on the seventeenth floor. Access is restricted to employees only."

She cocked her head to one side, grimacing as she stared at him. "If you are waiting for an appointment," she added, "might I suggest you visit our cafeteria located down the hall to your right. Our kitchen staff will be happy to prepare a wide variety of dishes, and the coffee is free."

Clapping a hand over his mouth, Jack shut his eyes. He tried not to chuckle. "That's alright, Aveena." Holograms... customer service was built right in. "I'll pass. Who is the department head for Applied Sciences?"

The hologram wavered, slowly fading out of existence. Her voice still came out of the speaker, however. "Gerald Hamilton is the department head of the Applied Sciences Department." A new image formed: a transparent man in a lab coat with thin glasses and a receding hairline.

Next to him, text appeared out of thin air. His name, phone number and e-mail address. It was almost as if the system had generated a holographic business card. *Will wonders never cease?*

Jack retrieved a USB stick from his pocket and slipped it into a port on the nearby terminal. Now for the most important part of his performance. Anyone who was passing by might wonder why he was asking these questions, so he'd give them a reason. "Please upload my resume and cover letter and forward them to Mr. Hamilton's e-mail address."

"Certainly."

Aveena reappeared with a bright smile on her face. "Your credentials are excellent, Mr. Trevor Conrad." He had invented a degree in applied physics from the University of Toronto along with a few entry-level science jobs, but there was no way a hologram could assess his qualifications. Still, it wouldn't surprise him if some moron on the seventeenth floor put stock in her – in *its* – opinion. "I'm sure you'll be an asset to the team."

Meeting her gaze, Jack flashed a wry smile. "You're a sweetheart, Aveena," he said, batting his eyes. "I think so too. Thanks so much for all of your assistance today."

"Logging you out."

Chapter 10

A stack of papers landed on his desk with a *flap*. Della stood in front of him with her arms folded. "Custody papers," she said with a nod. "The girls live with me. You'll get visitation rights. That's my final offer."

Tilting his head back, Harry stared into her eyes. He squinted. "You just don't know when to quit," he said, shaking his head. "Della, you've got a history of negligence and substance abuse. No judge in the world would give you custody."

The smile she offered was enough to freeze his blood cold. What was the woman planning now? "You expect me to give up?" she asked, raising a golden eyebrow. "Oh, Harry dear, if our marriage is any indication of what I should expect, you'll be begging to settle after two weeks."

Harry frowned, a flush burning through his face. He closed his eyes and bowed his head to her. "Now isn't the time, Della," he rasped. "In case you haven't read the news, I have a major case on my hands.

"Fine."

She turned away from him, allowing him to see the back of a sheer white blouse that revealed a tank-top underneath. Della marched to the door, pausing there. "We can pick this up again tomorrow. And the next day. And the day after that."

Harry groaned.

Was the woman so ill-informed that she knew nothing about the major disturbances around the city? People were starting to whisper, wondering what could have punched a hole in solid concrete and scraped up a layer of pavement. From what he'd heard just this morning, some people were afraid to go into work. Rumours circulated, naming everyone from Al-Qaida to the little green men as culprits. Under circumstances like these, it wasn't long before people started imagining bombs going off in the street. If he didn't wrap this up soon, they might have panic on their hands.

The phone rang.

He brought the receiver to his ear.

Mopping a hand over his face, Harry winced and let out a soft sigh. "Yeah, what is it?" he muttered. "For the love of God, Teresa, tell me it's not my wife's lawyer."

"Vitello wants to see you, sir."

"Send him in."

A moment later, Harry found a tall man with a barrel chest standing in his doorway. Vitello had a jolly face that seemed to be frozen in a permanent smile. His cap threatened to slip down over his forehead.

Leaning back in his chair, Harry smiled at the man. "To what do I owe the pleasure, Mike?" he asked, eyebrows rising. "I take it you have some results on the search I asked for? Reports on the blonde woman?"

"Actually, yeah," Vitello replied with a nod. "Eighteenth Precinct picked up a pair of yahoos down in Centre Town. A couple of small-time dealers selling Synth, but they were beat up pretty bad. Said a blonde woman did it. Couldn't have been more than five-foot-three."

Harry restrained himself from pummelling the other man with questions. A few days ago, he'd have dismissed those claims as nonsense from the mouth of an addict, but now? It seemed this woman had a tendency for starting fights. "Any leads?"

"Yeah, there was a vic," Vitello explained. His face darkened as he lowered his eyes to the floor. "Kid by the name of Hunter. Got beat up some. Funny thing is, our perps are willing to plead to everything – assault, trafficking, you name it – so long as we keep 'the blonde psycho' away."

Harry shut his eyes, tilting his head back. He took a deep, soothing breath through his nose. "These are the moments you live for, my friend," he said. "I think it's time that I pay Mr. Hunter a visit."

"The seventeenth floor…"

Jack was stretched out on his belly with an old yellow legal pad sitting on the floor in front of him. For the past hour, they had been trying to brainstorm ways to allow Anna to slip inside the Penworth building and take a look around. It bothered him that most of his ideas felt like they belonged in a bad Bond film. One more fantasy about ziplines and he'd bang his head on the wall.

Resting his elbow on the gray carpet, Jack leaned his cheek against the palm of his hand. "We must be missing something," he said. "There has to be another way to get you in unnoticed."

Anna sat across from him with hands on her knees, a serene expression on her face. Or maybe that was just perceptual bias. Either way, she seemed to be mulling it over, lost in thought.

Frowning thoughtfully, she glanced down at the legal pad, then looked up to fix her gaze on him. "You mentioned key cards," she offered. "What if we stole one from one of the scientists? If I'm careful, he may not notice."

Jack clenched his teeth, wincing so hard his face hurt. He shook his head in dismay. "Wouldn't work," he explained. "For one thing, the security office will just disable it the minute it's reported missing, and for another, it might tip them off."

He rolled onto his back, letting the ideas percolate. Unfortunately, the only thing he came up with was hacking the building's employee database and creating a fake ID. Only one problem with that: he didn't know the first thing about hacking. Ripping the guts out of a computer and putting it back together, sure, but not hacking. Besides, those scenes of people typing furiously at keyboards were all fake.

"What we need is a way to get the key card away from someone just long enough for you to use it…" He sat up. "Or take it in a way that he doesn't notice and use it before he realizes it's gone."

"What if we *copied* a key card?"

Jack stood.

He turned around to find Anna sitting with her legs crossed, hands resting on her knees with thumbs touching middle fingers. Her eyes were closed, almost as if she was meditating. "I think I know a way to do it."

"How?"

Anna reached into her blue jeans' pocket and pulled out a small circular device that she held between thumb and forefinger. "This is called a multi-tool," she explained. "It can help us."

Holding the device in the palm of her hand, she tapped a small button with her ring finger. The air wavered, creating a rectangular field of transparent blue light with script he didn't recognize. And icons. In fact, the more he thought about it, the more it looked like a desktop interface. Oriented toward Anna, of course, but a desktop interface just the same. Amazing that a people light years away would design something so similar to what he himself would have.

Only then did he realize what he was looking at. A portable holographic generator? Holograms were a new-fangled technology that had cropped up over the last decade, but they required more power than you could put into a handheld device. At least, that was true on Earth. "With this," Anna began, "I can copy the magnetic signature of one of those key cards. It's designed to learn how to interface with foreign systems."

Throwing his head back, Jack blinked at the ceiling. "It might work," he said with a bit of strain in his voice. "But the hardest part would be getting your hands on one of the key cards. Unless you can scan one from afar."

Anna looked up to stare at him through a field of transparent blue light. "Sadly, we cannot," she replied with more than a hint of dismay. "You'll have to get within a few feet of the target."

"Okay," Jack said. "I have an idea."

He turned around and took a moment to peer through the rectangular window in the wall next to his bed. Outside, the evening sky had faded to a deep blue with a few bright stars twinkling. The small variety store in the building across the street was lit up like a Christmas tree, its yellow sign flickering. "Are you hungry?" he inquired. "I was going to head to the store to pick up a few things."

When he spun around, the hologram had vanished, leaving Anna sitting cross-legged on the floor. "Why don't you save that for tomorrow?" she said. "I noticed that you have everything I need to make *creeshai,* and that happens to be one of my specialties."

"You want to make a Leyrian dish?"

Anna tilted her head to the side, smiling at him with impish glee on her face. "Well, I thought we could stay in," she said, her eyebrows shooting up. "And you could tell me all your deepest, darkest secrets."

Creeshai turned out to be quesadillas: three of them on a green plate in the middle of the small wooden table. Anna had prepared them with some grilled chicken, peppers and three kinds of cheese.

They sat at the little table in the corner of Jack's kitchen – a table that he normally reserved for his laptop. In truth, that was all it was good for. The single plate took up just about every inch of space.

Jack took a bite, strings of cheese extending as he pulled the tortilla into his mouth. He sucked them up with a slurp. "Now, that's delicious…" he said with his mouth full. "I don't know who taught you to cook, but you're an expert."

Anna wore a big grin as she stared down at the table. "I thought you might enjoy them," she said, eyebrows rising. "Now about those deep dark secrets that you promised to tell me."

Blushing hard, Jack shut his eyes. "We're still on that, are we?" He slouched in his chair, stretching out his legs beneath the table. "You know, we have a similar dish here on Earth. Really makes you wonder how much our peoples have in common."

"No changing the subject."

"I don't have a lot of deep dark secrets, An." He found himself grinning up at the ceiling, trying to ignore the heat in his face. "Really, I'm just a boring guy who works in a thrift shop."

Anna set her elbow on the table, leaning her cheek against the palm of her hand. "I find that hard to believe," she said, deep creases stretching across her brow. "To me, you seem *very* interesting."

"Well, I guess I should give you the profile," he muttered. "My name is Nathaniel Jack Hunter. I'm a Taurus. My turn-ons include gruelling death marches by the freeway, the Dewey Decimal System and tax evasion. I once told a woman that I'm deathly afraid of sock puppets just to see the look on her face. I did this over e-mail and then decided I need better planning skills."

Clamping a hand over her mouth, Anna squeezed her eyes shut and trembled with a fit of laughter. "You have a well-developed sense of humour," she murmured into her own palm. "But then I already knew that."

"All right," he said, "your turn. Tell me about yourself."

Anna pressed her lips together, tilting her head back. A look of concentration passed over her face as she chose her words. "Our school system is similar to yours," she began. "With the younger students separated from the older. I excelled in languages and physics. I bonded with my Nassai at the age of sixteen."

Jack blinked.

Crossing her arms, Anna grinned and bowed her head to stare into her lap. "It's very young, I agree…" A heavy sigh escaped her. "Most people are not bonded until they reach the age of twenty-one, but my case involved special circumstances."

"Care to share?"

"My father and I were on journey to Alastra," she explained, "a colony world near the edge of Leyrian Space. It was my first time off world. My father is a diplomat and he was attending trade negotiations with representatives of the Antauros Dominion. They're human as well, in case you're wondering.

"Relations between Leyria and Antaur have always been strained. Sometimes the colonies along the border attack one another despite the objections of both governments. Our transport was hit by raiders.

"The Nassai I carry was on board in a containment unit. It was supposed to have bonded with a young Justice Keeper who had just completed his training on Alastra. But during the attack, the containment unit was damaged.

"Nassai cannot survive in our environment without a host; however, the chances of a successful bonding get slimmer and slimmer once you get past the age of twenty-five. That left only six potential candidates on board, and two of them refused to join with the symbiont. As for the others...the Nassai touched each of our minds and chose me."

Jack wasn't quite sure what to make of that. Her story sounded like something out of a sci-fi flick, but then, why should that surprise him? It felt strange to realize that he no longer doubted Anna's extraterrestrial origins, but now that he had made that leap, it was silly to nitpick the finer details.

Biting his lip, Jack stiffened and shook his head. "Okay, I'm confused," he said. "You said the Nassai rejected the first three candidates. Why wouldn't it accept the first offer?"

Anna studied him with a blank expression, clearly taken aback. By the look in her eyes, he could tell he had asked a very stupid question. "The symbiont gets a say in the matter," she said in exasperation. "Most Nassai would rather die than give such power to an unworthy candidate."

"And why would a human reject the symbiont?"

"Power comes with a price," she replied. "Now that I have been bonded, my cells cannot replicate without my Nassai's assistance. I would die if the symbiont were to leave me. As it is, my lifespan has been shortened."

"So, you're saying..." He almost didn't want to hear it. Now that he had met Anna, the thought of anything bad happening to her was painful. That in itself was unsettling. He didn't like the thought of being so concerned for someone he hardly knew.

"I'm saying that I can expect to live into my mid-fifties," she explained. "And not much longer than that."

Well...there you had it.

Though he knew it was irrelevant – it wasn't as though he'd ever get the opportunity – Jack found himself wondering if he would accept a symbiont. He wanted to say yes, but was he willing to cut his lifespan in half?

Knock, knock, knock.

Anna threw a glance over her shoulder, her face twisted in an expression that made him think of a startled wolf. "Are you expecting visitors?" she asked in a voice that was barely louder than a whisper.

"No," he answered. "Hide in the bathroom."

With serpentine grace, Anna stood and padded across the room without making a sound. She paused at the door to the bathroom, slowly pulled it open and stepped inside. *Now, let's pray this goes smoothly.*

Another knock. Louder this time.

"Coming!" Jack shouted.

He went to the door and pulled it open to reveal a man in a black suit. Dark of skin and hair, this guy had a chiselled jaw and eyes that seemed to smolder when he looked at you. "Mr. Hunter?" he inquired, lifting up his open wallet to reveal a small silver shield. "Detective Harry Carlson, Ottawa PD."

Lifting his chin, Jack squinted at the other man. "Good to meet you, Detective," he said with a curt nod. "I think I know what this is about. If you need me to come ID those perps, I'm happy to help."

The man's face was a stone mask: completely unreadable. It was an old trick but a good one. "Actually, they confessed to everything," Harry Carlson elaborated. "You gave a report in which you said you were saved by an unidentified woman. I don't suppose you could tell me more about her."

"Not off the top of my head," Jack said. "My vision was a little bleary at the time, and I was pretty out of it."

Detective Carlson kept his gaze fixed upon Jack. There was just something so very unnerving about having someone stare at you. Jack knew from a few high school psych classes that it was an intimidation technique, and yet that knowledge did nothing to ease his anxiety.

"Hospital reported you had a visitor," the detective said. "A blonde woman."

"Her name is Tracy."

Carlson frowned, his brows drawn together. "Tracy..." he said, nodding to himself, testing the name. "This Tracy wouldn't be the same woman who saved you, would she? I would love to meet that woman."

"Of course not."

"Does Tracy have an address?"

Burning up with anxiety, Jack buried his face in the palm of his hand. He groaned and rubbed the tip of his nose. "She's a friend from Toronto," he muttered. "Went back there this morning."

He almost tripped over his own words. Giving away too many details was a sure sign that you were lying, so he made it a point to keep his responses short and frank. "Is that all, Detective?"

"There's no chance that Tracy's here?"

Jack stepped aside.

He allowed the man to peer through the open door, allowed him to see the ugly gray carpet that stretched all the way to a brick wall with two rectangular windows. Except for the couch in the middle of the room, a small table and his bed in the corner, the apartment was devoid of furniture. "Do you see anyone, Detective?"

The man scowled, shaking his head. "No, I don't," he admitted, stepping back into the hallway. "That's all for now, but I hope you will make yourself available should I have further questions."

Jack shut the door and heaved out a sigh. Tension that he didn't even know was there began to drain out of his body. *I should have seen this coming,* Jack noted. Anna had a bit of a flair for the dramatic when it came to opposing injustice; sooner or later, her actions would draw the law's attention.

We need to step up our timetable.

Chapter 11

A slanted window that rose from floor to ceiling looked out on an overcast sky where tall buildings stabbed the heavens. Gray daylight fell upon the dozens of small tables that were spaced out on the tiled floor. The cafeteria in the Penworth building was bustling with activity.

Ah, the miracles of Facebook. What luck it had been to discover that one of his old high school friends – an older girl that he hadn't seen since the end of ninth grade – now worked in the IT department. With excitement at the prospect of catching up mingled with the fear of getting caught, Jack had to resist the urge to look over his shoulder every few minutes. Leah was a nice girl. He didn't want her caught up in this, but there was no other way to get close to Hamilton.

Tall and a bit gangly, Leah wore a pair of black slacks and a blue t-shirt with a lacy neckline. Her gaunt-cheeked face was marked by freckles, and she kept her dark hair tied back in a ponytail. "Jack!" she exclaimed, approaching the table.

He wore the same black pants and jacket that he had worn yesterday, sitting in his chair with arms folded. "Leah," Jack replied. "Thanks for meeting me. God, it feels like it's been forever."

She sat down across from him, her mouth tight as she looked him up and down. "And here we are…" she said, leaning back in her chair. "So, tell me everything. The last time we talked, you were trying to work up the nerve to ask out…Selia? No, Cecelia! Cecelia Abrams! How did that go?"

Grinning with a burst of laughter, Jack looked away in some sad attempt to hide his embarrassment. "It went about as well as you'd expect," he said. "She broke my heart and shook my confidence daily. My next crush will be a Roxanne."

"Why's that?"

"Because no one *ever* wrote a song about a Roxanne."

She smiled into her lap, trembling with a burst of giggles. "Same old Jack," she said, shaking her head. "So, what happened to that old computer programming club? Do you still talk to Ray?"

Chewing on his lip, Jack looked up at her. "Yeah, he's gone out West I think." It took a moment to rack his brain. "I want to say Edmonton, but to be honest, I'm pretty sure it's Red Deer."

"I see," Leah murmured. "And you came out here?"

"About a year ago," he explained. "Right after graduation. My sister was already living out here, and that made it convenient. Dad thought I'd have an easier time getting into a school in Ontario."

Leah looked up to appraise him with those questioning brown eyes. In a way, she was another older sister. "Somehow, I figured," she replied. "You always put a little too much faith in your natural abilities, Jack, and you never did take school seriously. I get that you were bored but..."

He let her have her moment. Lord knows, she had earned it. Leah had been on the verge of graduating when he started high school, and for some reason that eluded him, she had taken him under her wing. A common theme in their many, many conversations was the need for Jack to straighten up and fly right.

For a moment he had almost forgotten his purpose in coming here. Guilt welled up when he thought about using Leah. *There's a life on the line,* he reminded himself. *She'd want to help if she knew.*

A glance over his right shoulder revealed the entrance to the cafeteria's servery, and though he spotted many people in business casual, there was no sign of anyone in a lab coat. Gerald Hamilton was his primary target, but failing that, anyone in Applied Sciences would do.

"Something wrong?"

Leah wore an expression of concern as she watched him, an expression he had seen far too many times. "You seem upset," she went on. "I didn't mean to insult you…I guess I need to remember that you're not fourteen anymore."

He offered a sly smile that he hoped would melt away the tension. "Now, it's your turn," Jack said, arching one eyebrow. "I want to know all the juicy gossip, and if it will make you more comfortable, I can braid your hair."

"Jack!"

"Okay, okay," he relented. "We'll restrict ourselves to a pillow fight. But I insist we look at your posters of Ross Lynch and talk about how dreamy he is. If we're going to do this, then damn it, let's do it right!"

People were moving through the cafeteria, some carrying red trays that were laden with food while others flowed toward the exits. In an office like this, people took lunch at almost any hour depending on their schedules. There was a chance he might not be able to catch someone from Applied Sciences.

He couldn't afford to hang around once Leah went back to work; it would raise too many red flags. That meant he had to act, and he had to act soon. At best, he had another forty-five minutes to make a play.

Leah was blushing…blushing so hard her face looked like a ripe tomato. "I'll get us some food," she said, standing. "You stay here and try not to get in too much trouble."

Craning his neck to stare at her, Jack felt a grin bloom. "My dear, Leah," he teased, shaking his head. "It's like you don't trust me. Honestly, how much trouble do you think I could get into?"

"You? Plenty."

She stalked off at a brisk pace and Jack couldn't help but notice the way she folded her arms and huddled in on herself. Leah had always been shy, but he would have thought leaving high school would have helped with that. Maybe she just wasn't used to the thought of the awkward kid she had tutored in algebra growing up to develop a talent for snark.

Jack pressed a fist to his mouth, shutting his eyes tight. He cleared his throat with some gusto. *Easy there, Hunter,* he told himself. *Just because it makes your life easier to laugh all the time doesn't mean that works for her.*

He slipped a hand into his pocket, resting fingertips on the multi-tool that Anna had given him. The small metal disk was cool to the touch. Thanks to the instructions she had programmed, he would only have to push a single button to activate the scanner. Now, all he had to do was get close enough to someone with a key card.

The crowd was thinning. He spotted a trio of middle-aged women at a table in the corner, a man in a suit with silver hair slicked back, two young guys who sat side by side with phones raised up in front of their faces and several others. Any one of them could be part of the Science Department. Or none.

His attention was drawn to a member of the janitorial staff. A tall woman in a blue uniform and matching baseball cap, she carried a spray bottle to one of the vacant tables and began wiping it down. That gave him an idea, one that he quickly filed away in the back of his mind.

Leah returned, carrying two plates of lasagna that looked absolutely delicious. She set one down in front of Jack, then took her seat. "I figured you could use a little protein. That and it's my favourite."

"Thank you."

Something in the way that she looked at him reminded him of Lauren. Truth be told, he wasn't sure what he had expected in coming here – it had been five years since they'd seen each other – but somehow he thought they would be on equal footing. Leah, it seemed, still thought of him as a fourteen-year-old boy.

Jack sliced through the lasagna with his fork, then stabbed the piece that he had cut off. He popped it into his mouth. Words jumped into his mind, but he stifled them before speaking. The last thing he needed was to confirm her preconceptions by talking with his mouth full.

"You wanted gossip," Leah said, before bringing a can of soda to her lips. She took a sip. "Let's see, four years at Waterloo. I was dating a guy named Darrel back then. After that, I started job hunting. I was lucky to get a two-year contract here last summer. Been in Ottawa ever since."

"Mmm."

"Now, what's this really about?"

Crossing his arms over his chest, Jack leaned back. He frowned, keeping his gaze fixed on her. "What do you mean?" he asked. "I saw you were here in Ottawa. I wanted to catch up."

Leah was smiling into her lap, her cheeks flushed as she shook her head. "Nice try, kid," she said, scooching closer, "But I've known you long enough to feel it when you're up to no good."

"Up to no good?"

She looked up to stare at him, and suddenly he really *was* fourteen again. "Jack, I always found your antics...amusing." The tone in her voice told him that his antics were anything but. "However, we're adults now, and it's time to put high school behind us. So I ask again, why did you look me up?"

He should have expected this. Leah really was like another sister, and he had been so fixated on his anxieties that he must have been giving off all sorts of tells. How did he explain that he was trying to rescue a sentient being from people who might just be her bosses?

The truth was not an option. So, if Leah saw him as a mischievous little boy with a slingshot in his back pocket, he would just have to conform to her expectations. "Well, I was thinking about I-T," he said. "I can complete a three-year program, and then I thought maybe you could help me get my foot in the door."

"You want me to help you find a job." The pinched expression on her face told him precisely what she thought of *that* idea. "Honestly, Jack, didn't you once tell me that you were far too quirky for the business world?"

Tossing his head back, Jack rolled his eyes at the ceiling. "That doesn't sound right at all," he teased. "I'm sure I must have said *quarky*. I've got lots of quarks to go around. Billions and billions of them."

Leah slapped a palm over her face, groaning with frustration. "Jack…this is what I'm talking about." She looked up, blinking at him. "If you want a career in the professional world, you have to stop treating everything like it's some joke that only you get."

Out of the corner of his eye, he noticed something. A man in a dark gray suit came striding across the room. He was texting on a phone, pausing just in front of the entrance to the servery.

Something about him was familiar.

Jack shot a glance over his shoulder and caught a glimpse of the man's features. Tall with a receding hairline and thin glasses on his face, Gerald Hamilton stood there, staring at his phone.

"You got me, Leah," he said, standing up. "I'm sorry."

"Jack-"

He started across the room with his hands shoved into his pockets, keeping his head down to avoid attention. *Now, for the big moment,* Jack thought, caressing the multi-tool with his fingers.

The head of the Applied Sciences Division was standing right there, frowning as he read a message on his phone. It was all Jack could do not to stare at the key card hanging from a clip on his belt.

Before he could get close enough, the man turned on his heel and slipped into the servery, vanishing into the crowd of people who stood in front of the counter waiting for lasagna. Would that make this easier or far more difficult? His chest felt tight enough to implode under its own gravitational pull.

If he was clumsy – if his intentions became obvious – he would find himself sitting in the Security Office while the guards prodded at Anna's multi-tool. *Then I'll just have to be graceful.*

Jack followed him in.

Cut off from the natural light that came through the huge window, the servery felt clean and sterile under the glare of fluorescent bulbs. A long metal counter to his right was operated by women in black uniforms who doled out large pieces of cooked lasagna to customers with red trays. Gerald Hamilton wasn't among them.

He stood at a table in the far end of the room, hunched over as he poured himself a cup of coffee. The man's posture was stiff. Nervousness? If anyone here knew about the Nassai, he surely did.

Pressing his lips together, Jack stared into the distance. He narrowed his eyes. *You can do this, Hunter,* he thought to himself. *Just keep your cool and make it look like an accident.*

He pulled out the multi-tool.

Gerald Hamilton was still hunched over, muttering to himself as he inspected the contents of his cup. As Jack made his way across the room, the other man let out a sigh and set his cup down on the table. "Lukewarm…" he said with enough volume for the entire kitchen staff to hear. "Is fresh coffee too much to ask for?"

Jack crept closer.

Gerald Hamilton spun around just in time for them to collide, the impact throwing them both to the floor with Jack sprawled out on top of him. In that moment of confusion, Jack waved the multi-tool over the other man's key card and heard a satisfying *beep!* The scan had been successful!

Jack sat up, pressing a palm to his forehead. He winced and let out a painful little groan. "I'm sorry…" he muttered. "I was just completely lost in thought. I must not have seen you there."

Hamilton was lying on his back with his face scrunched up, a soft wheeze escaping him. "Yeah, it's fine…" he said, getting to his feet. "Just…watch where you're going next time, okay?"

He offered Jack his hand.

Taking it, Jack slipped the multi-tool into his pocket and allowed the other man to pull him to his feet. A small crowd had gathered around the two of them, concern on their faces. That was good. So far as he could tell, everyone thought this was an accident. Focus on the embarrassment. Everyone thought he was a clumsy idiot.

"I'm sorry about that," Jack said again.

"Just…watch where you're going."

"Thanks."

With that, he left the servery and returned to the cafeteria's seating area. There were people sitting at tables with their heads turned, no doubt intrigued by all that commotion. Jack let them gawk. His job was complete. If he could just get out of here without having another incident, he'd be fine. The rest was up to Anna.

He found Leah waiting at their table, watching him with concern in those big dark eyes of hers. She blinked a few times. "What was all that about?" she asked. "I thought you were getting coffee."

"It's lukewarm," he replied. "Really, is fresh coffee too much to ask for?" Before she could chime in with a response, Jack went right on talking. "Listen, Leah, I just got a call from my sister. I have to run."

"Oh…all right."

"Thank you for a wonderful lunch," he said, forcing a smile. "Let's keep in touch. I would love to do this again soon."

"Me…" she looked truly perplexed, "me too."

Jack offered an awkward hug, then slipped away down the corridor that led back to the lobby. Every second he spent in this building only increased the risk of being caught and having everything go to hell.

When he finally made it to the door, he had to stop himself from breathing a sigh of relief. *Home free,* Jack thought, stepping out onto the street. *Well, An, I came through for you. Now, it's your turn.*

Wesley Pennfield stood in front of the window in his office with his hands clasped behind his back, staring out at a forest of skyscrapers that tried to pierce the clouds. Tall and slim, he had a manner about him that made his pressed black suit seem more like a bullet-proof vest. "Have you conducted your initial analyses?" the man asked without so much as a flinch. "What can you tell me about the Nassai?"

Gerald Hamilton stood in the middle of the room with his hands shoved inside the pockets of his jacket, trying to keep his face smooth despite the anxiety in his belly. After fifteen years of working with this man, he still felt uneasy.

Gerald bit his lip, then lowered his eyes to the carpeted floor. He felt deep creases stretch across his brow. "I have performed some...preliminary tests," he began. "And I can confirm that the-"

"Only preliminary?"

A flush reddened Gerald's face. He shook his head in frustration. "Just the preliminary tests," he managed without too much difficulty. "I don't want to risk any harm to the creature."

Wesley Pennfield just stood there with his back turned, refusing to budge so much as an inch. The man's inability to acknowledge him left Gerald feeling queasy. "I would suggest you accelerate your timetable."

"There may be difficulties in doing so. I believe-"

Wesley Pennfield turned.

The man scowled as he studied Gerald through the thin lenses of his glasses. A reaction? That couldn't be good. Pennfield was a glacier: cool, calm and reserved. He only deigned to interact with his subordinates when such interaction was truly necessary, and if you forced him to resort to such measures, well...it usually didn't turn out well. "I am uninterested in the details. Will the creature survive the process?"

"I'm not certain."

Pennfield dropped into his chair with a sigh, resting his elbows on the surface of his desk. He laced his fingers and touched his nose to his thumb. "Need I remind you of what your purpose here is?"

"No, sir."

"Then provide me with the information that I need," Pennfield snapped. "Tell me if the Nassai will survive the process."

As if Gerald could just conjure that information into existence! It was difficult for him to keep a cool head, but losing his temper wouldn't get him anywhere. "The data we have is sketchy at best."

Pennfield turned his head. Just a glance, but when the man's eyes fell on him, fear seized Gerald's heart in icy fingers. "You have forty-eight hours to present me with a better answer," he replied. "By that time, one of my associates will have arrived, and we will begin the procedure with or without your consent. The Nassai's life is in your hands."

Chapter 12

Jack decided to take a shift at the restaurant after returning the multi-tool to Anna. With the insanity of the last few days, he needed something mundane, something simple to restore his sense of normalcy. He wasn't a spy; committing what was essentially a kind of industrial espionage left him feeling a little shaken. Fortunately, he'd gotten away with no real problems.

Four hours of waiting tables, mollifying disgruntled customers and listening to his co-workers banter was almost enough to make him forget that his whole world had been upended over the course of two days. Still, his legs were aching. Amazing how a couple days of rest could make you forget what it was like to work for minimum wage and tips.

The door to his apartment confronted Jack with a pinprick of light passing through the small peephole. After a long evening shift, all he wanted was to flop down on his bed, but if Anna was on a mission...

He pushed his way inside.

The familiar red-bricked walls set his nerves at ease. Curtains were drawn around the bed in the corner, but the light above his couch was still on. Anna was still awake and reading, it seemed.

Chewing on his lower lip, Jack shut his eyes. He took a deep breath through his nose. "Oh, my aching feet," he said, stepping inside. "I'm telling you, kiddo, thank your holy companion you don't live on this world."

Anna sat on the couch with his e-reader held up in front of her face. She let out a slow, thoughtful grunt. "Good evening," she said at last with a curt bob of her head. "I'm sorry your night was difficult."

From this angle, Jack could only see the back of her head, but he could pick up that sense of skeptical apprehension in her voice. Just what had she been doing over the last few hours? "I'm surprised you're still awake."

"I've been studying your literature," she replied without turning. "I hope you don't mind that I used some of your…Internet connection. I wanted to understand your people from a cultural perspective. I have to say, some of the things that authors write about are a little disconcerting."

Pressing a fist to his mouth, Jack shut his eyes and cleared his throat. "Well, I don't know about you," he said, approaching the couch. "But I consider *A Love Spell for Buffy* to be nothing but tasteful."

Anna glanced over her shoulder, then arched a thin eyebrow. She held his gaze for one very long moment.

"I'm joking."

He fell onto the couch with a sigh, tilting his head back. The dull throbbing in his temples made him want to pass out right there. "What have you been reading?" he asked. "If it's *Fifty Shades of Grey,* then I'd like to take this opportunity to renounce my status as a member of the human species."

Anna smiled into her lap, those thin strands of red hair dangling and framing her face. "I'm talking about the fascination with vampires," she said, nodding once. "Just how is sneaking into a girl's room to watch her sleep a sign of affection?"

"You got me there."

"I don't know, Jack," she murmured. "Our species has its faults but I wouldn't turn in my membership card."

"Are you sure?" he countered. "Because I filled out a form 52-J in triplicate and it'd be a shame to let all that paperwork go to waste."

"Alright, what is it?"

He froze.

Anna looked over her shoulder, a lock of hair falling over one eye. "You could tell me what's bothering you," she said with a shrug. "Or you could insist you're fine until I drag it out of you."

Jack forced a tiny smile as he stared into his lap. He shook his head. "It's Leah," he explained. "Speaking to her reminded me of all the ways I've screwed up, of all the things I should have done differently."

When he glanced over his shoulder, Anna was watching him with curiosity evident on her face. "You like this girl?" she asked, arching a thin eyebrow. "And you feel like you're unworthy in her eyes?"

Scraping a knuckle across the tip of his nose, Jack winced. "Not like," he muttered, pressing his back into the couch cushions. "Respect. Leah was somebody who was there for me when I was younger."

"And why would you be a disappointment to her?"

How could he explain this? Part of the reason that he had gone into work was to get the events of this afternoon off his mind. Anna's concern was genuine, however, and now that he had started this conversation, it seemed rude to shut her down. "My grades were a mess when I was in high school," he began. "That being the case, most universities won't even look at my application. Leah didn't quite say *I told you so* this afternoon but...well, the point is I turned out pretty much how everyone expected."

"So, everyone expected you to be a brave, kind-hearted, noble human being?" The playful grin Anna wore was almost enough to make him burst out laughing. What he wouldn't give to just hug her right then. "Because that's what I see. So, I cannot imagine why you're being so hard on yourself."

Squeezing his eyes shut, Jack buried his face in his hand. He let out a groan. "Oh, I don't know," he mumbled, massaging his temples. "Maybe because it's almost impossible to find well-paid work without a degree."

With a growl, Anna hopped off the couch and marched across the room to stand in front of the TV. She remained there for a moment, lost in thought. Whatever was going through her head was beyond him.

She kept her back turned, but he could tell she was clasping her chin. "I don't think it's wise to torment yourself," she began more evenly than he would have expected. "You made some mistakes as a teenager. So what? That describes most people."

"Those mistakes might affect the rest of my life."

She turned partway around and looked over her shoulder, her face pinched in an expression of contempt. "And whose fault is that?" she asked, raising an eyebrow. "If the system offers no way to remedy those mistakes?"

Closing his eyes, Jack leaned his head against the couch cushions. He took a deep breath and then let it out again. "Oh, there's a way," he said. "I could take a few remedial courses to improve my transcripts."

"Then why not do so?"

"Well, the cost." Giving her a lecture on the finer points of economics might prove fruitless; he wasn't aware of how Leyrians organized their society, and he hadn't taken the opportunity to ask. "Those remedial courses cost money, money that I had planned to use to pay my university tuition. It's not impossible to dig myself out of this pit, it's just very, very difficult."

Anna stood before him with arms crossed, frowning down at her feet. She nodded once, as if that settled matters. "I see. Well, that being the case, I suppose I stand by my original statement. If I want to go back to school, all I need to do is fill out some paperwork. Money is not a factor."

"Your people subsidize education?"

"We consider it a matter of human rights," she replied. "If you want to have a free society, you need to have an informed populace, a populace who can distinguish between information and misinformation, a populace who knows when to trust their government and why. People need to learn how to think."

"So how does your society organize itself?"

"A topic for another time, I think," she said. "It's getting late and we have a lot to do tomorrow."

"Speaking of which."

Jack nodded to the small table against the wall.

Perhaps Anna had failed to notice the gray plastic bag that he had left behind one of the small wooden chairs before going in to work. At his cue, she turned with a puzzled expression and went over to it.

Anna dropped to one knee in front of the table, her back turned as she inspected the contents of the bag. "What's this?" she said, lifting up a dark blue shirt. "More clothing? I thought I had everything I needed."

"Oh, just something I picked up this afternoon. You may not realize it, but those clothes look exactly like the uniforms the janitors wear in the Penworth building. So long as no one gets too close, they'll think you're just another member of the custodial staff, and the thing about custodians is, people tend to ignore them."

Anna started to laugh.

"I suggest you get some sleep," he said. "Because we leave bright and early in the morning."

The living room was lit only by the glow from a laptop monitor, soft white radiance washing over the blue sofa where Harry sat hunched over. Blinds on the window fluttered in the wind that came in from the backyard.

Harry frowned, shaking his head. He felt his eyebrows climb higher and higher. *So, where are you?* he thought, sitting up straight. *Don't try to hide from me, Goldilocks. I'm smarter than the average bear.*

His monitor displayed black-and-white security camera footage from the hallway outside of Jack Hunter's hospital room. People rushed up and down the corridor: nurses in scrubs, doctors in lab coats, the odd visitor who kept his eyes glued to the floor.

A restless sleep had ended in the wee hours just before sunrise, forcing Harry to stare up at the ceiling and contemplate his predicament. After half an hour of tossing and turning, it became clear he was not going to find any rest tonight, so he chose to put his agitation to good use.

Watching a video of security footage wasn't likely to pay off – it was entirely likely that the blonde woman had nothing but the most incidental connection to Jack Hunter – but he was out of options.

"Dad?"

Missy stood on the stairs that led up to the kitchen. Tall and slim in a pair of blue shorts and a white tank top, she wore her long hair loose over her shoulders. Her face was frozen in a look of disapproval.

Craning his neck, Harry smiled up at his daughter. He blinked moisture into his eyes. "What's up, honey?" he asked. "Can't sleep? You should try opening your window for a little fresh air."

Missy descended the steps to pad across the carpet on bare feet. She paused just in front of him, lifted her chin to stare at him. "I could ask you the same question," she said. "Are you still neck-deep in that case?"

Harry bit his lip, staring down into his lap. "Yeah, it's making me crazy." He threw himself back against the couch cushions. "But you don't have to worry about that."

His daughter wore a skeptical expression as she studied him, an expression that he had seen many times on his ex-wife. "I'm not so sure," she said, pacing around the coffee table to sit down next to him. "We've had indoor recess for the last few days. Some of the parents have been calling the school."

"What about?"

Missy shrugged, frowning at the computer. "They're afraid that terrorists are going to show up at our school…"

Slapping a palm over his face, Harry let out a groan. He massaged his tired eyes to ease away a headache. "I highly doubt that," he replied. "Your school isn't exactly a high-profile target."

Missy just stared at the computer screen. Moments like these were always the most difficult: moments where he had to wonder what his eldest daughter was thinking. With Claire, it was easy. She was too young to really understand the situation as anything other than "Daddy is going to catch some bad men."

Missy, however…Missy was growing up to be a young woman. There were so many moments when he could *see* the wheels turning in her head, and yet he had no idea what she was thinking. "You're not in any danger, sweetheart." That was probably true. "We'll bring these people in."

"What was that?"

"What was what?" Harry turned back to the computer screen only to find himself looking at a hallway where a pair of doctors hurried by with their backs to the camera. No sign of anything out of the ordinary.

Hunching over, Missy covered her mouth as she studied the screen. She narrowed her eyes. "Rewind it," she said in that imperious tone preteens often used. "I could swear I saw something."

Harry did as she requested and watched the footage. He caught a brief glimpse of the two doctors walking backwards at twice their normal speed, then an empty hallway. Seconds later, a tiny figure appeared, also walking backwards until she entered...Jack Hunter's room. Harry let the playback resume.

A woman emerged from Hunter's room, but just as she did, the image blurred, light refracting as though she were standing behind a window with rainwater running over its surface. She put her back to the camera and marched off with her arms folded, the image stabilizing so that Harry could only see the back of her head.

He recognized her clothing though. That brown jacket that dropped almost to her knees was the same one he had seen in the photos from Wesley Pennfield's security feed. No doubt about it – he had found Goldilocks.

"What was that?" Missy whispered.

Planting his elbow on his thigh, Harry rested his chin on the knuckles of his fist. He squinted at the screen. "Trouble..." he muttered under his breath. "Go back to bed, Missy. Your dad has work to do."

She gave him a look, a look that said she didn't want him leaving the house in the middle of the night, and Harry felt the fire in his blood die out. So far all he had was the knowledge that Jack Hunter had lied to him. He'd seen no evidence of Goldilocks during his brief look through Hunter's front door, and he would need a warrant to perform a more extensive search. That kind of paperwork would take a few hours in any event. He could get that underway and meet with the judge once the girls were off to school. "It's okay," he told his daughter, "I'm not going anywhere."

She nodded.

Missy stood and flowed around the coffee table with hands shoved into the pockets of her shorts. She paused in front of the stairs. "Thanks, Dad," she said without looking back. "I love you."

"Love you too."

Chapter 13

Morning sunlight came through the windshield of the car Jack had borrowed from his sister, illuminating flecks of dust that swirled about over the dashboard. They had pulled to a stop along the curb roughly half a block away from Wesley Pennfield's tower. Now, it was Anna's turn to be brave.

Jack sat in the driver's seat, watching her with earnest concern on his face. "You do promise to be careful, right?" he asked, deep creases lining his brow. "I'd hate to lose my newest friend so soon after meeting her."

It was difficult not to smile, but she covered her mouth with her fingertips. Best to remember that this was all new for Jack; he wasn't used to the idea of knowing someone who deliberately went into dangerous situations. "Yes, I promise," she assured him. "So long as no one pulls a gun on me, I'll be fine."

Jack clutched the steering wheel in both hands, frowning as he stared through the windshield. "Well, if they do," he said with a shrug, "you can just have your Nassai warp their guns to shoot sideways or something."

Anna flinched as if someone had slapped her. Pinching the bridge of her nose, she let out a grunt. "I forget how much you don't know sometimes," she muttered. "I can only affect space and time within a few inches around my body. Even a bubble of accelerated time is just large enough for me to stretch my arms out."

For a long moment, Jack was stone silent, scowling as he considered the implications of what she had just said. She decided to give him more information. "I can erect a small Bending that will direct incoming fire away from my body, or I can put myself into a warp bubble that will give me more time to react. But I can't, say, project a Bending across a room to defend one of my teammates, and if I wanted to affect someone else with my abilities, I would essentially have to be touching him."

"Well, you're pretty clever," he mumbled. "If it comes down to it, I'm sure you can get out of any situation."

He sounded only half convinced. It didn't take much effort for her to hear the voice of a man trying to put on a brave face. Still, there was a good chance of success. She was unsure of what else to say, so she opened the door.

Jack squeezed her hand. "Good luck."

Anna felt her lips curl, a touch of heat in her cheeks. She bowed her head to stare into her lap. "I'll be alright," she said softly. "Meet me back here in half an hour. With any luck, I'll be out by then."

The stairwell went up and up and up, flight after flight of tiled steps surrounded by cinderblock walls. Windows at every landing allowed daylight through, and gave Anna a view of other buildings across the way.

Slipping into the building had been easy enough – it shocked her that she could just walk through the lobby with her head down – and now all she had to do was find her way up to the seventeenth floor. She had ducked into the first stairwell she spotted, hoping to avoid attracting attention.

In truth, she should have been shivering, but this was not even the most dangerous assignment she had ever taken. She was a new Keeper, having earned her badge less than one year earlier, but facing down Denario's multiple attempts on her life had steeled her nerves more than she would have expected.

So, she climbed.

Anna pressed her lips together, staring down at the floor. Her eyes flicked back and forth. *So far, this has been too easy,* she thought to herself. *I half expected them to swarm me the instant I walked through the door.*

Craning her neck, Anna peered through the window. She squinted. *Pennfield went to a lot of trouble to capture the Nassai,* she noted. *With my luck, there will be a squad of people in tactical armour waiting for me.*

She started upward again. The fear that she had been so quick to dismiss suddenly gripped her chest and made her want to turn around. Funny how apprehension grew more severe the closer you came to victory. Not that she didn't have reason for concern.

Thanks to Jack, her multi-tool had Gerald Hamilton's security pass, but there was no guarantee he had access to the places she needed to go. Oh, it was highly likely that the head of Applied Sciences would be able to access any lab in the building – that would be the most logical scenario – but human beings seldom obeyed the laws of logic. No plan was foolproof; most fell apart as a consequence of some random, insignificant detail that would have been impossible to anticipate.

On the seventeenth landing, she found nothing more than a simple white door with a security scanner next to the handle. For a moment, she paused. Communion with her Nassai allowed her to sense the world around her, effectively giving her eyes in the back of her head, but she could not see through walls.

Anything could be waiting on the other side. Anything! If only she had the ability to know for certain that this wasn't a trap. If only she had the ability to affect space and time at a distance of more than a few inches from her skin.

Pressing a fist to her mouth, Anna shut her eyes tight. She exhaled, trying to remain calm. *Now, we'll see if this plan works,* she thought to herself. *If it doesn't… well, I guess I'm breaking down the door.*

She waved her multi-tool over the scanner.

The small LED changed from red to green, and she heard a harsh *cha-chunk* as the locking mechanism was released. Anna carefully took hold of the door handle and pushed it downward, opening the door to reveal…a hallway.

Just an ordinary hallway that stretched on for several dozen feet with doors at even intervals in its pristine white walls. Lights in the ceiling seemed to hum, and a yellow sign stood in the middle of a glistening floor. It seemed other members of the janitorial staff had been here recently.

Anna stepped through the door.

She started up the corridor with her head down, allowing the bill of her baseball cap to hide her face. There was no one in sight, but nobody ever regretted being careful. Halfway up the corridor, she found a metal plaque on the wall.

A few moments of examination and she deduced that she had located a map of the seventeenth floor. What luck that she had taken the time to learn how to read this overly complicated language. According to the plaque, the main research lab was just around the next corner. That was a good place to start.

Anna bit her lip, nodding to herself. She closed her eyes and took a deep, calming breath. *Not much longer now,* she told herself. *If the Nassai is here, they'll be keeping it in a lab. If not…deal with that later.*

She approached the corner.

The sound of voices in the intersecting hallway made her flinch and press her back to the wall. Anna held her breath, hoping, *praying* that they'd go the other way. *Come on! Come on! Use the elevator! No one takes the stairs!*

A quick glance around the corner revealed the backs of two men in white lab coats as they vanished into one of the nearby rooms. She would have to move quickly. Once again, anxiety welled up.

Anna stepped around the corner.

She pulled the bill of her cap down over her face and started up the corridor. On the wall to her right, she found a large metal door with a scanner similar to the one she'd seen in the stairwell. A wave of her multi-tool took care of that.

The research lab was a large room with counters on all four walls and bright lights in the ceiling that shone down on a rectangular island in the middle of the floor. There were only two exits: the one behind her and its twin on the opposite wall.

Chairs were tucked neatly under the counter at every workstation, and shelves at shoulder height displayed microscopes, test tubes and flasks. She saw many other pieces of equipment that she didn't recognize.

A jolt of elation shot through her when she realized the Nassai was here. A tank that might have been used to house fish was sitting on the counter to her right, but instead of aquatic life, it was home to a thin purple gas that flickered as if an electrical storm was brewing inside. She hadn't failed! After all that effort, she had come here in time to save the symbiont! At first it shocked her that the lab was empty, but, of course, Mr. Pennfield would want to keep this place sealed off from anyone but his most trusted researchers, and it was still quite early in the morning.

She practically ran across the room.

Pushing a chair out of the way – the sound of its wheels rolling across the floor almost made her jump – she examined the equipment. On closer inspection, she noticed that the containment unit Denario had used to transport the Nassai was still attached to the tank by a long clear tube. A small saucer-shaped device about twice the size of her palm, it sat on the counter with a red LED that blinked over and over.

Anna shut her eyes tight, shaking her head in disgust. "I'm going to get you out of here," she said, dropping to one knee in front of the tank. "I know you can't hear me but just hold on. Help is here."

The controls were in Leyrian! That made her job easier, but it also indicated a rather unsettling reality: whoever operated this device could read her language. There was more going on here than a simple case of kidnapping.

Anna licked her lips, then looked down at the floor. She tried to ignore the sweat beading on her brow. "This is getting uglier and uglier," she muttered. "After we get you home, I might have to come back here with a full task force."

She tapped the glowing screen at the base of the tank to bring up the main menu. The system asked for a password. Bleakness take her! To have come so close and then be foiled by the most basic of security measures. There had to be a way! Perhaps she could guess the phrase.

Take it easy, Lenai, she told herself. *Let's play 'what do we know?'* Well, most people were terrible at remembering passwords, and they tended to choose something of personal significance. In this case, however, there was another factor to consider.

Whoever operated this tank could read Leyrian, but without a Nassai's assistance, the task of learning her language would be slow and arduous. That meant the password was probably something simple. Possibly even the default. After all, using the default password would not be much of a security risk in this case because any employee who managed to bypass the scanners on the doors would not even be able to read the text on the screen. She typed in *password.*

Access granted!

"Am I good or am I good?" Anna mumbled as she keyed in a series of commands that would transfer the Nassai back to its portable containment unit. There was a strange hissing sound as purple gas began to flow through the plastic tube. Slowly, the gas inside the tank grew thinner and thinner until it was gone. Only a vacuum would remain.

Crossing her arms over her chest, Anna pressed her lips together. She nodded once in approval. "Easier than expected," she said, eyebrows rising. "We'll get you out of this building and then you'll be safe and sound."

The LED on the portable containment unit flipped from a blinking red to a steady green, indicating the Nassai had been sealed inside. It was time to go. Anna retrieved her multi-tool.

She pushed a few buttons with her thumb, and three little prongs emerged from the top of the disk, each one magnetized. She clipped the tool onto her belt and fastened the containment unit to the prongs. That would leave her hands free.

She turned back the way she had come.

The door behind her opened.

Tilting her head back, Anna squeezed her eyes shut. She let out a quiet little squeal of frustration. "Of course," she muttered under her breath. "Why should I have expected things to go my way?"

She spun around to find a man in a guards uniform standing in the open doorway. A tall fellow with a bit of stubble on his pudgy face, he looked her up and down. "So, I was reviewing the sign-in logs," he said, placing a hand on his holstered pistol, "when I came across an anomaly."

The man frowned at her, his face contorted into that ubiquitous expression security guards got when they found something amiss. "Seems Mr. Hamilton's key card was used to access this room," he went on. "But he's scheduled to be out of the office until late this afternoon. You wanna tell me who you are?"

Pressing her lips into a thin line, Anna looked up to blink at him. "I mean no harm to you or to anyone else," she said, shaking her head. "The people you work for have taken a sentient being into captivity."

He drew his gun.

"Of course, this wouldn't be easy," Anna said, backing away. "I would prefer to avoid the use of violence."

The enhanced spatial awareness offered by her Nassai alerted her that if she kept backing up, she would trip over the chair she had rolled into the middle of the floor. How to use that to her advantage?

The guard thrust his hand out, pointing the gun at her chest. His face was twisted into a snarl. "You just stay where you are," he growled. "You think I don't know who I'm dealing with? You put three of my colleagues in the hospital."

"Yes," she replied. "I'm truly sorry for that."

With his free hand, the guard squeezed the radio in his shirt pocket. "This is Olsen," he began in a low muffled voice. "Send back up to Science Lab A. Looks like we have a thief on our hands."

"You don't have to do this."

"Don't I?"

Anna lifted her chin to stare him down for a long moment. She raised a thin red eyebrow. "Do you really want to kill me, sir?" she asked. "Have you ever even fired that weapon before today?"

His expression softened, and he looked down at himself. It seemed as though she'd gotten through to him. "I've never shot anyone," he conceded. "But you are a dangerous woman. Stay where you are."

He pointed the gun at her knee. Of course, the fellow would opt for a non-lethal solution. Even knowing she had disarmed three men twice her size, he probably thought she was helpless against firearms. Anna felt a sudden queasiness when she realized she would have to disabuse him of that.

"I don't want to fight you."

"Stay still."

"But you're leaving me no-"

The man showed his teeth and let out a growl. A vein began to throb in his forehead. *Oh no…* Anna thought. *He's going to shoot.*

Bending her knees, Anna jumped. She back-flipped through the air just as his gun went off with a *CRACK*, his bullet striking the floor and tossing up chunks of linoleum. She flipped upright to land behind the chair.

Anna kicked it.

The chair went flying across the room as the guard tried to adjust his aim. It hit him square in the face before he could point his gun at her, the pistol tumbling out of his hand. He dropped to his knees.

Now!

She turned and ran.

The door to the hallway was maybe five paces away, and she would be able to exit the room without her multi-tool. Before she got near it, however, the damn thing swung open and she was confronted with another pair of guards.

The one in front drew a pistol from his belt. He thrust a hand out, pointing the gun at her and squinting as he took aim.

Anna threw up a Bending. The air before her rippled, the guard now a blurry image as he pulled the trigger. *CRACK! CRACK!* Bullets appeared several inches in front of her face, veered off to her right and spiralled toward the wall.

Anna let the Bending drop, pain flaring in her temples.

The guard was staring at her with his mouth agape, blinking as though he wasn't all that sure his eyesight was in working order. In that moment of confusion, she closed the distance between them.

Anna kicked the gun out of his hand. She spun and back-kicked, driving a foot into his chest. The impact sent him tumbling backward and he collided with the guard behind him. Both fell backward through the door.

Two bodies in the hallway and the man underneath struggled, flailing about as he tried to push his companion off him. The guard she had kicked was winded, gasping and unable to move.

She ran up the corridor.

Clenching her teeth, Anna winced. She tossed her head about, strands of blonde hair flying across her face. "Keep it together, Lenai," she panted. "You only have to make it to the bloody corner."

She rounded it.

At the end of this hallway, she saw a door that led to a stairwell. Escape was only a few seconds away, but there was a problem. Another guard was standing in the middle of the corridor.

He drew his pistol and raised it in a shaky arm, terror evident on his face. "You just stay back," he stammered, backing away from her. "I don't want to shoot you, but so help me God, I'll do what I-"

Anna kept on running.

She dropped to her knees and slid across the slick floor tiles just before a deafening roar filled the air. Bullets whizzed past overhead, cutting the air with a sharp whine. She slid right up to him.

Reaching up with both hands, Anna seized his arm and pushed it upward so that his gun was now pointed at the ceiling. A few more shots – each one like a gong in her head – then plaster rained down on her.

Anna slammed a palm into his chest.

The man went flying backward, landing hard on his ass and sliding across the floor tiles. He let out a groan, his arm flopping down to let the pistol fall out of his grip. Right beside him.

Anna somersaulted across his body. Snatching up the gun as she passed, she came up in a crouch. Just a few feet to the door, but she needed to make sure nobody was able to follow her.

Pressing her lips together, Anna looked down at the floor. She closed her eyes and took a deep breath. *You're acting in self-defence,* she told herself. *These people will not hesitate to put a slug in you.*

She turned, swinging her arm out behind herself, and fired. Her gun went off with a flash of its barrel, and bullet holes appeared in the wall of the intersecting hallway. Anna had a brief glimpse of one of the other guards ducking back around the corner.

No time to lose.

In a heartbeat, she was on her feet again and charging through the stairwell door. She raced across the landing, leaped and sailed over the railing. For one perfect moment, adrenaline was enough to overpower the fear.

She landed crouched on the stairs. *Come on, Lenai. Let's go.*

"What do you mean 'she slipped past you?'"

Vincent felt sweat coating his face. "There were *four* of you!" he bellowed. "How could one little girl get past four armed guards, all twice her size?"

His faint reflection in a blank security monitor stared back at him. His cheeks were flushed, and his double chin seemed more pronounced. Sweat drenched his coarse black hair. "This isn't happening!"

The Security Office – a tiny cubbyhole on the first floor – was completely empty except for himself and a young man named Sean Collins. Just out of high school, the kid seemed frantic as he watched the monitors.

"She's... quick!"

Vincent groaned. Mr. Pennfield would have his job for this! "Where is she now?" he said, scanning the active monitors. "Collins?"

"Southeast stairwell."

Calling up the appropriate video feed, Vincent found a black-and-white image of a set of stairs under the light of the morning sun. There was no sign of the young woman, but she had a tendency to slip past cameras before he could get a good look. How had she gotten her hands on a *janitor's* uniform?

"She made it to the thirteenth floor," Collins shouted.

"Watch the cameras," Vincent barked. "I want to know the *instant* that she decides to change her route."

He only had twelve guards on the day shift. The woman had already slipped past the three who had been close enough to answer Lewis's call for backup, and that left only eight warm bodies to intercept this...she-devil – six, if you excluded Collins and himself. Someone had to coordinate this whole thing.

It was unlikely she would use an elevator – that would leave her at their mercy – and so she would have to take one of the four stairwells down to the ground floor. Of course, she could switch stairwells at any floor, and tracking her was proving to be quite a bit harder than he would have liked.

That being the case, Vincent did the only thing he could: he divided his men among all four stairwells and hoped against hope that it would be enough. "Lewis!" he growled into his radio. "Have your men take an elevator down to the fifth. Divide up and rejoin the others. One to each stairwell."

"But-"

"No excuses! Just *do* it!"

"She's cutting across the eleventh floor!" Collins shouted. "Heading to southwest stairwell!" The monitors displayed a young woman running through a narrow corridor of cubicles while men and women in suits and skirts jumped out of her way. None dared to block her path. "Wilhelm is on six and Terrance is coming up to join him. Police cruisers have been dispatched: ETA ten minutes."

Not soon enough.

Anna was crouched on the landing of a stairwell with her pistol raised up beside her head. The pain that came with using her Nassai's more advanced abilities had dwindled to a mild tingle in her skin. So far, she had managed to avoid bloodshed and, with any luck, she would be able to get out of there without further violence.

Unfortunately, the sound of footsteps on the stairs below meant that her good fortune had come to an end. She had made it to the ninth floor, but if her guess was correct, there were two or possibly three men coming up to meet her.

Red-cheeked and gasping, Anna closed her eyes. She tilted her head back, taking a deep breath. *You've already slipped past four,* she reassured herself. *This will be a whole lot easier with the element of surprise.*

The footsteps drew nearer.

In moments like these, it was difficult to ignore the beating of her own heart as it tried to punch through her chest. The thought of dying didn't scare her nearly as much as the thought of taking a life.

She spun around to stand at the head of the stairs.

Two big men in black-and-white uniforms stood dumbfounded on the steps below, their mouths gaping as they stared up at her. Surprise lasted only a moment before they reacted. One already had his weapon drawn.

Raising her pistol in both hands, Anna squinted at them, then shook her head in warning. "Your weapons," she said in a harsh, grating voice, "keep them pointed at the floor and eject the clips."

The nearest guard frowned at her, his dark face twisting in an expression of distaste. He complied with her order, ejecting the magazine from his pistol and letting it fall to the floor with a soft *click-clack.*

His companion did so as well.

"Toss the empty guns away," Anna ordered. She watched as they obeyed, both men throwing their weapons down to the landing they had just crossed. That done, she felt an immediate sense of relief. "Now, you're going to walk past me and you're going to keep going upstairs. Understood?"

They nodded.

"Go."

Anna stepped out of the way to let them cross the landing. The brain picked up all sorts of insignificant details in tense situations; she couldn't help but notice the way sweat plastered the fabric of those white shirts to their backs.

In a moment, they were gone. Another situation resolved without lethal force, thank the Holy Companion. If she could get down to an exit without any further incidents, this *mission* might just be a success.

Anna ran.

She stopped for a brief moment on the stairs, pausing just long enough to collect the discarded ammunition. She wasn't stupid; those men would turn around and chase her the instant they thought she had gone far enough, and she wasn't about to leave them with anything they might use against her.

After that, it was a mad dash to the ground floor. Anna hopped over the railing to land on the next staircase over. She dropped to a crouch, ignoring the slight burst of pain in her knees.

She ran down a few steps, then hopped over the railing again. This pattern went on while she counted the floors. The seventh…the sixth…the fifth and fourth. So far as she could tell, there were no more guards in her path.

Her ears picked up the sound of footsteps up above – a whole lot of them. It seemed the pair of guards had rendezvoused with several of their colleagues. That meant they were likely to be armed again. *Hurry up.*

She paused on the landing between the first and second floors, staring through the window at a lush green lawn that stretched on for several dozen feet before stopping at the sidewalk. Beyond that, she saw several cars parked on the curb. Was Jack's one of them? No time for worrying. She had done her part; now, she had to trust him to do his.

I'm sorry, my friend, Anna told her Nassai. *But I'm going to have to call upon your aid one more time.*

She fired at the window, filling the stairwell with a thunderous roar. These Earth weapons were so damn loud! The pane shattered into a thousand little shards that rained down upon the ground below. *Companion, have mercy on anyone who might have been standing there.* The thought occurred to her too late.

Calling on her Nassai, Anna bent gravity, reducing its pull to less than half of what would be considered normal on this planet. Pain flared behind her eyes, but she ignored it with some effort.

Anna leaped.

She flipped through the open window, then uncurled to drop to the grass outside the building. She landed in a crouch, raising her pistol on instinct and allowing her Bending to die. In a heartbeat, she was on her feet and racing through the grass.

Jack's car was waiting on the roadside, just behind a parking meter. Through the passenger-side window, she could make out the silhouette of his head as he waited for her.

Anna dashed across the sidewalk.

She pulled the door open and dove into the back seat, landing face down upon the cushions. "Go!" she shouted before she could even get the door closed. "Hurry! They'll be on us any second!"

A moment later, they were moving, and she twisted around to slam the door shut with all her might. Aches and pains that she hadn't even noticed were suddenly blazing beacons in her mind; the adrenaline was fading.

Through the driver's-side window, she saw cars whooshing past on their left. One man slowed just long enough to proudly display his middle finger. An obscene gesture on this planet? Jack must have cut him off as he pulled into traffic. Still, the plan had worked and they were safely on their way to-

Sirens blared in the open air. Anna had heard that sound once before, on the night when she had made her first escape from this building. That meant the local authorities were on their way to investigate the disturbance.

Anna buried her face in her hands. She let out a groan, then looked up to blink at the back of the passenger seat. "This can't be happening," she said, shaking her head. "I will *not* lose the symbiont now!"

"Stay calm," Jack told her, keeping his eyes on the road. "See what they do."

Glancing through the back window, she saw several cruisers rounding the corner of a street in the distance. She watched them maneuver through traffic, then come to a stop in front of the Penworth building. They weren't chasing?

They weren't chasing!

Of course, they weren't chasing. The guards had been half a dozen floors above her, so they hadn't witnessed her escape through the window. Anyone on the ground who saw that little display would not have had the chance to inform the police yet. And that meant they had a few minutes to get away. "They aren't following us."

"Good," Jack said, nodding. "So, we're just going to go with the flow of traffic, not make any aggressive movements. With luck, we can put some distance between them and us before they start following."

"Maybe we're in the clear."

Jack shook his head. "Maybe," he said, "but maybe not. If anyone on the sidewalk got our plate number..."

She sighed.

"Hang on, An," Jack told her. "We're not out of the woods yet."

Dabbing his face with a paper towel, Vincent closed his eyes. He tried to keep his breathing steady. "You have to act professional," he muttered. "You did everything you could."

The men's room on the thirtieth floor was a bit classier than many of the others he'd seen in this building. Glossy black tiles upon the walls seemed to reflect the light, and the sinks were built into granite counters.

He checked his reflection in the mirror.

His pudgy face was flushed and glistening, and his dark eyes looked ready to start tearing up. Sweat slicked his black hair until it very nearly shimmered. How could that bloody woman be so *fast*?

Vincent winced, then hung his head. He wiped sweat off his brow with the back of his hand. "Mr. Pennfield will be angry," he noted. "You just have to approach him with your head held high."

He turned and left the room.

A long hallway stretched on to a set of glass doors at the very end. Even from here, Vincent could make out the white letters painted across the pane. *Wesley Pennfield: CEO and President.*

He swallowed.

Walking the eighty feet from the men's room door to Pennfield's office seemed to take forever. He felt very much like a dead man marching through that long black tunnel only to discover that hellfire waited on the other end. What would Teresa and the kids say if he lost his job?

He stepped through to find himself in a sterile office where gray carpets stretched from wall to wall. A kidney-shaped desk with a surface of perfectly polished glass was the only piece of furniture, Pennfield's monitor turned askew so that he could almost see what the man had been reading.

The CEO of Penworth Enterprises stood before the window with his hands clasped behind his back, staring out at a field of skyscrapers that glittered in the morning sunlight. "Thank you for coming, Vincent," he said in that dry, nasal voice of his. "I do hope your men were not seriously injured."

"No, sir."

"Excellent." Vincent very nearly lost his footing. Where was the explosion that he had been expecting since being paged up here ten minutes ago? Pennfield was…calm. A little too calm. "Did anyone get a good look at the car she used to make her escape?"

It didn't seem possible, but Vincent's flush burned even hotter. He lowered his eyes to stare at his shoes. "No, sir," he rasped. "No one on our staff anyway. Cops are starting to interview witnesses."

"Keep me posted."

"Sir…" Vincent couldn't bring himself to look up. "I-I just want to say I'm sorry. If we had only been faster…"

Pennfield said nothing.

Folding his arms with a sigh, Vincent backed away. He frowned, shaking his head with disgust. "That woman is just..." Just what? He had nothing. "Sir, I don't know what she took but-"

"That will be all, Vincent."

He nodded.

Turning around to leave this office made him feel as though a huge weight had been taken off his chest. He could see the hallway through the door and the letters that were now backwards from his perspective. Just a few steps and he would be home fr-

"Vincent."

Panic ripped through him. Vincent turned around to find the other man standing so that he saw him in profile. "If you could be stronger and faster," Wesley Pennfield began. "If there was a method to endow you with abilities similar to those of the woman who bested half a dozen of your guards, would you take it?"

"I...yes, sir."

Wesley Pennfield smiled. "Excellent," he said. "That was *exactly* what I wanted to hear."

Chapter 14

Pounding on the wooden door with the knuckles of his bare fist, Harry let out a hiss at the sting to his fingers. "Jack Hunter?" he called out. "This is Detective Carlson. I've got a warrant to search these premises."

He stood in the hallway in a gray suit with a sharp maroon tie, his dark hair combed neat and square. "Jack Hunter?" he said. "This would be a hell of a lot easier if you cooperated."

No answer.

The two uniformed officers at his side exchanged glances, apprehension visible on their faces. Rumours had been spreading like wildfire, and the idea that some kid might be involved with the strange crimes that had been popping up all over the city wasn't one that Harry could keep quiet. He supposed that was for the best; it made his people sharp.

Harry ground his teeth, then closed his eyes and shook his head. "All right, open it up," he said, gesturing to the man beside him. "If the kid's not here, it will only make this a whole lot easier."

The landlord shuffled forward.

A tiny man with a ring of gray hair around the back of his skull, he fiddled with a set of keys. "Just a moment," he grumbled, approaching the door and sliding one in. "I'm telling you the boy is harmless."

Harry would judge that for himself.

The door opened to a small apartment where gray carpet stretched from brick wall to brick wall. A bed in the corner was hidden by curtains, and the only pieces of furniture that Harry saw were a table next to the television and a couch in the middle of the room. Spartan. It reminded him of his college days.

He nodded.

The two uniformed men were the first through the door, glancing about as though they expected gunfire at any second. That was probably for the best as well, but it made Harry wistful. Was there ever a time when people hadn't been so jumpy?

Crossing his arms with a sigh, Harry frowned down at the floor. "The boy is a lot more clever than he looks," he said, nodding to himself. "Keep your eyes peeled, and don't touch anything you don't have to."

He stepped in.

One of his officers was already drawing back the curtains around the bed. He went stiff, back straightening. "Sir, I think you might want to have a look at this," he shouted. "Seems Hunter has a girlfriend."

Harry paced across the room to find clothes resting on the wooden shelf above the bed, clothes that were obviously meant for a woman. They were similar to the ones he'd seen in the plastic bag his people found outside the thrift shop.

Lifting his chin, Harry squinted at the shelf. He shook his head. "That's a start, but not enough for an arrest," he said, spinning around on his heel. "We need something to prove they belong to Goldilocks."

"What about this?"

Carmichael stood at the closet near the front door, holding a hanger that supported a beige trench coat. "Doesn't this look like the one that woman was wearing on the security camera footage?"

"Yes…it does."

Just then, his phone started screeching at him. He would really have to change that ring tone. He was tempted to ignore it and continue with the search, but after the week he had been through, it was probably something important. Harry brought the phone to his ear. "Carlson, go."

"Sir," Rawlins panted, "you have to get over to the Penworth building."

"What? Why?"

"Dispatch just got a call," Rawlins explained. "Seems that crazy blonde woman is back and man-handling their people."

"Damn it!"

There were people in this world with a hard-on for architecture; David Hutchinson was not one of them. So, when he looked up at the Penworth building, all he saw was another rectangular skyscraper that made his eyes sting when the sunlight bounced off its windows. Worst of all, the damage to the front wall took away any beauty the building might have had.

First, the window near the front entrance had been boarded up with plywood, and now there was a great big hole in the southwest stairwell. Whoever this blonde chick was, she really liked to make a mess.

People were crowded together on the sidewalk behind a line of yellow police tape, all gawking at the damage and muttering to themselves. He could already hear some of the rumours. A woman had jumped through the window! She was some kind of ninja! No, she was an assassin hired by the Socialist Party. No, not the Socialist Party. This hit was ordered by a rival company. Some even said she was an alien! A god damn alien! People believed the stupidest things. Why did he always end up working the crime scenes that attracted the most weirdos?

Pressing his lips together, David stared up at the building. He squinted, shaking his head. "Black Ops," he said to himself. "That's gotta be it. Some woman breaking into the place to recover government secrets."

Did the Canadian government *have* secrets?

His phone rang.

He checked the screen and felt a chill when he recognized the number. For a brief moment, he was tempted not to answer, but ignoring this call would be bad for his health and his career.

David brought the receiver to his ear. He closed his eyes and let out a sigh. "I told you not to call me at work!" he snapped. "You have any idea what would happen if the LT knew I was talking to you?"

"Now, now, Officer Hutchinson," Wesley Pennfield replied. "Is that any way to talk to the man who has generously agreed to cover your gambling debts? What do you think would happen if your lieutenant knew about that?"

David froze.

"I have a very simple favour to ask you," Pennfield went on. "Have you identified the car that the perpetrator used to make her escape?"

David glanced about. When he saw that none of the other officers were paying all that much attention, he turned away from them and whispered, "We did. The car belongs to a Lauren Hunter. The perp has been staying with her brother Jack."

"Can you provide me with contact information for this *Jack Hunter*?" The tone in the man's voice implied that saying "no" would be a mistake.

Tension formed a knot in the middle of David's chest. Giving out information like that was a serious breach of protocol, a violation of basic civil rights. "Absolutely not!" he shouted into the phone. "I won't put my career on the line for-"

"Very well," Pennfield cut in. "Then our association is at an end."

Squeezing his eyes shut, David trembled. "All right," he said, turning away from the others and marching toward the front entrance. "I'll get you the information. Damn it, Pennfield, you need to be discreet."

"What I need is none of your concern," the other man replied. "Now, here's what you're going to do next..."

The noonday sun was high in the sky, shining down on a field of lush green grass that stretched on to a line of trees with patches of brown dirt here and there. Off in the distance to her right, children played between two white goal posts, kicking a ball with black spots on its surface.

Jack had taken her to a place called Brewer's Park. According to him, this was far enough away from his neighbourhood in Centre-Town to let them stop for a few minutes and plan their next move.

Anna stood on the grass with her arms folded, smiling down at her feet. The wind blew tendrils of hair back from her face. "We did it!" she said. "I can't believe we did it."

She turned around.

Jack was smiling at her, his blue eyes practically sparkling in the sunlight. For some reason, she had taken a liking to that messy hair. "Yeah, we did it," he said, his eyebrows rising. "Now we have to figure out what to do next."

"I suppose we could run."

Bowing his head, Jack stared down at the grass with a solemn expression. His face seemed to flush. "We could do that," he replied. "And spend the rest of our lives running from the cops."

Guilt was a spear point that had plunged right through Anna's chest when she wasn't looking. In her excitement to free the Nassai – her *need* to complete this assignment – she had failed to consider how this might affect Jack. Though his intentions were admirable, he had broken the law of this world. There had to be something she could-

Of course!

Tilting her head to the side, Anna flashed a sly grin. She batted her eyes. "You can come back to Leyria with me," she offered. "Dex sent a distress beacon before our ship went down; with any luck they'll find us."

Jack kept his face smooth as he peered off into the distance. He nodded to himself, thinking it over. "That would be one hell of an opportunity," he murmured. "But I have a family that I can't leave behind."

So, travelling the stars was not an option then. A pity. In truth, she hadn't expected him to take the offer – very few people would be willing to leave their family behind – but she would have liked to have shown him some of the wonders she had seen. The Syl Nebula and the-

Wait, what was she thinking? Travelling the stars might not even be an option for *her;* all of that was contingent on her people detecting the distress beacon, and this world was far from Leyrian space.

That left her with another problem. The portable containment unit she had stolen would keep the Nassai safe for a few days, but after that, she would need to find another solution. Just as a space suit only offered so much air before the astronaut suffocated, the containment unit would only last so long. If help didn't arrive in that time, there were only two possibilities: the Nassai would either take a host or perish.

"I would really like to go," Jack said, bowing his head to her. Apparently, he had been thinking it over while she considered her options. "There's so much I wish I could see, but not without telling my family."

She slipped her arms around him.

Anna pressed her cheek into his chest, closing her eyes. She took a deep, soothing breath. "Could we talk to your authorities?" she inquired. "If we could prove to them that Wesley Pennfield had captured a living being..."

"It's worth a shot."

"Perhaps that Detective Carlson?"

"Maybe," he replied. "I-"

She was startled by a sudden beeping, and Jack pulled away from her. Fishing in his pants pocket, he retrieved a small rectangular device. A cellular telephone? They seemed to be the closest thing these people had to multi-tools.

Jack narrowed his eyes, staring at the screen. He shook his head. "I don't know this number," he said, answering the call and bringing the receiver to his ear. "You've reached Jack Hunter. How can I help you?"

As he listened to the person on the other end, his face went paler and paler, and his eyes looked ready to pop out. "It's for you," he whispered. "Hold on. I'll put him on speaker phone."

"Hello?" Anna said.

"Miss Lenai. This is Wesley Pennfield."

Anna bit her lip, then lowered her eyes to the ground. She felt the blood drain out of her face as well. "What do you want?" she grated. "Walk soft, *veksha.* I have half a mind to bring a fleet of Leyrian cruisers down on your head."

Soft chuckling came through the speaker. "You really don't know, do you? Tell me, Miss Lenai, don't you think it's odd that yours was the only shuttle to pursue my associate all the way to this system?"

"What. Do. You. Want?"

"I want my property back," he replied without a hint of inflection. The man seemed to pride himself on complete emotional control. Which meant he wanted her to hear him laughing a moment ago. "And I'm willing to go to great lengths to retrieve it. Were you at all aware of the Byward Market Street Festival taking place today?"

Jack looked puzzled, his brows drawn together as he stared down at the phone. He glanced up at her. "Why don't you just make your point, Wes?" he asked with a touch of contempt in his voice.

"Ah, Mr. Hunter, so good you're paying attention. My point is quite simple: the real currency in this world is not money but loyalty, and I have earned more loyalty in the last year alone than you will in your entire lifetime. At the moment, I have a squad of tactical mercs ready to rain death upon the street festival unless I get the Nassai."

Anna stiffened, turning her face away from the phone. It was difficult to contain the rage boiling in her chest. "You'd do that?" she hissed. "You'd kill hundreds of people just to have the chance to study an alien?"

"What I would do," Pennfield said, "and why I would do it are things beyond your comprehension, my dear. Doubt me if it pleases you; I would be happy to demonstrate my commitment. A few hundred lives are nothing compared to the destiny of the entire human race."

"You're bluffing."

"Test that theory at your leisure, my dear."

"Fine," Anna growled. "Two hours."

"307 Dalhousie Street, Apartment VI."

The line went dead.

Rubbing her nose with the back of her hand, Anna winced. She shook her head and heaved out a sigh. "You're going to take the Nassai and go," she instructed Jack. "Leave this city, and find someplace safe."

He stared at her with his mouth agape, sweat glistening on his face. "You cannot be serious," he said, backing away from her. "You're actually going to walk straight into the bastard's trap?"

Anna crossed her arms, then frowned down at the ground. "I can't take the chance that he'll make good on his threat," she said. "I will *not* have the deaths of hundreds of innocents on my conscience."

"But the Nassai-"

"Weren't you listening?" Anna bared her teeth in a vicious snarl, squinting as she studied him. "I won't bring the Nassai within ten miles of that man. The symbiont is in your care now, Jack."

He stared down at the ground, face reddening as he shook his head in disgust. "I'm not qualified to do that." Turning away from her, Jack walked a few steps before pausing. Her heart went out to him. "I wouldn't know where to begin."

"Have faith."

"Faith?"

Closing her eyes, Anna took a deep breath. She nodded to him. "You're far stronger than you give yourself credit for," she began. "Trust in yourself, Jack. You may not have all the answers, but I have no doubt you'll find them."

He stood with shoulders slumped, staring out across a field at a line of trees in the distance. "You don't expect to come back from this," Jack muttered. "You believe you're going to die."

Anna unclipped the multi-tool from her belt, leaving the disk-shaped containment unit attached. "You have to care for the Nassai," she said, approaching Jack. "It can only survive for a few days unless you find it a host."

Jack rounded on her.

For half a heartbeat, she expected an argument, but he simply took the containment unit in both hands. "I'll care for the Nassai," he said, nodding. "And I won't let Pennfield or his goons anywhere near it."

"One other thing."

She turned.

Their car was parked along the curb at a bend in the road, right in front of a set of tall red-bricked houses. It was what Jack called *a clunker*, but he seemed to have some affection for it. Strange.

Anna shuffled across the street with hands in her pockets. She paused, then bowed her head. "This won't be easy," she told Jack. "Pennfield will almost certainly send men to hunt you down."

She opened the car's back door.

Retrieving her gun from the seat, Anna held it up in one hand. She watched sunlight reflect off the sleek black barrel. "I'm giving this to you," she went on. "Leyrian firearms are more advanced than those of your world. It might give you an edge."

She flipped a tiny switch just above the grip, activating the weapon. Leyrian pistols used magnetic propulsion to fire a round at speeds comparable to those of chemically based firearms. Depowering the weapon also served as a safety precaution.

"There are three rounds left in this magazine, plus two additional clips," she began. "The power cell should be good for another hundred shots. After that, the weapon will be useless, but you'll run out of ammo long before that."

She spun around to find Jack scowling at her, shaking his head as if he thought she had lost her mind. "Won't you need that?" he inquired. "You're the one going into danger, and I don't like the thought of carrying a lethal weapon."

"*Shin vaki!*"

Speaking the words "stun rounds" in Leyrian caused the LEDs on either side of the pistol's barrel to turn blue. "Remember that command," Anna said. "Blue means that the weapon will fire rounds with a mild electric charge – just enough to immobilize a target for a few minutes. They'll fly at a much lower speed, which means they won't cause any permanent damage but will also be useless against body armour. *Nishto!*"

The word *standard* made the LEDs go dark.

Burying his face in his hand, Jack let out a groan. "Anna, I want you to keep it," he protested. "You're the one who's going into danger; I'm just leaving the city. You need it more than I do."

Idiot man!

Could he not understand that she was giving this to him because he had no other way of defending himself? Because...because she couldn't bear the thought of him being hurt? "I'm a trained Justice Keeper," she said, amazed by the lack of fury in her voice. "I can take care of myself."

He watched her with a flat expression, then nodded once. "All right then," he said, backing away from her. "But I want a plan to rendezvous once you've dealt with Wesley's threats. I expect you to come out of this."

"Naturally," she said. "Let's get moving."

Chapter 15

Jack sat in his sister's car with his hands on the steering wheel, trying to subdue the tension that threatened to squeeze his lungs until they burst. Somehow, despite herculean attempts to be positive, he had come to believe that he would never see Anna again. That left him feeling dead inside.

Clenching his teeth, Jack stared down into his lap. He shook his head. "Damn you, Pennfield!" he shouted in a rasp. "If you hurt that girl, I swear to God I'll dedicate every waking second to taking you down!"

Through the windshield, he saw an ordinary suburban street with cars parked along the curb and kids shuffling about in the middle of the road, eating popsicles. Hundreds of people might be dead in a few hours; how could everything look so *normal?*

The Nassai's containment unit was sitting in the front seat with its LED lit up in a steady green. Leyrian characters flashed on the small screen atop the device, presumably indicating that all was well. Too bad he couldn't read their script.

Jack winced, then pressed a palm hard against his forehead. He let out a groan. "If you could only comprehend what's going on," he said to the creature, "maybe you could tell me what to do next."

His phone rang.

Lauren's number flashed on the screen as his phone danced about in the little slot between the seats. Should he answer? It didn't seem prudent if he was planning to leave town with her car but...

Jack picked up the phone.

He closed his eyes and rested his head against the seat cushion. "Hello?" he said in a tight voice. "What's up, Lauren?"

"Oh, this isn't Lauren."

Those words hit him like a punch to the chest. The voice on the line belonged to a man that he had hoped to evade. Detective Harry Carlson sounded far too satisfied with himself. "Hello, Jack," he went on. "I thought we should talk."

Jack sat up.

It took some effort to keep his voice steady, but he managed it. "What are you doing with my sister's phone?"

"Well, right now, I'm standing in her living room," Carlson explained. "Making an arrest for aiding and abetting a known fugitive. Poor Lauren was foolish enough to lend you her car after all."

Jack ground his teeth, squeezing his eyes shut. He couldn't stop the rumbling growl that erupted from his throat. "That'll never hold up in court!" he spat. "Lauren could not have known what we were planning."

"You'd be surprised what a jury will believe," Carlson shot back. "But I'm willing to let her go. She's not the one I want anyway."

Blood drained out of Jack's face, and sweat broke out on his forehead. He couldn't turn himself in; ordinarily, he'd do anything for Lauren, but if Carlson got his hands on the Nassai, he'd give it back to Pennfield. "What are you proposing?"

"Meet me at your sister's house."

"And if I don't?"

"Well, you can run," Carlson replied. "But this will go up the ranks, and sooner or later you'll have the RCMP on your ass. Meanwhile, your poor sister will be tied up with legal battles and spending her days in a jail cell. Trust me when I say that no judge will allow bond, not with the chaos that your little friend has been causing."

Chewing on his lower lip, Jack shut his eyes. He nodded to himself, trying to stay calm. "Seems you've got all the bases covered," he said. "But there's something that you really ought to know."

"What's that?"

"Anna," Jack began, "that little chaos-causing friend of mine, is trying to *save* lives. Pennfield is the real criminal here."

"Why should I believe that?"

Why *should* he believe that? Think! There had to be something Jack could use to convince the other man. "She told me about what happened each time she escaped from the Penworth building," he said. "I'm betting that if you check the security footage, you'll see that she went out of her way to *avoid* lethal force."

Silence on the line.

"You know I'm right," Jack pressed. "And I would be happy to give you all of the details, but right now, I have what you might call a foreign dignitary with-"

"No, that's enough," Carlson interrupted. "You wanna talk? I'll hear you out, Jack, but you come here and meet me."

Could he go? He had promised to take care of the Nassai – and he couldn't do that if it was taken from him – but he couldn't allow his sister to rot in prison either. Not for something he had done. Why did it always feel as though he were a fly on the world's windshield, destined to be hit with the wiper blades? No matter what he did, everything fell apart.

No.

That was defeatism talking. His problem was that he had reduced the situation to two choices – go to Lauren or flee the city – when, in fact, there were several others. He had Anna's pistol and her multitool. He could prove that there was more going on than just a lot of violence. Maybe he could even convince Carlson to help him look after the Nassai. "All right," Jack said. "I'm on my way."

Dalhousie Street was a wide corridor between two lines of buildings of no more than three or four stories, most with red-bricked faces and windows on the upper levels. The road was devoid of vehicles except for a few cars parked along the curb. The nearby street festival had reduced traffic to a minimum.

Anna walked up the sidewalk with her arms folded, frowning down at her feet. The warm sun on her skin did nothing to take away the shivers that went through her. *So, this is how it ends for me.*

A few young women on the opposite sidewalk walked past, stopping in front of a purple building that housed a restaurant. They were laughing and chatting, completely unaware of the danger.

The address Anna had been given was located above a small pastry shop in what was obviously an apartment. She could see the buzzer next to the front door. No doubt her contact expected her to announce her arrival by asking for admittance. She intended to disappoint him; the first rule of survival was to never do what your enemy expected.

A red postal truck on the curb would keep her hidden from anyone on the opposite side of the street. The thing was rumbling, spitting out fumes from a stubby exhaust pipe. Perhaps if she made contact with her people, they could teach the citizens of Earth how to create cleaner energy technologies.

Gritting her teeth, Anna looked up at the building. She narrowed her eyes, focused on the task. "Well, my Nassai," she said, nodding once, "this might be farewell. But for what it's worth, you've been a good partner, if a silent one."

Her eyes caught sight of something in the window.

A figure in unrelieved black, barely visible through the glare on the windowpane, paced across the room and vanished from sight. Just a glimpse, and yet she was sure that was her contact.

Anna spun around to face the truck.

Reducing gravity, she leaped and sailed upward to land crouched upon its roof. She turned and leaped again, the windowpane coming closer and closer in her field of vision until she grabbed the concrete ledge beneath.

Anna pulled herself up. Her skin was tingling with sharp little pinpricks, and her temples began to throb. Holding onto the ledge was easy with gravity's pull reduced to almost nothing, but holding the Bending was extremely difficult.

She slammed her palm against the pane.

With the strength of a Justice Keeper, she pushed it inward, tearing the whole thing free of its mountings and creating a hole just large enough for her to squeeze through. *A moment more. Just a moment more.*

Anna wiggled through the gap.

She somersaulted across the carpeted floor, coming up on one knee and releasing her Bending. Instantly, the pain began to fade. She was alone, thank goodness, but that man in black would return.

This space might have been intended to be used as a bedroom, but it was devoid of furnishings of any kind. Blue carpet stretched from the window behind her to a door on the opposite wall. Through the opening, she could see what looked like a hallway, but she wasn't willing to take a closer look.

Anna got up.

The sound of footsteps announced the return of the man in black. He stepped into the room and froze, clearly surprised to find her there. One look, and she was certain this was the man Wesley Pennfield had sent.

He wore a pair of cargo pants with a pistol holstered on his belt and a shirt under a bulletproof vest. His face was hidden behind a dark mask with only thin slits for his eyes and mouth. "This," he said in a grating voice, "is surprising."

"I aim to please."

Crossing his arms, he looked her up and down, then narrowed his eyes. "You have the Nassai with you?" he inquired. "I would hate to think I came all the way out here for nothing at all."

"What's your name?"

"Excuse me?"

Squeezing her eyes shut, Anna shook her head in disgust. "I want to know your name!" she growled. "I can't pray for your soul if I do not know your name, and you're going to need my prayers."

Clapping a gloved hand over his mouth, the man closed his eyes. He trembled with laughter. "You're a cocky one, aren't you?" he mumbled. "My name is Vincent, not that it will matter to you. Now, the Nassai."

"Now which of us is the arrogant one?" Anna spat, fury boiling in her veins and surging through her muscles. It was difficult not to leap at the man and topple him to the floor. Anyone who threatened the lives of innocent people deserved no less. "You really think I'd bring the Nassai here?"

"You are far, far too predictable, Agent Lenai," Vincent replied. "Allow me to clarify something. This is what we call a diversion. Did you think Mr. Pennfield wouldn't anticipate such duplicity? The purpose of this meeting was to get you away from Hunter so that we could take the Nassai from *him*."

Anna bit her lip, a flush reddening her face. She lowered her eyes to the floor. "I guess I'm predictable then," she said, stepping forward. "But that's not going to matter because *Jack* isn't."

"Oh, please."

Anna looked up to fix blue eyes on him, then squinted. "He'll elude you time and time again," she said with a nod. "You'll spend the next three years hunting that man and you will *never* find him."

Vincent smiled, then bowed his head to stare down at the floor. He covered his eyes with a hand. "We already have him, girl," he muttered. "But take a moment and consider. We might be willing to let him go."

"Oh, I see," Anna shot back. "This is the moment where you tempt me by appealing to my gentle nature. 'Put on a black hat and we'll take care of your loved ones,' is that it? Tell me, how does the hero usually respond to that?"

"You have skills that we can use," Vincent rasped. "You have proven yourself to be a capable warrior. Men like Denario Tarse are disposable, but you, you are not. The old ways are failing. Justice Keepers will not be able to stand against what's coming."

"And what's that?"

"Come with me," Vincent said, stepping forward. He extended a hand toward her in a gesture of friendship. "You will find out."

Throwing her head back, Anna stared up at the ceiling. She rolled her eyes. "Let's see, if I join the bad guys, I'll learn their terrible secret," she mocked. "No thanks. I think I'd rather stay ignorant."

Vincent studied her for a long moment, lips together, gray eyes calculating. "Very well then," he said at last. "I've always wanted to test myself against a Justice Keeper."

Lauren lived in a small brown-bricked house with black shingles on its slanted roof and hedges under the large window that looked into the living room. Bright afternoon sunlight prevented Jack from seeing inside, and that made him nervous. True, Carlson was a cop, but that didn't mean he was trustworthy.

Jack stepped inside to find the detective sitting on a couch opposite the large bay window, poised and composed in a fine gray suit. "Hunter," the man said with a curt nod. "So good of you to come."

A uniformed officer stood across from Jack in the doorway that led to the kitchen. Tall and imposing, he kept his arms crossed, his thick face twisted in a scowl. "Oh, don't mind Hutchinson there," Carlson went on. "He's just here to make sure you don't go and do anything stupid."

Lauren stood with her back turned, facing the TV in the corner. Was it a bad sign that she refused to look at him? It certainly left him feeling anxious. *Don't let it show,* he scolded himself. *To these men, you're a picture of poise.*

Jack smiled, then bowed his head to the Detective. "Carlson," he said with a quick shrug of his shoulders. "Good to see you. To be honest, I'm glad you caught me. It makes me happy to know my tax dollars aren't going to waste."

Oooh... bad move.

Harry Carlson lifted his chin and squinted at Jack. Was that the hint of a flush in his cheeks? "You've got a smart mouth, kid," he said. "And a clever mind. It's a shame you're wasting it on crime."

Baring his teeth, Jack kept his eyes glued to the floor. He let out a soft hiss. "I told you, Anna's trying to save people." The words grated in his own ears. Why was it so hard to keep his voice steady? "Her people have a symbiotic relationship with a species called Nassai. Pennfield abducted one of these creatures."

The uniformed cop let out a wheezing laugh, his face twisting as he trembled with mirth. "You gotta be kidding, boy," he said, shaking his head. "You're gonna pull out science fiction to justify harbouring a fugitive."

The thing about acting was that sometimes, even when you were speaking the truth, you still had to sell it. Too much conviction would make him seem desperate. "I wouldn't expect you to believe me," Jack began. "Hell, on most days I'm the president of the Dana Scully fan club, but I've seen a few things that make me want to believe."

"Such as?" Carlson inquired.

Thrusting his chin out, Jack squinted at the other man. "I've seen Anna deflect bullets with her mind," he said. "I've seen energy fields used as weapons."

Carlson was frowning into his lap, sweat glistening on his brow. Could it be that he was starting to believe? "That would explain the strange trajectories," he mumbled. "The bullets in the wall and the pavement."

Clenching his teeth, the uniformed cop went beet red. He shot a glance toward his superior. "You can't honestly believe this!" he snapped. "The kid is making up this crap because he knows about the crime scenes."

"And how would he know?" Carlson replied. "We kept the details out of the press. He wasn't there, Hutchinson."

Only then did Jack see that Lauren had turned around. She was watching him with an expression of confusion, her face as pale as fresh-fallen snow. At least he was getting through to his sister.

"Even still!" Hutchinson protested. "How would Pennfield kidnap an alien?"

"The alien was brought here by a man named Denario Tarse," Jack said before the other man could speak. "There are humans elsewhere in the galaxy. As I understand it, they were taken from Earth over ten thousand years ago and scattered on other habitable worlds. So far as we know, Pennfield wanted to study the Nassai."

Carlson got up off the couch and started pacing, passing in front of Hutchinson as he marched to the wall. "There are too many unanswered questions," he said, staring at the plaster. "Can you offer proof, Jack?"

Wiping sweat off his brow with the back of his hand, Jack shut his eyes. "I can offer evidence," he replied. "But after that, you're going to have to decide for yourself."

"Show me this evidence."

The multi-tool was clipped to Jack's belt with the Nassai's containment unit held in place by those three magnetic prongs. He pulled it free of those prongs with some effort, causing them to retract into the tool's surface.

"This is a containment unit," Jack explained, setting it down on the small wooden table next to the front door. "It provides a habitable environment for the Nassai so that we can return it to its people."

Jack lifted the tool in the palm of his hand.

He pushed a button with his thumb, and a hologram rippled into existence: a blue rectangle with Leyrian script and large pictures that looked like the icons on his smartphone's home screen. "Have you ever seen a holographic generator this small?" he asked. "What about all the other technologies that we've never seen before? Tell me, what could burn a hole through solid concrete?"

Carlson looked nervous.

"You've seen my friend on the security footage," Jack went on. "You've seen how she goes out of her way to avoid the use of lethal force, how she does her best to inflict minimal harm on Pennfield's guards."

Carlson bit his lip, then bowed his head to stare down at the floor. He took a deep breath and let it out again. "So, she's not a killer," he muttered. "That doesn't prove that she isn't a thief."

"A thief with a conscience?" Jack offered.

Behind Carlson, the uniformed cop was grumbling to himself, pulling his pants up by the belt loops as he stepped into the living room. That one would be trouble. For some reason, he had it in for Jack.

Carlson was stroking his jaw, squinting as he studied the hologram, Jack saw him through a field of transparent blue light. "You make a good point," the detective said. "I might be inclined to believe you."

Jack pushed a button on the multi-tool.

The hologram winked out, allowing him to see the other man's face more clearly. That look of contemplation was unmistakable; the detective was assembling the pieces, building a case in his mind. Jack could already see the implications. If Anna was not the villain here, then what did that say about Wesley Pennfield? Should he push? Try to slam his point home with one final strike?

No.

He and the detective had one thing in common, and that was a vehement dislike for anyone who tried to tell them what to think. The man would be more amenable if Jack let him reach his own conclusions.

"Okay," Carlson said with a curt nod. "I'm not going to arrest you, but that offer is contingent on you and this...Anna...coming in to my office to answer some questions. I promise to be discreet for the-"

"Carlson, duck!"

Before the man could react, Hutchinson came up behind him and swung his baton into the side of Carlson's head. The detective staggered, his eyes nearly popping out of their sockets.

Then he dropped to the floor.

Hutchinson stood behind him with his eyes downcast, holding the baton at his side. "I didn't want to do that," he said, shaking his head. "But you can't trust this boy and his little alien bitch!"

He dropped the baton, then drew a pistol from the holster on his belt. He raised the gun in both hands, aiming for Jack. "Now, Mr. Pennfield wants that little round thing you have there."

Vincent stood with arms folded in the middle of the room, frowning at her through the hole in his mask. "You won't see reason," he said, stepping forward. "I would have preferred to make you an ally."

Anna grinned down at the floor. She shook her head, trying not to laugh. "So, you want to test yourself against a Keeper," she said, eyebrows rising. "Well, sweetie, if we're gonna get rough, I'll have to insist on a safety word."

"You mock me to hide your fear."

Tapping her lips with a single finger, Anna squinted at the man. "How do you feel about 'expurgations?' " she said with a shrug. "I always liked the way that one rolled off the tongue."

She was stalling, and the bloody man knew it. No one in her right mind challenged a Justice Keeper unless she had an edge. She had to determine the nature of that edge if she wanted to walk out of here. On instinct, she focused on spatial awareness.

Five steps backward would see her standing on top of the window-pane that had fallen to the floor when she had pushed her way in here. There were only two ways out of here: the door behind her opponent and a long drop to the sidewalk below. Besides, if she ran, Vincent would only come after her. That meant surprise was her ally.

Anna charged at him.

She punched with one hand but Vincent caught her fist. She punched with the other but the man caught that too. He pulled her close with a growl.

Squeezing his eyes shut, Vincent delivered a fierce headbutt to her face. Her vision blurred and a sense of queasiness nearly overpowered her. Anna found herself backing up until she felt glass crunch beneath her shoes.

As her vision resolved, she saw Vincent coming forward with fluid predatory grace. The man chuckled to himself, shaking his head ever so slowly. "The sweet young Justice Keeper meets her match."

He threw a punch.

Anna ducked.

She sent a pair of jabs into his belly, then rose and backhanded him hard across the cheek. The blow was enough to turn his head aside. Vincent went stumbling backward on wobbly legs.

Anna ran forward.

She leaped and turned sideways in midair, rolling like a log over his head. Calling on her Nassai, she used heightened spatial awareness to land on one foot with the grace of a ballerina.

In a heartbeat, she was facing him, watching the man recover and round on her. He brought up his fists in a guarded stance. *So, he doesn't underestimate me quite so quickly anymore.*

Anna kicked him in the belly. She spun and hook-kicked, her foot whirling around to hit...nothing at all.

When she came around, she saw that Vincent had crouched. The man stood up and seized her shirt in both hands. "You begin to aggravate me," he said, pulling her in close enough for her to feel his breath.

He gave a shove.

Bent gravity sent her flying backward across the room. Anna went right through the door, then collided with the wall of the hallway outside. She landed on her feet, hot pain racing through her body.

Baring her teeth, Anna squeezed her eyes shut. She tossed her head about, trying to clear her head. *Stay calm,* she thought, recalling her training. *Your symbiont will heal your body, but you can't-*

When she opened her eyes, she found Vincent standing in the middle of the room, drawing a pistol from the holster on his belt. He thrust a hand out to point that gun right at her.

Anna dove.

She somersaulted through the door, then uncurled to lie flat on her back. She kicked up to strike the underside of his forearm, knocking the gun askew just before the man had it pointed at her. *CRACK!*

Curling her legs against her chest, Anna growled. She kicked out with both feet to strike him hard in the chest. A Keeper's strength was over twice that of a normal human being's. Vincent went flying backward, the gun falling out of his hand.

His legs hit the windowsill, and his upper body fell backward through the opening. Just like that, he was gone. With a pounding heart, Anna waited for the sound of a scream that never came. Had he fallen to the ground below? Broken his neck? Had she just taken a life for the first time?

The thought left her numb inside. She had become a Keeper to preserve life, not to destroy it. Of course, she had known that this might be required of her – and Vincent had left her with no recourse – but that didn't make it any easier.

She sat up.

Hissing through clenched teeth, Anna shut her eyes. She tried to ignore the sweat that matted hair to her forehead. "Have to get to Jack," she said in a rasp. "Come on, legs. Don't quit on me now!"

She stood up with some effort and nearly fell over again. This little sparring match had left her weak and aching all over. Thankfully, her symbiont would help with that, but it left her with another unsettling question. How had Vincent been able to bend gravity like a Justice Keeper? It should have-

She saw the man's masked head pop up over the ledge of the window. With a harsh grunt, he crawled through the opening and dropped onto the shattered pane, screaming as he rolled across the floor.

He stood up before her, tall and imposing, seemingly unconcerned by whatever bits of glass had stabbed into his back. "You're far more clever than I gave you credit for," he whispered. "Join me."

Thrusting her chin out, Anna felt her cheeks burn. She narrowed her eyes to slits. "I don't think so," she said, shaking her head. "Somehow, I think high treason doesn't look very good on a resume."

"I am trying to save humankind."

Red-faced with rage, Anna lowered her eyes to the floor. She drew in a shuddering breath. "By killing people!" she snapped. "And kidnapping innocent life forms? Exactly how will *that* save humankind?"

Crossing his arms with a sigh, the man studied her for a long moment. He nodded to himself. "As I thought," he said, backing away.

"Too stubborn. Too indoctrinated with the outdated values of a dead society."

"Oh sure," Anna replied. " 'Thou shalt not kill' is really obsolete. Just when are the rest of us going to join the revolution?"

They paced a circle around the room, sizing each other up. Despite her bravado, Anna felt anything but brave. What this man did should have been impossible without a symbiont, and yet there had been no reports of missing Nassai. Suddenly, an unpleasant thought occurred to her. Just what had Pennfield been planning to do with the symbiont he had captured?

"You leave me no alternative," Vincent said, drawing a knife from a sheath on his belt. He pointed the razor-sharp blade at her chest. "I would rather have you on my side, but you cannot see the truth."

"Bleakness take you!" Anna shouted. "Stop gabbing already."

Vincent ran across the room.

He slashed at her throat – missing by inches – then spun like a twister. His knife came around in a tight arc.

Anna ducked.

She felt the blade pass over her head, then waited for him to round on her. When he did so – in that brief second while he was off balance – she rose and delivered an uppercut to his chin.

Anna fell over backward.

Slapping hands down on the floor, she brought her feet up to rest both heels on his shoulders. She squeezed his neck in a vise-grip, then flung him sideways. *And they told me acrobatics was a waste of time.* Vincent hit the floor to lay sprawled out on his side, groaning in pain.

Flipping upright, she kicked him in the belly. The impact sent Vincent rolling across the floor like a fallen tree down a hill. He went all the way to the opposite wall, slamming hard into the plaster and flopping onto his belly.

Slapping a palm over her face, Anna let out a groan. She looked up, blinking tears away. "Now, my friend," she began. "You're going to tell me who you really are and how you got your hands on a Nassai."

"Not a Nassai," Vincent said, rolling onto his side. "The symbiont I carry is called a Drethen."

"A Drethen?"

The Nassai within her recoiled at the sound of the word. Whatever it was, it must have been something profane, something bordering on blasphemy, for her symbiont to express such emotion.

"It is the future, Anna Lenai," Vincent said, staring at her through the holes in his mask. He seemed completely unconcerned by the fact that he was lying on the floor with bruises all over his body. "I'm sorry you can't be a part of it."

The gun that had fallen out of his hand was resting on the floor next to his shoulder. In her zeal to discover the source of the man's Keeper-like abilities, she had failed to notice it. Vincent snatched it up.

He pointed the weapon at her.

Anna tried to react, tried to summon a Bending, but the aches and pains in her body and the strain that she had already put on her Nassai today were too much for her. Anna clawed at space-time with her mind, but it just wouldn't bend.

CRACK!

Hot stinging pain ripped through her body as blood sprayed from a wound in her chest. She folded in on herself, dropping to her knees on the carpet. What was going on? Everything seemed so muddled.

It took a moment for her to identify the ear-piercing scream as the sound of her own voice. She clamped her mouth shut but the scream persisted. No...that was not her. This was a different scream.

The symbiont.

It wailed in her mind.

Through fuzzy vision, she saw Vincent stand up and march toward her. He pointed the gun at her head. "You've caused my boss all sorts of trouble," he rasped. "At least he will be free of one more nuisance."

Her frantic mind was unable to find enough lucidity, but on some level, she knew she was supposed to panic. She, Anna Lenai, was going to die here, unremarked in some room on some uncharted planet. She,

Anna Lenai, had done violence, had inflicted pain on innocent men, and now she was going to have to account for her sins.

Would the Bleakness take her?

Panic held Jack's guts in an iron grip. He had to focus, had to think his way through this. You could find a solution to just about any problem if you just used your brain, but... dear god, was this what it was like to have a gun pointed at him?

Hutchinson stood with the pistol held in both hands, his teeth showing like a growling dog. "The circular device," he said with a jerk of his head. "Step aside, son. Give me that device and this ends."

Dimly, Jack was aware of his sister gasping with her back pressed to the wall on the other side of the living room. She looked haggard, strung out. *This is your fault,* a small voice whispered. *You shouldn't have gotten involved. Why can't you ever just keep your mouth shut like every-*

No.

That kind of thinking would get him nowhere.

Closing his eyes, Jack took a deep breath. He bowed his head to the other man. "I can't do that," he said, stepping forward. "That's a *person* in there. It may not look like us or even think like us, but it's alive."

Hutchinson bit his lip, then lowered his eyes to the floor. He seemed to be wrestling with the decision. "Listen, kid," he began, "I don't wanna shoot you. But you don't know who you're dealing with."

"Pennfield?"

"Guy has connections everywhere." Hutchinson shook his head in dismay. "I cross him and it's the end for me, for my family. Now, I'm sorry, but I gotta look out for me and mine."

Jack pressed his lips together as he studied the other man. It took effort to keep his expression blank, but he managed it. "Isn't that what everyone does?" he replied. "Look out for themselves first? Isn't that why the world sucks?"

Hutchinson shuddered.

No, Jack didn't regret helping Anna. He refused to be just another schmuck who let evil men go about their business without protest. It wasn't his fault that Lauren had been dragged into this; he couldn't take responsibility for the actions of other men. All he could do was try to make a difference when the opportunity presented itself. "It doesn't have to be this way, Hutchinson," Jack began. "I have friends who can protect you, who can keep your family safe. You don't want to shoot me. Listen to your conscience."

"I can't, kid."

The other man looked away, staring at the wall while five kinds of anguish played across his face. "You're young; you don't get it," he murmured. "You still believe there's justice in this world."

Just like that, he was the picture of conviction again, raising the gun to aim at Jack's face. "Now, step aside!" Hutchinson growled. "I ain't gonna tell you again, kid. You step aside or I shoot."

So, would he do it? His mind flashed back to that morning outside the thrift shop. Sticking his nose where it didn't belong had earned him a beating on that day; now, it would cost him his life. It pleased him to realize that his answer was the same now as it had been then. Better to die than to live in a world where the strong preyed on the weak. "Then shoot," Jack said. "Or admit you're nothing but a ball-less sack of shit."

Hutchinson narrowed his eyes.

Now they came to it. It was time for Jack Hunter to meet his maker and see if he was really the man he aspired to be. So focused was he on keeping his nerves steady, he barely even noticed Lauren's scream.

It all happened at once.

A potted plant flew across the room and struck Hutchinson in the side of the head. He fell over sideways, his gun going off with a *CRACK,* and Jack felt a bullet whiz past his belly on the right side.

A fierce burst of relief lasted just a moment before he turned and saw the Nassai's containment unit. Hutchinson's slug had hit the side of the little gray saucer, punching a hole in the metal. Purple vapour rose from the opening.

No!

On instinct, Jack knelt down and covered the hole with his hand, noting the touch of warm moisture against his skin. There was a strange tingling sensation in his palm and then something else. "Oh...my...God..."

Power burned through him.

The end of Part 1.

Interlude

The little bar was lit by sunlight that streamed in through stained-glass windows, casting patterns of coloured light across the round tables that were spaced out on a black hardwood floor. Odd bits of paraphernalia were hung up on the walls: transit signs, news articles, pictures of famous athletes over a century old.

Jena Morane took a stool.

A tall woman in gray pants and a red t-shirt with a white diamond across the chest, she had the face of an eighteen-year-old girl and the hair of a twelve-year-old boy. "Lovely afternoon, Leras," she said, accepting the bottle of beer that the bartender set down on the counter. "Wouldn't you say?"

With a quick twist of the wrist, Jena popped the cap and watched thin mist rise from the skinny blue bottle. Chilled to perfection, as always. There were reasons why she came to this establishment.

The woman behind the bar was tall and slender, dressed in a black skirt and t-shirt that matched her long dark hair. Her face was breathtaking with smooth copper skin and large dark eyes. There were *reasons* why she came to this establishment.

Jena brought the bottle to her lips. She closed her eyes and took a long swig, tilting her head back. "Now, that was heavenly," she said, setting her bottle on the counter. "Just got in from the Outer Systems."

"Trouble?" Leras inquired.

Wiping her mouth with the back of her hand, Jena winced. "Rounded up a few Flash dealers," she muttered. "Three deaths before the locals even thought to call us."

Leras pursed her lips as she studied Jena. She arched a thin, dark eyebrow. "It took them that long?" she asked, her voice laced with incredulity. "Haven't they received the information packets the government sent out on that substance?"

Jena bit her lip as she stared down at the counter. She shook her head with a heavy sigh. "They've got it," she said, snatching up her bottle. "They just don't want to *believe* any of it."

"I know they'd rather be independent," Leras said with a skeptical expression. "But surely not at the cost of lives."

It was all Jena could do not to sigh. That was the problem with Core Worlders: they had grown so used to the comfortable lifestyle they had developed, they never thought to wonder why settlers on the Fringe would crave independence. Gentle, loving Leyria – the caring home world. If the government had its way, it would round up all the colonists who had gone into space and bring them home to "take care of them."

Leras, just like everyone else on this planet, had grown up with plenty, and so she understood little of the frontier spirit. Of course, the homeworld had a valid point; far too often, the colonies tried to tackle problems that were just too big for them.

"Why wouldn't they call for assistance?"

Jena grinned into her lap, a touch of heat singeing her cheeks. "Politics," she muttered. "Keepers have a tendency to ride in on a white horse and micromanage the entire situation."

"But…"

Jena frowned, then looked up to fix her gaze on the other woman. She blinked in confusion. "You still see us as the guardians of truth and justice," she said. "Maybe the Nassai see it that way too. But we have our faults."

"Sometimes," a man's voice proclaimed. "I think you might be a little too focused on those faults, Operative Morane."

Having dimmed the spatial awareness that came with a Nassai bond – there were times when you didn't want eyes in the back of your head – Jena had failed to notice the man who had slipped in through the front door.

He was a tall well-muscled fellow in black pants and a gray shirt with the collar open. Dark of skin and eye, Nate Calarin frowned at her. He nodded once. "Sometimes, I think you *try* to see the worst in us."

Red-cheeked with chagrin, Jena bared her teeth. She closed her eyes and let out a soft sigh. "And there are times when you're much too poised," she shot back. "Come to join me for a drink, Nate?"

She brought the spout of her bottle to her lips, threw her head back and took a long pull. That was guaranteed to aggravate Nate's Capitol-bred sensibilities. Good! The man needed someone to shake him out of his arrogance.

Crossing his arms over his chest, Nate lifted his chin. He frowned at her but said nothing about the beer. Instead, he tried to change the subject. "I came here to engage in a serious discussion."

"Sorry, sweetheart," Jena mumbled. "I don't do long-term commitment."

"How droll."

"I do pride myself on my talent for sass."

Nate buried his face in the palm of his hand. He let out a grumble as he rubbed his eyelids. "The Senior Director wants to see you," he said in clipped tones. "He asked me to bring you to his office."

Glancing over her shoulder, Jena quirked an eyebrow. "What does Slade want with me?" she asked cautiously. "I filed my reports on my visit to the Loranos System."

"Come with me and find out."

Jena sighed.

This was not going to be pleasant.

A long hallway stretched on for several hundred feet, illuminated by sunlight that filtered through windows in the wall to her right. At the end of the corridor, Jena saw a set of double doors. Slade's office. In all her years as a Keeper, Jena had met the head of their organization only once.

She ground her tooth, wincing as she marched down the corridor. "Tell me this guy doesn't creep you out," she said. "I mean, come on! He's just so smooth all the time!"

Nate walked along with hands clasped behind his back, chin lifted in the air. "Not all of us have your…difficulties with decorum," he muttered. "And I would suggest that you avoid voicing such opinions where they might be overheard."

For once, she took his advice.

The office was larger than what would be considered normal for a Justice Keeper, but she supposed being the Senior Director had its privileges. Gray carpets stretched from wall to wall, matched by plush chairs that faced a desk of polished oak wood. A window looked out on the city, revealing glittering skyscrapers in the distance. Of course, this room was not nearly as imposing as its occupant.

Grecken Slade stood with his back to her, tall and slim in a red coat that dropped to his knee. Long, black hair fell to his shoulder blades and shimmered in the sunlight. She made a note to ask about his shampoo. "Operative Morane," Slade began. "Thank you for meeting me this afternoon."

Folding her arms over her chest, Jena smiled down at the floor. "Oh, it's no trouble, sir," she said with a shrug of her shoulders. "I was just telling Nate that the one thing that would make life better around here was more staff meetings."

Slade turned.

His tanned face bore a strong chin and tilted eyes that seemed to be sizing you up whenever they glanced in your direction. "Indeed; I've rarely had the pleasure of working directly with you."

He waved a hand over his desk. Light sprang into existence over the polished wood, coalescing into an image of the galaxy that rotated slowly. Leyrian Space was marked by an amorphous blue blob about halfway between the Core and the Rim. "Operative, have you heard the rumours about our wayward daughter?"

"Sir?"

Grecken Slade lifted his chin as he studied her. He squinted, and Jena felt a shiver run down her spine. "Three weeks ago," he began, "one of our shuttles departed Petross Station in the Aranis System in pursuit of a man who kidnapped a Nassai.

"The shuttle's occupants were a Justice Keeper named Leana Lenai and a pilot by the name of Dex Aron. Against my orders, they pursued the perpetrator on a course that took them beyond our borders."

At a wave of Slade's hand, a red dot appeared near the edge of Leyrian Space and extended through the nearby starfield to a green blob that Jena recognized all too well. What in the Verse would possess them to go *there?*

"Dead Space," she said with a curt nod. "The woman has guts. Nobody flies into Dead Space voluntarily."

"Nobody flies into Dead Space for a reason," Slade replied. "The place is littered with abandoned Overseer outposts, some of which possess automated defense systems that attack passing ships."

Lifting a gauntleted forearm up in front of her face, Jena studied her multi-tool. The little silver disk blinked at her, indicating that its power cells were almost fully charged. "Multi-tool active!" she said. "Display dossier for Justice Keeper Leana Lenai."

A transparent blue rectangle rippled into existence in front of her, followed by the results of her query. Jena found herself staring at the image of a young woman with short strawberry-blonde hair and big blue eyes. Her biographical information was listed next to the picture. Leana Lenai, Serial Number: 5087421, commissioned…last year?

The hologram winked out when Jena let her arm drop. She couldn't believe this! By the Holy Companion above, what had this man been *thinking?* "Are you completely mad, Slade?" she found herself saying.

"I beg your pardon?"

Pursing her lips, Jena looked up to fix her gaze on him. She narrowed her eyes. "I must be going blind!" she snapped. "Because this report can't possibly say what I think it says. You sent a *rookie* to recover a Nassai?"

No doubt the girl never thought to question why this assignment had been given to someone with so little experience. Young Keepers were always eager to prove themselves and blind to the political maneuvering of their superiors.

Grecken Slade frowned at her, his cheeks turning red. It seemed the man was not used to being challenged. "Agent Lenai is quite capable," he replied. "Her work thus far has been exemplary."

"Until she questioned your orders."

"You're out of line, Operative."

"You sent a child to recover a captured symbiont," she hissed. "Then you called her back when she pursued the thief beyond our borders."

"I was unwilling to put her life at risk."

"Then why give her this assignment in the first place?" Jena spun around to find Nate standing just inside the door with a scowl on his face. He shook his head, warning her to back down. "There had to be other officers available. Why choose a child?"

"I'm not interested in explaining my decisions to you, Operative." No, of course not. She could tell that her questions were hitting too close to home. Sending an inexperienced pup on a mission like this was beyond idiocy.

The Nassai would be furious when they discovered that one of their own had been abducted by a human. Not quite furious enough to sever contact, but a few more incidents like this might just do the trick. Every Justice Keeper on this planet would tremble at the thought of such a thing; it would mean the end of their organization.

Slade knew this, and yet he sent a girl to recover the symbiont. That meant one of two things: either he wanted the girl dead – which was unlikely since he had called her back – or he wanted the mission to fail. Of course, she couldn't say as much. Jena Morane had been reprimanded on more than one occasion for her "conspiracy theories."

In the public eye, Keepers were a noble organization, and for most of the people in the trenches, that was true. Good men and women put their lives on the line every day to protect those who could not protect themselves. But there were some in the higher levels of the administration who seemed…untrustworthy.

In theory, the Nassai were supposed to be a check on such corruption, but theory was not practice. How long had it been since Slade had made use of his symbiont's gifts? They were not necessary for a desk job. Perhaps the symbiont was crying out right now, screaming its objection to what Slade was doing.

No one would know but the man himself.

People trusted symbiosis because the Nassai had proven time and again that they were willing to sacrifice themselves to save the lives of innocents. When Slade died, his symbiont would be returned to the Collective so that it could share its experiences with the greater whole. That would expose his corruption as well. But, if he could arrange to die in such a way that made returning the symbiont impossible…no one considered these things. No one questioned what was right in front of their faces.

Except Jena Morane.

"Are you just going to stand there, Operative?"

Gritting her teeth, Jena squeezed her eyes shut. "No, sir," she said, whirling around to face the man. "I assume you've told me all of this for a reason. You want me to go after Lenai?"

Grecken Slade stood behind the desk with his hands folded behind himself, his face as smooth as the finest porcelain. "We've picked up a distress beacon," he said, nodding once. "From Dead Space."

"Lenai's?"

The man pressed his lips together, bowing his head to stare down at the floor. He seemed visibly troubled for a moment. "Yes, it's hers," Slade admitted. "And the Prime Council wants to send a rescue mission."

Jena flashed a smile.

"This amuses you?"

"Only the fact that it's obvious to me that *you* were opposed to such a rescue," she replied. "Too bad you can't overrule the Head of State."

Slade wore a frigid expression as he fixed dark eyes upon her. "You're bordering on insubordination, Operative," he replied. "There's a reason you've been assigned a series of dead-end missions on the Fringe Worlds."

Blushing like the sun, Jena felt her grin widen. She closed her eyes and nodded to the man. "I have no doubt you're right about that, sir," she said, stepping forward. "Thing is, I like it out there."

"Then you will enjoy this assignment," Slade muttered, turning away from her. He stood before the window, staring out at the city. "You're to board the LMS. Renoko and conduct a search and rescue."

"You can count on me, sir."

She left the office without another word. So once again Slade had picked the worst Keeper for the job. Well, in actuality, Jena was far better at her job than most people gave her credit for, but her service record wouldn't reflect that fact, and Slade seemed like the kind of guy who put a lot of stock in service records.

He was expecting her to fail. How interesting. She would have to pull a few strings and have a new ship assigned to this mission. She couldn't trust one that had been picked by Slade. It would be far too easy for him to make a destroyed ship look like the work of an Over-seer trap.

Perhaps she shouldn't have been so overt in her defiance, but then, she was a Justice Keeper. Dying young was part of the job description. *This,* Jena thought to herself, *looks like it's gonna be fun.*

Part 2

Chapter 16

Through fuzzy vision, she saw Vincent stand up and march toward her. He pointed the gun at her head. "You've caused my boss all sorts of trouble," he rasped. "At least he will be free of one more nuisance."

Her frantic mind was unable to find enough lucidity, but on some level, she knew she was supposed to panic. She, Anna Lenai, was going to die here, unremarked in some room on some uncharted planet. She, Anna Lenai, had done violence, had inflicted pain on innocent men, and now she was going to have to account for her sins.

Would the Bleakness take her?

Clenching her teeth, Anna felt tears on her cheeks. She turned her face away from the man. "Do it…" she whispered. "If you're going to kill me, then by the loving Companion, hurry up and get it over with."

Vincent cocked his head to the side, frowning at her through the mask. "Stubborn even in the face of death," he mumbled. "I can give you treatment. Join us, Anna Lenai. Help us save this world."

The wail of a siren pierced the air.

Vincent shot a glance over his shoulder, squinting at the window. "No, I don't think I'll kill you," he said softly. "We win either way; if you die, one more nuisance will have been eliminated, and if you live, the chaos that will come when these primitives discover what you are will be… quite satisfying."

He turned on his heel and ran for the window. He dove through the opening like an arrow on course for its target, leaving her alone. Alone and cold. Why was it suddenly so cold?

Anna wheezed and gasped for air. Her face was cold and clammy, her hair slick with sweat. *Somebody help me...* she called out in her own mind. *Please... somebody help me!*

Lauren Hunter stared down at trembling hands that didn't seem to want to obey her commands. She had just taken down a cop with a potted plant. She had just assaulted an officer of the law.

When she looked up, she saw the uniformed man down on hands and knees, head lolling. He shuffled his way toward the fallen detective who lay sprawled out upon the hardwood floor. Only the latter man was coming to.

"I didn't mean to," Lauren whimpered. "I'm sorry. I don't know what came over me."

But she did know. That bastard had tried to kill her brother! She couldn't just stand there and do nothing no matter what sort of trouble Jack had gotten into, and by the gist of their conversation, she had the distinct impression that her little brother wasn't the bad guy here. Not by a long-

She noticed Jack for the first time.

He was down on one knee next to the small wooden table, turned so that she saw him in profile. And his skin was glowing! Streams of white light pulsed from his body, washing over his face and hands.

"What the hell?" Lauren said, backing up against the wall. "Jack? Jack, can you hear me?"

He didn't respond.

The detective sat up with a pained expression on his face. He pressed a palm to his forehead and let out a groan. "Where are we?" he muttered. "Hutchinson, where... did Hunter do this to me?"

"The kid knocked you out," Hutchinson breathed.

"He did not!"

Fists balled at her sides, Lauren strode forward. She flashed clenched teeth and seethed at the cop. "*You* knocked him down!" she said with a nod. "You knocked him down, then pulled a gun on my brother!"

"You can't believe-"

Harry Carlson silenced him with a glare. "Dear God..." the man said, trying to stand. "David, why the hell would you hit me with your baton?"

Jack was still on his knees, but the glow had intensified, transforming him into a figure of pure white radiance. Only then did she notice that his clothes were not glowing, just his exposed skin. What was happening to her brother? Could she stop it? She didn't dare try, not if doing so might kill him.

Carlson seemed to notice him for the first time as well. He shuffled backward on the floor, raising a hand to shield his eyes. Perhaps this would buy them time. If Lauren could get the gun away from them...

When Hutchinson looked up, he let out a shriek. The shock of it must have been too much because he quickly flopped down on his side. Lauren couldn't blame him. Each and every instinct in her body told her that this thing that had taken possession of her brother was nothing short of death incarnate. She remembered hearing Jack say that a life form of some kind had been inside the little container.

Hold on, Jack... she pleaded. *Hold on.*

The mist stretched on in all directions. A kind of uniform featureless gray that was strangely lacking in moisture, it flowed around his body in thin puffs and tendrils. Where was this place? How had he come here?

Jack moved like a ghost.

The mist clung to him, flowing over his blue jeans and jacket, streaming from his fingers in thin lines. It wasn't cold or wet. In fact, he couldn't feel it on his skin. Finally, it began to thin.

Chewing on his lip, Jack turned his head and peered into the distance. "Well, this is just swell!" he said, eyebrows rising. "I was really looking for some trippy, psychedelic crap to fill that empty four PM slot on my schedule."

Footsteps in the distance.

He winced and shook his head. "Okay, Jack, keep it together," he said. "This can't be any stranger than the guy with cyborg hands."

A silhouette in the distance became distinct to his eyes. A tiny woman who moved through the mist with a determined stride. Could that be Anna? He would know for sure in a moment.

The strange fog parted before her, and he found himself looking at a woman who stood just a few inches taller than five feet, a woman with a face that felt oddly familiar to him. It took him a moment to place it, but he *had* seen this woman's face before. Well, he'd seen her *faces.*

She was a composite of Buffy Summers and Vin Venture with traces of his mother and sister mixed in for good measure. There was even a bit of his kindergarten teacher, Mrs. Simms. She seemed to be a mix of every strong woman he'd known, both real and fictional. "Greetings."

"Hello," Jack said.

The woman smiled, a sudden burst of crimson in her cheeks. She bowed her head to him. "I believe I owe you my life," she began. "I am very grateful for everything you did to free me from my captors."

His mouth agape, Jack stared at her with wide eyes. "You're the Nassai!" he said, giving his head a shake. "That's right! Hutchinson took a shot at me, and then I put my hand over the containment unit…"

"That vile man is currently lying on your sister's living room floor," she informed him. "For the moment, he is incapacitated, but that will quickly change. We must work together if we are to survive."

"Where is this place?"

She grinned, turning her face up to the open sky. "This?" she said, her eyebrows climbing. "This is your mind, Jack. I could have produced another setting, but this had a certain appeal."

"I'm unconscious?"

"Not precisely." The puzzled expression that passed over her face left Jack feeling off-balance. How could an alien – a cloud of gas, no less – learn to emote with the skill of a master thespian? "Our two minds have blended, and you are currently processing an overwhelming amount of data. It feels to you as though several minutes have gone by, but in the physical world, less than five seconds have passed since your hand came into contact with the containment unit."

"So we have some time?"

"We have time enough for a brief explanation," she replied. "But as I said, the man who assaulted you will not remain incapacitated forever. We must act quickly if you wish to save your sister."

Jack closed his eyes, a single tear rolling over his cheek. "I put Lauren in danger," he whispered, shaking his head. "Don't get me wrong; I don't regret helping you, but I should have known better than to come here."

The woman stepped forward.

Craning her neck, she stared up at him with an earnest expression on that angelic face. "There is still time to help her," she said with a nod. "I believe you to be resourceful enough to do it on your own, but if you want my assistance, there is something else that I must ask of you."

"What's that?"

She took his hands in a tender grip, her skin warm to the touch. How was this even possible? Was she stimulating the parts of his brain that processed his sense of touch? "If you wish for my help," she said softly, "you must bond with me."

The offer hit him like a punch to the stomach. In a way, he should have expected as much – what else would a Nassai want under these circumstances? But Anna had made it clear that they would not bond an unworthy host even if failing to do so meant death. If she meant what she said…

Of all things, she chuckled, backing away from him with one hand covering her mouth. "Yes, Jack, you are worthy," she assured him. "You have repeatedly put yourself in danger to help a total stranger. You are courageous, intelligent and capable. But most important of all, you care."

Jack grinned, a sudden warmth in his cheeks. He looked away so that she wouldn't see. "Well, thank you," he mumbled. "But if you knew me half as well as you think you do, you'd know I tend to screw up everything I touch."

"How do you think I know any of this?"

"I'm sorry?"

She studied him with pursed lips, blinking slowly as if uncertain of what she saw. "Do you believe I learned all this while inside my containment unit?" she asked. "Maybe I overheard Denario Tarse while he spoke?"

"I-"

"I've been scanning your mind, Jack," she explained. "You will forgive me, but I need to determine the suitability of a potential host. I know everything about you from your first memory to the very moment that Hutchinson pointed that gun at you. I know you to your *bones,* Jack, and I'm telling you that you would make an excellent Keeper. Together, we can make this world a better place, but if you do not wish the bond, I will let myself pass."

Jack spun around.

He paced through the mist with arms folded, thin tendrils of vapour streaming over his body. "If I say no, you'll die," he said, freezing in place. "You have to know I'd never allow that."

Shutting his eyes tight, Jack tilted his head back. He took a deep breath through his nose. "You say we could make this world better?" he asked. "Well, if you think so, then I'm on board."

"Don't be too quick to accept," she cautioned. "There are several things you must know before accepting a bond. My cells will join with yours, and as such, you will carry me with you wherever you go. Once we are fully bonded, you will be unable to survive without me. This decision, once made, is permanent.

"You will be several times stronger, more agile and quick to heal, but your lifespan will be shortened by a decade at least. My presence will be necessary to facilitate cellular division in your body, and there will come a point when I am no longer able to do this for you. When that happens, I will be returned to my people, and you will be allowed to pass peacefully. There is one other price.

"You will be unable to conceive children with any partner. Meiosis becomes quite impossible once you have bonded a Nassai. If you are willing to accept those drawbacks, then I will gladly accept you as a host."

Pinching his chin, Jack squinted down at the ground. The mist flowed over him in thick waves. "You want to know if I can accept that?" he muttered. "You're giving me a chance to make a difference. I'd say it's a fair trade."

He spun around to find her standing in the fog with hands shoved into her pockets, a thoughtful expression on her face. "I like you," Jack went on. "So if I have to live out my days with you riding shotgun, I think I'd be okay with that."

"Then you accept?"

"Lay on, MacDuff."

She grinned as she strode toward him, spreading her arms wide for a great big hug. Quick as a blink, she was slipping her arms around his waist, resting her head against his chest. "I am honoured to join with you, Jack Hunter."

Her body began to glow with a light so fierce it should have burned him to cinders, and yet he felt only a gentle, comforting warmth. Radiance spread over him, sank into his skin and surged through every cell in his body. "I will bond with you now."

"Okay," Jack said, "but you better still respect me in the morning."

Chapter 17

Carlson and Hutchinson were both crawling across the hardwood floor, but the only thing Lauren could see was her brother who knelt before the little table, glowing like an angel. Light streamed off of him, rippling over his body.

Jack stood up, tilting his head back as the light faded away to nothing. He took a deep breath. "Well, then," he said, spinning around to face the two cops. "Where were we before I blacked out?"

He stood with his eyes closed, perfectly serene except for the sweat that matted his dark hair to his forehead. "Oh, that's right," he said, nodding once. "You were threatening to kill me, Hutchinson."

When he opened his eyes, they glowed with pure white radiance, as though each contained a tiny sun. "You threatened my family," he growled, striding forward. "You threatened my friend. For this, you will know divine wrath."

Hutchinson scrambled backward across the floor. He stared up at Jack, his mouth moving without a sound. "Please, God, have mercy!" He crossed his forearms in front of his face as if to shield himself. "I'm sorry!"

"Leave this place," Jack said. "And if I ever see you again, you will burn."

That was all it took; Hutchinson turned around, crawling on hands and knees to the kitchen before getting to his feet. Lauren heard the stomp of footsteps and the creak of the back door. *He's gone...*

With his mouth agape, Harry Carlson stared up at Jack. He blinked several times in confusion. "What are you?" he asked, shaking his head. "What in God's name , how did I get stuck in a horror movie?"

The light in Jack's eyes died, returning them to their normal shade of blue. Lauren didn't know whether to cheer or start crying. Had something taken control of her brother? Did it mean to kill them?

He dropped to his knees.

Jack buried his face in his hands, a painful groan escaping him. "All right, that was painful." He looked up, blinking tears out of his eyes. "Good to see you're up, Carlson. I was worried he might have done permanent damage."

"Jack…"

Biting his lower lip, Jack heaved out a sigh. He closed his eyes and nodded once. "It's really me, Lauren," he said, guessing her question before she could even ask. "Just a new and improved version."

Crossing her arms with a shudder, Lauren frowned down at the floor. "I liked the *old* version just fine," she said, her eyebrows rising. "Jack, what the hell is happening? First a detective shows up, then his partner tries to kill you and then you put on a light show."

"I'll explain everything," Jack said. "But now, we need to find Anna."

Patient has taken a gunshot wound to the chest.

The morning sun was high in a blue sky full of puffy white clouds, shining down upon a wooden fence behind a small garden with daisies. Anna liked daisies. Each one reminded her of a sunrise.

She knelt in the grass before the garden, dressed in a pair of blue jeans and a white shirt that she wore belted with an empire waist. Her red-gold hair was tied back into a short ponytail with thin strands framing her face.

Anna bit her lip, nodding to herself. "Well, it's not my best work," she said, wiping sweat off her brow with the back of her hand. "But it'll have to do. Sorry, Mom, but I just don't have your green thumb."

She stood.

Pressing her lips into a tight frown, Anna closed her eyes. She felt the wind caress her face, blowing those strands of hair back. "You should have expected as much," she muttered. "Alia was always the gardener. I was the painter."

What had possessed her to come out here and dig around in the dirt was something she couldn't remember at the moment. Perhaps it was just a desire to enjoy a warm spring morning. She so rarely had the opportunity to just bask in the sunshine because…because…she couldn't recall.

Pulse is erratic, respiration shallow.

Turning away from the little garden, she faced a small dome-shaped house where sunlight shimmered on photo-voltaic paint that coated the entire building. An arch-shaped overhang shaded the back door.

Anna marched through the grass with arms folded, frowning down at her feet. "It's almost noon anyway," she said with a shrug. "Dad will be home soon, and I have to make sure lunch is ready."

She approached the back door.

Once inside, she found herself in a large living room where gray carpets stretched from wall to wall and a crescent-shaped couch encircled a coffee table. Her wooden easel was set up in the corner with a painting of the garden outside on the canvas. She had used acrylic paint, blending colours together where soil met grass and flowers poked up before the wooden fence.

It needed a few touch-ups, but then art was never truly finished, was it? Alia kept telling her to leave it alone, but Anna was a perfectionist in this regard. It was a trait that vexed her more than anyone else.

Blood pressure eighty over forty-five.

Where was that voice coming from?

"Digging in the garden, huh?" When she turned, she found her sister coming out of a door that led to the office. "I guess I should feel sorry for the plants. Maybe I'll give them a little extra water today."

Alia was a short and slender woman in black pants and a gray t-shirt with a long V-neck. Her face was thinner than Anna's, her cheekbones more pronounced and she kept her reddish blonde hair at shoulder length.

Anna frowned, then lowered her eyes to the floor. She tried to ignore the warmth in her cheeks. "I figured I'd give it a try," she muttered "It wouldn't kill you to expand your horizons, Alia."

"My horizons are fine right where they are, thank you." The other woman shook her head as she paced through the living room with arms folded. "And the flowers might prefer it if you left yours alone as well."

Anna stuck her tongue out.

She turned her face away from her sister. Of course, that didn't stop her blush from deepening. "Maybe I just don't like the idea of being assigned to a role," she said. "Maybe I want to try new things."

Gardening would never be one of her favourite hobbies – having to check on those flowers every day would drive her crazy – but she was curious. She wanted to see what her mother and sister found so fascinating.

Their father would be home soon. On the far side of the living room, Anna found a small kitchen where wooden cupboards lined two walls and an island supported a few cloth place mats.

"Do me a favour," she called out to her sister. "Grab last night's leftovers from the fridge. We can heat up the chicken for a-"

Start an O-Negative drip.

"We can heat up the chicken for what?" Alia stood in front of the couch with her arms crossed, scowling down at her feet. "I know you love to daydream, kid, but could you at least finish your sentences?"

Something about this wasn't right. There was somewhere she was supposed to be, something she was supposed to do. Why did her chest hurt? No, that was silly. She was supposed to make lunch for her father.

Her father.

The front door opened, the sound of footsteps in the front hall. No, it was too early. She needed more time to complete her task! "Anyone home?" her father called out in a jovial voice. "Leana? Alia?"

"Not yet," Anna muttered to herself. "I need more time! I wasn't finished yet!"

Her parents emerged from the front hall, side by side and hand in hand. Beran Lenai was a compact man in black pants and a blue suit jacket. His square jaw was fringed with a coppery beard, and his dark red hair fell to the nape of his neck.

Next to him, Sierin Elna was only slightly shorter. A slim woman in a white dress, she wore her honey-coloured hair done up in a braid. "Someone's been busy," she said, glancing toward Anna. "Out in the backyard?"

"You're holding hands."

Sierin looked genuinely surprised, her eyebrows slowly rising as she studied her daughter. "Of course we're holding hands," she said at last. "We often hold hands. That's what you do when you're in love."

"You're not in love."

"Leana Delnara Lenai," her mother scolded, using the dreaded full name. You knew you were in trouble when one of your parents called you by your full name. "What a horrible thing to say!"

The bullet grazed her right lung. Once again, that disembodied voice distracted her with its constant nattering. Didn't anyone else hear it? *Something's odd; she seems to be in better shape than I would have expected.*

"This isn't real."

Her father stared at her with his mouth agape, blinking as if she had just sprouted wings. "Of course it's real, sweetie," he said softly. "What's going on? Did something happen while we were away?"

Covering her mouth with the tips of her fingers, Anna closed her eyes. "No, it isn't real!" she said, shaking her head. "The two of you are divorced, and we haven't lived in this house since I was ten!"

Beran frowned at her, then turned his head to stare at the wall. A heavy sigh escaped him. "You are quite strong-willed, my host," he muttered. "Your memories suggest that this has been a source of frustration to the one whose form I wear."

Her Nassai.

Prep for surgery; we need to get that bullet out of her. The voice. She had been shot in the chest. All of this was an illusion created by her symbiont? *Let's move, people This one still has a good chance of survival.*

"Where are we?"

"You are unconscious while the human healers attend to your wounds." Her father turned his head to fix his gaze upon her mother. She wavered out of existence, blurring into a smear of colour before vanishing completely. "For a time, it seemed as though we would pass. I wanted your last moments to be joyful."

Anna crossed her arms, then bowed her head to him. She hunched up her shoulders in a shrug. "That's kind of you, I guess," she said. "But I don't like being lied to, and you pick *now* of all times to make contact?"

The illusion of Beran wore a serene expression that she'd never seen on her actual father. "You were so young when we bonded," he explained. "You came eagerly, but your sense of self had not been formed. I did not wish to overwhelm your personality with my own. You had to grow into your own person."

"I don't think you could have if you tried."

Her imaginary father blushed as he stared down at the floor. "No, perhaps not," he said. "But I felt it best to allow you room to discover the world on your own terms. Even when you became a woman, I did not see."

Beran looked up to study her with blue eyes that seemed to drill through her defenses. "It was when you took that bullet," he said, nodding curtly, "when you chose to sacrifice your life for strangers that I began to understand."

Anna felt a grin bloom, her face as red as the setting sun. She bowed her head to the Nassai. "Well, that's what family does," she murmured. "They take care of you even after you stop needing it."

"Do you claim kinship with me then?"

Grinning down at the floor, Anna shut her eyes tight. She trembled with a burst of laughter. "You're the one who hitched a ride in my body," she teased. "I would say that makes us blood in a literal sense."

"I find that satisfactory," he said at last, "and if you would be willing, I would like to talk from time to time."

"I'm a very good listener."

Anna took one last look at her childhood home. In a way, the Nassai had done her a kindness by bringing her here. Perhaps she should have played along, pretended that she had a family again just for a little while. "So, what now?" she asked the Nassai. "Do I get to wake up after this?"

"The humans are tending to your wounds," he explained. "Yes, you will be fine. At least for now."

Anna arched an eyebrow.

Pressing his lips together, the Nassai looked down at the floor. He exhaled through his nose. "Something is coming," he said softly. "I cannot say what, but a word spoken by the warrior in black stoked feelings in me.

"Something buried deep in the Nassai collective memory, something from the days of Origin, when the Makers prowled the skies. A soft voice whispered in my mind, 'the Destroyer names himself. The Advent begins.'"

"Well," Anna mumbled. "Isn't that cheerful?"

Chapter 18

Jack would have expected his world to change after bonding with a symbiont, but aside from a strange awareness of everything around him, he felt very much as he always had. His fingers flexed when he ordered; his legs moved on command. When he sent a questioning thought at the Nassai, all he felt was a mild sense of amusement.

He watched the taillights of a white Nissan Versa flaring bright with red light as it pulled to a stop at the intersection. Tall buildings rose up on either side of the road, and pedestrians crowded the sidewalks.

"So, an alien..."

Lauren bit her lip as he stared through the windshield, sweat glistening on her thin face. "You're carrying an alien," she said, nodding. "You let it...merge with you? Bond with you? You let it inside you?"

Jack smiled, his cheeks flushed to a soft pink. He lowered his eyes to stare into his lap. "You make it sound so romantic," he said, eyebrows rising. "Yes, Lauren, I carry a symbiont. It was that or let it die."

His sister went bone-pale, keeping her eyes fixed on the road. "You should have let it die," she muttered. "Jack, you have no understanding of the consequences. This is an *alien*."

Tilting his head back, Jack closed his eyes. He took a deep breath and then let it out again. "A *kind* alien, Lauren," he replied. "One that cares about us and wants to protect us from men like Hutchinson."

"Your sister is right."

That from the back seat. Detective Carlson sounded a little more lucid than he had back at Lauren's house. With everything else that had happened, it was easy to forget that the man had taken a blow to the head. After checking with his superiors, they had learned that Anna had been taken into intensive care.

Jack felt a sense of dread that just would not relent. If he strained, he could almost sense an echo of his own emotion, one so subtle he would not notice if he didn't look for it. "How you doing back there, Carlson?" he asked. "Still awake?"

"I'm fine."

In the passenger-side window, Jack saw his faint reflection as the buildings rushed by. His expression was tense. "World's a lot bigger, Lauren," he mumbled. "You're not the only one who will have to adapt."

"I'm adapting fine."

Gripping the wheel so hard her knuckles whitened, Lauren refused to look at him. Perhaps she was afraid that this was an 'Invasion of the Body Snatchers' situation. Well, he couldn't blame her.

If a hostile alien really had taken control of his body, the first thing it would do was probe his mind and learn his mannerisms. His sister was a brilliant woman; this outcome would have occurred to her. "I'm fine, Lauren."

"What exactly are Mom and Dad gonna think?" she growled. "Christ, I'm supposed to take care of you! Instead, I let you go out and get it on with intelligent bacteria. Jesus! I can't deal with this."

Grinning like a madman, Jack slapped a palm over his face. "You have such a way with words, Sis," he teased. "Tell you what, if Anna gets a shuttle down here, we'll fly to the nearest space station and spray paint my number on the bathroom wall."

"Is he always like this?" Carlson inquired.

"Always."

They were moving again. Jack ignored his sister's mutterings and contented himself with watching traffic. The cars were moving at a good clip, but it was mid-afternoon, and rush hour would be on them soon. Things were already picking up.

He lifted a hand, wiggling fingers just to make sure they were still his. It was silly, but the whole experience had been a little overwhelming and... there was no scar on his right hand. There should have been a scar!

Jack squinted into his palm. He shook his head ever so slowly. "It can't be," he muttered to himself. "Never mind law enforcement. The Nassai missed their true calling as cosmetic surgeons."

"What are you talking about?"

"You remember when I cut myself in Wood Shop?" he asked, glancing toward his sister. "How it left a scar across my palm?"

She nodded.

"It's gone."

Jack lifted up his pant leg to expose smooth skin in place of a scar that should have left a small gash on his shin. The hair was even starting to grow back! "And the one from that time I went biking with Matt Sierpinski!" he exclaimed. "Remember? They put four stitches in my leg!"

Come to think of it, was his vision a little sharper than it had been before? Cars and buildings that were far off in the distance seemed clearer than they should have been. *You know, Buffy,* he thought at the symbiont. *I think this might be the beginning of a beautiful friendship.*

The hospital staff had given Anna a room to herself, a cramped little room where fluorescent lights in the ceiling shone down upon a single bed with metal bars on either side. Blinds on the two windows shut out the daylight.

Learning that she had survived her encounter with Pennfield's goons was a relief to Jack, and if he strained, he could almost sense that his Nassai felt the same. That would take some getting used to.

Anna looked almost serene, lying in bed with her eyes closed, blonde hair strewn over her face. Shot through the chest? It was a painful reminder that even Justice Keepers could be killed by simple firearms.

"She's alive."

When he turned, Lauren stood in the doorway with her arms folded, her dark hair tied in a ponytail. "I'm glad she's alright," she muttered. "But you'll forgive me if I'm a bit too frightened to celebrate. I'm sorry."

"Don't be."

"If you're going to apologize," Anna murmured through a groan. "Could you please make amends for disturbing my sleep first?"

Her face lit up with a smile when she saw him. Knowing that she would be all right was one thing; seeing it for himself was another. "Hey, you," Anna whispered. "We need to stop meeting in hospitals before it becomes the trendy new scene."

"We can't have that," Jack said. "If hospitals get too popular, it's only a matter of time before hipsters start coming here, ironically. Still, I kind of like the ICU. This could be our thing."

Anna went red, then turned her head so that her cheek was pressed into the pillow. She let out another soft moan. "You're just happy for the chance to see me in a hospital gown," she teased. "Maybe catch a glimpse of my backside."

Closing his eyes, Jack shook his head, a blush setting fire to his face. "It *is* a very nice backside," he said. "And don't you give me that glare. Not when you're the one who encouraged me to look."

"*Heh-hem.*"

Pressing a fist to her mouth, Lauren shut her eyes and coughed with enough force to wake the dead. "Big sister here," she said, striding forward. "So, if you want to keep your thinly veiled sexual tension to a minimum…"

"Do you bring all the girls home to meet your family, Jack?" Anna said in a rasp. Tears glistened on her cheeks. "Sorry. Still a little achy and sore in the chest."

"So, you're an alien?"

Jack tuned out the explanation that followed – he'd done his part to catch Lauren up on the exposition, and he was glad to let someone else have a turn – choosing instead to focus on contacting his Nassai. No matter how hard he tried, however, the only thing he got in return was a series of vague impressions.

After such a lively conversation, he couldn't help but wonder why his symbiont had put on her introvert cap. Perhaps the bond didn't work that way? Maybe they could only speak when he was in a trance-like state. The burst of approval that flooded his mind told him he'd found the answer.

"What do you think, Jack?"

"Hmm?"

"You're honestly willing to trust this woman?" Lauren squeezed her eyes shut, shaking her head. "Even when you know so little about her?"

Jack crossed his arms, then bowed his head to her. He offered a half-hearted shrug of his shoulders. "She saved me a few times," he said. "Besides, young men like me are helpless in the face of thinly veiled sexual tension."

"You're just so-"

"If we could put the family squabbles on hold." Anna glared at him, then turned her head to direct an equally frosty stare at his sister. "There are much larger concerns at the moment, like the safety of your parents."

"Lauren, give us a moment."

His sister scowled at him, and for a moment, Jack expected an argument. Then she threw her head back and let out a sigh. "Why do I even bother?" Lauren barked, turning away from him and marching to the door.

Anna frowned at the other woman, her cheeks stained with a touch of crimson. "So much for my hopes of making a new friend." She coughed and spasmed. "Do you have the symbiont with you?"

Jack sat in the chair next to her.

"I bonded with the Nassai," Jack said. "There was no other choice. We were attacked, and the containment unit was damaged."

He looked up.

Anna was grinning at him, her blue eyes practically sparkling. "You accepted the bond," she said in a breathy voice. "Oh, thank the Companion. I was afraid we wouldn't find a suitable host."

Pinching his chin with thumb and index finger, Jack squinted at her. He shook his head. "You wanted this," he said, sitting back in his chair. "That's what you meant when you told me to find a suitable host."

"I hoped for it." Anna had her cheek mashed against the pillow, strands of hair falling over her face. "A symbiont won't Bond with just anybody, and the Keepers need someone like you. But the decision was always yours."

"Is that why you never suggested it?"

"It's considered taboo for a Keeper to try to *persuade* someone to join our ranks. The decision had to be yours. If you accepted a Nassai with resentment in your heart, it would damage your relationship with the symbiont and make you far less effective at carrying out your duties. Commitment is essential."

"So, what happens now?"

Rolling onto her back, Anna stared up at the ceiling. The thoughtful expression on her face made him wonder. "Now, I teach you," she replied in a rasp. "I teach you what it means to be a Justice Keeper."

Jack stood.

Before he could move, Anna glanced in his direction, her eyes wide with fright. It made him freeze; twenty-four hours ago, he would have thought her incapable of fear. "I have a request," she whispered. "Will you stay here with me? You're the only person on this planet I trust, and I'm afraid to fall asleep without…"

Jack felt a smile bloom. Closing his eyes, he bowed his head to her. "Of course I'll stay with you," he said, sitting down again. "Justice Keepers protect, right? May as well get started right away."

The glare of a penlight was like a tiny star in Harry's field of vision, waving back and forth and drowning out everything else. Purple afterimages sparkled and shimmered when the light was removed. "Good," Dr. Tenant said, "I've seen no sign of any major neurological damage."

Tall and slim with tanned copper skin, she wore her black hair tied back in a long ponytail and her lab coat unbuttoned. "I think you'll be fine, Detective," she said. "But I want to keep you overnight for observation."

Harry frowned thoughtfully as he studied her. He nodded once. "I guess I'll have to find myself a babysitter," he muttered. "I don't suppose you have a college-aged daughter who might want some extra cash."

"Sorry, no."

Stiffening as he shuddered, Harry closed his eyes and quickly shook his head. "That's alright," he grumbled. "I'm sure I'll find someone. I have a big address book."

The doctor turned away from him, scribbling something down on a clipboard. She nodded with each word. "I'll have one of the nurses assist you with that." She drew the blue curtain aside and stepped out of the examination room.

Well, the word *room* might have been a bit generous. It was more of a cubbyhole between two cinderblock walls so close that he could touch both if he stretched out his arms. Whoever said the health care budget was too large had never had to spend fifteen minutes in one of these.

True, that was probably claustrophobia talking – Harry had never cared for small, enclosed spaces – but the point stood. Cops of all people deserved the finest treatment that money could buy.

Pressing a palm to his forehead, Harry winced. He massaged away a headache with the heel of his hand. "You sure everything checks out, doc?" he muttered. "'Cause I think I must have hallucinated most of this afternoon."

"I'm sure that you didn't."

The curtain slid sideways to reveal a woman standing in the doorway, a tall woman in a dark pantsuit. Her olive-skinned face was pinched in a no-nonsense expression, and her dark hair was tied back. "Good to see you, Detective," Aamani Patel said. "It seems you've been busy."

Harry frowned, then looked up to fix his gaze upon her. He squinted, shaking his head. "What are you playing at?" he snapped. "You wouldn't be here if you didn't know what happened this afternoon, so out with it."

The woman blushed, then bowed her head to him. "Apologies, Detective," she said, stepping forward. "I don't mean to put your back up, but I think we should discuss your new friends."

"My friends?"

Crossing her arms in a huff, Patel frowned down at the floor. She shook her head in exasperation. "We don't have time for this, Detective," she said. "The boy that you were chasing, Jack Hunter. He's in a room on the third floor."

"Your point?"

"With a certain young woman," Patel added. "One who we've seen repeatedly on various security cameras. Now, I would like some clarity on the rumours that have been running through my office. Are we dealing with aliens?"

"I believe so," Harry rasped. "Or at least humans from another part of the galaxy. Don't ask me how that's possible."

Patel wore a blank expression as she held his gaze, but the sweat on her forehead made it clear she was struggling with the information. "The girl then," she said at last. "She is one of these... offworlders?"

"Yes," Harry replied. "And she carries a symbiont of some kind."

"A symbiont?"

"Some kind of intelligent organism." Harry stiffened, shaking his head as he tried to put it into words. "Hunter has one too. At least he does now. I saw him bonding the thing this afternoon."

Aamani Patel glanced over her shoulder so that Harry saw her in profile, staring at nothing at all. "We have no choice then," she said, almost to herself. "We have to quarantine them."

"Or you could try speaking to them," Harry protested. True, he wasn't exactly on board with this whole symbiont thing, but he wasn't comfortable with CSIS getting their hands on those kids either. The word *quarantine* had all sorts of unpleasant implications he would rather not consider.

"We have no choice," Patel insisted. "We have absolutely no way to predict what kind of threat these symbionts represent."

Clapping a hand over his mouth, Harry shut his eyes. He took a deep breath through his nose. "You might want to consider," he said into his palm, "that if the girl's people are anything like us, they'll be looking for her."

Patel stared at him, her face glistening with sweat. "What precisely are you trying to say, Detective?" she asked, raising a thin dark eyebrow. "That we're in danger of a full-scale invasion?"

"Call it a hunch," he said, "but I don't get the sense that these people mean to harm us. The girl has gone to enormous lengths to avoid killing; that says a lot to someone like me. However, she *is* a guest on our planet. How might her people react if they learn we've been mistreating her? They can travel the stars, Aamani. After the devastation you've seen this week, do you really believe even our best weapons will stop them?"

The woman looked positively shaken.

Harry winced, pinching the bridge of his nose. "If it means anything," he muttered under his breath, "I think Hunter will be amenable to working with us, maybe the girl too. But you have to proceed with caution."

"Thank you for your insights, Detective," she said, backing away. "I will give them serious consideration."

A moment later, she stepped through the curtain and left him alone with his worries. The world had changed in one day; suspicions had become realities, and Harry Carlson was forced to redefine his place in the universe. Here on earth, people wondered whether humanity would ever travel the stars, completely unaware that humanity was doing just that. What kind of world would his children live in?

Christ, his children.

Every police officer who also happened to be a parent dreaded the possibility of having to tell their children they had been injured in the line of duty – or worse, having someone else tell them. True, the doctors claimed he would suffer no permanent damage, but this incident would only remind Missy and Claire that they might lose their father at any moment. Leaving them with a sitter tonight wouldn't help matters either.

With a frustrated sigh, he set about scanning through his phone's address book.

Some time later, after calling every available contact, Harry found himself sitting in a hospital room, contemplating the unthinkable. Madison, his usual sitter, was studying for an exam, and his neighbours were out. His brother was in Toronto on business, so that left him with only one option.

Harry tapped the screen of his phone with his thumb, dialling his ex-wife's number. Leaving the girls with her would be better than nothing, he was forced to admit, but only just. Missy was old enough to resent some of her mother's more questionable decisions, and he expected an incident.

"Hello?" Della said.

Closing his eyes, Harry brought the receiver to his ear. "Della," he said, nodding once. "How are you today?"

"What do you want, Harry?"

"The girls need a sitter," Harry began, trying to ignore the bile churning up in his stomach. Having to ask this woman for help was worse than facing down a pack of well-armed thugs. "You're the only one available."

"Oh really?" she replied in scathing tones. "And just why can't you be there? Work getting too hectic again?"

"I was injured."

Silence was the only reply. For a moment – a very brief moment – Harry actually wondered if the thought of him being injured had fazed her. "And this is why I should get custody," she said at last. "You're unreliable, Harry. You think only about your career and not about your daughters."

Tilting his head back, Harry squeezed his eyes shut. He couldn't stop the growl that rumbled in his throat. "For the love of God, Della!" he spat. "Can you put that issue aside for now and focus on your kids?"

"I *am* focusing on-"

Harry slapped a palm over his face, groaning in frustration. "I'm sorry," he broke in before she could say anything else. If he didn't appease her, she might refuse to help out of spite. "Look, the girls need dinner and someone to stay with them. And no fast food! Something healthy for God's sake."

"You owe me for this."

"Oh, don't worry," Harry snapped. "If there's one thing I've learned about you over the years, it's that you'll collect with interest."

It had taken a bit of gentle persuasion to convince the hospital staff to let him stay the night, but Jack had managed it. Lauren had required even more coaxing. She seemed to think he was likely to start chanting "you will be assimilated" any moment now. Jack tried to be patient.

The dim light and quiet gave him a chance to think. He had made a life-changing decision today, but his life didn't *feel* any different. He was even starting to get used to the added spatial awareness. As for the Nassai, for the most part she let him be. Perhaps she sensed he needed some time alone.

The room was dark except for a tiny light above Anna's bed that offered just enough illumination for him to make out her features. She was lying on her back with her eyes shut, her expression serene.

The sound of her breathing almost made him want to drift off as well. Bonding the Nassai had taken a lot out of him – he'd eaten *two* dinners – and he still felt like he could pass out at any moment. It probably wasn't wise to force himself to stay awake, but Anna was right; they couldn't trust Carlson or any of the local authorities. Once she was well enough to leave, he planned to rent a car and just drive in any direction.

Jack frowned, his head drooping from the weight of his fatigue. "Come on, Hunter," he whispered. "You promised to watch over her, so no dozing off."

He scrubbed a hand over his face, running fingers through his hair. "You can handle a little more exhaustion," he said, blinking to moisten his eyes. "Once you get her out of here, you can rest."

"You needn't be so distrustful."

Dressed in a black suit with brass buttons, a tall woman stood in the doorway with arms folded. She wore her dark hair up in a ponytail, her face an expressionless mask. "I take it you are Hunter."

Pressing his lips together, Jack looked up to stare at her. He narrowed his eyes. "I am Hunter," he said, nodding once. "And who might you be? Given your lousy sense of timing, I'm guessing 'watchmaker' isn't likely."

"My sense of timing?"

"It's the middle of the night."

The woman moved gracefully into the room, stopping a few feet from the bed as if she feared Anna might jump up and punch her. "My name is Aamani Patel," she said. "I came here to make you an offer."

He stood.

Clasping hands together behind his back, Jack maneuvered around the foot of the bed and stood before her. "I'm all ears," he said, eyebrows rising. "But I should tell you up front: I've already got a lifetime's supply of Turtle Wax."

Aamani Patel studied him with a flat expression, then nodded to herself. "Carlson told me you were defiant," she said, stepping forward. "Let me be equally forthright with you, Jack. I work for CSIS."

"Oh, that's awesome!" he exclaimed. "Hey, now that I've got you here, let me ask: is there a Canadian equivalent of that warehouse at the end of *Raiders*? You know, one that holds all our country's secrets, like the recipe for maple-glazed Timbits?"

Patel thrust her chin out, her dark eyes smoldering. "I'm well aware of your talent for verbal sniping, Hunter," she spat. "Has anyone ever told you it's a rather thin veil for the self-doubt that gnaws at you?"

Jack sucked on his lip, his cheeks flushed to a blazing red. He lowered his eyes to the floor. "What's your offer?" he muttered. "And if you think you're going to take Anna into custody, you're very mistaken."

"I want you to come work for me."

What?

When he looked up, he found Patel watching him with a completely straight face; her tone seemed even as well. "You and the girl," she said, glancing at Anna. "I'm told you both have talents that we can put to good use."

"I'm not sure I trust-"

"If what you say is true," she pushed on, "then Pennfield has been snatching up all sorts of alien technology. That represents a clear and present danger to the security of this nation and every other nation on this planet. Who better to devise a defense than a pair of experts on the subject?"

"You make a solid case."

Turning away from him, Patel marched to the door and paused there. "You would be consultants only," she went on. "Exempt from taking part in any assignment if you so choose. Though my operatives would welcome a woman with Anna's skills, and if what Detective Carlson tells me is true, you will soon be joining her at that level of…shall we call it combat proficiency?"

"All right, I'm on board." He still wasn't certain that he could trust this woman, but it was better to be working with CSIS than to be running from them. "For the moment, I'm happy to work with you, but I can't say the same for Anna."

Patel glanced over her shoulder, her lips curled into a small smile. She nodded to him. "Present my offer to her," she said as if it were already settled. "I'm sure that you'll find her amenable."

Chapter 19

Waves crested and fell beneath the starry sky, washing up over the sandy beach in a thin white foam. Teenagers gathered in the sand, many in nothing more than swimwear, and most carrying some form of alcohol.

From her perch on the wooden patio, Elora watched them with half-hearted interest. A young man in swim trunks and an open shirt led a bikini-clad girl off into the darkness. What she wouldn't give to have the last twenty years back, to relive them here, on this backward little planet.

A slim woman in a red sundress, Elora felt the wind tease her bob of dirty blonde hair. Her skin had been bronzed by the sun, but she would still be considered pale here in the Dominican. "If wishes were ships," she said, nodding to herself, "every last one of us would sail the stars."

She turned away from the railing.

The small bar with a neon sign in its front window had a roof of small red tiles and a few cracks in the white stone that made up its front wall. Plastic tables and chairs were spread out across the patio. Not exactly a palace, but the place was hers. She had always wanted to own a bar.

Elora glided across the wooden planks.

Pushing her way through the front door, she found herself inside a dimly lit room where wooden tables were spread out haphazardly on the dusty floor. The counter off to her left was occupied by a young man in a Hawaiian shirt who sat with his back to her, staring into his beer.

With a heavy sigh, Flora lowered her eyes to the floor. She felt deep creases stretch across her brow. "Still here, Emmanuel?" she asked. "I thought that I'd made my position clear to you."

He kept his back turned, but Elora could see the way he hunched up his shoulders as though a shiver had run down his spine. "You sell to Rolin," he growled. "Why should I be any different?"

"Because your mother would hate me."

"Forget that bitch!"

Lifting her chin, Elora narrowed her eyes to slits. "You will not say such things in my presence." The words came out as a rasp, but that suited her. "Your mother is kinder than I would be in her place."

He swivelled around on the stool.

Emmanuel was a handsome boy with copper skin and high cheekbones, his black hair kept short. "I know you need the money," he said, standing up. "Just this once, and I swear I'll never tell."

Elora felt her face burn.

It was becoming clear to her that the kid would not depart until she appeased him; he had come in a half hour ago, demanding a bag, and silencing him had taken more effort than she would have cared to expend. There were customers who only wanted to drink in peace, and alerting them to her *under-the-table* activities was a good way to run afoul of the locals.

Not that she feared imprisonment – the few trinkets she had brought with her to this technologically impoverished world would be more than enough to evade the police – but that would require her to move on. She had spent the better part of her adult life drifting from one port to another, but she liked it here. It was warm.

She had placated the boy with alcohol despite his lack of an adult bracelet, but with the last of her customers gone, his protests had started up again. At this point, it might be wiser to relent. Boys had a habit of letting their tongues wag, particularly when they felt slighted.

Allowing him to purchase his bag would provide him with plenty of incentive to keep silent.

Elora marched across the room with her fists clenched at her sides, her face twisted in a scowl. "You are a foolish boy," she said, shaking her head. "But if you insist on this, then I'll have your promise. Not one word to anyone."

"Of course!"

She dropped to a crouch behind the bar, rifling through a few cardboard boxes that she kept on a small shelf. So far, she had managed to keep their contents hidden from customers and government officials alike. When she found what she was looking for, she breathed out a sigh of relief.

Pulling a black glove over her hand, Elora squinted into her palm. She nodded once in approval. "One thing before we go on," she said, standing up. "Do you believe in black magic, Emmanuel?"

He leaned over the bar with a big grin on his face, his eyes as wide as a ten-peso coin. "What are you talking about, Lora?" he exclaimed. "Nobody believes in those old superstitions. Now, give-"

She seized his throat with her gloved hand.

The boy spasmed as pain shot through his body, arms flailing about, head bobbing from side to side. A Slaver's Glove was designed to do just that: stimulate those nerve-endings that sent pain signals to the brain.

She gave a shove.

Emmanuel fell backward, landing hard on his ass on the wooden floorboards. Tears glistened on his cheeks. "What did you..." He shook his head, groaning. "Why would you do such a thing?"

Elora lifted her chin to stare down her nose at him. "Do you believe in black magic, Emmanuel?" she asked, raising an eyebrow. "Perhaps your view of the universe has been expanded tonight."

Red-faced and gasping, Emmanuel hung his head. He sobbed and tears dripped from his chin. "Sweet Jesus, have mercy," he whimpered. "Mother Mary and all of the Apostles, I beg-"

"Pick yourself up."

The boy did so with some hesitation, standing on shaky legs as though surprised to find that the pain had receded. He looked up at her, terror on his face, "How are you able to do that?"

"That is not your concern." Elora took a small bag of cocaine from a drawer under the bar and tossed it onto the counter. "You will pay me two hundred for that, leave here and never speak of this to anyone. If you do, for any reason, I will inflict horrors on you that you have never imagined."

Emmanuel frowned, staring down at the floor. "Okay, Elora," he said, retrieving his wallet and fishing out a stack of bills. "I won't tell anyone; I promise. Just…whatever you did, don't do it again."

When he was gone, Elora heaved out a sigh. Inflicting pain on the boy had been a gamble – it might persuade him to remain silent, or it might convince him to bring the law down upon her – but she felt more assured of the former than the latter. Emmanuel would not want to talk to the police when there existed the possibility that Elora might reveal the purpose of his visit.

"Tormenting children," a dry voice said. "I thought that beneath you."

A sudden chill went through Elora, and she almost reached for the pistol she kept under the counter. Almost. A savvy woman learned to keep those reactions under control; they could interfere with business.

A tall man stood in her doorway, dressed in blue jeans and a black shirt with the collar left open. His thin, angular face was a little too pale, and the glasses he wore reflected the light. "Perhaps I underestimated your foolishness."

A flush singed Elora's cheeks, and she looked down at the counter to avoid glaring at him. "What do you want, Pennfield?" she asked. "I'm fairly certain my debts to you have been paid."

"To prevent you from drawing attention to yourself." Slipping his hands into his pockets, Wesley Pennfield strolled into the room, glancing about as if to study the décor. "I did not offer you refuge on this planet only to have you flaunt your stolen technology like a child with a toy."

Elora closed her eyes. She took a deep breath and then let it out again. "What I do in my own establishment is none of your concern," she said. "If you're worried that I might divulge-"

"Please."

The man turned on his heel, facing her with his chin thrust out. Being scrutinized by Pennfield made her feel very much like a worm that had been primed for dissection. "Nothing you could divulge would harm me. I've come here to arrange a simple business transaction. Nothing more."

"What sort of transaction?"

Wesley Pennfield smiled a smile that seemed forced somehow. "You have several battle drones, do you not?"

"I do not."

Crossing his arms, the man looked down at the floor. He seemed to be choosing his next words with care. "But you know where I can *find* some," he said. "Perhaps you can broker a deal?"

What in the Holy Name of Jada could this man want with battle drones? They were killing machines: robots that had been built for the sole purpose of destroying the enemy without hesitation. In fact, they often worked *too* well.

Drones could not think for themselves; they exterminated their targets by the most efficient means possible, blind to the ethical dilemmas of war. There was no algorithm in existence that would allow a machine to grasp the nuances of human judgment. Half the time, when their enemies offered a legitimate surrender, drones assessed the situation and labelled it a "false white flag," proceeding to slaughter their opponents long after they had laid down arms.

For that reason, use of drones in combat had been outlawed by the Leyrian Accord. Selling them on the black market was one of the few offenses punishable by death. "What are you offering in return?" If she was going to risk capital punishment, the pay-off had to be worth it.

Pennfield grinned, and this time, it was a sign of genuine pleasure. "I thought you might be persuaded."

Elora flinched, turning her head so that he'd see her in profile. She felt sweat prickle on her brow. "I deal in small merchandise, Pennfield," she said. "Not military hardware. But I may have a solution."

The man pursed his lips as he studied her, nodding to himself. "And what precisely would that be?" he asked, approaching the bar. "Do you suppose one of your compatriots is willing to deal?"

Setting her elbow on the counter, Elora rested her chin in her palm. She closed her eyes, thinking it over. "Raolan had some heavy weapons," she explained. "I saw them on the transport here. But the man is in Norway."

"What's he doing there?"

"He likes it cold."

Elora felt her mouth tighten at that. In her estimation, no civilized people ever built settlements in regions where the temperature dropped below freezing. "I'd be willing to make contact in exchange for a finder's fee."

"How much?"

"Three million," she said. "Cash."

Pennfield snarled at her, his lips peeling back from clenched teeth. "Do you think I'm stupid, woman?" he snapped. "You expect me to pay you three million dollars just to make one call?"

"I expect you to treat me with respect."

"I would only pay so much for the hardware itself," Pennfield went on. "No broker should charge so much just to set up the meeting. I think we will renegotiate your fee to a more reasonable sum."

"The fee is nonnegotiable," Elora said, reaching beneath the counter. She found a small cylindrical device about the size of a lipstick. "Three million in hard cash or you can forget about this deal."

Pennfield looked her up and down, his brows drawn together in a scowl. "I remember a time when you weren't so sure of yourself," he whispered. "When you would have done anything to escape the Justice Keepers, when you *begged* me for asylum. Do you recall those days?"

She thrust the device in his face, thumbing the switch. A high-pitched whine filled the air, and Pennfield doubled over, slapping palms over his ears. He dropped to his knees a moment later, crying out.

Gritting her teeth, Elora squinted at him. "They call it a Sonic Reducer," she explained. "A device that agitates the fluid in your inner ear, causing vertigo."

He shut his eyes tight, tears running over his cheeks. He tossed his head from side to side with enough force to send the glasses flying from his face. "And yet you remain unaffected by it."

Elora flashed a playful smile, bowing her head to him. "It isn't so remarkable," she said with a shrug. "A small implant just inside the ear canal is all you'll need to overcome a hypersonic pulse."

She retrieved a pistol from beneath the bar and held it up for inspection. Its sleek, black surface was cool to the touch. "Crowd Control!" Elora shouted, and the LEDS on its barrel turned green.

She pointed the gun at Pennfield and fired, launching a bullet into the man's chest with just enough force to send him toppling backward. When he was flat on his back, she pulled the trigger again.

A bullet struck him in the abdomen and bounced off. The man would have a nasty welt beneath his belly button, and possibly a scar, but nothing more than that. This setting was designed to inflict pain.

She deactivated the sonic pulse.

Wesley Pennfield sat up with his teeth bared, streams of moisture glistening on his cheeks. "You really have grown arrogant," he said, shaking his head. "Do you honestly think those trinkets are a threat to me?"

Pressing her lips together, Elora studied him for a very long moment. She nodded to herself. "*I* am not the arrogant party here," she said. "You have the audacity to step into *my* bar and dictate terms?"

The man was frowning down at himself, heaving out gasping breath after gasping breath. "Perhaps we can come to an understanding," he murmured. "Three million is not so much for battle drones."

"I thought you might see it my way." She still wondered what he wanted with such monstrous devices, but a wise woman knew better than to ask such questions. What men like him did with their munitions was none of her concern; she was here to make a quick profit and then leave before things got ugly. "Now," Elora went on, "let's get down to the specifics, shall we?"

Chapter 20

The window in Aamani Patel's office looked out on a green field that stretched on for about a hundred feet before ending in a line of pine trees near the edge of the property. Beyond that, the buildings of Ottawa were barely visible.

Sunlight streamed in through the pane, falling on a desk with a black surface where not even a single speck of dust glittered. Aside from a small picture of a man in a ball cap, there was no sign that any human being called this office home.

Anna stood before the window with arms crossed, frowning through the glass. "So, here we are," she said with a shrug. "Meeting with the representatives of the government's intelligence agency."

She turned, glancing over her shoulder, a lock of hair falling over one eye. "You're sure this is the right choice?" she said, eyebrows rising. "The few intelligence operatives I've met back home always gave me the creeps."

Jack smiled, a blush colouring his cheeks. He closed his eyes, then nodded once. "I think we should hear her out," he replied. "Normally, I'm not one to trust 'the Man,' but we have enough enemies already."

Anna turned her face up to the ceiling, blinking a few times as she thought it over. "I'm not so sure," she muttered. "Better an enemy who stabs you in the chest than a friend who stabs you in the back."

It had been three days since she had been discharged from the hospital, but mention of a chest wound still made her ache. Phantom pain, perhaps? She would be lying if she said that a brush with death hadn't fazed her.

"Ah, here we are."

Dressed to kill, Aamani Patel strode through the door with grim determination on her face. "I'm glad to see you've made it," she said, nodding to Jack. "Take a seat and we can get down to business."

"What do you want with us?" Anna inquired. "If you think that we can be persuaded to use our abilities for your personal gain…"

Jack slapped a palm over his face, groaning his displeasure. "Ladies and gentlemen, my friend Anna," he said. "Can you believe she doesn't have her own talk radio show yet?"

Patel smiled at him with a fond expression. She turned her gaze on Anna with just as much affection. "I can see you two will be among my more colourful agents," she said. "I have no intention of misusing your abilities, Miss Lenai."

"C-Span would love her," Jack replied. "Just sayin'."

Anna tried to fight down her chagrin, but when her efforts failed, she decided she had earned a little embarrassment. Patel had done nothing to earn her distrust, but she had an innate distaste for politics. The days that she had spent recovering from her wound had been filled with visits to special CSIS-approved doctors who were all amazed at the speed of her convalescence.

Hospital staff had been taken off her case to prevent them from uncovering any of the many tell-tale signs that Anna Lenai was not an average human being. Nassai cells in her blood would be a major tip-off.

CSIS, it seemed, had chosen a policy of non-disclosure, opting to keep knowledge of her existence and of events beyond the confines of this solar system a secret from the general population. To say that Anna disagreed with this course of action was a massive understatement. Any government that was unwilling to trust its constituents with the truth was unworthy of their trust in turn. People were far more capable of coping with the truth than their leaders gave them credit for.

Aamani Patel glided around the desk, trailing her fingers over its black surface. She paused for a moment to stare out the window. "Please, sit," she said, gesturing to the three gray chairs in front of her desk.

Jack sat down with hands resting on the chair arms, his expression as smooth as the finest silk. "So, you want us to work with you," he began. "Does that mean you're ready to go after Pennfield?"

Patel kept her back turned, standing with her arms folded as she peered through the windowpane. "I've come to suspect that your claims are accurate," she said. "If Pennfield has access to alien technology, we must recover it."

"And do what with it?"

At the sound of Anna's voice, Patel shot a glance over her shoulder, her dark eyes smoldering. "Study it, of course," she replied. "Understanding such technology will allow us to address any number of social ills."

Anna sat down prim and proper with her head bowed. "You want to study it," she said, hunching up her shoulders. "I don't suppose you've considered returning those items to their rightful owners."

"How precisely would we do that?"

"Pennfield has the means to contact my people."

With a soft hiss, Patel winced and shook her head. "I don't think so," she muttered, approaching the desk. "With respect, Miss Lenai, we know so little about your people, it's hard to trust."

Lifting her chin, Anna held the other woman's gaze. She narrowed her eyes to thin slits. "Perhaps now you understand my predicament," she said. "One that is made worse by the fact that I am alone here."

Before she could say anything further, the door flew open and Harry Carlson strode in. "Sorry I'm late," he said, shaking his head in dismay. "Bit of a mix-up with the kids... well, you don't need to hear about that."

"It's fine, Detective."

Patel studied him with an expression that said it was anything but fine, but that she wasn't going to make an issue of it. "Take a seat," she said, gesturing to the chair on the other side of Jack.

The man did so, giving Anna a moment to collect her thoughts. So, it seemed they were at an impasse. She wasn't willing to trust these people, and they weren't willing to trust her. At times like these, she wondered if it was truly possible to overcome human nature. Thousands of years of civilization and they were still afraid whenever they came across someone from another tribe.

Someone had to make the first concession, and on recognizing that, Anna saw no reason why it shouldn't be her. Her father would be proud. *You learn a thing or two as a diplomat's daughter. Maybe nurture isn't out of the ring yet.*

Anna rolled up her sleeve, revealing a gauntlet on her wrist with a touch-screen interface about half the size of the one on Jack's cell phone. Her multi-tool was attached, blinking away to indicate a full charge.

Anna swiped her finger across the screen and brought up the desktop. She tapped a few icons, bringing up files on medical research. "I'm sending you data that should allow your doctors to develop new and better cancer treatments."

Jack squinted at her. He shook his head. "I've never seen that thing before," he said. "Where were you hiding it? I did your *laundry* for God's sake."

"You never saw it because I didn't want you to see it," Anna replied. "A multi-tool is much easier to use with the proper interface. I trusted you not to harm me, but I knew that it would be hard for you to resist sharing this information if you got your hands on it. The data that brought about those cancer treatments can also be used to make biological weapons. I had to be careful."

Patel frowned at her, distrust evident on the woman's face. With a heavy sigh, she nodded acquiescence. "And yet you offer this data freely," she murmured. "So you aren't opposed to sharing knowledge."

"On the contrary," Anna replied. "I believe that we are morally obligated to share knowledge that will alleviate suffering. But such knowledge can be misused. You have to know who you're dealing with."

Patel smiled.

It seemed that Anna had gained some small measure of the woman's respect. Maybe there was hope for an understanding after all. "Pennfield will misuse the technology that he has acquired," she went on. "He's already made that abundantly clear."

All the while, Harry Carlson had been watching her, nodding slowly with each and every point. "So, exactly what kind of technology does this man have at his disposal?" he asked. "It would help to know what we're up against."

Anna grunted, nodding to him. "You aren't going to like it," she said, lifting up her forearm once again. She tapped away at the little screen. "Wesley Pennfield has a piece of technology that will broadcast your system's location into deep space."

The multi-tool made a whirring noise, and a cone of light shot up from the tiny silver disk, a cone that resolved into the transparent image of a triangular device that rotated on a central axis. "This is called a SlipGate," Anna explained. "Its primary function is to act as a short-range, point-to-point mass-transit system. Generally speaking, there would be hundreds of Gates spread out across the surface of a planet in a network.

"SlipGates have a secondary function that enables faster-than-light communication by creating microscopic wormholes. We theorize that they track each other's location by means of a central hub located at the Galactic Core."

A wave of her hand caused the hologram to vanish.

She paused for a moment to discover that Patel was staring at her with her mouth agape. "You...you've been to the Core?" she asked, blinking. "I-I'm sorry. This is all so new to me."

Anna pressed her lips together, staring into her lap. "No, my people can't get near the Core," she replied. "SlipGates are Overseer technology. We've learned to duplicate them, but that's all."

"Overseer?"

"The race of beings who scattered our people across the galaxy," Jack put in. It pleased her to see him demonstrate such confidence. Many people in his position would be tempted to keep quiet and let the experts do the talking, but a Keeper had to acquire some level of assertiveness. "From what Anna's told me, they were incredibly powerful and incredibly mysterious."

"With a SlipGate," Anna went on, "Pennfield will be able to make contact with any number of criminals. The man that I pursued – Denario Tarse – was brought here for the express purpose of delivering a Nassai symbiont. It stands to reason that there are other fugitives hiding on this planet."

Harry Carlson frowned. He wiped his forehead with the back of his hand. "That is an unsettling thought," he muttered. "So, what do you suggest we do? We can't just storm his building and take the Gate."

Patel's face was an expressionless mask, her eyes fixed on some point along the far wall. "Perhaps we should do just that," she said, eyebrows rising. "If what you say is true, it would be a step in the right direction."

"And violate due process?" Jack shot back. The look of skepticism that he gave her spoke volumes about what he thought of that idea. "No offense, ma'am, but if we throw civil liberties out the window, what will people think when this all comes out?"

"You didn't seem to mind when you and Miss Lenai were plotting your own form of corporate espionage," Patel said. "Now is not the time to lose your nerve. Not when lives are at stake."

"That was because the law offered no recourse."

Anna felt her mouth tighten, then lowered her eyes to stare into her lap. "Are there no other options?" she asked, her brow furrowing. "Surely you have more than enough evidence to request a search warrant."

"Indeed we do," Carlson offered.

Patel silenced him with a glare, the slight flush in her cheeks indicating that she was losing patience. "Evidence that we cannot submit," she insisted. "Revealing the existence of extraterrestrial life would be disastrous."

"No," Carlson said. "Anna's right."

Patel groaned.

Crossing his arms over his chest, Carlson leaned back in his chair and matched her stare for stare. "The law isn't just about rules," he went on. "It's about fairness. We have an opportunity to-"

"This isn't up for debate."

Well, that settled that then. Anna had thought that working with CSIS would give her the backing of legitimate authority, but it was back to a life of sneaking and secrets for her. "That being the case," she said, "the most logical course of action would be to sneak into the Penworth building and use the SlipGate to send a message to my people."

"Out of the question."

Anna winced, letting her head hang. She had hoped that her gesture of good faith would make Patel relent on this point. "My people have the means to retrieve the Gate with minimal violence."

"We can secure the Gate ourselves."

"No, ma'am, we really can't." Anna struggled to keep her face smooth as she held the other woman's gaze. "A SlipGate is heavy, approximately several times the mass of your desk. There's no way a strike team could get it out of there."

Jack lifted his chin to study the woman, his blue eyes as hard as forged steel. "One way or another," he began, "the Leyrians are coming. They're almost certainly searching for Anna's shuttle."

"That's true."

"So," Jack went on. "How much better would it be to begin our relationship with them by showing good faith? Miss Patel, if they're planning to wipe us out, there's very little that you or I can do to stop it, but if we can demonstrate that we're willing to work with them, we might just earn a powerful ally."

"It seems I'm left with little recourse," Patel muttered, staring down at the surface of her desk. She heaved out a deep breath. "I will bring your suggestions to the Minister of Defense. In the meantime, Jack, I'd like you to begin training-"

"No."

Patel stiffened at the sound of Anna's voice, then fixed a steely gaze on her. "You have an objection?" she asked, raising a dark eyebrow. "Do your people have some kind of moral aversion to combat readiness?"

Anna set her jaw and locked eyes with the other woman. She squinted, shaking her head. "He's my student," she said firmly. "I will train him myself. He needs to know how to think like a Justice Keeper."

"Will you at least make use of our facilities?"

Anna nodded. "That would be acceptable."

"Splendid," Patel said. "I'll make the arrangements."

Chapter 21

Anna stood with her back turned, peering through the large rectangular window that looked out on a park. "I guess it's all right," she said with a bob of her head. "But I'm still going to miss the old apartment."

Jack forced a smile, staring down at the hardwood floor. He shut his eyes and shook his head. "You're determined to hate this place," he muttered. "Seems very un-Leyrian of you, don't you think?"

She spun around with arms crossed, lifting her chin to glare at him. "You mean you like it here?" she asked, eyebrows rising. "Your old apartment was smaller, but you have to admit it had character."

With a deep breath, Jack turned his face up to the ceiling. He squinted, thinking it over. "I don't know…" he mumbled. "You haven't lived there for over a year. I bet if we had stayed, the lack of privacy would drive us crazy."

She stormed off with a grunt, passing him and making her way into the kitchen. If there was some rational cause for her dislike of this apartment, Jack couldn't find it. She had admitted the need for a change of residence – Pennfield could easily locate his old address – and the salary that CSIS had offered them was more than enough to cover the rent. Maybe it was just the fact that someone else had chosen this place for her.

Aamani Patel had arranged these accommodations – government clout had its perks – registering them as Mr. and Mrs. Peter and Linda

Marx. She would have offered Anna her own apartment, but Anna wasn't willing to let him out of her sight.

He turned around.

Their little kitchen had a tiled floor and white cupboards with wooden handles. Not to mention state-of-the-art appliances. He had never cared much for material possessions, but in all honesty, it was nice to have a dishwasher.

He started forward.

A frown tightened Jack's mouth as he walked through the kitchen. "Oh, come on, Anna," he called out. "You're usually the first person to look on the bright side. What makes today any different?"

On the other side, he found a hallway that led to the two bedrooms. His door was closest, left open to allow a small rectangle of daylight to fall upon the floor. Even from out here, he could hear Anna's muttering.

Jack bared his teeth, throwing his head back. He felt a vicious growl vibrate in his throat. "All right, that's enough," he said, marching down the hallway. "Are you going to explain why you're acting like a child, or should I let you sulk?"

Through the gap in Anna's door, he saw her standing with her hands on her hips as she inspected a pink bedspread. Pink curtains hanging over the window matched it to the exact shade. "They gave me a pink room."

"So?"

Anna whirled around to stare at him, her face a storm cloud that threatened to let loose with lightning. "I hate pink," she barked. "I've always hated pink. They gave me a pink room because I'm a woman!"

Pressing a fist to his mouth, Jack closed his eyes. He cleared his throat with some force. "I can see why that would piss you off," he began. "But don't you think you might be overreacting just a tad?"

She went beet red, then lowered her eyes to the floor. "You're absolutely right, Jack. I *am* overreacting." She spun around and marched across the room to the window. "I just feel so powerless!"

"Oh, I see."

Anna turned, glancing over her shoulder, her flush somehow deepening. "What do you see?" she asked, raising an eyebrow. "A psychotic woman who you regret letting into your apartment?"

"No," Jack replied. "I see a woman who's trying to assert control over every little bit of minutiae, because she can't control the very big problem that's staring her right in the face. You want to go home."

The sudden slump of her shoulders told him that he had hit the nail square on the head. In truth, he should have expected as much. He had grown fond of Anna's company, but it was ludicrous to assume that she didn't have a life of her own, friends and family that she missed.

Here she was, living in an environment that she couldn't escape, and every aspect of that environment that displeased her only served to remind her of just how trapped she really felt. "I'm sorry."

"It's not that I hate it here!" Anna protested. "There are good things, but I would be lying if I said I didn't miss my family."

He stepped into the room.

Pacing across the hardwood floor, Anna frowned down at herself. She grunted and shook her head. "I know I shouldn't be acting like this," she went on. "It's just that even with a distress beacon, there's a good chance they won't find me."

She looked up at him with big blue eyes that glistened, blinking as if to force her tears away. "I may have to get used to the idea of living out the rest of my days here on this little planet."

He could only imagine her frustration. How would he react if he learned that he had to spend his life away from the people he loved, away from Lauren and his parents? The worst part, in his estimation, was knowing they would never stop worrying about him.

Jack sat down on the bed with hands resting on his knees. He stared down into his lap. "There has to be something we can do," he said at last. "Some way to make contact with your people."

Spinning around, Anna sat down beside him. "There really isn't," she mumbled. "The only guaranteed way to make contact is the Slip-Gate, and we both know how hard it would be to recover that. Like it or not, I'm stuck here."

Jack slipped an arm around her shoulder, pulling her close. Instinct alone had made him do it, and he very nearly pulled away when his rational mind reasserted control over his body. Vulnerability was not an invitation for affection, but strangely Anna didn't seem to mind. "Would it be so bad?" he asked. "Being here?"

She leaned her cheek against his chest, closing her eyes. A soft contented murmur escaped her. "I suppose it wouldn't," she whispered. "Not if I had my best friend to keep me company."

Jack felt his lips curl, his cheeks turning pink. He closed his eyes and touched his nose to her forehead. "Best friend, huh?" he said. "Well, if you insist on having such low standards, I can't stop you."

She gave him a playful little punch to the short ribs. "That's not nice," she said in a tone that almost sounded like sulking. "I happen to have impeccable standards. I only like truly exceptional men."

He stilled himself before instinct could kick in, realizing in a moment of terror that he had been planning to kiss her. That would have been incredibly inappropriate. He had to get a hold of himself.

Wanting to kiss her wasn't so bad – he could keep his hands to himself – but the real problem was that some part of him hoped they would be unable to contact Anna's people. Then he would never have to say good-bye.

That was a thought unbecoming of a Justice Keeper. These feelings were getting in the way of doing what he knew was right, and that meant he had to squash them. "Anna," he said. "I promise we'll find a way to get you home."

"Thank you," she whispered. "When we do…"

Jack raised an eyebrow.

She closed her eyes, her face turning several shades of scarlet, and leaned her head against his chest again. "Well, we can worry about that later," she added. "Thank you for being here for me."

"Any time."

When Jack was gone, Anna sat on her bed and shivered despite the warm afternoon. For a moment there, she had teetered on the brink of losing control. She could visualize it in her mind: touching his cheek and turning his face toward her, kissing him softly on the lips. Letting go.

She had almost given in to that temptation, and for a moment, it seemed as though Jack would have let her. Oh, she had no doubt that the attraction was mutual, but she was his mentor now.

Someone had to guide him down this very difficult path, and for the moment, she was the only Keeper available. That meant her personal desires had to be put aside. Hard as that was.

Anna bit her lip, squeezing her eyes shut. She felt sweat prickle on her forehead and shivered. "Cold shower," she said. "Long, uncomfortable, *icy* shower. Keep your head on your shoulders, Lenai."

The blazing sun dipped toward the western horizon, painting the sky with bands of orange and red. Sunlight glinted off the metal mesh behind the baseball diamond, and the sand over the infield sparkled with bits of debris.

Missy stood at the plate with the bat over her shoulder, the bill of her helmet shielding her eyes from the sun. "You can do it!" Harry called out despite himself. When his child had decided to play softball, he had promised himself that he would not become one of *those* parents.

The pitcher threw.

Missy swung and clipped the ball right in the sweet spot, sending it flying all the way to the outfield. Kids in red uniforms scrambled with gloves upraised, each one with his mouth agape.

Missy ran for first base in a mad dash, feet kicking up sand. She threw herself down and slid on her belly, fingers outstretched to touch the bag. Only then did it hit her that the first baseman didn't have the ball.

I told her to look before she dives, Harry thought to himself. *The coach is gonna tear strips off her hide.*

His daughter got to her feet and took off, but the kid on second turned to intercept the ball with his glove. He squatted down, tagging Missy before she could get past him. "Out!" the umpire called.

Harry covered his face with his hand. He pinched the skin of his forehead with the tips of his fingers. "Next time," he whispered, looking up. "It just takes practice. You'll get the hang of it."

Missy couldn't hear him, of course, but there were times when he felt like simply speaking the words would convey them to her mind. An odd thought, he knew, but Harry had long since stopped trying to hide his own idiosyncrasies. Parenthood changed a man. For the better in most cases.

Missy approached the bleachers with a ball cap instead of her helmet, a bright smile on her face. "Sorry," she said with a shrug. "I thought I saw... well, anyway. I'm glad you could come, Dad."

Harry smiled, his cheeks burning. He closed his eyes and nodded once to her. "Of course I came," he said. "And don't worry about it. Lots of people make those mistakes when they're still learning the game."

She climbed up over the bleachers – there were very few people; most of the other parents had brought lawn chairs – and took a seat next to him. He could tell that she was upset. "You'd think I'd learn faster."

"It's just a game, Missy," Harry replied. "Doing your best is important, but don't get your sense of self-worth tied up in it."

She nodded.

For a long while, they were silent. With the game over, both teams were gathered together while the coaches handed out popsicles. Harry suspected that his daughter was still too embarrassed to get one for herself. Fortunately, the freezer at home had several boxes full.

He had to give his daughter some credit; she maintained her composure quite well, given the circumstances. Not that he was an advocate of keeping feelings repressed, but it was good to know she could keep a cool head in a pinch.

"So, are you going to tell me?"

"Tell you what?"

When he looked over his shoulder, he found her watching him with a concerned expression, her face glistening. "What really happened that day when you got hurt," she went on. "What's been going on in the city?"

Harry stared into his lap, a frown tugging at the corners of his mouth. "If something were going on," he began, "I'd tell you, Missy. Honestly, it was gang violence and nothing else."

She crossed her arms and let out a grunt, frowning out at the field. "Gang violence. You expect me to believe that?"

His daughter was reaching that age where a child discovered that not everything her parents told her made sense. Missy would have heard the rumours just as much as anyone else. The advanced tech Anna had used had caused quite a stir.

Craning his neck, Harry frowned up at the sky. He narrowed his eyes. "There is no conspiracy, Missy," he muttered. "I promise that if something *were* going on, I wouldn't keep you in the dark."

"Who said anything about a conspiracy?" The sly little smile on her face made him want to slap himself upside the head. Amazing what a slip of the tongue could do. He had all but confirmed her suspicions.

"No one," Harry said. "Because there isn't one."

Missy got up and climbed down the bleachers, moving carefully over the wooden seats. "I'm gonna go talk to my friends," she said when she reached the bottom. "Meet you here in ten minutes?"

"Sounds good."

He sighed inwardly. When exactly had his daughter reached the point where she could best him in a verbal fencing match? Oh sure, he hadn't really given her anything concrete, but kids could speculate. And they got creative.

There were days when he wanted to grab Aamani Patel by the shoulders and shake her. It was almost a staple of pop culture that governments kept the truth from the people for their own good. He half wondered if that was part of what had motivated her decision to suppress knowledge of the Leyrians. Would people really panic if they learned about human beings flying around in spaceships?

His musings were interrupted by the high-pitched ringing of his phone. Checking the screen revealed that one of his officers was calling. So, this was almost certainly work-related then.

Harry brought the receiver to his ear.

He closed his eyes and took a deep breath, tilting his head back. "Mitchell," he said. "Does this mean you have an update on the matter we discussed?"

"We have a lead on Hutchinson."

"Go on."

"Well, he was smart enough not to use his own credit cards, but we got a few hits on his ex-wife's card out in Halifax."

"I'm not seeing the point."

"His ex lives here, sir," Mitchell went on, "and she hasn't been to Halifax once in her entire life. So, we can add credit card fraud to his list of charges. You want me to call the locals and have them pick him up?"

Clenching his teeth, Harry shielded his eyes with one hand. He blinked a couple times. "Negative," he muttered. "I've got contacts out that way. I can get in touch with them myself."

"Sir?"

Harry fixed his gaze upon the man and narrowed his eyes. "You heard me, Mitchell," he barked. "Leave this one with me. I'll bring the bastard in myself."

"Yes... sir... "

As luck would have it, Aamani Patel had assigned Jack and Anna a small workout room where they could begin his training away from prying eyes. A pair of ID cards were necessary just to get in the door. That was good, Jack supposed. Very few people at CSIS knew that Anna was the mysterious blonde woman who had been raiding corporate offices. Training in the main gym with the other agents would surely draw attention when she used some of her fancier abilities.

Or when I use them, Jack noted. It was still odd to think that he had the ability to bend space and time with his thoughts. So far, he had made no attempt to do so. That felt like the kind of thing you didn't attempt without supervision.

Four walls of white plaster surrounded a box-like room where blue gym mats were spread across the tiled floor. Fluorescent lights in the ceiling cast a harsh glare. What he wouldn't give for a window.

He stood on a mat in black sweats and a matching tank top, sweat glistening on his face and matting hair to his forehead. "Alright," he said, nodding to her. "Let's try this one more time."

Anna was just as soaked, her skin glistening and her face flushed. Worse yet, the way that gray tank top clung to her body was distracting in ways that he would rather not think about. "If you insist," she said. "Hit me."

"Can't you begin it?"

Tilting her head to one side, Anna frowned at him, her eyes scrunched into a pug-like squint. "I've come at you each time," she replied. "You must learn to initiate combat as well as defend."

Jack tried to keep his face smooth as he locked eyes with her, but the uneasiness in his belly made that difficult. "I can initiate combat just fine," he said, eyebrows rising. "I survived third grade after all."

"Then show me."

He knew what to do – a few years of Tae Kwon Do as a teen had given him a basic understanding of fighting stances – but the idea of striking someone nearly half his size made him feel like he was starring in an episode of COPS. Of course, he couldn't say as much to Anna.

She lifted her chin to stare at him, deep creases forming in her brow. "Well, are you going to begin?" she asked. "If you need a break, Jack, I'm not going to make fun of you. There's no sense in overtaxing yourself."

"It's not that."

"Then what?"

Jack felt his mouth tighten, staring down at the floor. He closed his eyes and shook his head. "Anna, you're barely five feet tall," he pleaded. "So, you'll forgive me if it takes a while to work up the nerve."

Crossing her arms, Anna grunted at him. It was a rare thing to see disapproval on her face – rare to see it directed at him, anyway – but today she was pretty damn liberal with her glares. "And while you hesitate," she shot back, "the small opponent you're so afraid of hitting pulls a gun on you."

"That's not fair at-"

"I think," she continued, pacing toward him, "that this has nothing to do with my size and everything to do with my gender. Are you afraid to hit a woman, Jack? If so, we can end this now."

"Thank you."

Anna pursed her lips as she studied him, squinting as though trying to be certain of what she saw. "I was wrong about you," she said at last. "You were never meant to be a Keeper. Not if you harbour such sexist attitudes."

"Sexist!"

"A woman can kill you just as easily as a man." She turned away from him, striding across the mat to stand facing the wall. "A woman can defend herself just as easily, and I can assure you that size is not a factor."

Gaping at her, Jack blinked in confusion. He shut his eyes and gave his head a shake. "I don't think that women are helpless," he began. "I'm just not comfortable with the idea of striking one-"

"Then prove it!"

She spun on her heel, glancing over her shoulder, her face flushed and twisted into a nasty scowl. "Attack me," she goaded. "Show me that you won't hesitate to defend an innocent man from an aggressive woman."

Jack heaved out a sigh.

Lifting fists into a fighting stance, he began to bounce on the balls of his feet. This would not be easy. Oh, he had no illusions that his superior size would be worth two figs against Anna, but biology was biology. The amygdala didn't really take years of training and a symbiont into account.

With extreme care, he closed the distance between them, feinting from side to side to keep her off balance. As if that would do any good. Still, he had to exploit every single advantage he could.

He threw a punch.

Anna seized his wrist.

She gave a twist and locked his arm in a most uncomfortable position. She pressed down on his elbow, causing him to wonder if she intended to break the bone. Just a little more pressure and she would do just that.

Grinding his teeth together, Jack squeezed his eyes shut. "I think you've made your point," he said, pulling away from her. "Look, Anna, I don't mean to offend you."

"Then let's go again."

Of course they would go again. Jack had only known her for a few weeks, but in that time, he had come to realize she was like a puppy with a chew toy whenever she felt she had something to prove. It seemed she was going to hammer the point home. "If you insist."

Jack stood before her with fists up in a guarded stance, bouncing on the balls of his feet. He stepped forward with a jab.

Anna ducked.

She slipped past him on the right, then kicked the back of his knee. The next thing he knew, he was down on all fours while a sharp strike to the back of his neck sent a jolt of pain through his spine.

Biting his lower lip, Jack squeezed his eyes shut. He felt his face grow redder and redder. "A woman can defend herself," he whispered. "I'm sorry, Anna. From now on, I promise to take you seriously."

"Thank you."

He glanced over his shoulder to find her standing over him with a pleased smile on her face. She nodded once in approval. "It's a lesson that many young men need to learn, even those who grew up with feminist ideals."

"Well, that's comforting."

She chuckled.

So they began again and again with Jack initiating combat each time. He landed on his ass more times than he could count, and those were among the more pleasant ways to be taken down. Sometimes Anna managed to get him doubled over with his arm locked into a painful hold.

But he was learning.

Jack could feel his Nassai working, reinforcing muscle memory every time he tried to deflect one of Anna's punches. They could not communicate abstract concepts unless you put yourself into a deeply meditative state, but they could speed up the rate at which you learned.

He'd grilled Anna on this topic and learned that Nassai preferred to avoid doing this whenever possible. Apparently, forcing the brain to rewire itself at an accelerated rate was risky. Anna's symbiont had only done it because she would have been helpless without the ability to speak English. Likewise, Jack's Nassai understood the need for him to be battle-ready in just a few weeks. After only two hours, fighting made *sense* to him in a way that it hadn't before.

Anna switched things up, of course, attacking him before he could decide how he would attack her. At one point, he found himself fending off a flurry of blows that drove him all the way back to the wall only to realize he had deflected every one. Months of training condensed into a single day.

There were advantages to symbiosis.

Hesitation was his biggest obstacle. There were moments where, after deflecting one of Anna's punches, instinct demanded he deliver a quick jab to her nose. Jack always managed to restrain himself. That was the problem. In those precious seconds where he stood frozen, Anna would snap-kick or knock his leg out from under him. Each time, she assured him this was normal. No one *liked* the thought of inflicting harm on someone else – no one worthy of a symbiont, in any case – so almost every Keeper had to overcome the urge to pull his punches.

When it was over, Anna turned away and wiped sweat off her face with a towel. "I think that's enough for now," she said in a breathy wheeze. "You're coming along, Jack. You're probably dreaming up all sorts of reasons why you aren't learning fast enough, but trust me when I tell you to put that out of your head."

"So, when do we go again?"

"Tomorrow," she said. "And the day after. Your body will heal quickly enough that it shouldn't overtax you. Normally, I wouldn't insist on such a fast pace, but there are only two of us here and we need to get you to a point where you can back me up."

Face glistening with sweat, Jack bit his lip and closed his eyes. He shook his head to clear away the cobwebs. "They're going to put me in the field, aren't they?" he asked. "I thought it would be a long while coming."

Anna somehow managed to keep her face smooth, her emotions under tight control. "You're a valuable member of the team," she replied. "Pennfield has access to advanced technology, and there's no way to know what he's going to throw at us. Without us, these people don't stand much of a chance."

"Yeah," he said. "I understand."

So, he might be put into a situation where he had to use force against someone else. Maybe even lethal force. Could he live with that? Well, it was too late to back out now. He'd just have to muddle through as best he could.

Still, the thought gnawed at him. After staring down the barrel of a gun, Jack had been convinced he would make a good Keeper. But giving up your own life was far, far easier than taking someone else's. He mulled it over well into the evening, wondering if he had made a mistake.

Maybe the symbiont was wrong to choose him.

Chapter 22

Through the back door in his sister's kitchen, Jack could see the wooden deck that overlooked a lawn of dead brown grass. A wooden fence was less than a stone's throw away, rising to jagged peaks under a cloudy sky.

Lauren was kneeling on the deck with her back to the door, hunched over as she inspected something. Dressed in jean shorts, she wore her brown hair tied into a short ponytail. *Well, this isn't going to be fun.*

Jack slid the door open.

His sister glanced over her shoulder, a frown putting wrinkles in her brow. "I didn't expect to see you today," she said, turning back to the potted plant she had been fussing over. "What's up?"

"Mom and Dad are safe," Jack informed her. "Patel has some of her best people on them twenty-four-seven."

"That's good."

Jack slipped his hands into the pockets of his blue jeans, marching to the edge of the deck with his head down. "I figured you'd want to know," he said with a shrug. "You've been pretty worried ever since this started."

Worried didn't even begin to cover it. His sister still thought the Nassai had taken over his body. Talking her out of calling their parents had been a daily chore. In fact, he wasn't entirely sure she hadn't done so against his wishes.

Lauren went as pale as a ghost. "I have been worried," she whispered, "about you mostly. Jack, how could you let an alien share your body?"

Jack gritted his teeth, then slapped a palm over his face. He groaned. "We've been over this," he said in exasperated tones. "It was that or let Hutchinson kill you. He wasn't going to leave any witnesses."

Lauren knelt with arms folded, shivering. She kept her head down so that he could only see the top of her scalp. "Yeah, so you've said," she murmured. "It just...I can't even tell if it's still you."

The sudden burst of anger came on so fast it took him a moment to realize the emotion had not been his own. Apparently, his symbiont was offended by the insinuations Lauren threw her way.

Baring his teeth, Jack shot a glance over his shoulder. He narrowed his eyes, sweat matting dark hair to his brow. "It's me," he said coldly. "The same little brother who used to hide your iPod."

"I still think we should tell Mom and Dad."

Jack frowned, tilting his head back. He blinked as he considered the issue. "If you do that," he began, "you upset some very powerful people in the government. They could hit you with charges."

Lauren spat.

She got up and marched down the wooden steps, making her way across the brown grass. "You know me, Jack," she said, staring at the fence with all its pits and cracks. "I can't leave things unfinished."

Wasn't that the truth. Growing up, his sister had been the kind of girl to colour code her notebooks and leave little sticky tabs on everything. No doubt she was applying that tenacity to the fence. He had listened to her complain about it before. The fence and his refusal to involve their parents.

Lauren seemed to think there was some innate order to the world. Families just did not keep secrets from each other; it went against nature. He had every intention of telling his parents. Eventually.

When he had a handle on things himself.

Jack felt his mouth tighten, a sudden warmth flooding his face. He closed his eyes and let his head hang. "What do you want me to say,

Lauren?" he asked. " 'Okay, let's go against the wishes of my superiors and commit treason?' "

She turned so that he saw her in profile, looking over her shoulder. "I want you to think about how your actions affect me," she growled. "How they affect Mom and Dad. Think of someone else for a change."

"What the hell are you talking about?"

"Correct me if I'm wrong," she snapped, "but right this moment, CSIS operatives are keeping watch on our parents because the billionaire you pissed off might decide to come for a little revenge."

"That's the gist, yeah."

Lauren spun around to face him, crossing arms over her chest. She lifted her chin to fix an icy glare on him. "So, why did you have to get involved?" she asked. "How come this couldn't be someone else's problem?"

Jack winced, turning his head so that she wouldn't see his expression. "Because I'm not willing to let an innocent creature die," he said, backing away from her. "Some things are bigger than you and me."

He turned around.

In the glass door that looked in on the kitchen, he saw his own dim reflection like a shadow against the gray sky. How fitting. That was how he felt right now: submerged in darkness. "Is that really the kind of world you want to live in?" he asked. "A world where people turn a blind eye to injustice?"

His Nassai provided him with a mental image of his sister standing there with her arms folded. It was almost sharp enough to let him see the grimace on her face. "Do not make this about some larger social issue."

"But it *is* about some larger social issue."

"No, it's about *us!*" she shouted. "It's about the danger you've put me in, the danger you've put Mom and Dad in."

Jack closed his eyes, a single tear running down his pale cheek. "Well, that's good to know," he said, nodding. "I'm not going to argue this point further. If you'd feel safer with me keeping my distance, that's fine with me."

He left without another word.

Despite sunlight that came in through the front window, the small bar on MacLaren Street was dark. Neon signs up on the walls cast a colourful glow over tables and booths with leather seats.

Anna found Harry Carlson sitting on a barstool with his back turned, lifting a mug of beer to his lips. Why the man had called her here was uncertain. Mastering the use of one of their cellular phones had been simple enough. Not so different from a multi-tool in all honesty. True, removing all the superfluous applications to allow for faster processing time had been cumbersome, but once she had that done, making and answering calls had been as easy as breathing.

Dressed in blue jeans and a white t-shirt with red flowers, Anna approached the man. "Well, here I am," she said. "So, what precisely did you want to talk to me about?"

He turned.

Carlson wore a troubled expression, his eyes hard as he studied her. He lifted his mug. "Something to drink?" he asked. "Don't worry about the expense. It's on me today."

Anna hopped onto the stool beside him. A drink sounded lovely, but her symbiont didn't care for alcohol, and she disliked the bubbly beverages that most restaurants in this city offered. Too syrupy. By the look of this place, it was highly unlikely she would find decent fruit juice.

Pressing her lips together, Anna shut her eyes and took a deep breath. "A glass of water, please," she said with a nod to the bartender. "With ice and a slice of lemon if it's not too much trouble."

The young man smiled, his cheeks turning red. He bowed his head to stare down at the floor. "Coming right up," he said, hunching over to fill her glass with ice. At times, she wondered what it would be like to work in the hospitality industry. It gave one a chance to meet so many interesting people. What would the young man think if he realized that the woman he served had been born on a different planet?

He set the glass down in front of her.

Anna flashed a smile.

"Thank you kindly," she said, setting a five-dollar bill down on the counter. Harry Carlson had offered to buy the drinks, but she could leave a good tip. She wouldn't want to seem rude. "I appreciate your hard work."

The bartender left with a grin on his face.

Frowning in confusion, Carlson studied her over his shoulder. He shook his head in disapproval. "I thought you were sweet on Hunter, Anna," he said. "Is there some reason you're playing the role of shameless flirt?"

"Excuse me?"

Harry leaned in close enough for her to feel his breath, a scowl twisting his face. "I don't care who you flirt with or sleep with for that matter," he began. "But getting close to that boy would risk exposing things we'd rather keep secret."

"I am *not* flirting."

"Then what *are* you doing?"

"*Vaneesh del vaneeshari,*" she said in her own language, speaking softly enough to avoid being overheard. "Serve the servants." When Carlson looked confused, she felt a sudden queasiness. Didn't these people understand basic courtesy? "When someone is in a position of deference, you go out of your way to be as polite as possible. Behaving as though you're ordering him around is the height of rudeness."

"But he *has* to take your order," Carlson said. "That's his job."

"Precisely the point. In accepting this position, he surrenders a small portion of his freedom. It would be so easy to abuse him or demean him. And, therefore, those of us who avail ourselves of his services must be on our best behaviour."

"Not on this planet," Harry whispered, lifting the mug to his lips. He took a drink, then set it down on the counter once again. "On this planet, you state your order, then pay and go about your business. Most people try not to notice their server."

Anna ground her teeth as she stared into her glass. The heat in her face matched the fire in her veins. "Because you see them as objects," she said, "not as people. They exist only to serve your whims."

Harry Carlson threw his head back, rolling his eyes at the ceiling. "Anna, you are praising him for bringing you a glass of water," he snapped. "My, what a terrible burden it must have been for him."

"And I suppose that's all he did today." Anna threw a glance over her shoulder. "He certainly didn't clean a filthy restroom or tolerate another customer's belligerence with good humour. Learn some manners, Carlson. It won't kill you."

"I'm not going to debate whether this is right or wrong," he muttered. "If you want to avoid drawing attention to yourself, you need to do as we do."

The more Anna learned about *what they did* on this planet, the more she wanted to go home. Of course, she couldn't say as much. And a tiny part of her had to acknowledge the arrogance in thinking that the Leyrian way was the only way. Other cultures had as much right to their customs; there were other valid ways of living.

Of course, there were plenty of *invalid* ways of living as well. Being open-minded did not mean you had to tolerate a custom simply because it *was* someone else's custom. If custom dictated that husbands beat their wives, she wouldn't blink an eye at putting a stop to it, and diplomacy be damned. Besides, there was just as much arrogance in a man thinking that a woman desired him just because she had been polite. "You know, Carlson, a woman should be able to demonstrate common courtesy without every man in earshot mistaking it for sexual attraction. The words *please, thank you,* and *I appreciate your hard work* are not secret code for *would you like to go to dinner?*"

"I see," he said into his mug. "And what do you say when you want to ask someone to go to dinner?"

Slapping a palm over her forehead, Anna let out a frustrated groan. "Well, I generally go with *would you like to go to dinner?*" she said. "It's crazy, I know. You'll just have to blame my estrogen-addled brain."

"Let's talk about Jack," he said, changing the subject.

Anna frowned, her face tight with anxiety. She jerked her head toward the tables by the window. "If we're going to talk," she began, "then let's do it somewhere a little more private, shall we?"

Without waiting, she got up and marched across the room with her drink in hand, making herself at home in a small wooden chair. A little sunlight was a welcome change. Why Carlson would want to meet in a dingy old bar was beyond her.

The man sat down across from her, a tight frown on his face. His dark eyes were intense as he looked her up and down. "Do you think Hunter's ready?" he asked. "You haven't been training him long."

Planting elbows on the table, Anna laced her fingers and rested her chin on top of them. "Ready for what?" she asked, eyebrows rising. "You have to give me some context before I can answer that."

Harry Carlson grimaced, bowing his head to peer into his lap. He seemed genuinely upset. "I've located Hutchinson," he said. "The officer who assaulted me and pulled a gun on Jack. I'll need both of you to bring him in."

"What's the plan?"

Carlson winced, shaking his head as though the thought of discussing it sickened him. "Not here," he insisted. "You two can come into the office tomorrow. We'll lay out the plans then."

Anna heaved out a sigh. Why had the man brought her here if he had no intention of telling her anything concrete? "Well, I can't answer your question, then," she said. "I need specifics."

"Give me a general assessment of his tactical abilities," Carlson inquired. "Can we trust him not to panic in the face of danger?"

Anna bit her lip, nodding to herself. She lowered her eyes to stare at the table and chose her words carefully. "He no longer hesitates before throwing a punch," she began. "Thanks to his Nassai, he's learning at an accelerated rate, and his competence with the basic forms of hand-to-hand combat is solid."

"Will he panic?"

Pursing her lips, Anna looked up to fix her eyes on the man. She squinted, holding his gaze. "There's no way to answer that," she said. "A Keeper never knows how she'll perform until she faces real danger."

Harry looked a tad confused, and it took her a moment to realize that her use of the word *she* was to blame. Curse this language and its lack of a gender-neutral pronoun for living beings. Perhaps Anna should have gone with *he*. No matter. "I believe Jack can handle it."

"Based on?"

"You saw him when Hutchinson pulled a gun on him," she replied. "Did he panic then?"

"No," Harry mumbled. "Kid has guts."

"Then trust him," she said. "And trust me."

Anna brought the glass of water to her lips and downed more than half of it in a single gulp. Dear Companion, she was thirsty. "Thanks for the drink," she said, setting it down on the table. "It was…educational."

When she got home, she found Jack standing at the dining room window with his back turned, peering out at the street. She couldn't quite say what made her think so, but gloom seemed to radiate from him.

With her mouth agape, Anna blinked at him. "Well, the tables have turned," she muttered. "In the interest of fairness, I won't get angry if you snarl at me."

Jack stiffened, refusing to turn away from the window. He clasped hands together behind his back and stood there like a statue. "It's Lauren," he said softly. "She almost accused me of putting my family in danger."

Closing her eyes, Anna trembled as a shiver went through her. "Oh, Jack, I'm so sorry," she whispered. "I never meant to bring such turmoil into your life."

He turned so that she saw him in profile, then glanced over his shoulder. "Meeting you may just be the best thing that ever happened to me," he said. "For the first time in my life, I feel like I have a purpose."

Anna bit her lip, nodding to herself. "Bonding a Nassai will do that," she said, her eyebrows shooting up. "But it never occurred to me that it might also alienate you from the people you love."

"Why should it have?"

"In my culture, symbiosis is considered an honour," she explained. "Only the best and brightest are chosen. I was so driven, so focused on saving the Nassai. I decided that you would make an excellent Keeper after knowing you for only two days. I never once considered the personal consequences for you."

Guilt squeezed her insides into a little ball, so tight she felt as if she might pass out from lack of oxygen. Oddly, her Nassai offered... something. The emotional equivalent of soothing words. The logical part of her mind knew this was the best possible outcome. If Jack had refused the symbiont, it would have perished – a sentient being's life was more important than family drama – but that didn't change that she felt very much like an unwelcome interloper.

She sat down in a chair with hands folded on her knees, frowning into her lap. "I'm sorry," she said, shaking her head. "Sometimes I wish that I had never followed Denario to this planet."

"Right, because it's all your fault."

He leaned against the windowsill with arms folded, shaking his head in dismay. "It couldn't possibly be Denario's fault," he went on. "Or Pennfield's fault. We can only try to do the right thing, An. We can't blame ourselves for what other people do."

Pressing her lips together, Anna looked up to study him. She narrowed her eyes. "It seems you really are a Keeper at heart," she murmured. "Dray Adarus himself could not have said it better."

Jack went red, bowing his head to her. He clamped a hand over his mouth to hide his blush. "Well, I'm full of surprises," he said into his palm. "Lauren is my problem. So please don't tear yourself up over it."

Anna nodded.

Tilting her head back, she stared up at the ceiling, then blinked. "There might be something we can do," she offered. "Maybe if I talked to her, gave her a chance to really know me."

"You think that's wise?"

"Right now, she sees me as the strange alien woman who stole her brother." Anna had been mulling this over for a few days now, trying to put herself in the other woman's position. How would she feel to learn that Alia had been drawn into some scheme by aliens with technology beyond her wildest imaginings? "If she can see me as a person, as a friend even, it might change her mind."

Jack frowned, staring over her head at nothing at all. "That might actually work," he said, nodding to himself. "I hope."

"It's settled then," she said softly. "We need to get down to CSIS."

"What for?"

"What do you think?"

He winced in anticipation of a sudden blow, then rubbed the back of his hand over his forehead. "Yeah, I get you," he said, turning around. "Give me a minute. I'm going to go get the Advil."

Anna bounced on the gym mat with her fists up, a light sheen on the surfaces of her boxing gloves. The look of determination on her face gave him some encouragement. He was actually giving her a challenge.

Face glistening with sweat, Anna frowned as she studied him. She blinked. "So, are you ready?" she asked, coming forward. "We can rest for a few minutes if you need a bit of a breather."

Jack sucked on his lip, then lowered his gaze to the floor. "Ready as I'll ever be," he said, his brow furrowing. "Let's do this."

She charged at him.

Jack leaped and somersaulted over her head, allowing her to run past beneath him. He flipped upright to land hard on the mat, then raised gloved fists into a boxer's stance. With a growl, he spun around.

Anna was ready for him. She kicked him in the belly, then spun and backhanded, her fist whirling around.

Jack leaned back.

The sight of her boxing glove passing in front of his nose was enough to make him flinch. When she came around to face him, he snapped himself upright. He slugged her right in the jaw.

Anna stumbled backward, raising gloved hands to shield her face "Ow!" she said. "You're getting good at this." Now was his chance. Jack knew he had to act quickly to press his advantage.

He charged forward, then dropped to his knees and slid across the mat. He threw a hard punch to her stomach. Anna went flying backward, landing hard on her bottom with a grunt. Against all logic, she recovered.

She curled her legs against her chest and sprang off the floor, landing upright with fists raised. "Not nice, sweetie." She raced across the mat with all the force of a tempest, howling like a mother wolf.

Anna dropped low, sweeping her leg across the mat in a wide arc that would take his feet out from under him. Instinct kicked in before he could think. Jack bent his knees and leaped.

He back-flipped through the air, heart pounding ferociously. He uncurled to land poised upon his feet, bringing up both fists.

Anna was one step ahead of him.

A blur in his field of vision, she charged in while crouched low. She punched him once in the stomach, then rose to deliver a backhand strike to his cheek. Jack flinched, head turning from the force of the blow.

He fell over sideways, landing hard on the mat. A wheezing breath exploded from his lungs. "Jesus," he said, shaking his head. "You're so damn quick. How do you move like that?"

Anna frowned down at him, her eyes narrowed to slits. She nodded to herself, as though deciding to answer. "Practice," she said. "I knew what you were going to do and made myself ready to counter."

"That sweep kick," he said. "It wouldn't have knocked me down. My weight was evenly distributed."

She flashed a wicked grin, her blue eyes alight with mischief. "No, it wouldn't," she said, shaking her head. "But it made you react. It made you act on instinct and set you up for me to take you down."

Jack wiped his face with a towel, then looked up to blink at her. "Well, at least I'll remember that next time."

She offered an impish grin, a touch of crimson in her cheeks. "That's the spirit," Anna said with a quick bob of her head. "Just keep that in mind. We're about to put your abilities to the test."

"More sparring?"

Anna closed her eyes, shaking her head with a heavy sigh. "Afraid not," she said, turning away from him and marching across the mat. "I just got news from Patel earlier this morning. We're going after Hutchinson."

Chapter 23

"Dropping out of warp."

The young navigation officer who sat at a station on the captain's right side wore a black uniform and kept her blonde hair tied back with a clip. Jena could only see the back of her head, but she was fairly certain the woman was scowling.

The bridge of this Viper-Class frigate was large enough to comfortably hold about twelve people, and its gray carpets and curved walls made her feel as though she were standing inside of a very large egg. Captain Taborn, a stern-faced woman with bronzed skin and raven hair, sat in her large swivelling chair. "Show it on main display."

The large screen at the front of the room flickered, displaying the image of a dark circle against a field of stars. They had approached the planet on the night side, and the sun was just barely visible from behind.

Jena looked up to watch the screen. She wrinkled her nose in distaste. "Any sign of Lenai's shuttle?" she asked. "Metal deposits, wreckage. Anything to indicate she was here?"

A young man on the captain's left frowned down at his console. Dark of skin and bald except for a layer of stubble, he had that brash look that was oh-so-common among anyone under twenty-five. "No, ma'am."

Baring her teeth, Jena winced. She heaved out a sigh. "It was too much to hope, I guess," she muttered. "Just to be on the safe side, I suggest we run a full scan."

Taborn swivelled around in her chair, facing Jena with an expression so imperious you might have thought her a queen. "Every system we've scanned so far has turned up no results."

"Which is why we're going to keep scanning until we find something." Even with the faster-than-light properties of SlipSpace, a distress beacon this far out had very little hope of making contact. That its signal had been detected by anyone – a passing cargo hauler, no less – was a miracle. By the time this mission got underway, the beacon had burned out, leaving them with only a vague idea of where to search for Lenai.

They narrowed down the process by searching for star systems similar enough to their own for human life to have a fighting chance – the message transmitted by Dex Arin had been clear on that point – but after searching three systems, they had found nothing. The planet they now orbited had a nitrogen-oxygen atmosphere, but the balance was off. If Lenai was down there, she was probably delirious and gasping for breath.

Touching a finger to her lips, Jena closed her eyes. She took a deep breath, then let it out again. "Full scan," she said. "Let's be as thorough as possible. We do not leave our people behind."

She turned away.

"Operative Morane," Taborn called out.

"Yes, Captain Taborn," she replied in the mildest tone she could manage. "What can I do for you?"

When she turned, she found the other woman sitting with her chin thrust out and a frown on her face. "Need I remind you that this is my ship?" she inquired. "I'm happy to assist in your search, but-"

The alarm started blaring.

Young Lieutenant Noran – the man on the captain's left – grimaced as he scanned his console. "Picking up energy signatures, ma'am," he shouted. "Readings are consistent with Overseer technology."

"Get us out of here!" Taborn bellowed.

The young blonde navigator – Jena didn't know her name – went bone white as she looked up from her console. "They're generating a disruption pulse through SlipSpace," she said. "We can't establish a warp field. Gravitational engines not responding."

"Conventional drives!" Taborn shouted. "Reverse thrusters. All stations, brace for inertia!" The navigator gave a count of five before executing the order.

Jena was suddenly thrown forward, stumbling toward the front of the bridge with hands upraised to shield her face. The bridge officers had secured themselves with seatbelts, but she had been standing.

She went face-first into the wall with just enough force to send a jolt of pain up her arm. "Damn it!" Jena said as she steadied herself. "What's going on? Are they trying to fire on us?"

"Drones rising from the planet's surface."

"Show me!" Taborn ordered.

The screen flickered, producing the image of a small cylindrical object that might have looked like a missile if not for spokes that rose out of its body and curved toward the front. The drone's outer shell looked like flesh...and that was precisely what it was. Overseer technology had been *grown,* not built.

Jena counted three, all breaking orbit and flying toward them. Suddenly, the tip of each spoke burst alight, and particle beams streamed from each to the drone's rounded nose. It released a stream of brilliant energy.

The room swayed in a way that reminded her of a boat on a very turbulent sea, but so far as Jena could tell, there was no real damage. "Shields holding," Noran shouted. "No damage to the outer hull."

"Captain, I've found the reason our main drives aren't working," the navigator said. "There's some kind of structure on the southern continent that's matching our maneuvers. Every time we try to generate a gravitational field, it generates an equally powerful one in the opposite direction."

Taborn had her lips pressed together, her eyes narrowed as she stared at the screen. Right then, Jena would have been happy to be anywhere that wasn't in her field of vision. "Are there any signs of civilization?"

"No, ma'am."

Gritting her teeth, Zai-Ella Taborn shook her head. She leaned forward in her chair, hands gripping the armrests. "Then hit that thing with the biggest nuke we've got. We're going to have to resort to brute force."

Lieutenant Noran complied, and Jena found herself watching the screen. She caught a brief flicker of motion as something erupted from the ship's nose, then waited for what felt like a minute.

The planet hung there before her with its night-side exposed, visible only by the absence of stars and a small crescent of light along the edge. Just when she was about to ask if the warhead had somehow been disabled, a flash of brilliant radiance expanded on the southern continent.

"We're free."

"Reverse course!" Taborn shouted.

Stars wheeled along the screen until they were pointed away from the planet. This time, Jena felt no inertia. Universal acceleration. Everything on the ship had moved at the exact same time.

"No sign of Lenai's shuttle?" she called out. "We haven't detected any of the standard alloys?"

Zai-Ella Taborn was staring at the monitor, her face as red as a roaring campfire. "In case you haven't noticed," she said through clenched teeth, "we're just a little busy at the moment, Operative Morane."

Jena returned her attention to the screen.

Stars began to stretch into thin lines, growing longer and longer until it seemed as though they were flying through a blizzard of narrow white streaks. "We're at Warp," a man's voice called out. Jena was barely cognizant of the speaker. "Heading toward the outer system at 2.25C."

"Maintain course," Taborn instructed. "When we've cleared the system, accelerate to 31kC and head for the next system on our list." She swivelled around in her chair. "If I could speak to you in private, Operative Morane."

Bleakness...

Being the captain of a starship afforded you your own office, which was a generous perk even if the room was not much bigger than a closet. Little more than four walls with a curved desk of reinforced glass, Zai-Ella Taborn's office was decorated with paintings of gardens and forests.

The woman sat in her chair, turned so that Jena saw her in profile. A frown had put creases in her brow. "Let me ask you something, Operative," she began. "Are you under the impression that we're not doing all we can to find your missing Keeper?"

"No," Jena said. "I'm not."

The Captain leaned back in her chair with elbows sitting on the armrests and fingers steepled. When she spoke, her voice was calm and quiet. "Then why is it that you insist on micromanaging every aspect of this search?"

Jena crossed her arms, lifting her chin to fix a steely gaze on the woman. "Well, I don't know," she said, shaking her head. "I suppose it could be my desire to be thorough, though that might be too straightforward an answer."

Taborn grimaced.

Licking her lips, Jena bowed her head to the other woman. She closed her eyes and took a deep breath. "My apologies, Captain," she said. "Your people are all good officers. I just feel responsible for this Keeper."

"Why?"

Jena took a chair across from the other woman. Knowing that she'd have to choose her words with care made this conversation feel a lot like navigating a mine field. "The girl should never have been given this assignment," she said. "Too young."

"I can understand that," Taborn replied. "But it doesn't answer my question. Do you know this Leana Lenai personally?"

"No."

"Then why…"

Several possible responses came to mind, but Jena rejected them all before opening her mouth. There was no way to know if this woman was in Grecken Slade's pocket, and if she was, she might deliberately try to sabotage the rescue.

The only way to be sure that they made a genuine effort to find Lenai was for Jena to oversee every aspect of the process, but doing so was exhausting. "We don't leave our people behind, Captain."

"We also don't put them in unnecessary danger," Taborn said. "They don't call it Dead Space because there's virtually no traffic through this part of the galaxy; they call it Dead Space because coming here *kills* you. The entire sector is littered with abandoned Overseer outposts like the one we just saw. I have half a mind to turn the ship around and set a course for home."

With her mouth agape, Jena blinked at the other woman. "You can't be serious," she blurted out. "We've been to five systems thus far, and this is the first time we've encountered resistance."

"Resistance that might kill us."

You're going to have to tell her the truth.

"I don't trust Grecken Slade," Jena said softly.

Her mouth a thin line, Zai-Ella Taborn studied her with eyes that were cold and calculating. "Grecken Slade is one of the most respected Keepers of our time," she began. "*Why* don't you trust him?"

"A feeling," Jena said. "And the fact that nothing adds up."

"What do you mean?"

"How did Denario Tarse get his hands on a symbiont?" she replied. "The Nassai in our care are well guarded. Why would he take it to Dead Space of all places? Why was Leana Lenai – a girl so green she's probably stopped eating in favour of photosynthesis – sent after him? Why not a more experienced Keeper?

"Why was Leana told to turn back when Denario entered Dead Space? Recovering that Nassai would be worth the risk. Why weren't other ships sent to assist her? And then there's the distress beacon's transmission. The data we received suggests that her shuttle went down over a world nearly identical to our own. Denario Tarse wouldn't have flown here unless he had a buyer. Someone was waiting to receive that symbiont."

Zai-Ella Taborn was frowning into her lap, shaking her head as if she disapproved of what she had heard. "You make a solid case," she said. "But my people aren't trained for investigation."

"That's why I'm here," Jena replied. "We don't have precise coordinates, but we do have a general idea of where the shuttle went down, and we can narrow down the search by focusing on star systems with the right characteristics. That leaves us with about two dozen systems. Let's check them and get to the bottom of this."

The other woman looked up to fix her gaze on Jena, her expression unreadable. "Very well, Operative," she said. "You've convinced me. For now."

Then at least one thing worked out today.

Chapter 24

The small plane was lit mainly by the oval-shaped windows on either side of the cabin, bright sunlight spilling in over leather seats. The constant hum of the engines had faded to a soft buzzing in the back of Jack's mind, but he still felt as though he'd float like an astronaut if he jumped.

He made his way down the aisle toward the back of the plane, passing Patel on his left. The woman sat with laptop open, her eyes focused on the screen. Speaking to her would probably be unwise.

Carlson was in the seat behind her, leaning back with eyes closed, his black hair in a state of disarray. How the man could sleep at a time like this was something Jack would never fathom. But then, Carlson had survived life-threatening situations before.

Two of the TAC officers sat side by side over the wing, conversing softly with each other. One shot Jack a glare as he passed. Doubtful of the new Keeper? Jack really could not blame him.

He found Anna sitting in the window seat and staring out at the clear blue sky. She was the one person on this plane who looked as apprehensive as he did, but Jack figured it had nothing to do with impending danger.

He sat down next to her.

Anna clamped a hand over her mouth, shutting her eyes tight. She looked positively nauseous. "I have to admit I'm not used to this," she whispered. "My stomach's been doing flip-flops for the last hour."

Tilting his head back, Jack closed his eyes. He took a deep breath and then let it out slowly. "You only have to worry about turbulence," he said. "I, on the other hand, have to worry about gunfire."

Anna bit her lip, staring down into her lap. She brushed a lock of hair away from her face. "You're ready for this, Jack," she promised him. "You know what you need to do. Confidence will come in time."

"I'm not so sure."

Jack shut his eyes and turned his face away from her. The touch of leather on his cheek felt sticky. "You're the experienced one here," he went on. "I don't mind dying, but if I screw this up, Pennfield wins."

She laid a hand on his arm.

When he turned, he found her watching him with a solemn expression, blinking as she chose her words. "Every Keeper fears the consequences of failure," she said. "I was much the same on my first mission."

He decided not to press the issue any further. Every new recruit needed a pep talk before his first big assignment, but there came a point where you were only bellyaching. It wasn't gunfire that frightened him – Jack had discovered that he was all too willing to martyr himself – it was the possibility that he wouldn't be fast enough, wouldn't be strong enough. That Hutchinson might escape.

"It makes more sense to send you in," Anna said, repeating the sentiments of just about everyone at the briefing this morning. "If you get into trouble, I can respond with greater speed than you could manage, and Pennfield's goons might know my face."

Anna set her jaw, staring resolutely ahead at nothing at all. "I *will* make sure you get through this," she said, nodding to herself. "That's a promise, Jack. I'll be right there with you the whole time."

She sounded less than convinced. Perhaps, deep down inside, Anna secretly wished she were the one going undercover. Her rational mind understood the necessity of sending Jack in to look for Hutchinson, but she still didn't like the thought of putting him in danger. There were times when Anna reminded him of a mother lioness who saw just about everyone else in this world as one of her cubs.

Chewing on his lower lip, Jack closed his eyes. He nodded once in approval. "You have my complete confidence, An," he said. "I know I'm safe so long as I've got you by my side."

She beamed at him.

Apparently, that had been the right thing to say. A mother lioness indeed. When he was in tenth grade, he had listened to Megan Lowell wax poetic about how important it was for a woman to feel safe in the company of a man. Anna, it seemed, wanted men to feel safe in *her* company.

This should be interesting.

According to their intel – Jack still felt odd using that word – Hutchinson liked to frequent a bar down by the waterfront with several of the same men every night. Patel suspected he was really meeting with Pennfield's contacts. Either way, this was the best place to find him.

A wide black parking lot stretched on toward a box-like building with a big red sign that read "Billy's" over the door. Beyond that, the ground sloped downward to the rocky beach.

Jack stood in the lot dressed in blue jeans and an old flannel shirt that he had left untucked. He had avoided shaving to put a little stubble on his jaw, and the Blue Jays cap on his head would shade his eyes.

Slipping hands into his pockets, Jack started forward. He shook his head and let out a sigh. *Well, now you're into it,* he noted. *Are you sure you wouldn't rather take Lauren's advice and mind your own business?*

No one was waiting for him at the door.

Jack pulled it open to reveal a room that looked like it had once been used as a meat locker. Small metal tables were spaced out on the floor, and the lights hung upon the wall seemed unable to pierce the gloom.

A bar-counter along the wall to his left was home to a wiry little man with tanned skin and short silver hair. He gave Jack a withering glare the instant he stepped through the door. Clearly, strangers weren't welcome here.

"I'm right here with you, Jack," Anna's voice said through the small ear-piece he wore. "We've got our eyes on you, and we'll be there to back you up at the very first sign of trouble."

He couldn't reply, of course.

Three men at the nearest table looked up when he came in. Their leader, a big guy with a brush of short black hair, stood up. So this was the enforcer. Jack didn't know if he would have trouble just getting in here, but it seemed that luck wasn't with him tonight.

"I think you're in the wrong bar," Mr. Big said as he paced around the side of his table. He sauntered up to Jack and stood there like a statue of Hercules. "There's a nice dance club just a few blocks up the road."

Jack smiled, then lowered his eyes to the floor. "I'm looking for a close friend of mine," he said, eyebrows climbing. "Goes by the name Hutchinson. You wouldn't have seen him, would you?"

Mr. Big stiffened.

Grinning from ear to ear, Jack looked up to study the man. He blinked a few times. "Oh come on now," he pleaded. "We're all friends here, aren't we? I know my buddy Wes would like us to get along."

Big shot a glance over his shoulder, frowning at the man behind the counter. His expression softened a moment later. "Grab a beer at the bar," he said at last. "You and I can have a little chat."

Jack strode across the room, trying to project confidence. Somehow he suspected that trying too hard would only make him look nervous. Damn it but he could *feel* their eyes on his back.

He hopped onto a barstool.

The bartender looked up with a frown on his face, squinting as though he wasn't sure what to make of Jack. "What'll you have?" he muttered. "Don't ask for any of that fancy European crap."

"Beer?" Jack said. "Domestic?"

A moment later, the guy put a glass of fizzing lager down on the counter. Jack had no intention of drinking it – if these people really worked for Pennfield, it might well be poison – but he had to look the part.

Mr. Big came up on his right, standing at the bar next to Jack. He frowned down at the counter. "Now, we're gonna have a little chat," he whispered, "about what you know about our friend Wesley."

Through contact with the symbiont, Jack *felt* another man approach on his left. This one was tall and slender, kind of twitchy. Out of the corner of his eye, Jack saw a thin gray beard on his face. "A beer!" the guy shouted. So he was trying to make it seem as though he only wanted a drink.

"Sure thing, Tomas," the bartender replied.

Jack glowered at the countertop, pulling the bill of his hat down over his eyes. "I know only what you know," he murmured. "That you don't cross him if you want to live."

"Why are you here?"

"Isn't it obvious?"

"No."

Jack bit his lip, glancing over his shoulder. He squinted at the other man. "Wesley sent me to check up on Hutchinson," he growled. "The guy's been a little paranoid since that business in Ottawa."

Crossing his arms, Mr. Big frowned at the wall. He nodded to himself with a soft grunt. "Damn straight he is," the man agreed. "Hutchinson should have just killed that kid and ran."

Wiping his mouth with the back of his hand, Jack closed his eyes. He shook his head and muttered, "That would have been an even bigger spectacle. The boss wants to keep it all low-pro, you know?"

A grin broke out on Big's face, and he wheezed with laughter. "You ought to be a rapper, kid," he said. "Pity you won't be able to."

"Why's that?"

The man's face went red as his lips peeled back in a vicious snarl. Spit flew from his mouth. "Because no one knows about that business up in Ottawa," he barked. "The only reason I know is 'cause I'm the one who took Hutchinson in."

Jack whirled around to find three hundred pounds of pissed-off criminal baring his teeth and clenching his fists. "You really don't want to do this," he warned the other man. "I'm stronger than I look."

Mr. Big threw a punch.

Jack ducked and felt the blow pass within inches of his scalp. He drove both fists into the man's stomach like a pair of pistons. His opponent went flying back a few feet before landing on his ass.

Jack sensed motion behind him. His mind's eye perceived it almost as a series of transparent outlines. Tomas was reaching for a gun on his belt, trying to raise the weapon for a fast headshot.

Jack leaped.

He flew backward over the man's head, then landed on the floor behind him. Tomas spun around, raising the pistol.

Jack brought one hand up to strike the man's wrist and knock the gun askew. He slammed the palm of his other hand into the man's face. Tomas stumbled, blood dripping from his nostrils.

Spatial awareness flared up again, and Jack spun around to find a man with a thick black moustache raising a gun in both hands. The man squinted. Panic welled up and Jack reacted by instinct.

CRACK!

The air before him rippled, the image blurred and stretched as though something had refracted the light. Through the shimmering curtain, he saw a single bullet spiralling toward him, mere feet away.

He ducked.

Gritting his teeth, Jack squeezed his eyes shut. He felt sweat matting bangs to his forehead. "Well, this is new," he said, trying to ignore the pain in his temples. "I think I could get used to it though."

He let the bubble pop.

A bullet zipped over his head.

Running forward, Jack seized one of the wooden chairs. He flung it and watched it tumble through the air, striking Mr. Moustache in the face before he could reorient his aim. The other man fell backward.

Lifting his chin to stare down his nose at the fallen man, Jack stepped forward. "I hope we've learned something," he said, eyebrows rising. "Boys shouldn't play with their daddy's guns."

He felt more than saw three other men stand up from tables on the far side of the room. They each drew pistols, raising their guns to point at Jack. Apprehension from his Nassai told him that he couldn't outmaneuver all of them at once.

Biting his lower lip, Jack winced. "And I shouldn't pick a fight in a bar full of criminals," he said. "Okay, boys, let's not do anything that we will regret in the morning."

The front and back doors swung open, each releasing half a dozen agents in black tactical gear into the room. Armed with assault rifles, they dropped to one knee to point weapons at the criminals.

One by one, each of the three men dropped to a crouch and set his gun down on the floor. Only then did Jack realize that his heart was pounding so hard it might just burst right out of his chest. "None of us should underestimate Anna," he said.

As if drawn by the sound of her name, she stepped through the front door, dressed in black pants and body armour. For some reason, she hadn't bothered with a helmet. She likely didn't need one.

Anna shut her eyes and nodded to him. "You did very well," she said, striding into the room. "Now, let's round up these low-lives and escort them all to one of our nice, cozy detention cells."

"How…" one man in the back asked. "How do you move like that?"

Jack grinned, sheepishly bowing his head. "What can I say?" he muttered with a shrug of his shoulders. "Fabulous secret powers were revealed to me the day I held aloft my magic sword and said, 'By the Power of Grayskull!'"

Five minutes later, half a dozen men were on their way to jail.

The battering ram slammed into a door that led to the basement of a small house, forcing it right off its hinges. Inside, Harry saw a small room with linoleum floor tiles and white plastered walls.

Two women in TAC gear leaped through before him, both dropping to their knees and lifting assault rifles. "FREEZE!" one bellowed. "Do not move! I *will* fire; so you just stay where you are."

Harry stepped inside.

He found David Hutchinson sitting on an old brown sofa with a can of beer raised halfway to his mouth. The man was bone white, sweat glistening on his forehead. "Um...hello, Detective Carlson."

Harry narrowed his eyes. "So, here you are," he said, shaking his head. "You'd think Pennfield would spring for a five-star hotel after everything you've done."

Hutchinson closed his eyes and let his head hang. The sheen on his brow seemed to thicken. Or maybe it was just the light. "Look, Harry, it wasn't personal," he said. "I like you fine, but-"

Harry bared his teeth, his face suddenly on fire. He felt as though he might explode from the rage boiling inside him. "Do not give me your excuses!" he growled. "We were never friends, Dave, but I never thought you'd try to bash my skull in."

Maintaining a professional composure was going to be difficult. He would prefer to set an example for the TAC Team – some of them might one day climb the ranks – but at the moment, he just wanted to throttle Hutchinson. "Get on the floor, David," he ordered. "Hands behind your head."

The other man dropped to his knees, lacing fingers over the back of his skull. He flinched and let out a groan. "What are you gonna do, Harry?" he asked. "You arrest me, and it will mean exposing all this stuff you want to keep secret."

"I'll deal with it. Cuff 'em."

A third TAC officer – this one a tall man in a black helmet that hid his face – went over to Hutchinson and dropped to one knee behind him. He seized Hutchinson's wrists, placing a cuff on each.

"Get him out of here," Harry spat. "Is the car ready?"

"Yes, sir."

"Good," Harry replied. "Let's get him to the airport."

He couldn't wait to usher the other man into a nice, comfortable interrogation room where they could learn everything he knew about Wesley Pennfield. They would need a confession from Hutchinson if they wanted to put that bastard in prison. If they could get Hutchinson to admit that Pennfield told him to shoot Jack…well, that was Murder One. That would stick.

Harry felt very much like a cat hankering to sharpen his claws on a juicy, tender piece of fresh meat.

Chapter 25

The first thing Anna saw when she woke was the distant highrise behind the blinds of her bedroom window. A few puffy clouds were floating through the clear blue sky. Just enough for picturesque scenery.

Anna sat up, pressing fists to her eye sockets. She rubbed them and let out a groan. "I hate late nights," she muttered to herself. "If criminals could confine themselves to the afternoons, I'd be very appreciative."

Gritting her teeth, Anna winced. She tossed her head about to shake out the early morning fog. "*Very* appreciative," she whispered. "I might even let a couple go just to prove my point."

The flight back from Halifax had been taxing, and though she had been seated the entire time, her muscles ached worse than they would after a long workout. It was a miracle that she didn't throw up. She had been making a point to keep complaints to herself, but how these people survived with such primitive technology was beyond her. Next she'd be traveling by horseback!

A few moments later, she was pacing down the hallway in beige khaki pants and a gray t-shirt with laces over its deep V-neck. Her hair was tied back, but she could *feel* a few flyaway strands.

At the end of the hall, she found the small kitchen on her right with a pot of coffee already brewing on the counter. Odd. Jack usually slept later than she did. She hadn't expected to see him for another half hour.

Anna found him standing in the living room with a mug of hot chocolate in hand, staring out the window behind the small television. "Morning!" she said in a chipper tone. "Thanks for making coffee."

Jack just stood there with the mug raised halfway to his mouth, still as a statue with his back turned. What exactly was passing through his head just then? Concern dampened her otherwise good mood. "Jack?"

"Hmm?"

"Is everything alright?" she asked, brushing hair out of her face. "You look like that bald space-ship captain just before he launches into a speech about the burdens of command."

He took a sip of his hot chocolate, then lowered the mug again, staring straight out the window. "Just thinking," he said. "I woke up early and couldn't get back to sleep. Too many thoughts racing through my mind."

"Wanna tell me about them?"

Anna moved up beside him, resting a hand on his back. The gesture felt so natural, she didn't even consider the implications until he stirred. Snatching her hand away, she gave herself a silent reprimand. She was his mentor; these feelings were *not* appropriate. When he turned, she almost cringed in embarrassment.

Jack stared at her with a blank expression, blinking as he chose his words. "Just a mix of feelings," he murmured. "At first, I was thrilled – I faced down men with pistols, and I survived – but then…"

"But then?"

"Well, I woke up feeling like I could take on the world, but then it occurred to me that I was celebrating that I just beat up three guys. How can I possibly feel proud of that?"

"Those feelings sound perfectly natural to me," she said. "You *should* be proud, and you *should* be scared."

Bending over with a hand on his stomach, Jack shook his head. "I know I need to keep this under control," he said. "I know these feelings get in the way of doing our job."

Anna frowned, then lowered her eyes to the floor. How exactly was she supposed to explain this? "You've got it all wrong," she said, shaking her head. "Emotions don't get in the way of doing our job. They make it possible for us to do our job."

"But if we hesitate," he said, "it could get us killed."

"But you didn't hesitate, Jack," she replied. "You did what was necessary when it was necessary. That you feel remorse for doing harm to another human being is a sign that you understand the burden of the power you've been given. You *care* about people; so you will use that power wisely."

"And mope like a toddler?" He turned away from her, marching over to the wall, and stood there for a very long while. "Hell, I actually teared up this morning. Everyone always told me I was soft."

Crossing her arms over her chest, Anna scowled down at the floor. She hunched up her shoulders in a shrug. "I'm not saying it will be easy," she began. "But you'll learn how to manage these feelings once you stop lying to yourself."

"And what lie am I telling myself?"

Anger welled up when she considered her words, white-hot magma that burned in her veins. How could someone as noble as Jack not see the truth for what it was? "The lie that strength is the absence of emotion," Anna said, surprised by the gentleness in her voice. Her anger was not with him, she realized, but with the people who had taught him to equate empathy with weakness. "You have a right to your tears, Jack; we all do, men and women alike.

He shuddered, huddling in on himself and moving closer to the wall. The poor guy was really quite upset. "Turn around," Anna said softly. "You don't have to hide what you feel from me."

He whirled around to face her.

Jack closed his eyes tight, tears glistening on his cheeks. He shook his head with a shuddering breath. I'm sorry," he whispered. "I don't mean to dump all this on you; I just don't know what to make-"

Anna stepped forward, slipping her arms around his waist. She buried her head in his chest. "You don't have to be sorry," she said. "Having emotions is a good thing, and I *want* you to share them with me."

Face tight with anxiety, Jack went red. "So how do you do it?" he asked, squeezing her tight. A surge of affection made her return the embrace. Those damned feelings were popping up again. "How do you live with the knowledge that you've done violence?"

Anna looked up at him with wide eyes, blinking as she chose her words. "It takes time," she said, nodding. "But eventually you accept that it was necessary and that your actions protected the lives of innocents."

"Just like that?"

"Jack, believe me," she whispered. "The fact that you're upset says volumes about the quality of your character. Which is top-notch in my opinion."

He shuddered, wiping tears off his face with the back of his hand. "Has anybody ever told you you're a wonderful mentor?" he asked. "It's going to take a little while for me to learn to be as open with my emotions as you are."

His words hit her like a slap to the face.

Closing her eyes, Anna let her head hang. She reached up to brush a lock of hair out of her face. "Physician heal thyself," she mumbled. "Jack, there's something I have to tell you…and it won't be easy."

Every instinct told her to clamp her mouth shut or come up with something else that might follow her last statement – something that did not involve expressing her romantic feelings – but she had insisted on openness. If they were on her world, Jack would have a more experienced teacher, and she would be free to snuggle him up into a big warm blanket and fall asleep in his arms. But there were only two Keepers on this world. Perhaps that meant it was time to rethink the rules. "I think I'm falling in love with you."

Sniffling, Jack smiled at her. Had anyone ever told him he had such beautiful blue eyes. "Yeah, I kind of figured," he said softly. "And I feel the same way. So, what do you want to do about it?"

She turned away from him, pacing across the room with arms folded. "Well, that is a tough one," she said, stopping in front of the couch. "I'm your mentor. Indulging these feelings could create a conflict of interest."

"Normally, I would agree," he began. "But I think this case is different. Anna, you sometimes have to struggle just to be tactful. I have a hard time believing that you would ever lie to spare my feelings."

"A fair point."

"So..."

"So it seems to me there's only one logical thing to do."

In her mind's eye, she saw him standing behind her with hands clasped behind his back, his eyes glued to the floor. "Oh, really," he said through soft laughter. "Well, as long as we're being logical. How do you want to syllogism our way out of this one?"

Glancing over her shoulder, Anna flashed a wicked grin. "How 'bout you meet me downtown tonight?" she said, raising an eyebrow. "Say, at the corner of Bank and Queen around eight-thirty?"

"Yeah, sure," he said. "But-"

"No, no," she cut in. "No questions. It'll spoil the surprise."

Hunching over, Harry slammed his hands down on the metal table and snarled at his prisoner. "Let's go over this one more time," he grumbled. "What do you know about Pennfield's plans?"

David Hutchinson sat across from him, frowning into his lap. Sweat glistened on the other man's face. "I already told you, Harry," he whispered. "Pennfield never shared his deepest secrets with me."

Harry trembled, shaking his head in contempt. "The guy was paying you to take care of his dirty work," he said, straightening. "I have a hard time believing you never made a few educated guesses."

The interrogation room in the CSIS office was very much like the one down at the station: bland and devoid of furnishings of any kind. A rectangular mirror on the wall to his left was actually a window that Patel could use to keep an eye on things. Someone had to keep Harry from throttling the other man.

Hunter and Lenai had been excluded from these proceedings. In his opinion, that was for the best. Though this alliance had served them all well, Lenai was an unknown element, and Hunter had made it clear that his first loyalty was to her. It was no good trying to reason with him. No young man of that age would see sense when he was in love. Harry hadn't.

"What's your answer?"

Hutchinson placed an elbow on the table's metal surface, then planted his face in his hand. "I already told you, Harry," he mumbled. "He ordered me to kill Hunter and bring that device to him. You've got my confession. That's enough to go after him."

"I want more."

Leaning back in his chair, Hutchinson folded his arms. He looked up to fix a dark-eyed gaze on Harry. "What are you gonna do?" he asked, raising an eyebrow. "Torture it out of me?"

Harry closed his eyes, tilting his head back. He took a deep, calming breath. "This is getting us nowhere," he said. "Look, Dave, we both know that Pennfield is dangerous. If you give me some useful information-"

"Pennfield will kill me!"

Resting both elbows on the table's surface, Hutchinson grabbed clumps of his own hair. "I can't help you!" he said, his voice muffled by his own arms. "Pennfield wouldn't tell me something if he thought it might harm him."

A knock at the door came before Harry could reply, and a good thing too. He had been on the verge of screaming at the other man. An officer of the law took an oath to protect the innocent. Only the worst kind of scum would betray that oath for cash, debts or no debts. Perhaps that was why Lenai was so volatile. The young woman had an oath of her own to keep.

When he stepped out into the hallway, he found Aamani Patel leaning against the wall with arms folded, scowling down at herself. "You need to ease off," she said. "Look at that man. He's afraid for his life."

"He should be."

Patel frowned, her face twisting in disgust. "I understand your frustration, Detective," she began. "But terrorizing that man won't get us anywhere."

"What do you propose?"

"If you listen carefully, you'll realize that we've already learned much of what we need to know," she said. "Hutchinson is afraid that Pennfield will kill him even while he serves his time in prison. That suggests connections to the underworld."

"It suggests a lot more than that," Harry said. "But we already knew as much. He's been in contact with aliens, Aamani. We know the Slip-Gate is his means of doing so. It's a variable that we need to remove from the equation."

With a heavy sigh, Patel studied the floor. She nodded, though the gesture came with some reluctance. "My superiors agree," she said. "I'll contact Hunter and Lenai. We should include them in this."

Bill let the body drop.

Elora Sempressa's corpse landed face-down on the floor, her hair dishevelled, her black dress rumpled. The poor woman hadn't even expected him to come up behind her and snap her neck with a quick twist.

"I can't say I like this, Boss," Bill muttered. "Mom always told me never to hit a woman, and now I killed one."

Lights flickered in the ceiling of the cramped underground bunker, shining down on wooden crates that were spaced out on the concrete floor. Wesley Pennfield stood there in jeans and a leather jacket, smiling down at the body. "She thought she could dictate terms to me," he said.

"You are a ruthless man, Pennfield."

A portly man in jeans and a sweatshirt stood across from Bill's boss, his beard so scraggly that Bill half expected to see flies buzzing around his head. "I will not miss Elora," Raolan Carso went on. "But I had not expected her to die quite so violently."

Wesley Pennfield showed teeth in the most vicious smile Bill had ever seen, bright light reflected in his glasses. "The woman is dead," he said. "That's all that matters. Now show me the drones."

Hooking thumbs into the waistband of his pants, Raolan waddled over to the nearest crate. Its side had already been pried open and now leaned against the box to hide what was inside.

Raolan pulled it down.

It fell to the floor like a tree that had been chopped down, exposing two metallic creatures inside. Robots? They were shaped like people with arms and legs, but made of something that might have been steel. In place of a head, each had a device that looked a bit like a TV camera.

Bill felt his jaw drop. He blinked a few times, then looked away from the bloody monstrosities. "You really gonna buy those, Boss?" he asked. "Seems like it'd be pretty damn obvious you're up to something."

"Be quiet, William."

Pennfield stepped forward with a greedy smile that grew larger and larger the closer he got. "Yes," he said, nodding once. "These will do nicely. How much do you want for them, Raolan?"

"Ten…twelve million?"

"Done."

Rubbing his mouth with the back of his hand, Bill closed his eyes. He took a deep breath. *The Boss gets what the Boss wants,* he reminded himself. *But maybe now's a good time for a vacation.*

Pennfield stood there with his chin pinched in one hand, squinting at the dormant robots. "I suspect even a Justice Keeper will find it hard to destroy these," he mused. "Is there any new information?"

The question was directed to the other aide that Pennfield had brought with him on this trip to Europe. James Phillips, a slim man in a black suit, stood off to the side with a tablet PC. "We just had a report from our contact at CSIS," he answered. "Aamani Patel has ordered several of her deep-cover agents to keep an eye on Hunter's family."

"For what purpose?"

"I think they're expecting you to take a shot at them," Phillips replied with a wry grin on his face. "A bit of revenge for the theft of the Nassai."

Crossing his arms with a sigh, Pennfield shook his head. "They really expect me to be so petty?" he asked, turning away from Bill. "I suppose that we should be grateful. Small-minded enemies are easily defeated."

Raolan threw his head back and roared with laughter, his thick face flushed to a fierce red. "They do not know you, my friend!" he exclaimed. "This is most unfortunate for them, no?"

It was most unfortunate for whoever stood in Pennfield's way. The man kept Bill well paid for his services as a low-profile enforcer, but it was not money that bought his silence. Bill knew damn well that if he ever crossed Pennfield for any reason, he would never hear the shot that killed him.

"You're planning to use those?" Phillips said, eyeing the side of the crate. "Weren't we instructed to keep Earth isolated from the rest of the galaxy at all costs?"

"It's too late for that now," Pennfield replied. "My contacts on Leyria have assured me that a rescue ship has been dispatched to recover Anna Lenai. Even if they do not find this system, CSIS has been made aware of the existence of extraterrestrial life, which means the government knows as well. Their next move will most likely be an attempt to access the SlipGate."

"Then we should move it," Phillips insisted.

"No!" Pennfield barked. "I want them to come for the Gate. When they do so, we will activate these drones."

"Two drones?" Phillips said. "Against a team of CSIS operatives?"

Wesley Pennfield spun around with a hand clamped over his mouth. He closed his eyes, breathing deeply. "You don't understand the devastating power of this technology," he said at last. "Furthermore, our goal is not to prevent Lenai from accessing the Gate; if we manage to do so, I will consider it a serendipitous bonus, but our real goal is to create a public spectacle. I want people to witness the violent power of Leyrian weaponry."

Pennfield was genuinely pleased with himself. The only time Bill ever saw the man smile was during these moments where one of his plans came together. "Prepare a media campaign highlighting the dangers of alien technologies. Begin by leaking rumours to the tabloids with emphasis on the devastation we've already seen. Anna Lenai has been kind enough to supply us with plenty of fodder for the rumour mill.

"The firepower unleashed by these drones will cause enough damage to squash any hope of a cover-up. Even if the government denies any knowledge of alien involvement, we will release evidence to the mainstream media with an added dose of fear mongering. If we cannot keep Earth and Leyria apart, we can at least make them despise each other."

Chapter 26

The sky was a deep blue with the onset of twilight, the last rays of the setting sun bouncing off the windows of tall office buildings. Cars whooshed past on Bank Street, headed for the waterfront.

Summer was in full swing with teens and twenty-somethings shuffling along the sidewalk under the light of bright neon signs above storefront windows. Guys in shorts and tees and young women in sundresses. Most weren't that much younger than Jack – and some were older – but they felt like children to him. Children for whom he'd become responsible. Now, that was an odd thing to consider.

Jack stood on the street corner.

He wore blue jeans and a black t-shirt with a V-neck, his dark hair combed so that messy bangs fell over his forehead. "Cheer up, Hunter," he said with a shrug. "You have as much of a social life as them."

Slipping hands into his pockets, Jack frowned down at the sidewalk. "Everybody says you're the life of the tactical briefings," he muttered, shaking his head. "You make covert affairs seem fun!"

The sense of someone approaching made him turn.

Anna stood on the corner in a pale green sundress with thin straps and a bow on the waist. Her hair was tied back with tiny beads on the strands that framed her face, and somehow she had found a pair of green ballet flats.

Grinning like a toddler with a stolen cookie, Anna went beet red. She bowed her head to avoid eye contact. "So with full knowledge of the considerable effort I put into this," she began, "how do I look?"

Jack felt his jaw drop. He squeezed his eyes shut, then gave his head a shake. "Um, you look incredible," he managed without too much trouble. "So, does this mean what I think it means?"

"Well, we've both acknowledged certain feelings." Anna bit her lip, nodding as she chose her next words. "So that being the case, I think you'll be able to figure out what's going to happen next."

"Oh! Oh! I know this one!" Jack exclaimed. "Your old boyfriend Laszlo wakes up from his five-year coma and comes to town in a hackneyed attempt to draw out the will-they won't-they plot for one more season."

"No, silly."

Grinning like an idiot, Jack bowed his head. He chuckled softly to himself. "You mean that's not it?" he exclaimed. "Geez! I guess all those teen soaps really steered me in the wrong direction."

"We're going on a date," Anna said, stepping forward. She looked up at him with the most earnest expression, and for the first time Jack realized she was even more nervous than he was. "So, how should we begin?"

"Frozen yogurt."

"Frozen yogurt?"

For the love of God, how was it possible that hearing her use the word *date* only *strengthened* his anxiety? Jack wasn't an expert on the subject, but he had always figured that knowing a woman reciprocated your affections took the edge off. Apparently not. If those soaps were to be believed, feeling so nervous your nails dug furrows in your palm was supposed to be part of the fun. "Yeah, I know a place," he said in a voice so steady he half wondered if it was really his own. "Come on. It's just a few blocks from here."

She walked next to him, staring down at the ground, deep in thought. "So, I've done some thinking," Anna said, shrugging her shoulders. "And I think that I could learn to like it here."

Jack was a little too wrapped up in his feelings to process what she had just said. In fact, it took him a moment to realize she had been speaking. Christ! Not two minutes into their first date and he had already developed the fabled male attention span. "Earth does have some unique features."

"Such as?"

"The Grand Canyon, the Great Wall of China, global warming. A *thriving* novelty t-shirt industry that I'm told represents point three percent of the GDP."

Anna shuffled along with arms folded, shaking her head as she laughed at his joke. It was good to know that he could make her giggle. "Really?" she said. "Point three? See, I would have figured point two at most."

Jack grinned, pinching the bridge of his nose with two fingers. "And that's why I'm essential to this operation," he said. "Where would you be without me?"

"Lost."

When he looked over his shoulder, he found her watching him with an intensity in those big blue eyes. "Completely lost," Anna went on. "Hungry, frightened and so very, very lonely."

That left him taken aback. He found himself staring up at the skyscrapers on either side of the street, watching the people as they frolicked on the sidewalk. "Then I'm glad I could be of service."

"Can I tell you something?"

"Sure."

Anna walked beside him with her arms crossed, smiling down at the sidewalk. "This is the first real date that I've ever been on," she said with a shiver. "And I'm glad you're the one I get to share that with."

Jack took her hand, twining his fingers with hers, and gave a squeeze. This was a side of her that he'd never seen before. The Anna he knew was the very image of poise and confidence. She could be defiant or gentle or delightfully charming, but he would never have thought it possible for her to be anxious. So far as Jack was concerned, that word didn't exist in her lexicon.

Anna very deliberately stumbled sideways, nudging him with her shoulder. When he looked, she was wearing that impish grin of hers. "I wanted to go in that direction," she said. "You just happened to be standing there."

Business was booming down at Froyo and Sam's with over a dozen young people packed between four walls that were painted in bright neon green and orange. Each and every one of the small round tables was occupied.

Anna stepped in front of him with hands clasped behind her back, turning her head as she scanned the room. "It's colourful!" she said with a bounce in her step. "I like that a lot. What flavour should we get?"

Tapping his lips, Jack turned his face up to the ceiling. He felt deep furrows stretch across his brow. "That *is* a tough one," he said. "But I have to go with chocolate-mint for the win."

"I was thinking about strawberry." Anna whirled around to face him with a big grin on her face, a mischievous glint in those blue eyes. "With real chunks of fruit blended in. Maybe we could share?"

Crossing his arms, Jack gave her a withering glare. He shook his head. "Are you actually turning down chocolate-mint?" he teased. "It's only the most heavenly flavour ever created!"

Anna stuck her tongue out.

Well, it seemed he was going to have to prove his point. Before she could say one word, Jack marched across the room to the yogurt dispensers. He grabbed a cup from the wall and filled it with a blend of chocolate and mint. Thankfully, they kept the spoons on a small shelf nearby.

Through the bond with his Nassai, he saw her coming up behind him. Well, maybe *saw* was the wrong word. It was more of a mental image that began as a silhouette. His knowledge of the room and of Anna's appearance let him add colour without having to think about it. "Oh come on," she said. "Yogurt is always better with fruit."

Jack spun around.

"I love real straw-"

He shoved a spoonful of yogurt into her mouth before she could finish her sentence, and her eyes nearly popped out of their sockets. The spoon waggled up and down as she spoke. "The deliciousness of this confection in no way diminishes the truth of my well-reasoned argument."

Jack slapped a hand over his face, trembling with laughter. "Very well," he said. "If you can still hold out after that, I yield to your superior tenacity. Though I'll point out that I've already filled a bowl, and now I *have* to buy this."

"Damn it!" Anna teased. "He's more clever than he looks."

The lack of seating presented a problem, so Anna suggested they go for a walk. She wanted to see the waterfront, which was fine with him. Hell, he was making this up as he went along anyway.

Was this how most people approached a first date? Nineteen years of Western pop culture had inculcated him with the idea that he was supposed to plan something fairly elaborate. Dinner at a fancy restaurant. It dawned on him that he could actually afford that now, but somehow he had the impression that wasn't the kind of date Anna would enjoy. What she wanted most was to see the city.

That was easy enough to arrange. He led her down Queen Street where skyscrapers stood tall and ominous with lights in their windows. Anna seemed genuinely intrigued by the architecture, and he was almost tempted to ask whether her world had such buildings. That was a silly question, of course; any world that could build star ships would have no difficulty with skyscrapers.

Maybe it was just the thrill of seeing a new place. He'd often dreamed of travelling to Europe and parts of Asia. Mainly just to see what was there. Anna hadn't had much of a chance to really *look* at the city since arriving here.

It pleased him to realize that his initial nervousness had dwindled; in fact, he felt very much at ease. This felt the same as every other time he'd hung out with Anna except that he didn't have to pretend he wasn't just a wee bit infatuated.

Christ, but she was beautiful.

It wasn't that he had never noticed before – this wasn't one of those Rachel Leigh Cook on the Stairs moments – but until today, Jack had never allowed himself to really contemplate it. He had always stifled such thoughts. The idea that she might actually want such attention from him was so novel that he still had trouble believing it.

"What?" she asked when she caught him looking.

Covering a grin with one hand, Jack shut his eyes. He shook his head and tried not to laugh. "Nothing, An," he managed after a moment. "I'm just amused by the number of improbable things that also happen to be true."

A quick walk up Metcalfe brought them to Wellington Street where the Parliament buildings stood tall and proud. With floods of light shining on its facade, the Centre Block – home to both the House of Commons and the Senate – had been visible for quite some time before they finally arrived at its front gate.

Two wings stretched out from either side of a clock tower with dark windows lining each of their five stories. The slanted rooftops had been restored to their proper shade of copper, but a patina of green still covered the tower's peak.

Craning her neck, Anna squinted at the building. She seemed to be lost in thought. "So this is the seat of your government," she said with a nod. "Somehow I had expected something that resembled an asylum."

"I choose to postpone my feigned outrage just long enough to inform you that I've taken the tour, and I can assure you that the walls are sufficiently padded. So why would you go and say a thing like that?"

"If I understand matters correctly," she replied, "your government is well aware of the fact that much of the technology you use is harmful to the ecosystem. Several viable alternatives exist if you would only create the infrastructure, but despite over fifty years of warnings, you do nothing."

"You obviously don't comprehend the situation," Jack said with a nod. "This is all part of our fiendish plan to fend off an alien invasion."

"Oh really?"

"Mmmhmm," Jack went on. "You see, we figure if we act like complete morons, the galactic community will think there's something in the water supply and deem this planet unsuitable for colonization."

Anna crossed her arms, smiling down at herself. She shook her head with rueful exasperation. "Well, I take it back then," she said. "Clearly yours is a nation of brilliant strategists and tacticians."

"Don't be too hard on yourself," Jack teased. "Not everyone can be as clever as the folks in Canadian Parliament."

"Apparently not."

"Come on," he said. "I've got more to show you."

To her great delight, the anxiety that had tightened Anna's chest had melted away to be replaced by a sense of warmth and affection. Relationships were new territory for her; oh, there had been boys in her past, but never anyone with long-term potential. She was only twenty years old, after all.

Revealing her intentions had been difficult. She had been terrified that Jack would look at her like a madwoman when she said the word *date*. Of course, those were the thoughts of a woman who had departed Logic Station on a one-way train to Crazy Town, but you stood a better chance of winning a gunfight with a butter knife than you did of subduing your anxieties with rational thought.

Jack had taken care of that for her.

He had a way of disarming her, of making her feel safe. At first, she had feared it might have been her own naivety – she wanted to see the best in people – but weeks of living with him had proved to her that his kindness was genuine. And his bravery. His intelligence. What would he be capable of if he only saw himself for what he really was?

The black waters of the Ottawa River lapped against the foot of a grassy slope, light from a nearby lamp reflecting upon the rippling waves. In the distance, a bridge stretched across the water to the city of Gatineau where tall buildings stood beneath the starry sky.

Anna sat on a bench with hands folded in her lap, staring off into the distance. For the moment, she was content to just sit quietly and enjoy the view. If she were fated to live the rest of her life on this world, Ottawa would be a fine place to do it.

"So, you've never been on a real date?" Jack asked.

Smiling down into her lap, Anna closed her eyes. She shook her head with a soft sigh. "There's never been anyone to go with," she explained. "When I was a teenager, I had a boyfriend, but it was what you'd call puppy love."

In the dim light, she saw Jack smile. He nodded, staring out at the water. "Well, at least you avoided the drama," he said. "From what I'm told, high school relationships are overflowing with it."

"From what you're told?"

"I never had one," he admitted. "There were girls, but I never quite worked up the courage to talk to them."

Pressing her lips together, Anna stared out on the water. She blinked, considering his words. "How very sad for you," she said. "Of course, it resulted in you being single, which is very good for me."

"I'm glad you have your priorities straight."

"Indeed I do," she teased. "Now that we've got that settled, let's move on to more pressing matters."

"Like what?"

Anna scooched closer, slipping an arm around his waist. He seemed to understand the message and wrapped an arm around her shoulder. Now all she had to do was resist the urge to tickle him.

Leaning her head against his chest, Anna shut her eyes. She murmured contentedly when he squeezed her tight. "Much better," she whispered. "It's not nice to let your date get cold, you know."

At that, he slid both arms around her. Being snuggled up with him brought a sense of warmth and safety that was almost enough to make her forget how far she was from home. A burst of resolve followed. Jack was her friend...her lover, and she would protect him no matter what.

No matter what.

She knew that she would give her life for him without hesitation just as she knew that he would do the same for her. They would fight side by side, drawing a line against injustice, and when all was said and done, the world would be a little better.

Before she could wonder whether he felt it too, Jack touched his fingertips to the underside of her chin. He tilted her face up and brought his lips to hers.

At first it was the most gentle kiss she could imagine, coupled with the soft caress of his fingers on her cheek, but it wasn't long before a hunger came over him. Jack pulled her close.

She seized his face in both hands and broke contact just long enough to nuzzle his nose with hers. Then she was kissing him again, slipping her arms around his back and grabbing his shirt.

Anna pulled away from him, blinking over and over. She tossed her head about to clear the fog. "Wow..." she said breathlessly. "That...that was...where exactly did you learn to do that?"

"For a guy who never had a girlfriend," Anna began, "you certainly know a thing or two about kissing."

Jack was smiling into his lap, shaking his head with amusement. "Well, this might not be a shock to you," he rasped. "But I've been thinking about doing that for quite some time now."

"Really?"

"Yeah," he whispered. "Sorry."

Anna brushed that lock of hair out of her face, squinting as she thought about his response. "Sorry?" she mumbled. "Why in the Verse should you be sorry for wanting to kiss me?"

He scrubbed a hand across his brow, wiping sweat away. Despite his best efforts, his skin still glistened. "It might have made things awkward," Jack said. "I wasn't sure you returned my feelings."

Well, she could understand that. After all, she *had* spent quite a bit of time trying to hide those feelings from him. Trying and failing, but that didn't change that it had probably sent some mixed signals.

Should she tell him that she had imagined kissing him too? That she had imagined *more* than kissing? Images of waking up naked in his arms flashed through her mind, and the heat in her face made her wonder if her skin might catch fire. "Well, Jack, I suppose I can forgive you on one condition."

"Oh?" he asked. "And what's that?"

"Whether or not you're willing to share some of the *other* things you've thought about doing with me."

The apartment was dark except for a bit of moonlight that streamed in through the dining room window, passed through the narrow kitchen and left a rectangle across the hardwood floor. In the silence of night, the only thing she heard was the soft whoosh of cars as they passed on the street below.

Anna stood in the hallway with her arms wrapped around Jack's neck, her nose buried in his chest. "So, here we are," she murmured, clinging to him. "As dates go, this one will be pretty hard to top."

In the pale moonlight, Jack smiled down at her. He kissed the top of her head. "I'm glad to hear it," he whispered. "And I think you should know that tonight exceeded my very lofty expectations as well."

"You had lofty expectations?"

"Mmmhmm," he said, nodding. "They may have included pink unicorns and little heart-shaped notes that read 'Mr. Jack Lenai.'"

Anna giggled, clamping a hand over her mouth. She squeezed her eyes shut and wheezed. "That's not nice!" she teased. "Making fun of me for sharing my feelings! So much for your gentle, sensitive side."

She understood that all too well. The whole way home, all she could think about was what she planned to do when she finally got him alone. There young women – most of them religious – talked about saving themselves for that one special person. Anna had never been one of them.

To her, sex was neither magical nor mysterious; it was simply part of human nature, nothing more, nothing less. She might have experienced it long before, but for the fact that she had bonded a symbiont at such a young age. She had often daydreamed of becoming a Justice Keeper, but most people did not join with a Nassai until they were

Jack's age or older. The last few years had provided her with very few opportunities to socialize with young men. Most male Keepers had been at least five years older than her and not at all interested in teenage girls.

Now, she realized that physical intimacy was something that she very much wanted to experience with Jack. She just...didn't want to experience it right this moment. Telling Jack how she really felt, going on dates, passionately kissing him – this was all new to her. She wanted time to let it sink in before she moved on to the next step.

"Anna?" Jack whispered. "My God, you're trembling!"

"I'm sorry."

Jack stared at her with his mouth agape, blinking in confusion. "You don't have to be sorry," he said, shaking his head. "Anna, I didn't mean to upset you. I really did have the most wonderful evening."

"It's not that," she said. "I just...Jack, I'm sorry. I know we talked about all of the wonderful things we want to share, and I *do* want to experience them with you! I just don't think I'm ready for-"

She didn't have to say another word.

Jack slipped his arms around her in a tender hug, letting her rest her cheek against his chest. He placed one hand on the back of her head, gently stroking her hair. "It's all right. You don't have to justify yourself to me. I'm not sure I'm ready to go that far either – not yet, anyway – and I would never be angry with you for wanting to take it slow."

"Really?"

"Really," he whispered. "I know this should go without saying, but even the most magical evening does not entitle me to expect anything more than you're willing to give. Sex isn't compensation for a job well done; I get that. I wasn't sure what to expect when we walked through that door, or how I would react if *you* had wanted to go further. I'm glad we're on the same page."

"Oh, it's official," Anna mumbled. "I'm so in love with you right now."

His lips curled into a tiny smile, just before he pressed them to her forehead in the softest kiss. "Right back at you," Jack whispered. "There is one thing I'd like to ask... if that's okay. Would it be alright if we fell asleep in each other's arms?"

Covering her mouth with her fingers, Anna closed her eyes. She felt hot tears slide over her cheeks. "Yes," she said, nodding. "Yes, I would like that very much. You have no idea how happy that would make me."

"Really?"

"When I go to sleep each night," she said, "I find myself thinking of all the people I miss. My family, my friends. It's so easy to just keep my mind busy all day long, but once I get in bed, it's just me and my worries."

"And then I think of you," she went on. "I close my eyes and pretend you're there next to me, and I feel so warm and safe that I just drift off. From the very first night I fell asleep in your bed, I've always known that I was safe with you."

"I..." Jack shook his head. "Wow."

"Give me five minutes," she said. "I'll come join you."

Thin curtains billowed in the breeze that came in through the window, and silver moonlight made his furniture stand out as dark shadows against the blackness. The air was just cool enough for sleep, a welcome change from the heat wave that left you warm and sticky in the middle of the night.

Jack found himself pleasantly drowsy, ready to slip away into dreamland. Anna hadn't been kidding when she mentioned feeling warm and safe. Right now, he honestly believed that everything would be all right. Tomorrow, he would likely worry about Pennfield's next move – or the problems with his sister, or how he would tell his parents about the symbiont – but for tonight, he could put his worries aside.

"Hey..." Anna said softly.

She stood in his doorway in a pair of shorts and one of his old gray t-shirts. On her tiny body, it may as well have been a circus tent. Her hair was left loose in a bob that fell to the nape of her neck.

"You're beautiful," he stammered.

Anna smiled down at herself, shaking her head. No doubt she was blushing like an open fire. "It's just an old t-shirt," she said, stepping into the room. "Not exactly the most flattering thing I could wear."

"You still pull it off."

She moseyed over to the bed, pulled back the covers and hopped in next to him. Rolling over, she smiled at him in the moonlight, and the look of joy on her face was quite possibly the most beautiful thing he'd ever seen.

"Thank you," she murmured.

"For what?"

"For letting me stay with you."

Mashing his cheek against the pillow, Jack shut his eyes. He took a deep, soothing breath. "Thank *you* for joining me," he whispered. "You aren't the only one who benefits, you know."

Anna snuggled up to him, slipping an arm around his chest where she rested her head and murmured, "I'll keep that in mind." After that, she was silent, drifting off to sleep.

For a long while, Jack just lay there, stroking her hair with one hand while he stared up at the ceiling. Anna felt safe with him; that brought him joy. After knowing her for only three days, he realized she would fight tooth and nail for the people she loved. He could always count on her. It was good to know she felt the same way.

Some time later – maybe fifteen minutes, maybe twenty – he became aware of the sound of her breathing. Slow and steady. She had fallen asleep in his arms. He could only imagine the weight she carried. Light-years from home with only a few years of training and no one to back her up. She was quite honestly the strongest person he had ever met, and he was honoured to call her a friend.

Drowsiness came a few moments later, his thoughts melting away to be replaced by the soothing sound of her breathing. For the first time in several years, Jack Hunter fell asleep feeling perfectly content.

Chapter 27

Anna had never been one to spend much time musing on interior design, but even she could see that someone needed to give the CSIS briefing room a – what was that odd English word? A *makeover*.

Little more than a long wooden table between four white walls: the briefing room seemed to embody the concept of blandness. There were no paintings or sculptures, no plants, not even a window.

Aamani Patel stood at the head of the table in front of a white projector screen. As usual, she wore a black pantsuit and kept her dark hair tied back. "Thank you both for joining me today," she said. "We have much to discuss."

Dressed in gray pants and a black short-sleeved blouse, Anna sat with hands folded in her lap. "Thanks for having me," she said, nodding. "I assume you want our help with another operation."

"Not that we'd mind," Jack added.

He sat on the other side of the table in a brown jacket, his dark hair combed forward so that bangs fell over his brow. "The enemy of my enemy and all," he went on. "It's good to work together."

Standing before them with hands clasped behind herself, Patel frowned and turned her head to stare at the wall. "We've reached a decision," she said with some reluctance. "We're going to take out the SlipGate."

Anna felt her mouth tighten as she studied the other woman. "That's an ambitious plan," she said, blinking. "As I said, it will be extremely difficult to move the SlipGate, and disabling it will be just as hard."

"What about destroying it?"

Anna licked her lips, then lowered her eyes to stare into her lap. She heaved out a sigh. "It's not that simple," she murmured. "I have no doubt that you could find enough explosives, but that Gate is located in an office building."

Jack bit his lip as he stared off into space, nodding to himself. "Lots of potential civilian casualties," he said. "There's got to be some other way to disable the Gate without risking any lives."

"That's why I've called you here." Patel crossed her arms, shaking her head with frustration. "Can you offer any suggestions?"

Well... could she? There were ways to disable SlipGates, but she was no expert on Overseer code. Bleakness, the best software engineers on Leyria had learned to parse out the algorithms, but she was no programmer. Each Gate had security measures, and most multi-tools could interface with them, but...

Pursing her lips, Anna stared into her own lap. She closed her eyes and nodded to herself. "I might have one idea," she began. "I could put a security lockout on the Gate. A password that would prevent anyone from accessing it."

"What will that do?"

"Think of it like stealing Pennfield's car keys," Anna explained. "The SlipGate will remain in perfect working order, but Pennfield will be unable to activate it."

Patel was no fool; it took only a few moments for her to work out the unfortunate implications of this plan. "Won't he eventually crack the code?" she asked. "What's the use in a temporary solution?"

Anna winced, shaking her head. "There *is* no use in a temporary solution." With a sigh, she swivelled around to face the table. "Our best bet is to contact my people."

"My government does not support that plan."

"Why not?" Jack asked.

Patel scowled at him, her cheeks suddenly aflame with anger. "You may be willing to accept them on face value, Mr. Hunter," she began. "The rest of us are not. Is it really so hard to understand why we might fear people with such advanced technology?"

"This might be moot in any event," Anna cut in before the two of them could start arguing. Jack had more patience with this kind of political wheeling and dealing, but no good would come from debating something that might not even be a factor. "If Pennfield already has a security measure in place, I won't be able to do much."

Patel heaved out a sigh, slumping over as though a huge concrete block had been strapped to her back. "Then our best bet is to destroy the Gate," she said. "How much of a blast will it take?"

"I won't support such a plan."

"Me neither," Jack said. "Not if civilians might get hurt."

Anna wanted to kiss him right then.

"Then it seems I have no choice." Patel spun on her heel and began pacing across the room with her arms crossed over her chest. "I will consult my superiors. If your plan is approved, Anna, we will move forward.

"We intend to go in through the parking garage. The two of you will be responsible for getting the rest of us in the front gate. I assume getting over the fence won't be much of a problem."

"It shouldn't be," Anna replied.

"Good," Patel said. "We meet back here in three hours. I should have a final go-ahead by then."

A fence of green metal bars walled off a line of pine trees that swayed softly in the wind. Beyond that, Jack could see the Penworth building rising up toward the night sky with lights in the windows.

They were on a small street behind Wesley Pennfield's property, and if he strained, he could just make out the top of the parking garage. Going in the back way had seemed like a good idea, but now that he saw that fence, he wondered if he could actually make that leap.

Crouched on the sidewalk in black cargo pants and a Kevlar vest over a matching t-shirt, Jack let out a groan. "Can we jump that high?" he asked, "I know we bend gravity, but there has to be some kind of limit."

Anna stood beside him in identical gear.

She turned her face up to the sky and blinked a couple times. "The only limit is time," she said. "Can we hold a Bending long enough to make it over those trees? It will tax our Nassai."

Jack sucked air through his teeth, staring down at the sidewalk. He felt sweat break out on his forehead. "Can't say I like that idea," he muttered. "We'll need them both at full strength if we come up against resistance."

Anna chewed her underlip with a thoughtful expression, nodding when she reached a conclusion. "There may be a way," she said at last. "If we stand close enough and make a Bending together, our Nassai can share the load."

"Let's do it then."

"Whenever you're ready."

Jack stood.

Closing his eyes, he focused and imagined a small dent in space-time that lessened gravity's pull. His Nassai responded with a burst of encouraging emotions that told him she could make such a Bending. He felt Anna beside him, felt that odd warping sensation as she got to work.

It was slightly different from the Bending that he had imagined, but Jack's Nassai assured him that she could improvise. He formed the image in his mind – this had to be a team effort, symbiont and host working together – and felt space warp around him.

He nodded.

Bending his knees, Jack sprang off the ground and shot up into the air with Anna right beside him. They crested the fence together, and the tree line beyond it, dropping to a grassy hill at the edge of the parking lot.

He landed in a crouch, hanging his head from the mild throbbing in his temples. "I guess that wasn't so bad," he muttered, releasing the Bending. "How you holding up over there, Anna?"

"Fine."

When he opened his eyes, he saw an empty lot that stretched on to the three-level parking garage behind the building. Tall lampposts at even intervals shone cones of light down on the yellow grid that stretched across the concrete. There were a few cars – most of them near the front – but they would be exposed as they crossed the open ground.

The parking attendant's booth was near a gate in the fence off to his right. People entered this lot through a side street to avoid slowdowns in traffic on the main road. "You ready for this?" he asked.

"Ready."

Anna was up and racing across the concrete in half a second, re-markably fast for someone of her short stature. *Well, all right then,* he thought. *I'll just bring up the rear and watch your six.*

Jack started after her.

Clenching his teeth, he winced and shook his head. *You're so bloody impetuous, my love,* he thought. *It doesn't seem to occur to you that Pennfield might have snipers up on his rooftop.*

Office building or no office building, he wouldn't put it past the man to do such a thing. Pennfield was obviously willing to rely on black-market assistance for his security needs. As he considered the possi-bility, however, he felt a burst of information flood into his mind. A gift from his Nassai.

He could sense the rooftop – there were no obstructions in the way – and he felt nothing up there. Of course, his perceptions couldn't be trusted at this range. Even Nassai had their limits.

Anna ran straight toward the passenger side of an old SUV, then fell to her knees right next to it. She was doubled over, drawing that fancy Leyrian pistol from the holster on her belt.

Mopping a hand over his face, Jack shut his eyes. He tilted his head back, breathing deeply. "How do you want to play this?" he asked. "It's probably smarter if just one of us takes out the attendant."

Anna glanced over her shoulder, strands of hair falling over her face. She blinked sweat out of her eyes. "I'll get up close and stun him," she said. "You watch my back in case he has help."

"Got it."

Anna held the pistol in front of her face, squinting as she studied it. "Stun rounds," she ordered, causing the LEDs to turn blue. Only she didn't say *stun rounds*. The pistol only responded to commands in Leyrian.

"Anna, let me ask you a question," he said, startled by the sensation of new words on his tongue. "What language is this?"

She smiled into her lap, her cheeks flushed to a soft pink. "It seems your symbiont has taught you to speak Leyrian," she said, eyebrows rising. "Be glad. It took three days of sounding like a toddler for me to learn English."

As if that wasn't a miracle in and of itself!

"Come on," she said. "Let's move."

Anna got to her feet and ran around the back of the SUV. The only thing he could do was follow. *Have a little faith in your best friend,* Jack told himself. *She's been doing this a lot longer than you.*

Anna went charging toward a small booth where a man in a white shirt stood with his back turned. He seemed to be reading a newspaper. Jack had to give his partner this much credit: she was fast and quiet.

She dropped into a crouch right next to the booth, holding the pistol in both hands. From here, Jack could see that she was frowning, nodding to herself as she planned her next move.

She knocked on the door.

A moment later, it swung inward, allowing the attendant to step out into the cool night air. He turned his head, scanning the parking lot for the source of the disturbance. He had just enough time to fix his gaze on Jack when Anna fired.

A stun round hit the side of his belly.

The man spasmed, his arms and legs flailing as though he had been hit by a Taser. In a way, he had. Stun rounds were charged with just enough electrical current to give a grown man a good zap.

The attendant stumbled forward, landing face down on the pavement. Poor fellow. This was better than killing him or beating him senseless, but it could still do harm. If the guy had a heart condition...

Clamping a hand over his mouth, Jack squeezed his eyes shut. "Will the guy be alright?" he asked. "I'm not a doctor, but that *couldn't* have been good for him."

"He should be fine," Anna said. "The Gate?"

"Right."

Inside, the little booth was so cramped that Jack could barely raise his arms without hitting both walls. A workstation with a computer monitor and keyboard was positioned under a window that looked out on the street. He saw only a few shops on the far side of the road, but he knew his team was out there.

Biting his lower lip, Jack squinted down at the console. He nodded to himself. "It has to be here somewhere," he muttered. "If I were the switch that raised the guard rail, where would I be?"

A big red button.

He pushed it.

Instead of the explosion that he more than half expected – some clichés were far too obvious – the black-and-white guardrail moved upward to make a clear path for vehicles to enter the parking lot.

He left the booth just in time to watch a large gray van pull up through the narrow lane that led to the street. Headlights blinking, it settled to a stop right in front of him, allowing him to peer through tinted windows on the driver's side.

The door slid open. "Come on!" a harsh voice beckoned from the darkness. "We don't have all bloody night!"

Jack didn't waste another second. Hopping through the opening, he dropped to his knees on the van's floor. He couldn't see much, but enhanced spatial awareness allowed him to sense half a dozen people buckled into seats on his left and another half dozen on his right.

Anna followed mere moments later, grunting as she knelt down on the floor. She muttered something in Leyrian – something about pig-gish men with nasty BO; he had been studying the language – and then pulled the door shut.

Before he could so much as think, the van was moving again. He had been bonded to the Nassai for several days before he noticed an improvement in his sense of direction. That has always been pretty solid – Jack had been able to find his way home from almost anywhere – but the symbiont had made it even easier.

Even trapped in the pitch-dark van, he could tell they were driving toward the building and then turning toward the parking garage. So far, the plan had gone smoothly. That made him nervous.

Nothing was ever this simple.

After a quick ride in a very cramped space, Anna felt the van settle to a stop. The side door slid open, giving her a view of a huge parking lot beneath the glare of fluorescent lights in the concrete ceiling.

To her surprise, there were still about a dozen cars parked between here and the back wall, staggered at uneven intervals. It seemed the janitorial and security staff liked to shield their vehicles from the elements.

She hopped out.

Jack followed her, trailed by a line of half a dozen men and women in black tactical gear, all wearing helmets with visors pulled down. They were quick to form a perimeter, the ones in front dropping to one knee and swinging their rifles back and forth to identify any potential targets.

Anna pinched her chin in one hand, closing her eyes tight. She took a deep breath and let it out slowly. "Does this seem a little too easy?" she asked in a quiet voice. "After my last visit, I'd have expected more security."

Jack was frowning into the distance, blinking as he considered the question. "Right there with you, An," he said, nodding. "I've had a strange sinking feeling in the pit of my stomach ever since we jumped the fence."

Anna felt her lip quiver, then turned her face away so that he wouldn't see her anxiety. "Maybe we're just being paranoid," she muttered. "A good habit so long as it doesn't get in the way of your job."

There was a gap of perhaps ten feet between the side of the van and two cars that were parked nose to nose, a gap that was very quickly filling up with warm bodies. Anna had a very uneasy feeling.

In the corner where the back wall intersected with the one to her right, a door led into a stairwell. That was to be their point of entry. If this mission went as planned, they would descend the steps to the basement and navigate a series of corridors until they reached the room where Pennfield kept his storage crates. From what she had been told, most of those contained parts for jet engines.

Aamani Patel came striding through the gap between the van and the nearest car. Like the others, she wore black pants and an armoured vest, but her face was uncovered. Anna understood that. Morale went up when soldiers saw their captain's face. "So far, so good," she said, approaching them. "We should get a move on."

"This is too easy."

Patel lifted her chin and studied Anna. She narrowed her eyes, no doubt wondering if everything was on the up and up. "It's too late to back out now, Anna," she said. "And we're well-armed. There's little that Pennfield can do to stop us."

Anna frowned, then lowered her eyes to the floor. She felt her eyebrows climb up and up. "If you insist," she muttered. "But I've learned the hard way not to underestimate that man."

Her multi-tool began to beep.

"Something's wrong," Anna barked, checking the display screen on her gauntlet. "The Gate just started broadcasting its location into SlipSpace. Anyone within a dozen light-years will know it's here."

Patel's face crumpled as though someone had just kicked her in the stomach. "We need to move quickly then," she said, turning and making her way toward her tactical officers. "Head for the stairwell."

Men and women in tactical gear sprang into action, hoisting up rifles and filing out of the space between the van and the two cars. They turned left, toward the back wall, heading for the stairwell door.

Anna hesitated, placing a hand on Jack's arm to prevent him from following. Why would Pennfield activate the SlipGate? Why would he broadcast their location? Earth's solar system was smack dab in the middle of Dead Space. There would be no one within a dozen light-years to receive that broadcast. Activating the Gate would serve no purpose unless...unless Pennfield knew perfectly well that alien ships were in the area.

"Pull back!" she bellowed.

Three men who brought up the rear of the group suddenly turned around...then froze. In a heartbeat, they brought up rifles to point at something on the other side of the van. "Hold!" one shouted.

"Am I interrupting?" someone called out.

That voice...it had come from the other side of the van, somewhere between here and the entrance to the parking garage. Anna would know those harsh, grating inflections anywhere. That was the voice of the man who had shot her.

"Vincent..." she whispered.

Jack looked up, his face suddenly pale. "Vincent?" he said, deep creases forming in his brow. "That guy is *here?*"

Now halfway to the stairwell door, the tactical officers halted and spun around to face the newcomer. The front rank dropped to one knee, lifting rifles to point at Vincent while those behind aimed over their heads.

They formed a firing squad in the roadway between two lines of parking spaces. A few cars on their left and their right would provide a safe haven, but every one of those officers had a sprint of at least five paces between himself and cover.

"Now, now," Vincent said. "Let's not be rash."

"Bleakness, take me!" Anna growled. With the van in the way, she couldn't use her Nassai's talents to see what was happening. That left her with only one option. Motioning Jack to follow, she crept forward, past the driver's seat. She saw a man through the small window sitting with his hands clenched on the steering wheel.

When she peered around the corner, she saw Vincent standing with his back to the open garage door, flanked by a pair of metal soldiers that stood head and shoulders taller than him.

Battle drones.

Both robots waited with arms at their sides, camera lenses pointed toward the group of TAC officers. Their sleek metallic exoskeletons reflected the light from the fluorescent bulbs overhead.

Dressed in black pants and a vest of his own, Vincent stood with his arms crossed, the ski mask pulled tight over his face. "So glad you could join me," he said. "Put down your weapons, and I promise you a swift and painless death."

Patel was crouched at the end of the front rank with a sub-machine gun in hand, her face grim. "At my count," she said, nodding. "There are three of you and over a dozen of us. Stand down."

"Shut up, Patel!" Anna shouted.

"Would that be Miss Lenai's voice?" Vincent asked, shaking his head. He let out a soft, satisfied chuckle. "You should listen to her, Director Patel. You have no idea what you're up against."

Pressing her lips together, Aamani Patel squinted at the man. Even from here, Anna could see sweat on her skin. "Would you be one of Mr. Pennfield's employees?" she said in soft tones. "Consider yourself under arrest."

"*Magak,*" Vincent ordered in Raen.

At his command, both drones started forward, moving past Vincent, then coming together to shield him from oncoming gunfire. They continued on their inexorable march forward, feet clanking on the concrete.

"Get to cover!" Anna screamed.

The TAC officers ignored her.

Assault rifles flashed while the harsh growl of automatic weapons' fire filled the air. It did no good. Screens of white static appeared before both drones, intercepting every bullet and sending slugs dropping to the floor.

The force-fields vanished.

A few bullets sparked against the robots' chest plates, but did nothing to slow their advance. In unison, both drones lifted their right arms and took aim at people along the front rank.

One man spasmed as blood fountained from his neck, falling forward to land facedown atop his rifle. Other officers followed, all tumbling to the floor after a quick shot to the throat.

The people in second rank started backing away, keeping their rifles up to loose a barrage of bullets at their attackers. Idiots! Apparently, they still didn't comprehend the futility of doing so.

The drones halted side by side, erecting force-fields to shield themselves from the incoming fire. Enough physical damage to their bodies would eventually cause them to shut down, but unlike organic soldiers, their bodies were powered by several high-yield fuel cells. They could recharge their force-field generators in seconds.

While the drones took shelter behind their kinetic barriers, the TAC officers were offered a brief reprieve. Force-fields were essentially walls of electromagnetic energy. Nothing could get in, but nothing could escape.

Of course, they could...

The force-fields sped forward side by side: two screens flew down the roadway and slammed into the tactical officers with the momentum of a pick-up truck. Men and women were tossed about like leaves in the wind.

Lifting her pistol up in front of her face, Anna squinted at the weapon. "EMP!" she said, nodding once.

The three LEDs on the barrel's surface turned white. Now all she had to do was get a clear shot before one of those robots put a slug in her head. A time bubble might protect her from a single drone, but she needed something to distract the other.

Patel had taken refuge behind a cute little green car with the Earth letters V and W on its hood. "Aamani!" Anna called out, silently cheering when the other woman turned her head. "Have your people fire on the one on the left!"

Patel nodded.

Three TAC officers were crouched behind a black sports car not far from Patel. They nodded as well. "On three!" one said. "One! Two! Three!" They aimed rifles over the hood of the sports car and fired.

The drone on the left suddenly staggered as bullets pounded its body. Halting its advance, it raised a buzzing force-field to intercept the slugs. Now was her chance. *Have to make this count.*

Anna spun around the hood of the van.

She raised the pistol and fired. Blue tracers sped toward the other drone, which paused just in time to erect a force-field. The screen of static flickered, disrupted by the EMP rounds, and bullets slammed into the robot's chest.

The residual charge that each slug carried shorted the drone's circuitry. Stumbling like a drunken man, it raised both arms to steady itself. "Threat level reassessed," it said in Raen. "Recalibrating targeting parameters."

Anna ducked behind the van.

Jack stared at her with an open mouth, then quickly gave his head a shake. "What now?" he asked. "I don't suppose you have one of those fancy guns for me, huh?"

"The one I shot is coming after me now," she told him. "These things do not stop until they have eradicated all targets. But I think I can handle one. You'll have to help the others."

"How?"

"Improvise."

Anna got up, pressing her back to the van, sweat drenching her hair. "You can do it, Jack," she said, screwing up her courage. "Remember, no matter what happens, I believe in you."

Anna charged forward, toward the pair of parked cars. With a thought, she put up a small Bending behind herself. Sure enough, bullets struck the patch of curved space-time, turned and went off toward the wall.

She leaped.

Anna somersaulted over the parked car, then fell to the floor behind it, crouching down. Releasing her Bending, she tried to ignore the tingling in her skin. The loud pings of bullets striking the car's body made her flinch.

Gritting her teeth, Anna winced and felt tears slide over her face. "Don't give up on me now, my friend," she whispered. "They're counting on us. We just have to hold out a little longer."

Not far ahead, a black pick-up truck took up most of the space between two yellow lines. After that, it was a short run to the concrete pillars near the back of the room. There were two: one on this side of the lot and one on the other.

Anna ran.

She leaped and twisted in mid-air, landing hard on her side in the bed of the pick-up truck. Seconds later, bullets whizzed through the space above her. Luckily, that other car had prevented the drone from getting a clear shot.

Bending gravity – reversing its pull – Anna lifted herself into the air and then threw herself over the side of the truck. She landed on all fours. This time, the tingling became sharp little stabs of anguish.

Staying low, she started forward.

Spatial awareness told her that the truck would provide cover until just before she rounded the pillar. At the very last second, she threw up a Bending – the pain worsened – and heaved a sigh of relief when bullets curved away from her body.

She slipped around the pillar.

Pressing her back to its surface, Anna shut her eyes. She took a deep breath through her nose. *Rest now,* she thought. *If you keep using your abilities, you're going to pass out from the strain.*

No time to rest.

Tiny vibrations surged through the concrete as the drone began shooting the other side of the pillar. If nothing else, the damn thing might just decide to spend the next ten minutes chipping away at her only source of cover.

With any luck, the thing had ignored Jack. Trapped as he was between parked cars, the drone could have gunned him down in seconds as it passed, but Anna was its primary target now. Battle drones tended to prioritize targets by threat level. *He's a clever man,* Anna told herself. *He'll adapt.*

But what was she to do?

Jena didn't know why she insisted on remaining on the bridge; she was useless up here. Perhaps it was just a deeply rooted belief that sitting in the Mess Hall and reading her novel would not count as doing her job.

About ten feet in front of her, the back of the captain's chair blocked her view of the large display screen at the front of the room. A young man was seated at the station on her left and a woman at the one to her right, both hunched over so that she could only see the backs of their heads. Lorans and Helani, respectively. She had made it a point to learn their names.

Jena frowned into her lap, closing her eyes tight. She heaved out a deep breath. *It won't be much longer now,* she told herself. *We've checked almost every system on our list. Either we find Lenai, or-*

"Captain," Lorans said. "I've found something."

The chair swivelled toward him.

Spinning around to face his commanding officer, the young man wore a puzzled look on his face. "It's the distress beacon, ma'am," he mumbled. "Someone's reactivated it."

Jena stood.

"Point of origin?" Taborn asked, turning so that she faced forward once again. It irked Jena that she could not see the other woman's expression. Even a Nassai could not help with that.

Lorans turned back to his console, hands dancing across the touch-screen interface, sliding application windows over the desktop. "A main sequence star roughly two-point-three light years from here," he said. "We can be there in about half an hour."

"Set a course," Taborn ordered.

Finally, Jena thought. *Some answers.*

Chapter 28

The instant Anna took off, Jack slipped into the narrow space between the van and the concrete wall. That hulking monstrosity would be passing soon, and he wasn't about to let himself be caught with his pants down.

Heavy metal footsteps thumped on the floor. He took a quick peek and found that the drone had already passed him. It stood with its back turned, raising its arm to fire a tempest of bullets at one of the pillars near the back wall.

Chunks of concrete went flying, dropping to the floor. No doubt Anna was behind that pillar. He had to do something, but what? The only thing he had was a crappy nine-millimetre pistol and no fancy ammo.

Pressing his lips together, Jack closed his eyes. He forced out a sigh. "Think, Hunter," he scolded. "Your greatest weapon has always been your brain. Start using it."

He moved carefully to the other side of the van, then, with a lot of courage, took a peek around the corner. The second battle drone had moved off toward the garage's front entrance and now stood with its back to him, firing at the wall.

There were several cars parked along that wall, and from the way the battle drone shredded their windshields, it was a good bet that several of Patel's men had taken cover behind them. *Think! Think! Think!*

Symbiosis

About ten paces away, the man called Vincent stood with arms folded, observing the mayhem with casual confidence. The drones weren't targeting him, even though his attire was almost identical to that of everyone else in the room. That meant he likely had some device that flagged him as a friendly.

If Jack could steal it...

Vincent had taken position near a door in the wall that led to another lot identical to this one. No doubt the man planned to make a timely escape if events should fail to go in his favour.

Only one thing to do. Jack drew the pistol from the holster on his belt, released the safety and stepped out of cover. With the aid of his Nassai, he watched the battle drone while keeping his eyes on Vincent. For the moment, it seemed to be ignoring him.

Jack lifted the pistol.

Without warning, the other man's head whipped around, and he studied Jack through the holes in his ski mask. Anna had said that the man possessed a symbiont. Not a Nassai but something else.

"Call off your drones," Jack ordered.

"You must be joking."

Jack frowned at the man, shaking his head. He felt sweat rush over his face in thick waves. "I don't want to pull this trigger," he said, "But either you put a stop to this, or we find out if you're really as good as a Keeper."

Vincent looked down at the floor, no doubt frowning behind the ski mask. "You do have guts, boy," he muttered. "I'll give you that much. You don't have to die with Lenai. Join me."

"Like hell."

Crossing his arms, Vincent shook his head and chuckled. He seemed to view the whole thing as a joke. "It won't work, boy," he mocked. "You can't intimidate me. We both know you don't have it in you to pull that-"

CRACK!

The air in front of Vincent shimmered, transforming him into the rippling image of a black shadow. A bullet struck the pulsating curtain, turned lazily in a wide arc and flew off to the left.

The blurry Vincent backed away, grabbing the door handle in one hand. He pushed it open and stepped through just before the Bending vanished. As the door swung shut, he disappeared out of sight.

Pink-cheeked, face slick, Jack lowered his eyes to the floor. "Just let him keep you talking," he said, approaching the wall. "I mean, it's not like that's the oldest trick in the book or anything."

Pushing the door open, he found himself staring at yet another empty parking lot, this one blessedly devoid of gunfire. He saw no sign of Vincent, but the guy could not have gotten very far.

Jack stepped through.

A boot kicked the pistol out of his hand. Only then did he realize that Vincent had been standing next to the door. A hand seized the back of Jack's shirt and flung him hard onto the concrete floor.

He landed on all fours, bracing himself against the impact. With blessings offered by his Nassai, he perceived Vincent standing behind him with arms crossed, shaking his head in disgust.

Jack turned his head, shutting his eyes tight. He felt a single tear slide down his cheek. "Of course, it could be worse," he muttered. "You could fall for the *second* oldest trick in the book."

The onslaught of gunfire continued, sending tiny vibrations through concrete that shielded Anna from a storm of bullets. Battle drones carried half a dozen magazines of nearly a hundred bullets.

The pain in her skin had faded to a dull tingle – a sign that her Nassai was starting to recover – but if she used her talent again, it would return. Still, she couldn't stay here. Something had to be done.

Anna shut her eyes, leaning her head against the concrete. She drew in a shuddering breath. "I may need your help again," she told the symbiont. "A few good shots and we'll destroy that thing."

She felt encouragement.

"Alright, then."

She drew the gun from her belt, releasing the safety. "EMP!" she growled, watching the LEDS turn white. If she could inflict enough damage to the drone's circuitry, she just might be able to destroy the thing.

With a thought, she warped space-time and erected a bubble that was large enough for her to move around the pillar. The inside of its spherical surface became a shimmering curtain that made the walls and floor look as though they were under water.

She stepped around the pillar.

The tingling became a stabbing pain, but she saw the drone as a blurry figure with its arm thrust out, firing a line of bullets at the pillar. With any luck, that Bleakness-taken monstrosity hadn't seen her.

Raising her gun in both hands, Anna squinted. She fired and watched blue tracers appear beyond the bubble's surface, electrically charged bullets slowly spiralling toward their target.

The bubble popped.

Charged bullets punched through the drone's exoskeleton, blue sparks flashing over its metallic body. It stumbled backwards, unable to maintain its balance. Anna fired again and again.

More bullets pounded the robot, causing it to dance about. She saw a tiny flash of sparks from the force-field emitter on its chest. So that had been shorted out. Good. Now all she had to do was-

Something emerged from the robot's hip, a tiny cannon about the size of her closed fist, pointed right at her. Anna reacted without thinking. She ducked behind the pillar and waited for the blast.

With a loud *POP,* the cannon tossed a grenade that landed on the floor and skittered to a stop right next to her. Panic welled up within her, nearly overwhelming her ability to think straight.

Anna threw herself sideways.

She flew as straight as an arrow with her arms outstretched, then landed on the floor and somersaulted over the concrete. In the blink of an eye, she was crouching behind the other pillar.

She glanced over her shoulder.

The grenade exploded with a thunderous growl, shattering the damaged pillar into a hundred shards that flew off in all directions. Anna threw up a Bending, the air behind her rippling just in time to deflect several large pieces of shrapnel.

She slumped against the pillar, vision fading.

Closing her eyes, Anna let her head droop. She felt sweat mat drenched hair to her forehead. "Have to hold on," she groaned. "Come on, symbiont, you're up for some more adventure, aren't you?"

Bullets whizzed past the pillar, striking the back wall of the garage and pounding holes in the concrete. The pattern they made looked like a child's scribble, back and forth and up and down. Was the drone just waving its arm about drunkenly? Had she damaged its targeting circuits? That would explain why it hadn't gunned her down when she moved from one pillar to the other.

Her body felt as though it had been pummelled by a herd of stampeding rhinos, but if the drone was damaged, she might have a chance. The LEDs on her pistol were still glowing white.

Anna aimed around the pillar.

The drone stumbled backward through the roadway between parked cars, one arm upraised to fire bullets at the ceiling. Chunks of concrete rained down upon the floor, and light bulbs shattered.

Anna fired, sending blue tracers toward the capering robot. They slammed into its metal chassis, sparks flashing over its body. With a sound like thunder, the drone fell to its knees.

"High impact!" Anna bellowed. The LEDs on her gun changed from white to red, indicating that each round would be launched at twice the normal speed. She'd be unable to use full-automatic fire with this setting.

Anna squeezed the trigger.

A bullet crashed into the robot's chest with enough force to put a deep crater in the metal. Several more ripped holes in the drone's body, leaving its innards exposed to the open air.

The drone dropped to all fours, landing in a pose that reminded her of a cowering man begging for his life. It was over at long last. With muscles that felt like wet noodles, Anna heaved out a sigh of relief. *Thank the Comp-*

The drone prostrated itself, and she noticed the small bulbous protrusion where its spine should have been. Like the top of a dome, or half of a perfect white sphere. She had a sudden sinking feeling in her belly. *It can't be...*

The sphere emerged from the socket in its master's back, floating upward and then reorienting itself to point a lens at her. Seconds later, that lens began to glow with fierce orange light.

Anna ducked behind the pillar, crouching down.

No! No! No! she screamed inside her own head. *Not another Death Sphere! The universe can't be that cruel!*

She watched an orange particle beam slice horizontally through the pillar, leaving red-hot concrete in its wake. Had she been standing, that beam would have lopped her head off at the shoulders.

The air sizzled, painfully hot.

She had to move before the sphere recharged its emitters, but the moment that she emerged from cover, it would gun her down. Death Spheres were programmed to react to motion, and-

Of course!

Anna twisted around, raising her gun in both hands. She took aim at the other pillar and fired. High-impact bullets ripped chunks of concrete out of what had already been a ruined mass of jagged stone.

They fell to the floor.

Before she could so much as blink, an orange particle beam hit the other pillar and sliced right through it, heating the concrete until it glowed with crimson light. The sphere reacted just as she'd hoped it would, assuming the falling rocks indicated the presence of a target. Those things weren't nearly as sophisticated as true battle drones. They fired on anything that moved. Period. Now she had a few moments before it recharged.

Anna got up.

She turned and ran for the stairwell door, sweat coating her face in thick waves. She didn't even bother shooting at the sphere; those things could bob and weave until you had emptied your entire clip. She had to lure it into a trap.

Pushing the door open, she found a set of steps that led up to a landing with lights on the concrete walls. Another set led down to the basement, but instinct told her the high ground would serve her better.

She started up the stairs.

Clenching her teeth, Anna squeezed her eyes shut. She became aware of the furious heat in her face. "Just a little bit longer," she told herself. "After killing a drone, this thing will go down easy."

She rounded the landing, then started up another flight of steps toward the second floor. The parking garage was only two stories high. From the railing that overlooked the stairs below, she could watch the sphere as it came up in search of her.

"You can do it," Anna told herself. Those words sounded hollow but she repeated them several times. One way or another, this was going to be over soon; she just hoped it wouldn't end with her body reduced to a pile of ash. "EMP!" she ordered. The gun made a soft beeping noise as it changed settings.

Strangely, she found that the anxiety that twisted her stomach in knots had nothing to do with fear for her own life. Now that she had a moment to breathe, she realized that she was very worried about Jack.

There was a crackling squeal that could only be the sound of the sphere burning through the door below with its particle beam. The wretched stench of scorched plastic confirmed her suspicions.

Moments later, the sphere came floating over the stairs below, pivoting from side to side as it searched for her with its lens. *Now. Before it sees you!*

Anna leaped.

She flipped over the railing, turning upside-down in mid-air. Thrusting her arm out, she fired several blue tracers right through the sphere's polished surface. Sparks flickered as the thing fell to the stairs and rolled down to the first floor.

Anna landed crouched on the top step.

She threw herself sideways, sprawled out upon the landing as the sphere exploded with a violent cacophony. Shards of metal flew up from below, most bouncing harmlessly off the stairwell walls.

One left a rather nasty gash across her calf, tearing through the fabric of her pants. The stinging pain that followed rivalled that of overtaxing her symbiont.

Anna bared her teeth, wincing so hard she thought she'd burst a blood vessel. "Bleakness take you, Pennfield!" she said. "Who gives you these damn weapons?"

So far, Jack's plan to attack Vincent had not gone well. The other man stood with his back to the door, arms folded as he stared down at Jack. "What a pitiful little thing you are," he said. "Who would make you a Keeper?"

Baring his teeth, Jack snarled at the man. He felt sweat roll over his face. "A very kind symbiont," he whispered. "One with a lot more integrity than you could ever hope for."

He stood.

The sounds of gunfire in the other room sent shivers down his spine. He had to end this soon if he wanted to save his team. Fear seized his heart in an iron grip at the thought of something happening to Anna.

Vincent looked him up and down, squinting through the holes of his ski mask. "Ah. Is that fear I see?" he asked, coming forward. "Well, boy, at least you demonstrate some small amount of wisdom."

Something about the way he speaks...

Jack veered off to his left, moving deeper into the lot. The last thing he needed was a stray bullet to the head while he was trying to survive a fistfight. His symbiont told him there were several cars behind him.

"I'll make the offer one more time," Vincent said, rounding on him. The man now stood with his back to the garage's open front entrance. In the distance, Jack saw the pine trees that lined the fence he had jumped. "Work with me. Use your talents for the benefit of humankind."

Frowning to himself, Jack looked up to fix his gaze on the other man. He narrowed his eyes. "Does that line actually work?" he inquired. " 'Cause I'm pretty sure you'd have better luck with 'Did it hurt when you fell from heaven?' "

"Hide behind your japes, boy," Vincent said, coming forward. He moved with a kind of predatory grace, like a wolf about to run down a squirrel, stopping right in front of Jack. "If you wish to die, it can be arranged."

"Did you just say 'jape?' "

Vincent threw a punch.

Jack's hand came up, striking the man's wrist and knocking the blow aside. With his free hand, he drove fingertips into Vincent's throat. The man gurgled, eyes flaring behind the holes of his mask.

Jack snap-kicked.

Vincent caught his ankle, holding it pinned against his stomach. He gave a tug, and the next thing Jack knew, he was falling over backwards. Spatial awareness kicked in and gave him a chance to react.

Slapping hands down on the concrete, Jack thrust his feet into the air and rose into a handstand. He flipped upright just in time to see the other man coming forward with fists upraised.

Vincent slammed a palm into his chest.

Bent gravity sent Jack flying backward over the empty parking space. He landed hard on his ass, skin torn from the friction. Damn it, this guy was good. Anna had said so, but until now, he hadn't understood the extent of the danger.

The other man came striding toward him. He lifted his chin to stare down his nose at Jack. "Is that the best you can do?" he asked. "The power of a symbiont, and all you can manage is some pitiful flailing about?"

Curling his legs against his chest, Jack sprang off the ground. He landed on his feet, bringing fists up in a boxer's stance. "Hardly," he replied, drawing upon every last scrap of martial arts training he had ever had. His opponent drew near, and Jack squelched the sudden burst of terror.

Vincent kicked high.

Jack ducked and felt the man's foot pass over his head. He watched Vincent's leg come down, watched the other man begin a spinning back-kick. Pure instinct took over before he could think.

Dropping to his knees, Jack seized the man's ankle just before a rubber sole made contact with his nose. *Now, before he recovers!* He flung Vincent's leg aside, forcing him to turn around.

Quick as a blink, Jack stood.

He punched Vincent's chest with one fist, then the other. He drew back his arm and slammed his open palm into the other man's nose. Blood soaked through the fabric of that black ski mask.

Jack threw another punch.

Vincent caught his wrist, twisting in a way that forced him to stand with his side exposed. The other man kicked him hard in the belly. Jack was made to double over as he tried to catch his breath.

A blow to his head fuzzed his vision. Before he even realized what was happening, he was down on all fours, trying desperately not to empty his stomach. The world spun in circles. "Come on, Hunter..."

No matter how badly his body hurt, his sense of spatial awareness remained as clear as the noonday sun. The silhouette of Vincent drew a pistol from the holster on his belt. He released the safety.

Calling on his Nassai, Jack pushed himself off the floor. He used bent gravity to fling himself sideways, colliding with Vincent and knocking the other man off his feet. They both fell to the floor.

Jack rolled away.

When his vision cleared, he saw a gray sedan parked with its nose to the concrete wall, blocking his view of the door he had come through. If he could get there before the other man got his bearings...

Jack stood up and ran.

Clenching his teeth, he winced and felt spittle fly from his open mouth. "Come on, Hunter!" he rasped. "You can do this!"

In his mind's eye, he saw Vincent sit up and reach for the gun that had landed at his side. *Come on! Come on!* The other man picked up his pistol and got to his feet, groaning audibly.

Jack leaped.

He flew like Superman with his arms outstretched, passing right over the top of the car. He landed flat on his belly, skidding on the concrete. Seconds later, the car's windows shattered as bullets punched through them.

"I'm going to kill you, Hunter!" Vincent bellowed. "Rest assured of that!" Jack had no doubt that the man meant every word, and with the car in the way, he couldn't monitor Vincent's movements.

His own pistol was lying on the ground not far from the door that led back to the other garage. If he moved a few feet, he would reach it. Jack crawled toward his weapon, keeping low to make use of the car's protection.

The sound of gunfire drowned out Vincent's footsteps, but his Nassai told him that the other man was not in a line of sight. Not yet. He had to retrieve the pistol before that happened.

Glass crunched beneath his gloved hand, tiny shards digging into his palm. Jack suppressed the urge to scream. That might send the other man running over to finish him off with one quick shot, and-

Glass!

Jack scooped up a handful of it, ignoring the jagged edges. Calling on his Nassai, he readied a Bending that would change the pull of gravity. A burst of reassuring emotion told him this would work.

Vincent stepped around the car, lifting his pistol.

Applying the Bending, Jack whirled around and flung the glass. Tiny shards flew toward the other man – *fell* toward the other man – and Vincent backed away, raising an arm to shield himself.

Jagged glass punched through his vest and buried itself in his forearm. Kevlar armour was not designed to deflect sharp things. Knives would slip right through without any real difficulty.

Vincent's arm flailed, his pistol going off with a *CRACK! CRACK! CRACK!* and launching slugs toward the ceiling. *Now!* Jack thought, snatching up his fallen gun. *Let's even the odds!*

He spun around, extending his arm. He fired several times, and the recoil sent a jolt of pain through him.

Bullets slammed into Vincent's stomach, deflected by his vest, but the impact threw him to the floor. He landed on his backside, wheezing and gasping in pain. *Now, for the fun part.*

Jack stood up.

Raising the gun in both hands, he snarled at his opponent. Sweat seemed to gush from his pores. "Drop your weapon," he ordered in a voice that sounded so very unlike his own. "I'm serious."

Vincent complied.

Marching over to him, Jack seized the top of the ski mask and yanked it off in one quick motion. The bruised face of Wesley Pennfield stared up at him, blinking as tears rolled over his cheeks.

"It's old man Pennfield!" Jack exclaimed. "The guy who used to run that haunted amusement park." When his mocking provoked no response, he added, "You're supposed to reply with, 'And I would have gotten away with it, if it weren't for you snooping kids!'"

"You have no idea what you've unleashed," Pennfield said. "The re-union of the Lost Sons is a sign of the End."

A loud *ca-chunk* from the back of the room startled Jack, but rather than take his eyes off Pennfield, he used his spatial awareness. Someone had opened the stairwell door, the one in the far corner.

Anna stepped out, limping on her right leg. Elation burst through him the instant he realized it was her. Fighting for his life had left him little time to contemplate what was happening in the other room, but he had been quite afraid for her safety. "I see you have things well in hand," she said.

Stepping away from Pennfield – a moment's inattention would allow the man a chance to reach for his gun – Jack grinned. "I could say the same for you," he replied. "I should have known you'd carve that robot into little chunks."

Blushing hard, Anna smiled down at the floor. "Well, what can I say?" she asked with a shrug. "Fabulous secrets were revealed to me the day I held aloft my sword and said, 'For the Honour of Grayskull!'"

"Nice reference!"

"Thank you," she said. "I Googled."

"What should we do with him?" Pennfield was gritting his teeth, snarling into his lap. He shook his head and growled. "Even with the two of us for guards, shoving him into a cell will be hard."

"You are both fools!" Pennfield looked up to flash clenched teeth in an ugly scowl. "Do you honestly believe you can *hold* me?"

"Way to break a guy's heart, Wes," Jack mocked. "I was thinking we could spoon on the couch with Jewel playing in the background."

Anna frowned, looking down at herself. She heaved out a soft sigh. "We still have people out there, Jack," she said. "People who need our help. Order him to deactivate the second drone."

"You heard the lady."

"I think not." Pennfield stiffened, turning his head so that Jack could only see him in profile. "Why would I give away my single bargaining chip? If you want to save your friends, you'll have to make me an offer."

Jack felt his face redden, nodding to the man. "You make a very good point," he said, stepping forward. He pressed the barrel of his gun to Wesley's forehead. "So either you turn off the machine, or I fire."

"You don't have the stomach."

Could he do it? Could he really kill a man in cold blood? Sure, he had fired on this guy earlier, but at that time *Vincent* had been another combatant on the field. Now, he was at Jack's mercy. "I suspected as much," Pennfield muttered. "You Keepers are all soft and unwilling to do what must be done."

Wincing so hard that he trembled, Jack looked away from the other man. He felt a growl rumble in his throat. "Fine," he spat. "I guess my paragon score goes up. We'll just have to make another deal."

The tiny smile on Anna's face told him that she agreed with his decision. She kept her eyes on the floor, remaining silent, but he knew. "I hope you're not modest, An," Jack said. "'Cause we're about to see some naked billionaire."

"Excuse me?" Pennfield said.

"I figure if I strip you down to your birthday suit, there'll be a pretty good chance that whatever's protecting you from the drones will no longer be an issue. Then we're gonna take a little walk to the other garage."

Pennfield looked up at him with cold gray eyes that reflected the fluorescent bulbs overhead. "How would that be different from shooting me?" he asked. "Murder by proxy is still murder."

Jack grinned, bowing his head to the other man. "You're forgetting something," he said, eyebrows shooting upward. "I'm not the one who turned on the drones. Technically, this is *suicide* by proxy."

"Devious," Anna murmured. "But I'll allow it."

"I will not comply."

"That's fine," Jack mocked. "Anna never really got to have her college-girl phase; so I'm sure she's happy to start ripping your clothes off. Do a little dance, and she might even give you a tip. You have a belt knife, don't you, An?"

She produced it with a flourish.

Pennfield bit his lip, his face turning red. "Very well," he growled, pulling a small rectangular device from the pocket on his vest. "I will do as you ask. But this isn't over, Hunter."

"Yeah, yeah," Jack said. "You can give me the villain speech tomorrow. I'll make it a point to visit your cell. Tonight, I just want a shower."

The roar of gunfire went suddenly silent, leaving Jack with an uneasy feeling in his chest. He had grown so used to the cacophony that its absence felt wrong. Now, all they had to do was wrap up.

The metal monstrosity came lumbering out of the door that led into the garage, one arm raised to point a closed fist at them. With dents and chips in its gleaming armour, it turned its head to fix the camera lens on Aamani.

"Not yet," she whispered, lifting her sub-machine gun. "We need to hold on just a little while longer. Lenai won't let us down."

The red sports car that had been parked beneath the open air provided cover for the time being, but that didn't stop her from flinching when bullets started zipping over her head. Lenai had managed to destroy one of these beasts – and she would see to it that the other woman received a Medal of Honour for that – but her crew had had no luck with the other one.

Two men in black gear were hiding behind cars on her left and her right, each with a rifle in hand. As one, they aimed over the hoods of their respective vehicles and then let loose.

The robot stumbled just before a screen of flickering white energy shimmered into place, intercepting each slug. Aamani could see them falling uselessly to the ground. Her weapons had no effect.

Pursing her lips, Aamani shut her eyes tight. She shook her head with a gasp that all but drained her lungs. "There has to be something we can do," she said. "Allah above. It can't be invincible."

The screen of energy shot forward to slam into the other side of the car she'd used for cover. The impact was enough to rock the vehicle and shatter all windows, sending glass raining down on her. If any of it cut her skin, Aamani didn't notice. Adrenaline had taken care of that.

Sparks flashed across the robot's body as it tried to lift its arm to take aim, causing it to stumble about. Aamani didn't bother to watch what happened next. She hid behind the car with fingers laced over her head.

Bullets zipped through the air above her.

"I bear witness that there is none worthy of worship but God," Aamani whispered. "I bear witness that Muhammad is the Prophet of God." It was a prayer that she'd been taught as a child. She only half believed, but now seemed like a good time to find what faith she could.

Just like that, the thing stopped firing and lowered its arm to point at the ground, the light in its camera lens suddenly going dark. Had someone shut the thing off? By Allah, why would Pennfield do so now?

"Is everyone alright?" she called out.

"I'm fine," McConnell shouted. "Bruce is down."

Aamani spun around, putting her back to the van. She tilted her head back, shutting her eyes tight. "All right," she said. "Start rounding up the wounded. Michael, Maaz, you two are on first aid."

She ventured out of cover.

The robot just stood there with arms at its sides, head pointed down at the ground. For all intents and purposes, the thing was dead. Or at least off. "Call in back-up. Let's get these people to a hospital."

The garage door behind the robot was still open, and for the first time, Aamani truly noticed the damage that had been done. Cars had been shredded to pieces of scrap metal with shards of glass on the floor.

The large pillars at the back of the garage looked as though they had been gnawed on by giants, and both bore scorch marks. Lights flickered in the ceiling, one going out in a shower of sparks.

Aamani shuddered

She was so focused on the devastation that she barely noticed as somebody came stumbling up on her left. A man in black pants and a turtleneck walked with his hands in the air, his face bloodied. Despite that, Aamani had no problem recognizing his features.

She closed her eyes and let out a deep breath. "Wesley Pennfield," she said, removing her helmet, tossing her head about to let her black hair fly loose. "It seems you're a man of many surprises."

"Heh-hem."

Anna Lenai stood a little ways off with fists on her hips, a stern expression on her face. "I think someone else deserves your compliments," she said, jerking her head to the side. "*He's* the reason you're still alive."

Hunter leaned sideways, peeking at her over Pennfield's shoulder with a big grin. "Uh, hi there, Director," he said. "If it's all the same to you, can we skip the praise and segue directly into securing that SlipGate?"

"Agreed."

"The Gate will do you no good," Pennfield muttered. "You cannot begin to comprehend what you-"

"Hey!" Jack said, nudging him. "What did I say about gloating, Wes?"

The man went silent.

Aamani turned, surveying the empty parking lot. Several cars had been turned into smoking wrecks beneath the tall streetlights, and several of her people spread out on the ground. Anna Lenai had already chosen the nearest victim, and now knelt near his body with her back turned.

The gibbous moon was high in the night sky, casting silver light across clouds that floated over the city. It would have been a pretty night if not for the carnage. Her stomach did flip-flops.

"Director Patel!" A young man in black gear came running toward her, panting with every step. "You need to hear this, ma'am."

Lifting her chin, Aamani fixed her gaze on him. She arched a dark eyebrow. "What is it, Karl?" she inquired. "Is everything alright?"

He stopped in front of her, hunching over her and heaving out a breath. "Radio is out, ma'am," he said, shaking his head. "Can't get a cell phone signal either. Something's flooding every frequency."

"What?"

He removed the small radio from the pocket on his vest, turning up the volume with a quick twist of the knob. "*Endo ori en valis,*" a voice said through the speaker. "*Enasko an teyglar kaine ronis enday Leana Lenai.*"

Anna perked up.

An icy lump found its way into the pit of Aamani's stomach. She didn't much care for the implications of those words. "It means 'we are here peacefully,'" Lenai provided. "We seek a Justice Keeper whose name is Leana Lenai."

Aamani breathed deeply.

"Director," Jack added. "I think the Leyrians are here."

Chapter 29

Anna stood in the parking lot with hands in her pockets, watching as the shuttle settled to a stop and hovered just above them. Nearly six weeks had passed since her arrival on this world, and in all that time, all she could think about was how much she wanted to go home. Now, all she could think about was how much she wanted to stay.

The shuttle was a small craft, shaped like the head of an arrow with a large canopy window that looked in on the cockpit. Lights on the wings blinked, and the soft sound of anti-gravitation engines was almost soothing.

It began to descend.

Chewing on her lip, Anna looked down at the ground. The wind whipped at her hair, blowing strands back from her face. "Here we go," she said, stepping forward. "Papa's home, and you might have to explain the raging house party."

Little struts extended from the shuttle's belly, allowing it to settle on the pavement with its nose pointed off to her right. The lights along the wings went dark. Anna briefly wondered if she might get a reprimand. What would they think when they learned that a young man of this world had bonded a Nassai?

A hatch in the shuttle's side opened, flopping down to create a series of steps that led to the ground. In the dim light, she could just make out the inner doors of the airlock. They opened with a hiss.

The woman who emerged was tall and slender, dressed in gray pants and a blue t-shirt under her dark trench coat. Her face was pretty, but boyishly short hair would have turned off many men. "You're Lenai?" she asked.

Pressing her lips together, Anna looked up to meet her gaze. She blinked. "I guess it depends who's asking," she said with a shrug. "You're the one who showed up in a well-armed shuttle. How 'bout you answer first?"

The woman looked up to study her with a hard expression, street-lights reflected in her deep brown eyes. "Jena Morane," she said. "Operative Jena Morane. I was sent here to rescue you."

Jena Morane lifted a forearm, displaying the gauntlet that housed her multi-tool. "If you'll just give me a moment," she said, tapping away, "I'd be happy to offer you some *real* proof."

Anna's tool beeped.

When she checked the screen, she saw that Jena had transmitted one of the security ID codes that she had been given before departing Petross Station in pursuit of Denario. That meant her orders did indeed come from Grecken Slade.

Anna frowned as she looked up at the other woman. She felt her eyebrows draw together. "I guess that'll do," she said with a curt nod. "So, I'm guessing that you have a ship in orbit?"

Jena closed her eyes, nodded once in confirmation. "We do," she began. "And if it's not too much trouble, maybe we could continue this conversation after we're safely *aboard* that ship."

"What's going on?"

"I don't know if you realize this," Jena said. "But the lovely people of this planet have scrambled aircraft in an attempt to defend themselves from what they no doubt see as a hostile invasion. We've tried standard greetings, but we just can't communicate with them. I assume you know the local language?"

"I do."

"Good," the woman barked. "Then you can help us make first contact before they decide to start shooting things."

Anna looked back over her shoulder.

Jack was standing on the grassy hill that bordered the parking lot, keeping his head down. If she got in that shuttle, would she ever see him again? Did it matter? She had a job to do. "All right," she said. "Let's go."

As he watched the shuttle rise into the air, Jack felt a pang of anxiety mixed with sadness. Anna had insisted that he hang back in case the people onboard weren't who they claimed to be. Now she was gone. He didn't really think anything would happen to her – not really – but being shot at tended to make a man paranoid.

Patel approached.

The woman's face was haggard, her long dark hair in a state of disarray. She let out a deep breath. "Are you alright, Jack?" she asked with more sympathy in her voice than he would have expected. "I'm sure they won't hurt her."

Crossing his arms with a sigh, Jack frowned down at the ground. "I'm holding up okay," he said, nodding. "I don't think they'll hurt her, but I can't help but wonder what this means for the rest of us."

"I suspect there will be many changes," she said. "We've got the wounded on their way back to headquarters, and Pennfield's on his way to a maximum-security detention cell. I think we should get you down to the Med-Wing as well."

"I'm fine."

Patel thrust her chin out with a glare that reminded him of his third-grade teacher. "You're sure of that, are you?" she asked, raising an eyebrow. "Sure that those blows to the head did no permanent damage?"

He felt fine, but he lacked the energy to press the issue. So ten minutes later, Jack found himself in the back of an ambulance as it rumbled along the city streets. His Nassai offered feelings of comfort.

Jack closed his eyes.

When he opened them, he was standing on the front lawn of the home he'd grown up in, staring at the front porch. The sloping black-shingled roof had a pair of windows sticking out, and the green front door had a few scratches in the paint. "What the…"

He felt someone approaching, and when he turned around, he found himself facing a small woman in a white sundress who walked along with her head down. Golden hair spilled over her shoulders.

When she looked up, he caught a glimpse of her face and had a strange feeling that he should know her. It took a moment for him to recognize her as a composite of all the women in his life. There were bits of Lauren, bits of his mother and even some Anna all mixed together. A touch of Buffy as well. And a little Vin. "I thought we should talk."

"Sounds good."

He watched cars roll along the suburban street that she had constructed in his mind, watched children playing on the front lawns of houses across the way. They were fuzzy images, drawn from his memories, but the few that he recognized would be in their mid-twenties now. "What did you want to talk about?"

His Nassai stood beside him with arms folded, frowning down at the grass beneath her feet. "Changes are coming," she said, nodding. "I feel it in my bones…in your bones, I suppose."

Jack frowned as he stared across the street, sweat matting dark hair to his brow. "I feel it too," he said, nodding. "And I get the distinct impression that these aren't changes we would like."

"The Leyrians know of your people now," His Nassai turned her face up to the sky, studying the clouds with a serene expression. "They have some interesting beliefs about the planet of your species' origin."

"Earth."

"Yes," she said. "And they aren't alone. Your species has built several empires that stretch across the stars, and not all are as benign as Leyria. So far, only the vast distances of space have kept them from each other's throats, but that is changing. Your world will be a focal point of attention."

"Can we trust them?"

"You can," she said. "Most of them. I have discussed this quite extensively with my brother, and we believe your two peoples should coexist."

Glancing over his shoulder, Jack arched a dark eyebrow "Your *brother?*" he asked. "I didn't know Nassai had families."

She offered a tiny smile, her cheeks suddenly stained with crimson. "The symbiont carried by Anna Lenai," she explained. "The two of you were in contact for quite a long time last night. We joined."

"You *what?*"

"My people exist in a shared consciousness," she said in tones that sounded like the ones math teachers used when forced to explain the Quadratic Equation for the fifteenth time. "We become distinct when separated from the whole, but while in close proximity, we may join and share thoughts."

The response shouldn't have surprised him. Joining was as natural to a Nassai as swimming was to a fish. Why wouldn't they take the opportunity when it presented itself? "We discussed the two of you at length," she went on. "My brother believes that his host is lonely. We think you should join with Anna."

"This discussion is over!"

He turned around to watch the sun shine down on the house he knew so well. The chairs on the front porch were ones that his father had sold when he was nine. For some reason, his symbiont had constructed the image from some of his earliest memories. "We have concerns," she said. "There are things you do not know.

"For nearly five of your centuries, my people have had a covenant with the humans of Leyria. We choose only the best and the brightest, those who will use our power in the service of their peers. The Nassai are meant to be a check on corruption. But this Wesley Pennfield carries one of my kind. That should not be possible."

Jack felt the blood drain out of his face. He let his head hang, breathing out a soft sigh. "No, it shouldn't," he agreed. "So how did a sociopath like that manage to get his hands on a symbiont?"

His Nassai kept her back turned, folding her arms as she shivered. "I sensed it as the two of you battled," she said. "Such malevolence. I would never have thought a Nassai capable of such feelings."

"What was that saying?" he asked. "Something about pride and falling?"

"Your point is well taken, my host." She turned around slowly, a solemn expression on her face. "I believe that Pennfield's symbiont has been tortured. That being the case, I feel doubly indebted to you and to Anna for saving me."

The thought left him cold. If men like Pennfield could get their hands on symbionts – symbionts who willingly took part in the carnage – it meant that powers that had once been reserved for those who would use them to protect the innocent were now available to almost anyone. The Justice Keeper could rot from the inside out. "We might just have a problem here."

"We do indeed."

Jack marched across the lawn with arms folded, smiling and shaking his head. "You know, it occurs to me," he said. "If we're going to be chatting like this on a regular basis, you're going to need a name."

"A name?" she asked. "What would you call me?"

Jack looked down at the grass as he considered the question, deep creases forming in his brow. "Now, that's a tough one," he said, nodding. "I wanted to call you Buffy, but that feels like copyright infringement."

Tilting her head to the side, she offered an impish grin that was an exact duplicate of Anna's. "I would prefer a name of my own," she mused. "I would be the first Nassai to receive one. It should be original."

"Hard to top Buffy Summers."

"I'm sure you'll think of something."

"Wait, that's it!" Jack snapped his fingers. "Summer!"

The warmth in her smile was proof that the name fit. "Summer," she said, testing it. "It's a lovely name. You should speak to Anna about what we've discussed. It seems like a good time to have allies."

After a brief trip to the Med-Wing – a wasted fifteen minutes in which a doctor shined a light in his eyes, inspected his face from all angles and then concluded that he was fine – Jack made his way home. That proved to be a rather difficult task. Whatever the Leyrians had done had screwed with phones, making it impossible for people to call a cab, and now there was a backlog.

The cabby who picked him up – an old Italian man with stubble on his chin and a bit of silver at his temples – looked back over his shoulder as the car lurched into motion. "You hear that crap on the radio, kid?"

Jack frowned, staring down into his lap. He felt sweat break out on his brow. "No, I didn't," he muttered. "But I heard some people talking about it. Whatever those idiots did has everyone spooked."

"Bunch of gibberish on every station," the cabby said, his eyes fixed on the road. A stream of headlights zipped past them on their left, each spilling a glare that made Jack want to groan.

He scrubbed a hand over his face, wiping sweat away. "I'm pretty sure it's nothing to worry about," he said, looking up. "Probably some disgruntled employee who figured he'd go out with a bang."

"On every station?"

The guy had him there. Jack decided to leave the task of crafting a cover story to someone more qualified. He didn't know how Patel was going to weasel her way out of this one. "You ask me," his driver went on, "we've got little green men in this city. With all the strangeness, my wife wants to pack up and leave."

"What do you say to that?"

"Leave and go where?" the old man grumbled. "We got no family in this country, son. The both of us came over here in the nineties. Our kid moved back to Europe. And I figure if it's invasion time, no place is safe."

They were silent for the rest of the trip.

Once he got home, Jack took a shower and delighted in the sensation of hot water easing the pain from his muscles. There were cramps that he hadn't even been aware of until they vanished. He usually preferred not to shower before bed – that tended to keep him awake – but tonight there was little choice.

Of course, he couldn't sleep; he couldn't even will himself to get under the covers. Too many thoughts kept rolling through his head. Would the Leyrians reveal themselves? What would happen to him if his situation became public knowledge? Where was Anna? Would he see her again?

Jack paced up the hallway in jeans and an old gray t-shirt. "Take it easy, Hunter," he told himself. "They won't hurt her."

With a bit of effort, he managed to coax himself into the bedroom, but he wasn't ready to go to sleep. Three AM would be making its appearance any minute now. He needed to get some rest. Just as he was about to start pacing again, he heard the front door swing open. "Anna?" he called out.

"I'm here!"

She joined him a few seconds later, pushing open the bedroom door to stand before him in black pants and a t-shirt, her hair in a state of disarray. "Hey. I'm glad to see you're all right."

Jack sat on the bed with his hands on his knees, smiling into his lap. "Well, that's a coincidence," he said, eyebrows rising. "I was about to say the same thing. I was starting to think I might not see you again."

Anna stared at him with tears glistening on her cheeks, sniffling. "Oh, Companion, I swore I wouldn't cry." She wiped those tears away. "I have to leave, Jack. I'm being reassigned."

"Reassigned?"

She nodded.

Jack looked up at her with a blank expression, blinking as he pondered the possible implications. "What does this mean?" he asked, his brow furrowing. "Why are you being reassigned? Where are they sending you?"

Anna pursed her lips and looked up at him with stony resolution on her face. She took a deep breath. "They're sending me about as far from Earth as I can get and still be in Leyrian Space," she explained. "They want their most experienced people working on Earth. That's not me."

Licking his lips, Jack looked down at the floor. He felt a blazing heat in his face. "So that means I won't be seeing much of you," he said. "Is this the part where you give me the big good-bye speech?"

"No good-bye speech," she promised. "See the wonderful thing about living in an interstellar society is that we have this little thing called faster-than-light communication. I plan to keep in touch."

"Well, there's that."

He stood.

Anna moseyed toward him with hands clasped behind her back, keeping her eyes downcast. "So," she said with a shrug of her shoulders. "I'm glad I found my way to this quirky little planet. Because this is where I met my best friend."

He offered a small smile, shutting his eyes tight. "I'm glad you made it here too," Jack said, nodding to her. "Because you, Anna Lenai, played a big part in changing the destiny of this quirky little planet."

He wrapped his arms around her.

The hug lasted for several minutes in which they said nothing, content to just stay there in each other's embrace. Damn it, but he was going to miss her! "There's something we should discuss," he managed at last. "I was talking with Summer."

"Summer?"

"My Nassai."

Cocking her head to one side, Anna arched an eyebrow. "Getting creative with names, are we?" she teased. "Alright, what did Summer say?"

He shared Summer's reflections on Pennfield's symbiont and the implications that went with it, their fears that something might be eating away at the Keepers. Anna didn't like that one bit. Most people were raised to take a bit of pride in their homeland, and it shouldn't have surprised him that Leyrians were no different from anyone else in this regard. But there was a fine line between pride and jingoism.

Eliminating hunger and poverty were notable achievements – there was simply no arguing with that – but any society that started to think of itself as the pinnacle of human achievement was setting itself up for a massive collapse.

There was just no sleeping after a conversation like that. So, they made their way to the living room and sat quietly for a little while. For the moment, Jack was content just to share her company. In a few weeks, she would be getting on a shuttle and leaving him here. And when that day came, he would wonder why he had ever thought himself capable of enjoying any of "the little things" in the face of such a loss, but for now, he was content. Tomorrow's problems could wait until tomorrow.

They sat quietly and watched the sun come up.

The First Contact celebration had closed down Albert Street, resulting in a crowd of several thousand people all packed into the narrow corridor between two rows of office buildings. Every single one of them was cheering, tossing confetti into the air with wild abandon. Anna felt sorry for whoever had to clean this up.

They were calling it Friendship Day. For generations to come, the eighteenth day of July would be remembered as the day the citizens of Earth had embraced their long-lost cousins with open arms. After nearly ten thousand years, humanity had come home. Her people had spent decades searching for the lost home-world of their ancestors. Well, here it was in all its glory.

How exactly did one make contact with a planet full of people who might just whip themselves into a frenzy at the revelation that they were not alone in the cosmos? Her people had started with benevolence. Filling Earth's airwaves with the message of their arrival had been simple enough once she had provided the words. Choosing those words had been the hard part.

Anna was the only one aboard the LMS Valiant who could speak English. Her days had been filled with conference calls with panels of her world's most esteemed diplomats while the Valiant took refuge from prying eyes behind Earth's moon. She had arranged a tour of the ship for Jack – he deserved a chance to get to know the people that he would be working for – but when they'd met for lunch, the only thing he would say was, "I'm in space!" over and over with occasional outbursts of "Space! Space! SPAAAAAACE!" for variety. After fifteen minutes, she gave serious thought to punching him

"So what do you think of the ship?" she had asked him.

"So much space. Gotta see it all."

With a great deal of editing and hand wringing from diplomats, she had managed to craft a statement explaining the existence of human life on other planets throughout the galaxy. Then her people had broadcast it for the entire planet to hear, followed by a series of detailed outlines of some of their more useful advancements: medical treatments, food production methods, clean energy.

It wasn't long before scientists on Earth started confirming the information. That was when her people made their first public appearance. Now here they were, nearly a month later, celebrating that appearance.

The Valiant hovered over the buildings.

A huge bird-like ship with long, curving wings, it stretched on for nearly the length of a city block. Anti-gravitation technology. It took quite a bit of power to keep the ship from falling to the ground, but Captain Taborn thought it worth the trouble.

Lauren Hunter stood before her with her back turned, staring up at the ship as it provided some shade from the sun. "So, these are your people," she said. "It pains me to say it, but I keep wondering if they're about to start shooting."

Anna felt her mouth tighten, nodding to herself. "These are my people." She closed her eyes and bowed her head. "And we have no interest in shooting you. Honestly, Lauren, I don't know what else to say."

She crossed her arms, stepping forward with a heavy sigh. Anna frowned, shaking her head. "If I haven't earned your trust by now," she began. "I'm starting to think that I might never manage it."

The other woman cast a glance over her shoulder, her face as smooth as the finest ivory. "My brother cares about you," she said, eyebrows rising. "For the moment, I guess that's enough."

"Glad to hear it."

"But he does care," Lauren said. "So be careful with him."

Anna felt her lips curl, a sudden warmth in her cheeks. The Companion bless all big sisters. "I'm well aware of how much he cares," she said, nodding. "And I promise to be exceptionally careful."

Craning her neck, Lauren scowled up at the belly of the ship. She blinked, clearly lost in thought. "Good enough," she said at last. "To be honest, Anna, there are times when I forget you came from the stars."

"We're all human," Anna said. "Separated by light-years but human nonetheless."

"I know," Lauren muttered. "That's what scares me."

Anna chose to leave it at that. Humans were capable of a wide range of behaviour; they sailed to the highest heights and sank to the lowest depths. The thought of Pennfield with a symbiont made her stomach twist.

Was there any merit to Jack's suspicions? She didn't know. She wanted to believe that the Keepers were a force for good in the galaxy, but a chat with Jena Morane had left her with some nagging doubts. Doubts that she couldn't stamp out. It pleased her to know that her people had turned over control of the SlipGate to the Canadian government. Even now, Leyrian engineers were spearheading an initiative to find other Gates that had been left behind by the Overseers. Soon Earth would have its own network.

"It's a new world," Lauren murmured.

Anna nodded. "Earth is part of the galactic community now," she said. "I suspect you're going to see a number of interesting developments."

Bathed in sunlight that came in through the window behind him, Harry Carlson sat on the edge of his bed with a baseball and glove. "Missy?" he called out when he caught the sound of footsteps. "Is that you?"

His daughter had been out since about four o'clock yesterday afternoon, insisting on spending the night with her friend Sarah. This was becoming a trend. Last week, she had spent an entire weekend at Tracey MacMillan's house. She seemed to be trying to get out of the house as much as possible. "You want to tell me why you decided to duck out of our trip to Pizza Hut? Claire was upset."

Missy appeared in the doorway.

Tall and slim, she wore a pair of blue jeans and a red t-shirt, her dark hair pulled back into a ponytail. "Nothing's going on, Missy," she said, mimicking his words from so many of their recent conversations. "If something was going on, I would tell you. It's nothing important...just first contact with aliens. No big deal."

Harry frowned, shaking his head. "You don't understand, kiddo." He looked up and blinked at his daughter. "If that information got out, people could have been hurt. I had to keep it a secret."

Missy bit her lip, her cheeks suddenly a deep crimson. She looked away, as if the sight of him pained her. "So, in other words, you don't trust me," she whimpered. "You don't think I can keep a secret."

"That's not what this is about."

Lifting her chin, Missy gave him that frigid glare that she had learned from her mother. "No, it isn't," she said. "This is about you lying to me, and me wondering how *I* can ever trust *you* again."

Those words hit him like a punch to the gut. His daughter didn't think she could trust him? Didn't she understand that he was just doing his job? No, of course she didn't. That wasn't how it worked in the mind of a teenager. "Listen, Missy, I'm sorry that I had to mislead you, but-"

She turned around, putting her back to him, and marched off down the hallway. "I don't want to talk about it," Missy called out.

A heavy sigh escaped Harry. He had known that the arrival of the Leyrians would create all sorts of complications, but he hadn't anticipated anything quite like this.

Chapter 30

Raindrops pattered against the windshield of Lauren's car, sliding over the glass in thin streams only to be pushed aside by the wiper blades. Through the pane, Jack could see a sidewalk on his right and a tall chain-link fence. He had taken Anna to a small airfield just outside of Gatineau.

This is where they would say good-bye.

Breathing deeply, Jack closed his eyes and shook his head. "So I know we've been putting off this conversation," he said, ignoring the queasy feeling in his belly. "But I'm guessing you don't want to do the whole long-distance thing."

Anna pressed her lips together, her eyes downcast. "It would be difficult," she said, eyebrows rising. "We will be living on different planets. It's highly unlikely that our time zones will link up."

He had expected as much.

"But…" she began.

Jack shut his eyes, resting his head against the seat cushion. "No," he said, shaking his head. "I'm not going to do that. You deserve a chance to be with someone who can be there for you."

Anna was frowning, staring through the windshield with a solemn expression. He had no clue what she was thinking. In all likelihood, she was about to tell him that she could make her own choice. He didn't dispute that, but he didn't want to force-

Anna turned her head to look out the passenger-side window, giving him a glimpse of her short little ponytail. "You're my best friend, Jack," she said softly. "You'll always be my best friend."

"Yeah."

Outside, the rain poured down on the slick road and left puddles on the sidewalk. The fence glistened with moisture. If he looked carefully, he could make out the nose of the shuttle that would take her away.

Jack stared into his lap. "So, I guess this is good-bye then," he said, nodding. "For what it's worth, I think I learned more from you than I did from any of my previous teachers."

"Likewise."

Anna studied him with sadness on her face, tears glistening in those big blue eyes. "I'm a different person than I was a few months ago," she said. "And that's a good thing. This is not good-bye."

"But-"

"No," she interrupted. "I refuse to listen to it. This is not good-bye because I say it's not good-bye, and you should know that when I put my mind to something, I bloody well get my way."

Anna leaned in close to give him a peck on the cheek. She pulled away, blinking at him. "Take care of your sister," she said, opening the door. "And don't worry. Everything will be alright."

The days after Anna's departure were hard on Jack, but he got by as best he could. She had promised to make contact as soon as she was settled on Alios, and that was good enough for now. She'd be spending the next year or so in a tropical paradise. As far as Jack was concerned, there were worse fates.

He went about his business, trying to build bridges with his new bosses. Many of the Keepers that he met were really quite friendly, but a few rubbed him the wrong way. He could only describe them as stuffy, or in some cases, remote. That left him a tad unsettled. Anyone who made it his business to protect the innocent ought to be the kind of person who projected warmth.

The conversation with his parents went about as well as he could have hoped. He still felt pangs of anxiety when he recalled the sight of them standing there blinking at him in confusion. Their son was one of these new super soldiers who carried an alien symbiont? In the end, his motherr had been supportive. Well... as supportive as anyone could expect under such circumstances. His father had been very quiet for a very long time. *Well, at least she isn't as vocal with her objections as Lauren.*

For the moment, his biggest concern was impressing his handlers. The e-mail had shown up in his inbox that morning: he had been assigned to a new mentor. Jack stifled a burst of anxiety as he went to meet her.

The small office that CSIS had given the representative from the Justice Keepers was really more of a cubbyhole. A simple wooden desk sat in the middle of gray carpets, roughly halfway between two white walls without a spec of ornamentation. Blinds on the back window shut out the sun.

The officer Jack found waiting there stood with hands clasped behind her back: a slender young woman in gray pants and a short-sleeved shirt. Her black hair fell to the small of her back. "You are Hunter?" she asked.

Turning, she revealed her face. She had a statuesque appearance with smooth dark skin and thin eyebrows. "I am Sarissa," the woman said. "I will facilitate the completion of your training. I'll see to it that you are properly instructed."

Jack thrust his chin out, blinking at the woman. "I wasn't aware that Anna's tutelage was improper," he said, stepping into the office. "If you ask me, I think she's done an excellent job under difficult circumstances."

Sarissa frowned, then looked down to study her shoes. "We are well aware of your fondness for Agent Lenai," she began. "She has some unorthodox beliefs regarding the role of a Justice Keeper."

"You don't say."

The woman looked up, and when her eyes fell upon him, they all but smoldered. It was clear that she resented this position. "From this point onward, you will report to me. You will follow my every instruction."

Dropping into the chair across from her, Jack considered his options. Something about this woman rubbed him the wrong way. Those fears about symbionts ending up with unsuitable hosts came bubbling up. He could hardly imagine a Nassai choosing her.

Jack craned his neck to stare at her, squinting as he chose his words. "That should not be a problem," he said, shaking his head. "After all, it's not like you're going to order me to violate my conscience."

She gave him a tight-mouthed frown, then tossed hair back over her shoulder with a flick of her head. "We will begin with an assessment of your self-defence technique," she said. "I expect you in the gym at-"

"Am I interrupting?"

An ugly writhing sensation like spiders crawling over his skin popped into Jack's head just before a man stepped into the doorway behind him. With Summer's help, he was able to make out the newcomer's features.

The guy was tall and slender, dressed in a pair of pants and a long coat that fell to his knees. His hair was long as well, falling straight back over his shoulders. "I wanted to meet our newest recruit."

Jack stood.

When he turned, he was able to add colour to the mental image. The coat was red, the man's hair black and his face had distinctly Asian features. Of course, the guy had never *been* to Asia, but-

"Director," Sarissa mumbled.

A smile stretched across the other man's face, a smile that somehow failed to touch his eyes. "My name is Grecken Slade," he said with a nod. "And you are the first Justice Keeper from this planet. I hope you're comfortable attending diplomatic functions."

Grinning sheepishly, Jack lowered his eyes to the floor. He reached up to scrub a hand through his hair. "Well, I'm told I clean up real nice," he muttered. "So bring on the glitz and the glamour."

Slade pursed his lips as he looked Jack up and down. "Well," he said, eyebrows rising, "it's been a pleasure to meet you. I am quite certain that you will be a welcome addition to the team."

Jack left the office with his skin writhing. That man was a snake; he was sure of it. He probed Summer for her reaction and found nothing. Apparently, his symbiont didn't know what to make of the man who led their organization. From what he had been told, Slade was one of the most highly decorated Keepers in the last hundred years. So how did a man like that fall from grace?

You want to know the thing that pushed Lucifer over the edge? he asked Summer. *Too many people lavished too much praise on him.* In Jack's opinion no man should ever feel too good about himself. You ought to be your own worst critic, and the instant you stopped doing that, disaster happened.

He made his way down to the detention cells. He was suddenly very much in need of answers. A little careful prodding might be enough to extract a morsel of information out of Pennfield.

The cellblock was little more than a narrow corridor with barred doors on either side, though Pennfield's had been electrified to prevent him from trying anything. The man had ignored just about every attempt to question him.

Jack crossed his arms as he made his way down the corridor, staring down at his feet. "Rise and shine, Wes!" he called out. "We need to have a serious talk about who you've been slumming around-"

He reached Pennfield's cell.

It was empty.

He found nothing but a bench along the back wall, a sink and a toilet with no sign that anyone had ever occupied the space. The spatial awareness gained from contact with Summer confirmed what his eyes told him. The cell was empty.

"Oh crap…"

Wesley Pennfield rolled onto his back on the soft, moist ground. Consciousness seeped into his mind like drips from a leaky faucet, beginning with a sense of trepidation that he could not identify. He felt strangely calm for a man on the verge of panic. A few seconds passed before he realized the fear was not his own.

His symbiont was terrified.

As blurred vision solidified into recognizable objects, he took a moment to inspect his surroundings. He was in a cavern of some sort…or a tunnel. A tunnel unlike any other that he had ever seen.

A kind of ambient light permeated the space, allowing him to see dark brown walls of some membranous substance. Tubes rose from the floor like large jagged stalagmites, twisting and turning as they intersected with the walls or ceilings. On closer inspection, he saw that they pulsed with some kind of liquid.

Not tubes then.

Veins.

Touching the walls revealed a texture like smooth skin, warm to the touch, and he could swear that he saw tiny capillaries pulsing as he made contact. This place was *alive*. He was inside a living organism.

Wesley sat up.

He still wore the black pants and turtleneck that he had worn on the night when he had been captured by CSIS. Head hanging, he let out a deep breath.

Wesley frowned, shutting his eyes tight. He shook his head with a heavy sigh. "Is anyone out there?" he called out. "Anyone."

His symbiont practically screamed.

Only then did he open his mind to the sensations that it had been trying to share. With the Drethen terrified out of its wits, he had been afraid to risk contact with its mind. Spatial awareness filled his thoughts.

And he noticed it.

Perched at the top of a slope, a little ways up the tunnel, it sat there watching him, the large bulbous protrusion that he could only assume was the creature's head tilted like a sparrow inspecting a worm. Determining the creature's exact shape was impossible; it seemed to huddle in on itself.

Worst of all, he could not see it!

As far as his eyes were concerned, he was completely alone in what appeared to be a long tunnel of living tissue. The creature was there – he could *feel* it watching him – but the damn thing was completely invisible.

Closing his eyes, Wesley drew in a shuddering breath. "Well, at least we've come this far," he whispered. "Do you intend to speak with me, or would you rather just consume my flesh now?"

The creature shuffled off.

"We are pleased."

The sound of his own voice made his heart seize up with a sudden jolt of pain, and when he looked around, he saw another version of himself standing a little ways off. This Wesley was clad in Armani – a fine gray suit with a white shirt. His hair was combed to perfection, and glasses rested on his face.

"Pleased?" Wesley asked.

"Yes," his doppleganger replied.

Wesley unbuckled his belt. It was the only thing he had on him after so long in that bloody holding cell. He slid it free of the belt loops with enough gusto to leave a whistle in the air, then hurled it at his doppelganger.

As expected, his belt passed right through the other Wesley. His twin was nothing but an illusion, a telepathic projection beamed directly into his head by the creature that had scrambled up the hallway. He had communicated with such constructs before. That could mean only one thing.

Wesley Pennfield was in the presence of his Gods, the beings that fools like Anna Lenai called Overseers. Overseers! A banal term spoken by banal people who failed to comprehend the majesty of their creators. He preferred the term *Old Ones*. Their true name was unpronounceable by human mouths.

With sweat slicking his face, Wesley looked up at himself and blinked. "You are pleased?" he asked, deep creases forming in his brow. "I allowed the Leyrians to make contact with this world."

The other man frowned, then lowered his eyes. He shook his head with a sigh. "It is of no consequence," he explained. "Our projections suggested a very high probability of this particular eventuality."

"You are not angry?"

The other Wesley tilted his head, studying him. The question was probably absurd. For all he knew, these beings had no concept of anger. He had been ordered to keep Earth and Leyria apart, and he had done so to the best of his ability, but there were other goals that he had been told to accomplish, goals that required the procurement of a symbiont.

Bringing Denario Tarse to Earth had been worth the risk. If Slade had done his part, the Lenai girl would never have ventured into Dead Space. Perhaps the blame was not entirely his own.

His doppelganger clasped hands together behind his back, standing prim and proper with his chin thrust out. "There are contingencies," he said, nodding. "We will amend our plans as needed."

Red-faced, Wesley stared up at the man with his mouth open. He blinked over and over. "I am not to be punished then?" he whispered. "You will not make an example of my failure?"

Again, the other man stared at him with a flat expression, as if the master who pulled his strings did not know how the puppet should respond. Wesley scolded himself. Of course, he was not to be punished; that was a human way of thinking. If he understood their reasoning correctly, contact between Earth and Leyria was an undesirable but highly probable scenario, one that you planned for in much the same way that people who lived in the Caribbean planned for hurricanes. When a storm came, you didn't get angry; you just followed your contingency plan. "Why are you pleased?"

"Your initiative has not gone unnoticed," his other self replied. "When it became clear that contact between your people and the Leyrians was inevitable, you acted to ensure that such contact would produce favourable results. This proves you worthy of the gift we have given you."

The gift. His symbiont.

His twin spun around, allowing Wesley a glimpse of the back of his well-tailored gray suit. "Come," he said, starting down the tunnel. "There are many things that you should see."

Wesley stood.

Wiping his mouth with one hand, he closed his eyes. "I have seen more than any of my kind could ever dream," he said, following his clone. "I am dust beneath you, but you honour me with your presence."

The tunnel stretched on for what felt like the length of a city block, sloping upward every now and then, only to flow back down. He saw more tubes rising out of the floor, connecting to the ceiling. When he past, he could hear the fluid surging through them.

Through his bond with the Drethen, he *felt* the creature following behind him, always hovering at the very edge of sensory range, making it impossible for him to discern its true shape. He had experienced this sensation before. The feeling of being watched had been present in every interaction with one of these telepathic constructs. Apparently, the Old Ones had to be nearby to maintain the illusion. When he looked back, he saw nothing except... sometimes it shimmered like heat rising off black pavement.

The tunnel curved to the left with an angle that felt like a ninety-degree turn. His double stopped there. "Approach."

Wesley did.

The tunnel wall seemed to pulse with thin veins that sent a dark reddish fluid into the membranous tissue. There was a soft slurping sound. Wesley was amazed that the air didn't stink. In fact, it was as fresh as a cool breeze through an open window.

A seam appeared in the wall like an incision made by a surgeon's steady hands, the tissue pulling apart to reveal... the Earth. He was looking down on North America from orbit, watching as clouds swirled over the eastern United States and parts of Quebec and Ontario. Wesley nearly panicked. That was no window! He had been exposed to vacuum! His masters intended to punish him after all! He-

No air bled through the gap.

Only then did he notice the slight flicker of what looked like white static. A force-field? How was it possible to create a force-field that was almost entirely undetectable to the human eye? He had never imagined such a thing.

"Truly your power is great, Oh Lord," Wesley said, repeating a catechism he had learned in church.

The other Wesley stood beside him with hands clasped behind himself, frowning as he stared through the window. "The next phase begins," he said softly. "We have decided to afford you greater latitude."

Wesley noticed something.

A streak of orange light – no bigger than a spark rising from a campfire – making its way northward over the clouds that hid the Eastern Seaboard. "What was that?" he asked his master.

"The Leyrians," his doppelganger replied. "Like insects drawn to bright light, they have been sending shuttles down to the surface."

"And you've remained in *orbit*? What if they see you?"

The other man looked askance at him, an unreadable expression on that face. If he had not been frightened by the realization that he might have spoken out of turn, Wesley would have laughed. He had used that exact glare on so many of his subordinates. "Your species has a remarkable inability to notice the things that dangle right before your eyes."

Wesley swallowed.

As he peered through the rip in the ship's... skin, he wondered what would become of him. Somewhere down there, agents of just about every law enforcement department on the planet were looking for him. With the existence of the Leyrians public knowledge, he would be Public Enemy Number One on Earth and just about everywhere else in Leyrian Space. "I cannot go back," he said softly. "They'll be looking for me now. I cannot serve you as I once did."

His twin flashed a smile that made Wesley's blood run cold. "Other opportunities will present themselves," he said. "The galaxy is vast."

"Then my service is not at an end?"

The other man spun around to face him with arms folded, thrusting out a bold chin. "We'll be needing you a little while longer," he said, nodding. "You are an important part of the computer."

The End of the First Book of the Justice Keepers Saga.

Dear reader,

We hope you enjoyed reading *Symbiosis*. Please take a moment to leave a review in Amazon, even if it's a short one. Your opinion is important to us.

The story continues in *Friction*.

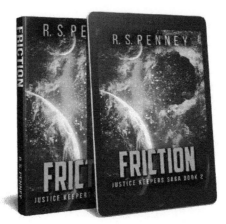

To read first chapter for free, head to:
https://www.nextchapter.pub/books/science-fiction-adventure-friction

Discover more books by R.S. Penney at
https://www.nextchapter.pub/authors/ontario-author-rs-penney

Want to know when one of our books is free or discounted for Kindle? Join the newsletter at http://eepurl.com/bqqB3H

Best regards,

R.S. Penney and the Next Chapter Team

Acknowledgments.

To my loving family: Glenn, Sandra and Alyssa. To my grandparents: Joan, Clayton and Remo. To Noel, Jess, Jonathon and Mason, you have my sincerest thanks.

To Jourdan Vian, a talented writer and editor who helped shape this book into what it is today. I could not have done it without you. To Gina Fusco of Re:Word Communications. Your contributions to this project have been invaluable.

To everyone who donated to my Kickstarter, thank you all.

About the author

The most important thing I can tell you is that I wrote this book while suffering from a severe visual impairment. At the age of thirty, I was diagnosed with keratoconus, which is a condition where your cornea is slowly warped. This led to some rather severe headaches and nausea; it took a while to learn how to adapt. This is the first book I wrote since being diagnosed with this condition. That makes it a real triumph for me.

Follow me on Twitter @Rich_Penney

E-mail me at keeperssaga@gmail.com

You can check out my blog at rspenney.com

You can also visit the Justice Keepers Facebook page
https://www.facebook.com/keeperssaga
Questions, comments and theories are welcome.

Printed in Great Britain
by Amazon